I0619773

The

Of the Sergeants Club

Thomas S. Mulvaugh

ISBN 978-0-578-48490-7

First Edition

© 2019 Thomas S. Mulvaugh

Golden Roads Publishing, a division of PAH Publishing

Acknowledgements and Dedication

If it were not for the assistance of many, this book would have not been possible. During the writing of this book I was diagnosed with stomach cancer and had to undergo surgery and chemo treatments, which just zapped my strength. However, with the help of my wonderful doctors and nurses I was able to get back to the story and complete it. I thank my wife Karla who has gone through this with me, along with my family and my church who offered up countless prayers and help.

I would also like to thank a good friend Christa Stout for reading over this and catching my mistakes, you have been a great blessing.

This book is dedicated to the memory of a wonderful friend Connie Davis, Connie was always the first one to read my stories, and she would stop and give me a call in tears either from laughing or crying at a scene in the book. Or asking what was Ryder up now. When I would see she always had a smile to greet me with that just warmed my heart. She will be truly missed and there will not be a day I don't think about her.

Thomas S. Mulvaugh

The

Blood Covenant

Of the Sergeants Club

"Faith and faith alone is the answer to all of life's riddles." *Thomas S. Mulvaugh*

Chapter 1

There is a technique to following someone, much like the cat pursuing a mouse. You let the mouse run without ever letting it know you were right behind. Rick Ryder knew the modus operandi well, it required a special car, a sedan, light colored preferably gray or light blue, as these are colors that the human eye does not notice well. The car could not be new or too old, between five and ten years old seemed to be the best. Also it worked best if there were two vehicles, different makes and models and colors. One running point- that is the car right behind the pursued- and the other one on a parallel course, that could come in, take the place and run point should the followed car become spooked.

Ryder selected a ten year old Ford sedan gray in color, and for his partner Isabelle Alexander, a mint green five year old Chevrolet sedan, it was another color that worked well. They had been trailing their suspect, Gerald Muller, across Joplin.

Muller 69 years old from Lenapah, OK, was well known to authorities in the four-state region with a rap sheet that ranged from receiving stolen goods, molesting teen and pre teen girls, and his latest, a suspect in the murder of a former employee of his father's pawn shop. To the police it became a cold case, but the victim's brother hired Ryder and his team.

For several years Ryder was a lead homicide investigator for the Kansas City Police Department, but quit and with his last dollar bought a Powerball® ticket and won the biggest jackpot of all time one billion dollars. Now Ryder uses his wealth to help those that need a detective but maybe can't afford one, by charging only a dollar a day.

He had spent two months on this case, all evidence showed this was the killer but he needed the murder weapon, a Remington 22 revolver that was reported stolen from the pawn shop. Hoping he could trick the suspect into leading him to it, he told Muller in a phone call that he had seen him hide it. Good thing some criminals are just stupid.

Muller had turned on to a side road that ran along Interstate 44, it was a narrow strip of pavement that did not have much traffic and making it even worse was the fact that it was in the middle of a residential area. Ryder had been following for a few miles now, as his partner tried to navigate her way back to the side road. If it had not been the dead of night, Ryder couldn't have gotten away with it. At two hundred feet away he was nothing but a pair of headlights in the rearview mirror. However, he couldn't keep following Muller who was going to get suspicious and like the rat he was, he would run for his hole.

"Alex you got a copy?" Ryder heard his wife Yakira say into a walkie-talkie as she held it up to her lips. Isabelle went by her nickname a shorter version of her last name. Ryder glanced over at Yakira. It was early summer, the air was still warm and blowing through her hair that was dark as the night itself, but as they passed under the street light there was just a hint of auburn showing through. It flowed down over her shoulders and the light blue long sleeve shirt of Ryder's that she was using as a jacket had the cuffs rolled up to fit her petite frame.

The full moon was high in the sky and was casting enough light that he could see the shadows of her face. She was pretty, but not glamorous, definitely the girl next door. As she spoke her tone had a mixture of Ozark Hillbilly and Jewish culture which she was. "We are running out of road here. *Ferhtay?*"

"I understand," a firm sounding female voice came back over the radio. "I am coming right up on your bumper." Ryder glanced up and saw the glow of headlights filling the interior of the car painting over the side of her face.

"Have her play teenager." Ryder said glancing over at his wife. She lifted the walkie-talkie to her lips and asked.

"Alex did you hear that?"

"Got it windows going down, radio coming on."

Ryder's eyes drifted up to the inside mirror again and he watched as Alex's car quickly accelerated passing by, once again leaving them in the dark. He could hear the stereo blasting through the open windows, as she continued to pass the suspect's car. At great speed and the stereo blasting Ryder's hope was that Muller would just think it was a young kid out speeding. He watched as Alex pulled back into the lane in front of Muller. It was a forward tail that Alex was doing and it was not a great place to be as the suspect could turn off behind her and she could lose him, with Ryder on point it still might work. Ryder reached over and took the radio from Yakira and placed it to his lips.

"Keep him in your sights. He is coming up on the I -44 exit. If he gets on the interstate we will lose him for sure."

"Roger," He heard Alex reply. "What do you want me to do?" Running ahead she would pass the exit.

"Just go forward, but be ready to back track." Ryder said. "How well do you know your way around down here?"

"Pretty well!" She replied. "We are getting close to the Horner Spooklight aren't we?"

"Yeah it is right over the Stateline."

"I am crossing over into Oklahoma right now."

"Slow down!" Ryder warned into the walkie-talkie. "You may have to quickly back track He didn't take the I-44 exit. He is heading down Stateline Road. Backtrack. BACKTRACK!" He shouted into radio.

" Roger." Alex replied, slamming down on the brakes sliding the car around.

Stateline Road was the zipper that held Missouri and Oklahoma together. One would think that for such a grand name it would be something more than just a strip of pavement that looked more like a country road. There were no dividing stripes, white lines or rough tracks that warned pavement ends here, you just had to trust the serpent that twisted into the cavern of trees on both sides. Striking into Oklahoma and then twisted again and one was back in Missouri.

"This is the way to Devil's Promenade." Yakira said her tone starting to sound stressed. "You know what that is don't you?"

Ryder followed keeping the taillights of Muller's car, a 2000 Camaro in his sights but staying far enough back that it didn't spook the driver. He glanced up into the mirror and could see the warm glow of the headlights of Alex' car behind. The signal light on the Camaro flashed, the bright amber glowing over the weedy lined bank as the red brake lights glowed. He took the walkie-talkie and spoke, "He is turning on Spooklight Road. Take the back way in."

" Got it." Alex replied as she signaled turning off the main road to a graveled dirt road to her right.

"We are not going down there are we?" Yakira asked as they got closer to the turn off.

On a Saturday night it was the destination of many couples, hoping the devil's light would show and the young lady would become frightened and cuddle closer to her love. The legends of the light were many. One of the most common is the Ozark version of Romeo and Juliet, of young Indian lovers torn between two tribes that leap off a cliff together to be sealed together forever in death. Another tale was that of an old prospector slaughtered by Indians who now roams the road holding his lantern, searching the back road waiting and watching for the young lovers there now.

"You don't believe in that stuff, do you?" Ryder asked.

"I am Jewish!" She shot back as Ryder slowed the car and made to switch off the headlights, and still following the Camaro he made the turn on the side road. "I grew up with relatives thumping me on the nose telling me I should wake up or Lilith will get me. Or when they heard an owl it was her calling and if someone said your name she would come and get you in the middle of the night and take you to the devil. We would hear an owl and Annalisa would say my name you know how many nights I spent afraid to sleep?"

Ryder had heard tales from Yakira's grandmother, of Adam's first wife before Eve, a blonde beauty that was banished from the Garden of Eden for being too independent and not worshiping God. She was sent to the far edges of the earth, but she molested boys and young men in their sleep allowing her to give birth to the demons. Jealous of children she flew in, perching on the limbs as an owl, asking their name. If someone would reply she would swoop in and take the child's life. The way to save them was to thump them on the nose and wake the child up as a child's cry would scare her away. He himself was likely thumped on the nose, but it was just a tale, the same as those that fed the frights of the Spooklight.

He heard a crumple of wrapper in the dark and he only had the glow of the dash light filling the interior, "What are you doing?" He asked then heard her crunch down on a snack. "What are eating?"

"Hot Fries," she said reaching into the bag and taking another bite. "Want some?" She held the bag over to him.

"Don't like spicy food."

"They are good." Yakira said reaching in and taking another bite. "You don't know what you have been missing, especially if you crunch them up over strawberry ice cream."

"Girl you are weird."

Even in the dark he could tell she was smiling as she said, "Is that why you love me and married me because I am unlike any other girl." She started to reach into the snack bag again but stopped and asked. "We really are going down here aren't we?
"You do believe this stuff don't you?" Ryder asked, quickly turning to her and then back to the road.

"The tale of homicide yes."

"Murder?" Ryder quickly looked at her again. "What murder?"

"You haven't heard that tale?" Yakira twisted slightly in her seat and began to explain. "The legend goes that a when a group of braves returned to camp they found their Chief and great medicine man murdered in his wigwam. His head severed from his body, and the head missing. It was told that the light was him searching for his missing head, and if the light came towards you he was after your head."

It was the third week in May, the summer was just beginning and tomorrow would be the last day of school. The sky was clear, as a plate licked clean by a starving dog. Ryder could see the Camaro slowing in front of them, its brake light shining brightly as it pulled off the side of the road and stopped. Ryder slowed the car and also pulled it off the road parking a few feet away from the Camaro.

"You think this can get dangerous?" Yakira asked.

"It could," Ryder said as he looked over his shoulder and out the back window where he could see the glow of a single headlamp way down the road.

The windows still down, the sound of a barred owl could be heard from the woods in the field on the side of the road. She turned back to him as she reached down to pull up the pant leg of her jeans and remove a Magpug® Snub nose 357 revolver from the holster strapped to her calf. She flipped the chamber open and checked the ammunition and closed it. The owl called out, Who who, who."

"That Lilith calling?" Ryder asked with a grin.

"You say my name, I will hit you."

He leaned over and grinned broadly, uswed his finger he flipped her on the nose and said, Wake up!" Then he looked back into the mirror, the glow of the single headlight was gone. Ryder picked up the walkie-talkie again. "Did you call Sam?"

"Yeah," he heard Alex's reply. "He will be coming in behind you."

"Did you tell him to come in code 1?"

6

"Negative."

"Do it," Ryder replied into the walkie-talkie. "I don't want to spook Muller."

Muller left the headlights of the Camaro shining like a security blanket in the darkness. "I can't get a hold of him, must be a dead spot down here." he heard Alex say over the walkie-talkie.

"Going to radio silence," Ryder whispered and then turned the walkie-talkie off.

Yakira held the snub-nose to her side as she calmly said, "Have you heard the cries down here? I have."

"It is the wind," Ryder replied back as he watched the light fill the interior of the coupe, and heard the door squeak as the suspect opened it and Muller stepped out. He was of average height but skinny, his hair dark and hung loosely on his shoulders, his face covered with a full beard. He was dressed in dark coverall's. The man took a drag from the cigarette he was smoking and crushed it under his foot before shutting the car door. He had a flashlight in one hand and a small shovel in the other. He clicked the flashlight on.

Yakira started to reach for the door handle when Ryder pointed to the open window and said softly, "Out the window." Ryder knew he could not open the car door as the interior dome light would come on and alert Muller. Instead he reached through the open window and grabbed the edge of the roof and slid his over six foot athletic frame out the widow. Stopping, resting on the door, his behind pressing down on the door lock button. He sat and watched as the man crossed the road and crawled over the barb-wire fence.

Ryder crawled out of the car as Yakira started to slide out of the car, her feet dangling from her just over five-foot frame, when she dropped to the ground softly. Ryder reached down and slipped the Glock 33 from the holster under his sport coat.

Muller shined the beam of the flashlight across the field to a group of trees in a row, he seemly counted from left to right shining the beam on each tree; one, two, three, four and then on the second tree behind that one and walked towards it. Ryder walked across the road, and crawled through the fence to get closer, the man counted off ten paces and began to dig into the ground. Then he kneeled down on the ground using his hands to remove the remaining soil from the hole. He reached into the hole and pulled out something wrapped in a stained shop towel. Ryder watched as the man unwrapped the towel, inside was a handgun, a Remington .22 caliber revolver, black steel with wood grips- the murder weapon.

The man stood up and using his foot he kicked the soil back into the hole and headed back towards the fence. He passed Ryder, had just pushed down on the barbwire when Ryder shouted using the man's last name. "Muller hold it right there!"

Muller turned and looked at Ryder and threw the shovel at him. Ryder ducked as the shovel twirled over his head and hit a tree he was standing next to.

"Yakira, Stop him!" Ryder yelled as he raced for the fence. Muller turned and threw the flashlight at him, again Ryder ducked.

He heard the crunch of gravel under tires as a dark blue Ottawa County cruiser pulled in behind Ryder's car. It was Deputy Sam Redfox. Suddenly there was a flash of red and blue lights, stroking across the field and over trees. Ryder's eyes blinked trying to refocus adjusting to the bright flashing lights.

BANG! BANG! Two loud pops rang out; breaking the stillness, sounding like firecrackers. They were gun shots, as flames and smoke poured out of the barrel of the revolver in Muller's hand. The birds of the night took flight

"Ottawa county" Ryder heard the call from Deputy Redfox. "This is thirty-two. Shots fired. E 50. I am on Spooklight Road."

"All units respond East 50 road,": Ryder heard the dispatcher respond. "Unit 44, what is your 20? Are you in that area?"

"Yakira!" Ryder yelled out as he dove to the ground aiming the Glock towards Muller .

"I am fine." She replied.

"Redfox!" Ryder yelled again.

"I am safe!"

"Muller give this up," Ryder shouted as he belly crawled along the ground towards the barb-wire fence. "You are surrounded; you are not going to get out of here. You heard that call. This place will be will crawling with OCSD." The last wire of the three wire fence was broken and Ryder crawled under the fence and rolled down in the ditch. He rolled on this belly and gazed out across the road, he could feel the warmth of the pavement rising up slowly in the night sky. Ryder gripped the Glock and stared down the sights across the pavement to Muller who was standing next to his Camaro, his head twisting and turning, jumping at every little sound that was made, from the high pitched song of toads mating in a nearby pond or the whistle of a night hawk resting on a limb that did not take flight.

"You don't understand!" Muller shouted out as he twisted back towards Ryder. "He was blackmailing me. I couldn't pay anymore." He twisted back and faced down the road. "He just wanted more and more. He said if I didn't pay he was going to give the story to Rolling Stone magazine."

"Just put the gun down," Ryder said as he slowly pushed to his feet, still crouched down in the ditch he began to inch closer. "We can talk this all over." Ryder took a step forward. CRACK! A stick broke under Ryder's foot

Muller fired off another round this time hitting the windshield of the cruiser. Cornered like a rat and a clowder of cats closing in, what else can a rat do but run. He quickly got into his car and fired it up and sped off, the back tires ripping into the grass ditch, throwing gravel and dirt. Ryder leaped to his feet and aimed the Glock and fired off two quick rounds shattering the right taillight. He heard the howl of an engine and quickly turned and saw that Yakira was behind the wheel of the sedan. Her foot pressed to the floor as the tires spun. The Ford rocketed up out of the ditch onto the pavement. The tires grabbed hard and the tail end swung around, Yakira fought the steering wheel, straightened as the car raced down the road after the Camaro.

Ryder stood there for a moment, it seemed to be happening in slow motion, the Ford catching up with the Camaro, just as Alex pulled out from an intersection blocking the road. The Camaro swung over hard to the right to avoid her. Smashing into a red pipe gate, the nose of the car crumbling as the gate bent and weakened sprung open the car, continuing sideswiping a tree before coming to a rest in the wooden area by the side of the road.

"Ryder!" Deputy Redfox yelled out. Ryder looked over his shoulder at the officer standing next to the patrol car. Ryder dashed to the patrol car and got in on the passenger side. The scream of sirens filled the air and the flash of red and blue light spanned over the pavement as they raced down the road.

"What the name of Yo-He-Waah is that?" Deputy Redfox said, pointing through the windshield at an orb of light that seemed to be racing down the road at them.

"The Spooklight!" Ryder said as he watched as Yakira stopped the car, got out and dashed over towards the Camaro.

"I have never seen it look like that" Deptuy Redfox said his hands gripped around the steering wheel and his eyes fixed on the red flashing orb that was getting closer and closer and was getting brighter. The flashing orb filled the windshield, he couldn't see and the deputy slammed down on the brakes as the car slid to a stop.

"DROP THE GUN!" Ryder heard Yakira shout, followed by loud bang that seemed echo all around as if another shot came from somewhere. "Ricky!" He heard her shout with desperation. Just as quick as the Spooklight appeared, it was now gone. Ryder opened the door and sprinted across the road and over to the woods, as the sounds of distant sirens began to drift through the timber. Ryder looked down.

There within a couple of paces from his wrecked car, the driver's door wide open and the window lying shattered across the brown leaves like a million dollars of diamonds, Muller lay on his back on the ground, staring straight up into the sky, two bullet wounds in his chest, just to the side of his breast bone. Yakira was kneeling beside him, she had removed the shirt she was using for a jacket and was using it as a bandage, applying pressure over the open wound.

Muller let out a gurgle as bloody bubbles formed in his mouth. Yakira's hair had fallen down over the sides of her face as she looked up at Ryder. "Ask her—tell her—" Muller struggled to get the words out. Yakira lowed her head to his lips and whispered something, before her he became still.

"I didn't have any choice!" She pleaded. "He pointed it right at me." Still clutched in Muller hands was the revolver. Ryder pulled out his cell phone and quickly took a photo of the weapon. "I had to shoot!"

Deputy Redfox walked up behind Ryder and quickly secured the weapon from Muller's hand, making sure it was empty. Yakira continued to keep applying pressure, the blood oozing between her fingers, dripping down over her nails like a deep red nail polish. The gurgling stopped and Ryder noticed the blood was no longer oozing between Yakira's fingers. The sounds of sirens grew closer.

"What did he tell you?" Ryder asked.

"He said, 'He hopes she will forgive him."

Chapter 2

A troop of deputies showed up storming the Devil's Promenade as if it were beaches of Normandy, the soldiers Ottawaa County sheriff deputies. Dark blue county cruisers lining up along the side of the road . Olkohoma Highway Patrol sliding to a stop, the flash of their emergency lights raping through the woods, each flash frightening the critters that called it home. A coyote quickly scampered away hiding in the remains of an abandoned badger hole wondering what the invaders in his homeland were doing here. Sniffing as Muller's body was removed by the County Coroner, and Yakira, Ryder, Alex and even Deputy Redfox were escorted to the back of a squad car and routed back to Miami.

When people think Miami, their minds fill with thoughts of long white sand filled coasts with clear blue water slapping playfully into the beach of a brightly colored city, not the wide open meadows of the Native State. That is my-am-ee this is my-am-uh, and don't dare call it anything else, or they will know you are an outsider.

Miami was the comma of the west before the nation took a breath and cities east of the Red People started to become just a little more jammed together. The age of the town was clear to see from the red brick buildings that were once the proud crown that the town wore, as newer buildings were placed up and around the town span. The Ottawa county Sheriff's Department was made of sand colored bricks, stained with rain that would pour off the roof during a down burst.

Inside was no different, cramped, every space that could be used, being used. Desk of over worked deputies stack yet more work. The interrogation room nothing more than an empty office with a small table and a few chairs.

Gary Nelson, the county DA, sat in one of the chairs; he was a large man, heavy set, with a belly that pushed at the buttons on his dark blue shirt. He gazed across the table at Yakira where she sat sipping a glass of water in a white foam cup. Holding it tightly, she lifted it up to her lips, her hands trembling; sitting next to her was Alex. Her long legs crossed, she was leaning back in the chair, her green eyes staring at the undersheriff.

Seated in another chair was Deputy Redfox, a full-blooded Cherokee, who was tall and leanly built, his hair dark as Oklahoma oil, his skin showing his heritage. He was dressed in uniform. Ryder stood his back up against the wall one foot crossed in front of the other, his arms folded in front of him, his sapphire eyes narrowed slightly and a gaze that did not blink as he stared at Nelson.

"Okay," Nelson said as he repositioned himself in the chair. "Let's go over this one more time!"

"Damn it Nelson!" Deputy Redfox cursed. "It was a clean shoot! He was going to kill her."

"And how do you know that Redfox? Did you see the shooting?"

"Yes, I did!" Deputy Redfox said.

"Sure it wasn't the Spooklight that shot him?" Nelson asked with a tone of disbelief. "Maybe you and your pal here, Mr. Moneybags, could say that and we just let it go." He laughed and added, "That would be something for the news media huh?" He turned to Yakira and asked. "One more time! Tell me what happen."

"I told you," Yakira replied placing the cup down on the table in front of her. "He tried to run; I forced him off the road. He got out of his car. He raised his weapon at me. I ordered him to drop it. He didn't, so I shot him!"

"One shot?"

"One shot!"

"You had no choice?" Nelson question was harsh. "You are not an officer! You were never trained. You were doing something that..."

"I trained her," Alex said who was sitting in a chair next to Yakira.

"You did?" Nelson snorted as he looked at Alex, pretty, with legs as long as the freeway and blonde hair that curled around her slender face. "And who trained you? Mr. Moneybags here?"

"Oh for God's sakes, Nelson!", Sheriff Cliff Cooper bellowed as he opened the door and came into the room. He was in his early fifties, his hair instead of showing its age was dyed sable brown, neatly cut but messed up as he had been fast asleep. He was dressed in jeans and a dark blue t-shirt with the Wardogs logo on the front - the local school's mascot. "Don't have clue who these people are? You stop getting your damn news from something besides the *Comedy Channel,* you might know Rick Ryder and his team."

The sheriff entered closing the door behind him. He looked at Alex. "Want to know who she is this Isabelle Alexander? She is the former Special Agent of the FBI known for taking down the terrorist group Black Midnight." Sheriff offered his hand to Alex, she stood and shook it and then reseated herself. He then turned to Yakira and said, "Weapons expert Yakira Rosen." Again he offered his hand. "But it is Ryder now isn't it." She shook his hand as he smiled and added, "Congratulations Mrs. Ryder. " He turns to Ryder and says, "And this is Rick Ryder former Chief's quarterback, Kansas City Homicide Detective and Powerball winner, who uses his riches to help those that can't afford a private detective. So, I guess if you are in my county you have solved a case for me?"

"The Dickerson murder," Redfox said. "He was blackmailing Muller."

"And she killed Muller." Nelson said pointing over to Yakira.

"Gerald Muller!" Sheriff Copper shot back. "That worthless piece of skunk squeeze. I would say she did us a favor."

"There needs to be an investigation. I am not going to stand for vigilantes coming into my county."

"Oh shut the freaking hell up Gray!" Sheriff Copper said. "You are an elected little ass just like me. You bring charges onto her for killing

Muller and you will be lucky you live till the trial. Hell there isn't a person in this county that didn't have a reason for killing that jerk. Myself and Redfox here included," the sheriff paused and his eye brows knitted down as he stared at the DA before he added, "Including you! Or do you not remember what he tried to do to your little girl? How he pulled her pants down behind the laundry mat. The only witness a teenage boy that was scared to death to say anything because he was afraid that Muller would kill his family? You wanted to hang him back then, so why now do you want to bring charges against a woman that took him out." Again the sheriff paused and then asked "Could it be you are trying to hide something?"

"What are you trying to accuse me of?"

The sheriff turned to Ryder and asked, "You did say you thought you heard two shots?"

"They came at the same time but yes I did." Ryder replied.

"What about you Redfox?"

"I can't say for sure sir?"
"And you Ms Alexander did you hear that?"

"No I just heard one shot." Alex said.

"And you Mrs. Ryder," Sheriff Cooper asked. "How many times did you shoot?"

"Once."

"Positive,"

"One hundred percent!" Yakira said again picking up the cup taking a drink before she continued. "He was going to kill me."

"And you were using a .357?"

"Yes!" Yakira said. "A Magpug snub nose."

"Isn't that a big gun for a little girl?" Nelson smirked.

"Not if you know how to handle it," Alex spoke up rolling her gaze towards the sheriff then back over to Nelson and added, "What about you? Can you handle your gun? Or do you need help? Or maybe you are the one that sits down on the toilet. "

"I don't need any of your mouth! " Nelson snapped back.

Alex looked back at the sheriff and said, "I saw the whole thing." She turned back again to Nelson and continued. "I came in from the north; it happened right in front me. Muller turned to avoid me. Yakira sealed off the road. He had no choice but to go through the gate. His car slammed against a tree. At which time he exited the vehicle. The weapon was in his hand. Yakira warned him to drop the gun. He brought the gun up, she fired. One time! He went down. As Redfox said, 'It was a clean shoot.' "

Nelson looked down at a file on the table in front of him, then with flick of his eyes he stared at Alex as he asked, "How come there are two wounds in the body?"

"Someone else fired," Yakira said. "I fired once and only once. My weapon shows that."

"Ms. Alexander," Nelson asked. "What weapon were you using?"

"Sig Saucer P320 9mm."

"And you Redfox?"

"Glock 17 9 mm."

"And you Mr. Ryder?" Nelson asked with a smirk that he knew the answer before Ryder could answer.

"Glock 33, 357."

Chapter 3

After all statements were taken and signed Ryder, Yakira and Alex headed for the double glass doors of the front of the sheriff's department. The morning was just beginning to break across the horizon; there was just something about that time of the day, which seemed that life was beginning again. The golden light of the sun was peering through the bright green leaves of the trees.

As Ryder pushed the door open they were greeted by birds that were awake and forming a chorus, of greeting the Lord in their own song. The town was coming alive, with the rumble of buses loading up with kids who were busy counting the last few days until school was over. Yes another day had begun, and another investigation had just come to an end.

They were met by another deputy who was walking up the front steps. He was an older deputy nearing retirement his once jet black hair now just a muddle of gray like storm clouds that form on the plains. He stopped in front of them and Ryder read his name tag "Darrin Matthews.' He was wearing large aviator style sunglasses, which he reached up and pulled down as he looked at Yakira.

"So it was you?" He asked. "You're the one that killed Muller." He grinned and added as he held out his hand to her. She shook it, "I just want to thank you. Miami wants to thank you. Hell the whole damn state of Oklahoma wants to thank you." He pulled his hand back and continued. "He was a piece of human filth! What he did to those little girls all his life even when he was kid. God bless you!"

Yakira moaned and held her stomach. Ryder turned to her. "Are you okay?"

"Just feel a little sick." She said. "Maybe it is because I am hungry."

"Maybe it's that big bag of hot fries you ate." Ryder said. She quickly placed her hand over her mouth and began to run for the door.

"Bathroom is just down the hall!" Deputy Matthews yelled at her as he pulled the door open. He turned and looked at Ryder "Well you just tell her we are all on her side. We had been waiting for this to happen one day. And when it did, we weren't going to investigate that hard."

"Why wasn't he ever brought up on charges?" Alex asked.

"Many arrests but each time the witnesses and victims would change their stories and charges would be dropped. I don't like to say it, because of the way the cop haters will see us but she is a hero in this town." With that the deputy walked inside.

The cars they had been driving were still part of an investigation, so Ryder called his uncle to come and get them. The Bail Bond across the street was casting long shadows over the street. In front of the sheriff's department was a porch with steps that led up to it.

Alex sat down on the top step and Ryder sit down next to her. "How was your first time?" Ryder asked.

"It was in the back seat of 1968 Camaro," she grinned mischievously at him as she slipped aviator type sunglasses over her eyes and laughed as she added, "It was over before I knew it."

"That is not what I meant. You know what I mean." He said as he reached into this jacket pocket and pulled out a pair of black framed Raybans ® and slipped them onto his face.

"You mean killing someone. I still see the face." She replied. "How about you?"

"I would like to say, they fade. Or it gets easier, but it doesn't."

"She is a strong woman. If anybody can get through this it is…"

"I know", Ryder said as he stood and walked out and gazed up the street, he was looking for his Uncle Tony 's car. Better known as Father Anthony Delany because he was the minster of St. Edwards in their hometown of Cassville, Missouri he was the only uncle that Ryder had on his mother's side. His mother was gone, she died when he was twelve. Ryder saw the nose of Father Anthony's car, it was a one of a kind 1970 Montego station wagon that had been turned into a pickup, much like a Ranchero but with a Mercury Cyclone Spoiler front end.

The dark metallic brown car pulled up in front of the Sheriff's Department and the driver's door opened. Out stepped a man with a round shaped face that showed his Delany Irish roots. With crimson hair parted on the side and his ruddy complexion, he looked as if he had just stepped off the boat Emerald Isle, but as soon as he spoke, out came what could only be considered true Hillbilly brogue.

"Only two seats up front. Who is going in the back?"

Ryder looked over his shoulder just as Yakira exited through the doors, he grinned and said, "You up to having the wind blow in your hair?"

"Why not!" Yakira replied as she walked down the steps. "The fresh air might make me feel better." He held out his hand and took hold of hers. He let his fingers wrap around hers, his large hand nearly swallowing her tiny hand. "Help me up?"

He scooped her up in his arms as she wrapped her arms around his neck, he drew her closer and he could smell her honeysuckle perfume that she always wore, as he lifted her up and over the side of the bed. He set her down in the bed of the vehicle. As Father Anthony and Alex got into the cab. Ryder went around to the back, putting one foot on the rear bumper, he swung his leg over the tailgate and crawled up into the bed.

Placed up next to the cab were two bucket seats that face the rear of the car and a chrome roll bar with yellow fog lights over them. Yakira was already buckled in when he sat down. He fastened the seat belt around him, slapped the side of the bed, and gave the thumbs up sign to indicate to his uncle that they were ready to go.

Father Anthony fired the car up, backed it out and headed back down the street the way he had come. Not a word was said as they passed through town noticing the many shops and diners, even a large flashing sign that was announcing that the rock band *Steelace* would be at the Buffalo Run Casino tonight.

"Maybe I should take her to a rock show?" Ryder asked as the wind was swirling around the cab, and making Yakira's hair flap like the flags at the car lot they passed by, Ryder looked over at her.

"Who?" She asked

"Marissa, her birthday is coming up." Ryder explained about his teenage sister. "I know she likes *Steelace*."

"Yeah that would be good." Yakira said. "They was hot when I was a teenager. They're back now?"

"According to Marissa they have a number one record now, *I Don't Need Love*." Ryder glanced over his bridge to watch her pushing her hair out of her face. "It is okay to feel you know."

"About what?"

"The shooting."

"Oh I am fine."

.Ryder didn't believe her; he had been in her shoes in the same way when a suspect drew a gun. There is but less than a twinkle of an eye, to decide to pull the trigger and live, or not, maybe take your last breath. But afterwards when you can breathe again, it plays over and over like an endless loop as you wonder 'did I make the right choice?'

"What did he mean when he said he wanted her to forgive him?" Yakira asked.

Maybe he was asking you to forgive him for making you...

Yakira interrupted, "That would not make since!" She shot back. Would he just asked for me to forgive him. But he clearly said he wanted her to forgive him." Again she pushed her hair back out of her face as the car slowed at a red light. She turned to him and Ryder said.

"Maybe it had to do with all the girls he messed with.

"Then why not hope they forgive him? He clearly said her? Who is she?"

I don't know." Ryder replied. There was a short break in the conversation before Yakira spoke again.

"I swear I heard him fire first. Didn't you?"

"I don't know for sure." Ryder said. Her hair had fallen down across her eyes, he pushed her hair backed and added, "It doesn't matter what I heard or anyone heard. He had fired at me and Redfox that makes it self-defense. You had no choice."

As the car got started going again, the wind began whipping at them, her hair and his jacket. He felt a little naked to the world with nothing on his side, his weapon had been held as part of the investigation. "Are you sure you only fired once?"

"Positive!"

"Are you sure?"

"*A brokh* Ricky!" Meaning damn it she cursed at him. "I know how many times I squeezed the trigger. It was one time!" She pushed her hair back out of her face again and said forcefully "One time!"

"I believe you." He said.

"Good!" She paused for a brief moment then added hoping to change the subject. "You ever think about getting a car for Marissa. She is going to be fifteen and will be getting her learners permit."

It was hard to explain but they had the same father but different mothers, like him she lost her mother when she was twelve, there were many years between them and she was more, age- wise like a daughter, than a half-sister. However in Ryder's house there was no half, she was his sister and that's all there was.

"I don't know," Ryder said with slight shake of his head.

"Well what a fifteen year old girl would really want would be a sixteen-year –old boy." She laughed and then added "I guess you wouldn't like that huh?" She paused and he didn't reply. "Have Gene build her a one of kind, like you did with the Killer Bee and this one for Uncle Tony. Have him build her a car just for her."

"That would take a long time…"

"Then give her what she really wants—you!" Yakira said interrupting him. She must have seen the confusion running through his mind, how could she want that. Since their father had died, she was living with him at his estate; he had even adopted her to make it legal. He made sure she had everything her little heart could desire. *What more could I give?* He thought. Yakira explained it. "Your time! We have been so busy with cases you haven't had time to be there for her, Bubbie has been staying with her. Why not give the gift of you, spend time with her."

"She is a teenager; she doesn't want to hang around with…"

"Sweetie you are not exactly the typical big brother, or parent here. And she is not the typical teenager either. She is having trouble fitting in. She isn't one of the jocks and isn't one of the nerds. You've seen her grades, she is a C student. She has one or two real friends, the rest of those girls she is hanging around with are only around her to get next to you."

They were still on Highway 10 heading back toward the Missouri state line. They were just crossing over the Spring River as he looked over her at the rocky bluffs that looked down upon the rolling water. There had been lots of rain this spring and what had been a small arm of the river was now a full rolling river. "What do you mean to get next to me?"

"Ricky you are good looking and a billionaire." She said, as she again pushed her hair back out of her face only to have it swat again across the face. "If it isn't the little teeny boppers that have the hots for

22

you, it is their mothers. You know what I hear when I go to get my hair done, at A Cut Above 'how can she get him? Look at her, she is no beauty queen, she has no body. It is tough for us that love you. And it is tough on her, she is not the sports star you were. She is still trying to find herself. Sweetie it is hard for us that love you,"

"Huh?"

"Give her two parties, one the blow out that will have the girls talking all summer." Yakira said, again trying to push her hair back out of her face. "Then give another party with the people that matter to her."

He reached and rubbed his hand on the side of her face as he said, "You are going to make a great mother someday."

"I hope so," She replied with hesitation. "But you know what the doctor said. The chance that I can carry another child is..."

He placed his finger over her lips leaning forward he said, "It is not zero. So there is a chance." She nodded and her lips curled up under his finger. He removed his finger from her lips and then gave her a kiss.

Chapter 4

Home! Cassville, Mo. A small town nestled in the Ozarks hills of SW Missouri where some of the best trout fishing could be found. Trout that would fight with every crank of the reel and make one work up a hunger for that fried up rainbow beauty. It was taken right out of a Norman Rockwell painting with even the bench where one could sit in the shade of a tree in front of the courthouse, and lift a glass of ice cold coke that you got from the soda fountain at the drug store on the square. Yes it was home and it felt good to be back.

There are two days that are celebrated in the Cassville R-4 school system by teachers and students alike, one is March the first, opening day of trout season when the school is closed. The other day varies and comes near the end of May, the last day of school.

No matter how old one gets you remember that day. It is just a half a day, students turning in books, clearing out lockers, sitting at desks eyes glued to the clock on the wall watching with each little tick of the second hand, each tick drawing just a little closer, till that bell rings, the cell doors open and the prisoners are free. Alice Copper's *School's Out*, blaring out over the intercom, as there is a mad dash to those outside doors and freedom.

They had dropped Yakira off at the house and Ryder and Alex had taken his custom blood red 1971 Dodge Charger known as the *Killer Bee* to pickup Alex's little girl Ceelia who was in kindergarten. The car with its high wing spoiler, gunmetal stripes and shark like nose cone was easy to spot going down Main Street and turned on to 14th street or as it is locally known as Kit-Kat Ave. "Things have really changed." Alex said.

He glanced up into the review mirror and saw the pink booster seat strapped into the back seat. Just a few years ago, he was a hard nose homicide cop on the streets of Kansas City and he and Alex were hunting the serial killer, the Kansas City Butcher. Now he was picking up a child at school, just like all the rest of the line waiting for their pride and joy to appear . Large long yellow buses lined up, their mouths open, waiting to fill up for the last time for another school year. Really changed," Ryder said. as he parked the car, he glanced over at Alex who had opened the door. "You ever think you would end up here?"

"Honestly?" She asked as she stepped out of the car. "No, but I wouldn't want to go back." She shut the door and he watched as Alex walked across the street and into the large cafeteria where she had to wait for teachers and helpers to guide the child to their parents.

With the window down, he heard the final bell ring, and turned, expecting to watch as the doors burst open, the convicts of edification breaking free and racing for the beginning of summer. The metal doors pushed open, not one child was running. No parent was scooping up their bundle of joy, just one hand held out, the other holding a cell phone, heads bowed to the information antichrist that they worshipped. Posting likes or comments on Facebook ® or scanning through the latest news, lifting a head only long enough to check for traffic as they crossed the street their child in tow trying to tell the excitement of the final day. Another bell rang and the middle school is released. Here the doors slowly opened as the preteens step into the mouths of the yellow beasts, they too head down in worship of the god they held in their hands. Where was the excitement of summer just ready to beam over the horizon, the feel of freedom he remembered feeling on this last day. No instead the magic was what they held, a piece of plastic, glowing, informing.

"Yeah things had really changed!" Ryder said out loud as he watched Alex hold her child's hand guiding her across the street. There was something dark red that was clutched in the child's hand. Alex opened the passenger side door.

"Hi Uncle Ricky." The little girl said crawling into the car as she grabbed him in a hug. He was not her uncle by blood, but by choice and that is how she knew him. She gave him a kiss and then held out what was in her hand. "I made this for you." He took it and looked at it. It was cut of construction paper, glued together to make a dog, and colored black and white.

"Well thank you Ceelia," he said holding it up and looking at it. "I will put this in my office," he started to fold it when she cried out.

"No Ricky. He is a border collie, he is a watch dog," Ceelia explained as she crawled between the bucket seats and into the booster seat, and Alex strapped her in. "He will watch over you when you and Mommy and Aunt Yakira are helping people." Ryder glanced up in the rear view mirror again, and saw Alex turn and look at him. He leaned over and opened the glove box door and reached inside and pulled out a roll of clear tape that he used to lift prints. He pulled off four small strips of tape and then taped the artwork to the dash of the car over the radio in front of the gear selector.

"See he will watch over us all now." Ryder said as he sat back up in the seat.

Alex got into the passenger seat and shut the door. She looked over at him and said, "All right, one down and one to go." Ryder fired the car up, on to the high school.

It didn't matter what city, what town it was, schools all looked the same, made of red bricks, a paved driveway in front and the mascot proudly looking down on the grounds. Here Wilbur the Wildcat, mouth opened in full growl, filled that duty, the school colors black and gold spelled out WILDCATS across the gym. Ryder parked the car and waited, watching as the buses pulled into the circle drive in front of the school.

"Mommy why were the teachers so nice to me today?" Ceelia said looking up at her.

"What do you mean?" Alex asked as Ryder once again looked at the little girl in the rearview mirror.

"Miss Ratcliff she gave me a hug."

"Well she was just—she was going to miss you. You are going into first grade next year."

"But she did when I got to school," Ceelia said as she turned and looked at Ryder. He could see the innocents in her sapphire like eyes. "She said I need to make a watch dog for Mommy."

"Then why did you give this to me?" Ryder asked pointing to the dash.

"Because, you watch after Mommy that she doesn't get hurt, you needed him to watch after you." Ryder took a deep breath trying to get hold of his emotions; he turned and looked at the school just as the bell sounded.

"They know what happened." Ryder whispered.

"Yes, the teacher asked me about it." She whispered back.

Kids began to push the doors open and began pouring out of the doors. Seniors saying good bye to the only life they knew, wondering where they would be going next, juniors looking to the next year when they will be the kings of the school, sophomores trapped in the ending cycle of being nobody. Freshman excited that, that year is over and they will no longer be first rung on this ladder, which everyone has to step on.

"Well at least another case is over." Alex said leaning her head back on the built in headrest of the seat.

"I am not so sure?" Ryder replied causing her to turn and look at him. "Did you see Muller fire?"

"No, he didn't fire. I didn't see any muzzle flash. But he did point the gun at her. You really think there could be two shooters?" Alex said and then looking across the school yard she added. "Here she comes. Or could she have shot twice? You know how easy it can happen in the heatof the battle."

"Not Yakira," Ryder said as he stepped out of the car. He leaned down, his arm resting on the roof of the car and looked across the interior of the car at Alex. "I know she has never had the training we have, but she was like she was born with a gun in her hand. If anyone knows how many times she shot it will be her."

"Then who else was out there?."

Marissa exited the school. She was with two other girls. A purple colored knapsack was draped over her shoulder. She was tall, with long legs, skinny and long milk chocolate colored hair that fell over shoulders and down her back and parted in the middle. Her face was and long and lean and she wore no makeup. Suddenly she stopped and looked at him. She dashed over and grabbed him in a tight embrace.

"What is this for? " Ryder asked. He heard her sniffle and felt her tremble in his arms. "Marissa!" He said pushing her back to look at her, tears were in his eyes. "What is the matter?"

"I heard you were involved in a shooting and someone was killed. It is all over the school." She said then she grabbed him again. "I was so afraid it was you! I tried calling you and you wouldn't call me back. I was so afraid—don't leave me, you're all I have."

Again he pushed her back and looked at her and said, "you're not going to get rid of your big brother that easy. We are all okay. Yakira shot a guy, he was the one who was killed."

"Oh my gosh! Is she okay?"

Ryder took hold of her backpack, and pushed the seat back forward as he said, "Why don't we go home and find out."

Chapter 5

Ryder's estate was just a few miles outside of Cassville. It was grand like a palace complete with a turret at the top where Marissa's bedroom was. Large wooden doors at the front of the house completed the castle look. Behind the black iron gates and the stone wall that surround the front edge of the yard was an elegant stone driveway that circled around and over to the three car garage at the side.

It rested on 1500 acres of farmland, with rolling hills, and a stream that cut through five acres of woods, that featured pine, oak, and walnut and hickory trees. Also on the ranch was another house, a three bedroom red brick ranch style house, just down the hill from the main house, where Alex and Ceelia lived, along several out buildings and a large barn that was nearly empty.

Next to the barn was a field with a *harras* of five horses, galloping at full speed, hooves being kicked up high in the air as if they were three year old toddlers enjoying a day out in the sun. Ryder stopped the car in front of the garage and got out, Marissa crawled out as Alex unbuckled her daughter from the booster seat.

Marissa looked over at the galloping horses there were three red ones, one a pinto, black and white, and another a beautiful mare, solid black, except for right around her hooves which were solid white. Her name…

"Socks!" Marissa called out as she quickly walked towards the white board fence that separated the field from the yard. "Socks!" She called out again as she set down the backpack and unzipped it.

The black horse suddenly stopped her tracks, flipping her head around, her mane tossing like the hair of a beautiful girl as Marissa crawled up and threw her legs over the top board of the fence. The horse came galloping up to Marissa. "Look what the ladies at the cafeteria sent you."

The horse let out a nicker, excited seeing the bag of slices of apples in her mistresses hand. Marissa opened the bag and pulled out a slice of the apple and placed her hand flat and the horse nipped it from her palm.

"Two beautiful ladies," Ryder said walking up to the fence, reaching over the fence and scratching the black beauty behind the ears. The horse tilted her head over, but only to quickly turn back to Marissa as she had yet another slice of apple in her palm.

Marissa turned to Ryder, grinned broadly and asked, "You think we could go riding today?"

"I will ask and see if...." Ryder replied as he leaned on the fence watching as the other horses continued to run in circles in the pasture.

"No!"" Marissa said interrupting him grabbing his arm. "I thought it could just be me and you." She grinned again showing her dimples. "I thought maybe we could take a picnic over to the creek. I know you want to be with Yakira and Ceelia but...can't you also have some time with me?"

"So Yakira was right?" Ryder said softly.

"What?"

"Nothing," Ryder said as he stood up. "Go get changed and get the horses ready." Marissa climbed down from the fence and dashed back towards the house. Ryder stood there for just a moment staring out across his ranch, reflecting on how things had changed. Just a few years ago he was in Kansas City, staring out across blocks and blocks of cement, not one person to care about, now he is surrounded by an entire family. Maybe there was a part of him, deep down, that might have missed that, but the biggest part of him, felt he belonged for once in his life. He turned and headed for the house. The front door was wide open. He shook his head at the excitement of his sister as he shut it behind.

"She forgot again!" He heard a woman say; he turned and saw an older woman standing next the stairs. It was Bubbie, Yakira's grandmother. Her hair short, like she was, and proudly silver, she was a little plump, but she made one think of a grandmother, she was always making something in the kitchen, her hands were covered in flour, and she was holding a white t-towel. "She came in and raced up the stairs. Your chicken is ready."

"What chicken?"

"The one Marissa asked me to fix this morning before she left for school. For your picnic" Bubbie said. "She is feeling left out you know."

"I know," Ryder said glancing up the stairs. "There just doesn't seem to be enough time."

"*Motek*," she said as a term of affection as she reached up and pinched his cheek. "There is always time to spread a little love. That young lady needs you just as much as Yakira or Ceelia does, just in a different way."

"How do I do that?"

"Listen to her Ricky. Be more willing to use these." She said pointing to his ears. "Instead of this." She put her finger on his lips. "She will tell you but you have to be willing to listen and not judge her."

Ryder leaned over and gave her a kiss on the cheek. "You are an amazing woman." He said.
"How did you get so wise?"

"It is a natural gift," she grinned. "It comes when you become a grandmother. Become a great-grandmother and you become a genius. So when are you going to make me one?"

Ryder felt a flush come over his cheeks, and masked his embarrassment with a small laugh before he asked, "I might need a little help in that , speaking of her, where is she ?"

"She went upstairs to take a bath." Bubbie said. Ryder started up the stairs when she added. "She said she wanted to wash it all away. What does she mean?" Ryder stopped and turned to her.

"Something she can never wash away." He said. "She is going to have to work this out herself. There is no one else that can help her." Ryder turned and walked up stairs, down the hall and to the master bedroom.

It was large, with a large bed, a fireplace and French doors that lead out on to a balcony. It was modernly furnished with a large king size bed, walnut end tables on each side. Matching dresser with a large mirror, a chest of drawers and above the chest mounted to the wall was a large flat screen TV. Over to the side was another set of double doors that lead into the master bathroom. It was a two part design with the front part being the dressing area and a small room that was for the toilet. There were two large sinks on counters one each wall, that faced two large mirrors, also on each side were two large closets, one for him, and the other for Yakira. A set of louvered doors separated the dressing area from the bathing area.

"Is there a beautiful woman in here?" Ryder asked as he lightly tapped on the doors.

"No, just me," he heard Yakira mournfully say from behind the door. He opened the doors and walked in. There was large walk in shower, with stones on the side wall and a large showerhead; it was like standing out in the rain. In front of him was the marble bathtub, rectangular in shape, it was big enough for two people. Around the back and side of the tub was dark colored glass, that allowed you to look out, but no one could see inside.

Yakira was sunken down in the tub covered with rich layer of foamy white bubbles. He walked over and sat down on the edge of the tub. "You can join me if you like." Yakira said looking up at him.

"It is tempting, but I am taking Marissa riding, we are going to have a picnic. I guess you are right she needs time with me. I think you are right, I think we don't need to take any more cases; we just need to stay here this summer. Just make it a family thing. We will have Marissa's party here, cookouts and just relax." As he spoke he sees it in his mind the fun they would have. "What do you say?" He looked back down at her in the tub. She was just staring out the window; there was nothing really to see just open sky and a field of fescue, the stalks drifting slowly in a gentle breeze. "Are you okay?"

"I told you I am fine." She said still staring out the window.

"Okay then." He leaned down and gave her a kiss. He stood up.

"Bubbie said she was going try to teach me to cook something." Yakira said.

"Don't burn the house down."

"I won't!" Yakira grinned as Ryder took a couple steps away, then she spoke again. "Why is it I see his damn face?"

He turned back to her and she continued. "Every time I close my eyes I see it happening over and over again." She turned and looked at him. "He was a little *Momzer*!", which meant bastard. "When I think what he did to little girls! What he could have done to Ceelia!" Tears puddle in her eyes as she continued, "Why should I give a damn that I killed him? She lowered her head and buried her face in her hands then softly added, "Why do I care? You think if he would have killed me he would be thinking about me?"

Ryder swallowed hard and walked back over to the tub and again sat down on the edge of the tub. "Because, darling, you are a good person. You have a soul." She raised her head and looked up at him. "That is the difference between murder and killing. One who murders has no regret. Those that take a life do. Let me ask you one thing. If you had it to all over again, would you still pull the trigger?"

"Yes."

Chapter 6

After consoling Yakira for a few minutes and changing into jeans and a t-shirt and boots he went back downstairs where he met with Bubbie and Marissa, his little sister now dressed in jeans, boots and western style blouse, they were both in the foyer. Bubbie was holding a small basket in her hand. As he descended the stairs she handed him the basket and said, "Got some fried chicken, potato salad, a blanket, plates and…" She leaned a little closer to him and added. "A chocolate cake for dessert."

"Your special recipe?" Ryder asked lifting the lid of the basket and sniffing inside. Her cake was different than most, one she made with fine chocolate and six eggs. It was ten times richer than other cakes. Topped with homemade candy icing, it was going to be hard to just get over to the back pasture where the creek was with having a smaple test.

"Of course!"

Ryder reached into his pocket of his jeans and handed his phone to Bubbie and said, "Could you put this on the charger please."

"You don't want it with you?" She asked

"Not today!"

Ryder took the basket, along with Marissa and headed towards the barn, where two horses were already saddled and ready to go; Socks and a beautiful, dark red, quarter horse with black mane and tail, and white blaze that was shaped like a tornado, giving him his name - Storm. Marissa mounted her horse as Ryder attached the basket to the saddle on Storm. With one foot in the stirrup he swung his other leg over the steed and pulled himself up into the saddle.

"Ready?" he asked.

"Always", she said with a grin. "Race you!" She said using the heels of her boots to prod the horse and the mare took off in a gallop heading across the pasture and up the hill. Ryder followed on Storm, his horse quickly galloping, trying catch up with her.

The ranch was laid out in several different fields, from a pasture where five head of cattle roamed including two calves that would become beef this fall and one 20 acre field that was growing hay for the horses, and the few head of cows. However, over the top of the hill, after a gentle ride through the woods and across the meadows at the back of the woods, was another hill.

As Ryder pulled back on Storm's rein at the top of the hill, he stared down the creek that twisted its way through the 1500 acres and ended up pouring into a small 3 acre lake with a waterfall at one end that drained into a smaller stream that continued out of his property and on to his neighbor.

It is hard to find stillness in this busy world, but here he could close his eyes and hear nothing, it was paradise. He leaned forward and the horse went down the hill, as he pulled back on the reins again.

On the bank of the lake was a woman. It his was his neighbor, Annie Harris. She was in her sixties, a little silver around the temples of her bob hair cut. Her legs seemed short for her body, and her khaki pants were rolled up revealing her tan and weathered bare feet. She was dressed in a fishing vest, and a wide brim hat with several colorful flies hooked into it. In her hands was a red fishing rod with a Zebco® 33 reel. She quickly reeled in the line as Ryder dismounted and tied the horse to a small sassafras tree.

"Hey Annie, how are they biting?" Ryder asked as his sister stepped down from her ride and tied her horses to another small tree.

"About like a vegetarian at a meat convention!" She complained, tossing the line out again. PLUNK! The line sank into the clear water. "Only two lousy Blue Gill."

"So no fried fish for supper?" Ryder asked as he untied the basket from the saddle. "How about some fried chicken?" Ryder held the basket up with one hand as he made his way over the lake. "It is still warm." She looked over at him a she handed the basket to his sister.

"Yeah…Okay." She said quickly reeling her line in. "Guess if they are not biting I can bite." She reeled her line again and placed her pole down on the bank and walked over to where Marissa was spreading a blanket out on the grass. Marissa placed the basket down and then sat down on the blanket beside his sister.   "So who made the chicken?"

"Bubbie."

Marissa took a paper plate and placed a spoon full of potato salad on it along with a couple of pieces of chicken, a leg and piece of white meat, and handed it to Annie. "So is this some celebration?"

"Yeah," Marissa said as she fixed another plate and handed it to Ryder. "School is out!"

"Not for all of us," Annie said.

"Mind if we say grace?" Marissa asked after fixing her own plate. Then she said grace and they began to eat.

"Got summer classes this year?" Ryder asked, knowing she was a professor at Crowder College in Neosho, where she taught biology.

"Oh yes!" Annie exclaimed as she took a bit of the chicken leg. "They got me on the summer line up this year. Hopefully I won't have a kid like I did this spring." She used the fork that Marissa had given her and Bubbie had packed in the basket, to scoop out some of the yellow potato salad. She set the plate down on the blanket and said, "This year I had a kid that answered the question 'What is a cytoplasm? And the little dimwit answered 'someone who makes money and should be killed.' I swear Ryder if I get more kids like that; you are going to have a new murder mystery. Some mystery though if I did it."

She looked over at Marissa and added, "You're not one of them are you?" Marissa shook her head as she reached in and put a drumstick on her plate along with some potato salad. "How many chromosomes in the human cell?"

"Twenty-three pair." She replied. "You taught me that."

"Maybe there is hope." Annie said as she picked up the plate and took another bite of the chicken. "But I can't take another one like that, we are talking Crowder College here not Berkley. Don't get me wrong when I was that young I had dreams to make the world a better place but never told a teacher I wanted to kill them."

"Someone threatened you Annie?"

"Oh it was no big deal," she replied as she finished the dark meat and moved on to the next piece of chicken. "He is just a mouthy little punk who tried to lead a walkout out of my class."

"So why don't you just retire Annie?" Ryder said as he filled his plate.

"Because every once in awhile you get a kid that gets it," Annie said holding the piece of chicken in her hand, her hand resting on her knee. That makes it worthwhile. I always try to teach my kids a lesson in life. By testing their beliefs."

 "Like what?" Marissa asked as she took a bite of the chicken.

"Life itself," Annie said "this kid I gave the assignment to proved life begins at conception."

"But it does!" Marissa replied assuredly.

"But he didn't believe that way," Annie explained. "His belief was that a child is not a human being until they could come into reasoning around two or three years old."

"That is crazy!" Marissa replied. "A baby is a baby."

"And you I would give the assignment to prove to me that life does not begin at conception."

"I couldn't do that!" Marissa said. "It is not what I believe. I prove to you otherwise. With facts and data."

A grand smile broke across Annie's face. "And there you got the real assignment! To stand up for your beliefs and prove them with facts, you would have got an A."

"An A really!" Marissa said. "Could you tell the teachers at Cassville to give me that?"

Annie looked over at Ryder and said, "You are doing well with this one Rick. Your mother would be proud of you." She shook her head not as in disagreement but as in where had all that time gone. "Your mother was my best friend at Crowder when we were going there. She looked at Ryder and added. "We thought we were something on that campus back then. We were all so close. You know when I look back at that I think you could have been my kid if things were different."

"So how is Harrell doing?" Ryder asked about her son.

"Don't get to see him much anymore," she said starting out past Ryder and into the distant field. "Now a renowned heart surgeon in Arkansas. Guess I would have to be getting married or dying the next time I see him." She took another bite of chicken and looked over a Marissa. "So what are you, thirteen now?"

"I am going to be fifteen in three weeks." Marissa said.

"Driving soon?"

"Getting my learners permit that day." Marissa said.

"That is a reason to stay at this fishing hole all summer. Another teenager on the road!" She turned and looked at Ryder and asked, "Going to get her a car, maybe a GTO like your mother had."

"We will have to wait and see," Ryder said. "Guess you and mom had some good times in that old goat?"

"Every time I see a GTO I think of her". Annie let out a sigh. "I miss her still." Annie stood up, and brushed the crumbs of the chicken from her pants. "Enough of this sad talk."

"Annie we got dessert," Ryder said as he looked up at her.

"I think I will pass," Annie said walking towards the water. She picked up her fishing pole and tackle box and then she turned back to him, "Rick there is something I need to talk to you about when you have the time."

"Sure Annie," Ryder said. "Come up anytime."

Annie took a few steps away, then turned and faced Marissa and said, "And you young lady I have a special gift for you for your birthday."

"What is it?" Marissa asked.

"You will just have to wait and see."

As Annie crawled through the barbed-wire fence that separated the properties, Ryder turned to his sister and said. "What do say we do some wading in the creek before we have our cake?" They removed their boots and socks and rolled the pant legs up their knees. He stepped into the water, even though it was a warm day the water was cold to his flesh as he felt the rocks and smooth pebbles on the bottom of his feet. He held his hand out and helped his sister take her steps out into the water.

"How are you doing?"

"I'm doing fine," She said. "You can let go now."

"Now I mean with school and everything that is going on."

"School is school!" She bemoaned. "I am glad it is over! I don't like it, it isn't hard to understand."

"And the girls at school, is it any better?" Ryder asked as he watched her hold her head down watching where she was walking in the water, her long locks flowing down like they were the long ears of a depressed hound, just flipping back and forth with each step she took.

"It is all cool now", she said, still not lifting her head, moving a couple of rocks with her toes and making a crawdad swim away.

"Don't lie to me."

She lifted her head and looked at him, "Do you mean the ones that ask me 'does my brother ever walk around nude and want to spend the night or the ones that tell me what they do in their bedroom to my brother's photo when he was a quarterback and was only dressed in his underwear shorts for that dumb advertisement you did." Again she dropped her chin down on her chest and used her bare toes to turn over more rocks, looking for more crawdads and then she added, "Thing have changed."

"How?" Ryder asked making her lift her head to look at him once again. "Don't get me wrong I love Yakira, Ceelia and Alex but..." She dropped her head again staring into the water. "Never mind it was just silly."

"It is no longer just you and me right?"

"I don't want it to be like I am some kind of bad person but..." Again she she looked up at him. "But I miss those times of when it was just you and I and a cup of grandmother's hot chocolate and I could tell you anything."

"You still can."

"I don't know", she said again dropping her head down to stare into the water. "Something's I can't."

He walked over to her and placed his hands on her shoulders. "You are not a bad person. I am."

"No, you're..." She said as she looked up at him.

"Yes, I am! And it is going to change. You're my sister and in about three years you are going to be heading off to college and you won't be here. So I was going to tell you about this later but I think now is the time. I am going to take the summer off and you and I are going to spend more time together. You are going to be driving on the permit; I guess that is up to me being in the seat next to you." Marissa grinned at him. "And there is nothing, I mean anything you cannot tell me."

"Anything? She said with a mischievous grin as she added, "Even sex?"

He felt his face turn a shade of red but added, "Yes even that!" He lifted his hands from her and placed one arm around her as they stepped back towards the bank. "What do you say we go back to the house and plan out a party? That will have those girls talking about that instead of me in my underwear."

Chapter 7

Ryder and Marissa rode back to the house. Marissa brushed the horses down and put them back into the pasture. For supper Bubbie made her specialty meatloaf, with a glaze of tomato sauce, honey, Worcestershire sauce and orange juice, with carrots and apples. It was one of Yakira's favorites but she didn't eat hardly anything she just pushed it around on her plate, before dismissing herself and going up stairs.

After supper Bubbie gave thanks for the meal, as was the custom in Jewish culture and began to clear the table as Ryder and Marissa sat at the table to plan out her 'party of all parties' for her birthday. Ceelia came to Ryder holding a golden haired doll. "Uncle Ricky can we play Barbie's?"

He looked down at her as she grinned flashing those dimples. He put her on his lap wrapping his arms around her as he explained, "I can't tonight darling. I have to help Marissa plan out her birthday party; her birthday is coming up next month."

"But we play!," the little girl replied sounding disappointed as she stared down at her doll she was holding. Then she tilted her back looking up at Ryder, allowing her long dark brown hair to fall back on his chest and asked, "How about tomorrow?"

"We will have to see."

Ceelia turned and looked at Marissa who was sitting on Ryder's side of the table and asked, "Can I come to your party?"

"Of course." Marissa said. With that Ceelia climbed down from Ryder's lap and went off to play by herself. The next three hours were spent making the plans for the party. After that Ceelia and Alex went back to their house down the hill and Ryder went upstairs and into the master bedroom.

Yakira had changed into her night clothes and was sitting up in bed, the dark blue comforter pulled up, and her back resting on several pillows against headboard. She was holding a bright pink glass bowl in her hands, watching TV eating something from the bowl. He found it strange that she was eating, because her excuse for not eating supper was that she felt sick.

"What do you have?" He asked as he walked over to the bed.

"Strawberry ice cream topped with hot fries." She held the bowl up and added. "Try some!"

"I don't think so."

"Oh come on, when we got married we were going to share everything." She said as she scooped up some of the ice cream and held up the spoon to him. He was still unsure of this concoction but opened his mouth and allowed her to put into his mouth. The first thing he noticed was the crunch of the fries followed quickly by the smoothness and sweetness of the strawberry ice cream. At first there was no notice of heat, he almost wanted to request another bite, then in an instant heat hit like a 380 pound linebacker and it lasted.

"Good huh?"

"One of a kind taste." He replied twisting his mouth around into a fake smile.

"Want some more?" She asked offering another spoonful.

"One is enough!" Ryder said grabbing her hand and pushing it back. He went into the bathroom changed into light blue sleep pants and a matching t-shirt.

As he exited the bathroom Yakira was just finishing up her bowl of ice cream and sat the empty bowl on the night stand. He walked over to the bed, picking up the remote that was lying next to her. "Mind if we turn this off?" He asked.

"I have seen it before; the good guys win in the end." She said as he pointed the remote and turned the set off. "Now I am ready for dessert." She said with a grin as she sat up on her knees and placed her arms around his neck and moved her lips closer to his, stopping as he said:

"I want to go over the shooting just one more time."

"No," She said releasing him and setting back down on the bed. "I have gone over it enough." She closed her eyes and continued, "I just want to go to sleep."

"I want you to do it different this time."

"How?" She said opening her eyes.

"I want you to close your eyes," Ryder said. "I will take you through it, and I want you to tell me what you hear."

"Hear?" She asked confused that he wanted this.

"Cut everything else out. Just tell me what you hear." She closed her eyes. As Ryder began taking her through it again, "Okay, Muller is crossing the fence. What do you hear?"

"Are you crazy?" She asked her eyes flying open.

"Just tell me what you hear not what you see. Only what you hear."

She closed her eyes again, "I hear his footsteps in the grass, now the scuffing of his feet on the pavement. I hear gunshots they are going over my head."

"Where are you?"

"I am behind our car."

"What do you hear?"

"The squeak of a car door opening." Yakira said her breath coming in short spurts as she was reliving it all over again. "I hear him firing up the car. Tires spinning. Another gunshot! It is you! You shot at the car." Yakira's breath is coming even quicker as she continues "I hear another car start I am behind the wheel. I can barely reach the pedal. I hear tires squealing, I nearly lose control. I hear an engine roar, I am speeding up beside him. I hear the tires rubbing against the pavement. It is Alex! She is pulling out in front of him."

"What do you hear now?"

"A crash!" She says with excitement. "He smashes through the gate, then into a tree. I hear my breath; I am racing for the gate. I hear the moan of his car door. It is opening! I hear a click it is the cocking of a gun. He raises up the gun. I am lifting up mine!" Her hands were trembling as she spoke.

"Honey!" Ryder said placing his hands on her shoulders. She opened her eyes, her breath was still quivering. "What cocking of a gun? I want you to try again. Cut out everything but the cocking of that gun where is it coming from."

She closed her eyes again. "I can't tell."

"Okay what does it sound like? Is it a hammer pulled back?"

"No," She said with a shake of her head.

"Come on Yakira you know the different sounds a gun make."

"Is it a slide hammer," he asked and she shook her head and he asked, "The bolt on a rifle?"

"It is a lever action." She said her eyes flying open. "It came from behind me."

Chapter 8

It was a couple days later, and each night was the same. With Yakira waking up every few minutes as the nightmare galloped through her memory like race day at the Kentucky Derby. Leaving her pacing the room like a prisoner in a cell, who was waiting for freedom, freedom that never seems to come. Each morning coming much too quickly, an alarm going off interrupting the final couple of hours of good sleep that was just the leftovers of the toss and tumble night. Each morning was greeted with a dash to bathroom as Yakira found herself throwing up.

Just as Ryder heard the flush of the stool in the bathroom, he heard his cell phone ding as a text message came through

Ballistic results in. Meet me at the C.S. at 11:00 a.m.
Redfox

As she exited the bathroom wiping her mouth with a wash cloth he turned to her and as he rolled out of bed he said, "Get dressed!"

"Why?" She moaned "I thought we were taking the summer off."

"We are," Ryder said heading toward the bathroom. "But we have something to do first. And we have to stop by your gun shop."

"What?" She asked confused as he passed by her. "Why?"

"Just some things we have to pick up." He said shutting the door behind him.

Ryder dressed as he usually did in slacks, dress shirt and sport coat. As Yakira got dressed, he went into the kitchen and fixed three cups of coffee and gabbed a box of doughnuts off the top of the refrigerator.

"All right where is breakfast?" He heard Alex ask as she walked into the kitchen. He handed her one of the cups of coffee and then opened the lid on the doughnuts. "Doughnuts?" She complained as she picked a chocolate covered one.

"Did you bring what I asked you?"

"Yes, I put it in the truck of your car." She took a bite of the doughnut and then continued, "So where are we going?"

"Spooklight Road."

****

By the time they crossed the Oklahoma line the dew that was holding to the grass was beginning to dry in the warmth of the rising sun, the trees intertwining their shadows with each other. Once again, they were at the corner of 50 and 680 known as Spooklight corner. He pulled the car over the side of the dirt road marked 680, stopped and got out.

Ryder looked up at the clear blue sky, his eyes shielded with Ray Ban® sunglasses; he watched a red tail hawk soaring in the sky circling the woods to his left. The twisted metal gate was pushed over to the side with the open side sealed with a single strip of yellow police tape, the ends tied to the fence posts.

Ryder popped the trunk and reached inside, getting the weapons that he had taken from Yakira's gun shop; a Tarsus 66 357 revolver, a Marlin XT-22RO Bolt Action Rim fire Rifle with 3-9x32 Scope; a Remington Model 7600 Pump Action Rifle, and the one type he had asked Alex to bring, a Henry Big Boy Lever Action. 357 Magnum Rifle that had been a Christmas gift last year from Yakira. He laid them all on top of the roof of the car except the pistol. As the hawk gave a flap of its wing and soared overhead into the field to his right, Ryder checked the cylinder of the pistol to make sure it was empty and then handed the black revolver to Alex.

"Where do you want me to go?" Alex asked holding the weapon to her side. Ryder gazed out across the road, to the fairly wide open field that was dotted with a few of trees that possibly could hide someone. "Go out and stand behind the forked tree." Alex went across the road and crawled through the barbed-wire fence and took her position behind the forked tree as Ryder and Yakira stepped across the yellow tape. He positioned her in the spot where she was standing when she shot Muller.

He took his place right next to her. "I want you to close your eyes and try to remember." He waved at Alex and she pulled the hammer back.

"No," she said with a shake of her head. "That is not the sound."

Ryder picked up the bolt action rifle and walked across the road and exchanged it with the pistol and asked Alex to try cocking the rifle.

"No that isn't it", Yakira said.

He switched the bolt action for the lever action and Alex cocked the gun. "That is it!" Yakira said. "That is what I heard."

"Okay but we have one more gun to check," Ryder said as he picked up the pump action rifle. He walked over to Alex and she began to switch, but he quickly shook his head and returned still holding on to the pump rifle. Again, Alex cocked the weapon.

"That is it too!" She said sounding confused.

"Are you sure?"

"Positive!" She said. "I don't understand it." She said opening her eyes and turning to him. "How could two rifles sound the same?"

"Because it was the same rifle, I tried to trick you." He turned to look at Alex and asked "could you make a kill shot from there?"

"With this Henry rifle, it would be like shooting a dead fish."

Afterwards she crawled back through the fence and handed her weapon to Ryder who was standing next to his car. "Well we proved there could have been two shooters." Ryder said.

"I guess we did," she replied not sounding assured for her own words.

"What's bugging you?"

"Look across there." She said for her to hear the cocking of the rifle, the shooter had to be no more than a hundred feet. Why didn't I see them? Or a muzzle flash."

"Where were you when the shooting happened?" Ryder asked. "I mean exactly happening."

She walked over into the road next to where the Charger was parked and said, "Right here." She was facing across the road.

"Where you facing that way?" Ryder asked.

"No I was…" She hushed as she turned to face where the shooting happened, the field to her back. "That is why, it was behind me ". She turned back around to the field and continued, "But how could someone get in there without us knowing it?"

"The single headlight," Ryder said remembering the night of the shooting. "It could have been a motorcycle. A motorcycle could have easily got in there."

Ryder heard a car approaching, he turned and saw an Ottawa Cruiser pull over to the side East 50 road and out stepped Deptuy Redfox. He glanced at the weapons resting on top of the Charger and said, "Getting ready for war?"

"Proving that there were two shooters," Ryder said as the deputy continued to walk towards him. In his hand was a file folder.

"That was what I wanted to talk to you about," Redfox said as he walked up to Ryder. "Ballistic showed two .357 rounds hit him, from two different guns. The one from Yakira's struck Muller's left lung, the other dead on into the heart. It continued on through him through the window and into the tree."

"So Yakira didn't kill him?" Alex asked.

"Legally no," Redfox said. "Coroner listed cause of death from the bullet to the heart. But he would have died from Yakira's shot."

"So what is Nelson going to do?" Ryder asked.

"After getting about five hundred phone calls, a couple thousand emails and every backer in the county telling him he would not get one damn dime if he brought charges. He has decided to call it a closed case. Your weapons will be returned to you within a couple of weeks."

"Well that is good news," Ryder said. "The sheriff said you had a reason to kill him, what was that about?"

"It is no secret!" Redfox said. "My cousin was one of the first girls he messed with. OH hell! Why don't we say what he really did!? He raped her! She was only 12 years old. So no, I am not shedding one tear that he is as cold as a freaking mackerel." His tone became angrier as he continued, "She tried to bring charges against him but she is a poor Indian girl and no one believed her. Hear all the time about how certain ones can't get justice, try being one of us!"

"Justice must be upheld," Ryder said. "Regardless of skin color, sex or how much money someone has. Justice must be justice!"

"In your perfect world Ryder, it would be, but this is Oklahoma." Redfox said as he stared out across the field. He turned back to Ryder and asked, "Are you telling me if you found the person who killed Muller you would bring him in? After all he did?"

Ryder didn't reply, instead he switched the subject, "Did anyone else know that you were coming out here?"

"No!"

"Any other deputy? The sheriff? Nelson?"

"No! And I told no one!" Redfox's eyebrows crinkled down as he paused before saying, "On the way in here I did see an old car a old Pinto parked alongside the road, it had one headlight broken out."

Chapter 9

Several days passed, and days turned to weeks, May had disappeared and became June. Yakira's nightmares were once again becoming sweet dreams, yet many days found her tummy hurting and throwing up. And as Ryder had promised his sister, the summer was going on without any investigations and life at the ranch had become routine, may be even some would have called boring.

It had been a while since Ryder had been on a tractor guiding a sickle mower, but it was like riding a bike, it all come back to him. Watching the blade slice through the stalks of alfalfa, the purple head stalks falling down in a row, drying and becoming tan in the sun, flipped over and then fed into a John Deere 328 Small Square Baler. The grass pushed tightly and dropped on to the field waiting for hands to grab its strings and toss it up onto a flat bed trailer being pulled behind the John Deere tractor. The last bale was put into place and then the trailer made the trip to the barn.

Alex was on the payroll, if it wasn't an investigation then she was driver of the tractor and since it was Marissa who wanted the horses, part of the deal was that she would take care of them and that included hauling and stacking hay. As Alex guided the tractor back down the hill and towards the barn Ryder sat on top of the stack next to his sister. He was in jeans and without a shirt, pieces of straw sticking to his muscular chest, some lodged in the curly hair that went across his Pecs and the breast bone, his stomach had not as much hair and showed his toned abs. He could smell the fresh cut hay, which he seemed to inhale as with the fragrance of a fine perfume. There was a red and white thermos in between them as the smoke belched out of the John Deer tractor. Ryder lifted the thermos unsnapped the cap and took a drink of water. It was getting low so he only took a couple swallows and then handed it to his sister. She was dressed in jeans and a western print blouse. She also had thick leather gloves on, which she had removed and laid down on the hay beside her so she could handle the thermos better. Her hair was tied back in a loose ponytail and pieces of straw were clinging to it, she also had on a black cowboy hat, one that she removed, wiped the sweat from her brow with the back of her hand and then took a swig of water from the thermos.

"Why do we have to have the little bales? When everybody else down this road has the big bales and they pick them up with the tractor?" She asked him as Alex turned the tractor down the small grassy lane that lead to the barn.

"Because you wanted those, darling," Ryder said pointing to the horses that had gathered up along the fence line to watch the hay being brought in. "They have to have the good stuff." Alex turned the tractor around and as Ryder directed her, backed the trailer into the barn.

Marissa pulled the gloves back onto her hands and climbed up on the inside stack that had been created with the new hay. Alex hand climbed down from the tractor and began to climb onto the trailer when Ryder handed her the water jug and asked her to go get it filled.

"I will get it filled and come back to help unload," Alex said. "How many more loads you think we got?"

"A couple," Ryder said. As Alex headed back to the house with the jug, Ryder gripped the strings of the hay bale, because it was alfalfa and baled tightly, the bales were heavy and his biceps heaved as he pushed the hay bale up over his head on the stack in the barn where Marissa grabbed it and drug it over to a waiting spot near the back of the loft.

"Ryder," he heard a woman carefully say. He turned and saw Annie, his neighbor, driving up in 1973 dark blue Camaro RS She stepped out of the car as Ryder grabbed another bale of hay and lifted it and heaved it up on the stack to his little sister. "Please," Annie begged, "I need to talk to you."

"Take a break," he told Marissa before jumping down from the trailer. He walked up to Camaro.

"This is new, "he said looking over the car, it was old, the paint rough and the passenger side light was broken. "How long have you had this?"

"Gene is working on my car," She replied. "He gave it to me for a loaner." She twisted her head. "Please Rick!" Annie again pleaded with him. "I need to talk to you alone."

He sat down on the hood of the car. She looked back at the tractor that had been backed into the opening of the barn. "It is so great to see you using all this stuff that it came with the place." She paused for just a moment to glance over the road to the old sorghum mill, and then turned back to him and continued, "You going to open up the old mill?"

"Annie as long as I have known you, you have never been one to beat around the bush. Did you really bring me out here to talk about the old mill?" Ryder asked.

"How long have we known each other?"

"Nearly as long as I have been alive," Ryder replied. "Now what do you want?"

"You know that they are planning new additions at Crowder?"

"Yes, I had seen something about it in the Neosho paper. You want me to make a donation or something?" Ryder was getting annoyed that she was playing this game of cat and mouse, yet he had played it many times, but he was always the cat. He didn't like being the mouse. He didn't even reply to her and she continued.

"That was where your mother and I met."

"I know," Ryder said sounding annoyed. "I heard her tell of the good times in the cafeteria playing cards, listening to the juke box"

"She ever tell you about the Sergeants Club?"

"The what?"

"It was a club we belonged to…" She hesitated a little before continuing "Well actually it was a club your mother created."

"What kind of club?"

"I can't tell you!"

"Damn it Annie! Do you know how annoying that is?" Ryder fumed. "You want my help but you won't tell me what it is?"

"I can't! We were all sworn to…" Again she paused and changed the subject. "Do you know what a blood covenant is?"

"Yes, it is a loyalty oath, a contract sealed in blood."

"Our pastor was talking about it last Sunday," Annie said. "You know I go to a church in Monett?"

"Yes I know the First United Methodist Church," Ryder was getting more and more annoyed. Tomorrow was Sunday, Marissa birthday, the big party was planned and rain was forecast for tomorrow night, so he had to get the hay put away today. "What does this have to do with what you want to ask me?"

"He was saying how a blood covenant can never be broken, and that is what we have with God." She sat down beside her on the hood of the car. She leaned over and and whispered, "they are going find it."

"Find what Annie?"

"I can't tell you," she replied then reached into her pocket and pulled out dollar bill, "you take a dollar a day right?" She held it out to him.

"No," Ryder said grabbing her hand pushing it back. "I promised Marissa!" He glanced back at the barn and saw her climbing down from the hay stack. "I am on vacation. No more cases." He let go of her hand. "No more cases this summer. I am spending it with my family."

"How much trouble could I get into moving a dead body and not reporting a murder?"

"A lot!" Ryder snapped back. "Did you do that? What murder?"

"I can't tell you. Please!" Annie begged still holding out the bill. "We swore our lives to our covenant. We tell, we are going to be killed.

Ryder stood up and stared at her. "I can't put up with the cloak and dagger stuff! Damn it Annie if you want help, you are going to have to tell me everything. And I mean everything."

"I will tell you everything. Tomorrow at Marissa's party."

Chapter 10

Birthdays are the celebration of life, of a day that God's own breath is breathed into a soul. It is the beginning step of life when one chapter ends, a new one begins. Today was Sunday, Marissa's birthday. Ever since her mother had been killed when she was twelve Marissa had lived with her big brother Ryder.

For someone who had spent most of his life on his own, Ryder's life had suddenly changed. He was now surrounded by people, people who loved him, each demanding their own time with him. It was reason to greet each morning with a cup of coffee raising the cup to the Creator.

The bright rays of the sun were just beginning to push up over the horizon, creating a masterpiece sunrise of bright reds and orange colors, the shadows of the trees growing out across the fields. The yard full of wrens and sparrows singing as robins bounced along fresh cut grass, stopping, turning a head to the side before grabbing a worm from the soil and then flying away to their nest to feed their young.

For today Ryder had several gifts for his kid sister, some costing grand dollars like the party planned for later today, and special gift. Another cost nothing monetarily but everything otherwise. It was her day. Whatever she wanted for the entire day, she would get. And it started with a special breakfast, made by her brother's hands that included scrambled eggs, beef bacon, and Ryder's own special shortcake pancakes.

He had sliced fresh strawberries and added sugar and a little water cooked over low heat till it became syrup as he allowed it to cool. He dumped flour, sugar, baking powder, baking soda, and salt into a large bowl, in another bowl he mixed up buttermilk, three eggs and some strawberry soda, and then gradually dumped the flour mixture into the buttermilk mixture, then added melted butter that had cooled, carefully stirring it in.

His kitchen was complete with professional style appliances, including the six burner stove, he had a griddle plate over two burners and using a dipper he scooped up some of the mixture and placed it on the griddle.

While the pancakes cooked he poured heavy cream and sugar into another mixing bowl and using the Kitchen Aid® mixer, he whipped the cream. As the cream was whipping he flipped the pancakes over, they were golden brown, perfect. He removed the pancakes to a plate, and then put more batter on the griddle.

The whip cream was now fluffy with stiff peaks. He layered three pancakes with whip cream and the strawberry syrup mixture and topped with whip cream and strawberries. He continued this process till he had six plates made up.

The kitchen was a bouquet of aromas from the bacon cooking in the oven, the scrambled eggs in a large electric skillet to the sweetness of the strawberries and fresh brewed coffee as it drifted through the kitchen and out to the dining room. The room wasn't used that much, as most meals were served around the kitchen table, but on special occasions, the chandelier with its rain drop shaped crystals would shine over the oval shaped walnut table covered with a lace tablecloth and set with the fine china. He could see five hungry faces in the reflection of the glass doors of the cabinet as he entered the room.

Ryder set a plate down in front of each one of them; Yakira and Alex on side of the table, Ceelia at the end, and Bubbie and himself on the other side, and the princess of day seated at the head of the table, Marissa. She was still dressed in her purple pajamas, her long hair tied back into a braided pony tail. Ryder returned to the kitchen and brought out Marissa's plate. It had a single lit candle in the center, as he carried it over to her, he began to sing Happy Birthday and the other's joined in, including Ceelia. He placed it down in front of her and said,

"I have you know I don't let too many hear me sing. So know just how special you are." He leaned over and kissed her on the cheek and said. "Happy birthday, darling! Make a wish!" She leaned over and blew the candle out. He removed the candle and laid it down on the table beside her. Then he took his place at the table that was to the right of Marissa.

After grace he cut into his stack pancakes and took a bite, savoring the sweetness of the fruit and the smoothness of the whipped cream and the slight tang of the buttermilk in the pancakes. It just balanced out the saltiness of the beef bacon. As he lifted his cup of coffee to his lips and took a sip before he looked over at Marissa. "So this day is mine?" She asked before she took a bite of bacon. "And you will do anything I ask?"

"Well…" Ryder drawled out. "I really don't want to go skinny dipping in the creek as there are turtles in there that like to nip at worms. Not that you ladies have anything to worry about that."

Alex laughed slightly at that statement and was just beginning to take a sip as Yakira who lifted her mug, but yet took a sip, said with a mocking grin, "Sweetie, a few of us seated here will tell you it is not a worm." At that point Alex choked her drink and spit it out on to the table as Yakira chuckled and Ryder felt a warm glow flow over him making him wanting to just sink under the table. With Alex still coughing and using her napkin to sop up the coffee she spewed, Yakira looked over to her and grinned mischievous smile as she said, "Well do I lie? Bubbie."

"It has been a few years, things change." The old woman replied.

At that point Alex's cheeks turned pink and then bright red as her daughter asked, "What is not like a worm mommy?"

"Nothing just forget it!" She huffed out in embarrassment.

"But Mommy…"

"FORGET IT!" Alex yelled before standing up her cheeks bright red as she asked, "Anyone mind if I turn the a/c down, it is a little warm in here."

"You are a bad little Jewish girl." Ryder said looking over the table to his still grinning wife as she now took a drink of her coffee.

"Let say I take after my grandmother."

Marissa dropped her head down have face glowing bright pink," All right I have my first demand for the day," Marissa said she looked ups and said.. "No more embarrassing the sister."

"Bacon?" Bubbie asked looking down at her plate. "You know I can't eat pork." As it was against her Jewish culture.

"It is beef Bubbie, Kosher beef in fact. I get it from Mother in Kansas City he said of his friend who ran a restraint in Kansas City," Ryder said. Try it."

She took a bite and said with glee, "This is good. She looked over at Marissa and asked. "So not being embarrassed, what else do you want to do today?"

"I want to go to church." Marissa replied taking a bite of her own bacon.

"Okay," Ryder said. "I will take you there."

"No!" She said leaning over towards him and looked at the others. "I want us to all go."

Ryder leaned back in his chair, picked up the cup of coffee again and took another sip. "I can't, the people are coming to set up for your party. I have to be here to show them where to set up."

"Oh *Motek*," Bubbie said placing her hand on his arm. "I can be here and show them. It is her day. You promised her."

"Okay, I am not sure if I know what to do in a Catholic church anymore."

"We are not going there." Marissa explained they were going to Annie's church, "she invited us last night." Marissa looked around the table Yakira across from Ryder, and Alex and Ceelia next to Ryder as she added "You said it was my day; I could get whatever I wanted."

"I guess we are going to church." Ryder said.

*****

First United Methodist Church sits just off the highway, at the North End of town, at the point where the highway bends and across from the cemetery. It was a large building but still inviting, made of red brick with a metal roof.

The parking lot was large, and there were several vehicles that ranged from brand new, to well used. Members were walking towards the covered entrance. On any given Sunday a car driving in would have gone unnoticed. However, driving up in a blood red classic Dodge Charger with a twin wing spoiler and shark like nose, more than one person stopped walking and twisted back as Ryder wheeled the car into a parking spot marked 'visitor'.

He stepped out of the car his gaze drifted upward towards the towering steeple, his eyes locking on the cross at the top. It had been a few years since Ryder's footsteps had trampled on the grounds of a church, and the last time was all business to question a minster about one of his flock that had been murdered. He repositioned his sunglasses and watched as the morning sun glared on the cross. As he held the door open, the driver's seat back pushed forward, out of the back seat crawled Alex and Yakira.

This was Marissa's day so she got 'shotgun' position. As she stepped out Alex walked around to help Ceelia out of her booster seat. It was then that a man approached them.

"Cool car!" The man said. "I don't think I have ever seen a car like this." Ryder looked the man over; he was about his age maybe a little younger, dressed in a red polo shirt and slacks. "What kind of car is it?"

"One of a kind," Ryder said. "1971 Dodge Charger Killer Bee. Custom made by Gene Weston. It is powered by a Hellcat Hemi."

"This is Lisa then?"

Gene had the habit of giving all his creations names, and this was his masterpiece that he named the Mona Lisa or Lisa for short. "So you know Gene?"

"Yes I would love to have him build me something, but with a wife and young kids." The man turned again to Ryder and said. "I am John Woods I am the pastor here." he offered his hand to Ryder, and Ryder shook it as he continued. "You are Annie's friend the detective Rick Ryder." Ryder introduced everyone.

"Annie mentioned me?"

"Yes, many times, she wanted to offer prayer for you," the pastor looked at them and said, "All of you. But it was after last week's sermon that she took a deep interest in, that she told me she was going to invite you all today."

"The blood covenant, right? What did she ask about it?"

"If it could ever be broken?"

"And what did you tell her?" Ryder asked.

"Never! God keeps his word," The pastor explained. "It is the shedding of the Son's blood that washes away our sin if we accept it, it is the basis of our faith, and if it is broken there is no faith. Even in Jewish there is a blood covenant."

"The Passover," Yakira said.

"Yes."

"Could she have taken it to mean something else?" Ryder asked. "Not about God, but something she did an oath she took?"

"I don't know," the pastor said as he looked over the parking lot. "Annie should have been here by now. Well come on inside and we will find you a seat."

They walked inside down a long hallway that opened into a wide space. To his left was the family life center, it was set up with round tables that was for the dinner that the church was planning to have after services. To his right just like cards being played in poker, there was three of kind, three sets of double doors that lead into the sanctuary. Each set of the doors were propped open and Ryder watched as a middle aged couple walked through in the middle entrance and took their seats in a pew, seventh one down on the right hand side. He knew no one here, but it seemed that many knew him.

"Ryder?" He heard a voice say as he saw a young man in his mid twenties walk up to him, he was well dressed, in suit and tie, wearing glasses. He held his hand out holding the church bulletin and with a smile continued, "Rick Ryder! Number seven. I saw you play at Arrowhead. Can I get your autograph?" Ryder took the bulletin, "You had one of the longest throws in the NFL history eighty-five yards"

"Sure." Ryder said reaching into his jacket and producing his pen.

"Think you could do that today?" Ryder lifted his gaze to the young man as he added, "Can you make it to Ronnie?" A half grin broke across Ryder's face As Ryder signed the bulletin and handed it back to him. "I was 23 years old then, don't think I could throw half that distance today."

There were three reasons that Ryder got recognized one was he was the biggest lottery winner in which case it was usually followed by plea for money, second was the former quarterback for the Kansas City Chiefs, and the other a little bit more morbid- because of his cases.

"Detective Ryder." He heard a pretty blonde woman say as she approached him, she was wearing a dark coral sleeveless dress with, drop pendent earrings that swung like the pendulum on a grandfather clock keeping its time as she continued to speak. Deep sea blue eyes shining as she looked up at him and continued. "My name is Sierra. I have been following all your cases. Are you here working on a case! Annie said she was going to try to get you to help her." She glanced over the interior of the worship hall and Ryder followed her gaze trying to see what see was searching for.

The church was laid out in four sections, two each side of the main aisle with another aisle separating the two remaining, one on each side with the longest pews in the middle. Glass windows on each side and the sound booth over to the far right, Sierra looked the entire church over, her eyes going each pew to each face she knew, even pushing up on her tip-toe to checking the tops of heads that could be seen in the sound booth. "She is not here! Annie never misses", she turned and looked back at Ryder and then added, "Annie has to be very sick or dead to miss. She glanced up at the stage and saw another woman wave at her. "Well guess they are calling my number. I better be going."

Though it was friendly and many others were coming up and introducing themselves, Ryder felt something uncomfortable as if there was someone watching him. He looked over the faces of the men, women, the old who could remember when everyone else joined and the young that laid in a mother's arm, only long enough for her grandmother to pry her away. The choir was in their red robes, candles being lit on the altar. Original artwork created with loving hands hung on the walls and the screen above began its countdown.

"Two minute warning," Ryder said softly.

"What?" Yakira asked as he sat down and stared out across the wooden pews, each one covered in a blue cloth fabric.

"Nothing," Ryder replied.

Ryder's eyes continued to scan over the room over to a round stain-glass window at the very back of the room. Suddenly a movement caught his eye. There was an old wooden cross near the piano on the stage. Standing behind the cross was Sierra she was staring at him. The clock was ticking down to the beginning of services; she took her place on the bench at the grand piano and began to play.

Each church has its own way, its own rhythm, its own dance; sit, stand sit, a laugh to give, a tear to shed, and blessings to receive like a child with eyes wide open as the members file out the way they came, the music playing, everyone hoping they can take a take piece of that blessing and hold to it.

Ryder was the salmon trying to make his way up stream weaving through the oncoming line of parishioners, many who would stop him and offer a "Hope you come back." He continued pushing himself forward and up the carpeted steps to the stage and over to the grand piano.

"Sierra!" Ryder said just as she finished up the music. "I would like to talk to you."

"What about?"

"Annie," Ryder replied. "You said that Annie wanted me to help her, do you know what it was about? Maybe something to do with the improvements at Crowder College? She sat on the piano bench, busily closing and arranging the sheet music as Ryder asked, "Or maybe about the Sergeants' Club?"

His words made her drop the sheet music on the floor, and she squatted down and started picking the sheets up. Ryder kneeled down on the carpet to help her."

"How do you know about that?" She whispered bundling the music books up in her arms.

"She told me." He said handing her the music he had picked up. "Can we talk?"

"Not in here," she said as she stood up. "In the Prayer Garden."

Ryder followed her down the steps from the stage and back up the aisle, passing by a thin man with long hair that was held back with a headband and long sideburns and a beard that was reeling from a strong sweet smell.   Sierra continued past the person, and in to the family life center where Yakira, Alex and Ceelia stood talking to the pastor, Alex turned her head following Ryder as Sierra continued through the room and headed for the back door, that she pushed open.

Sierra walked across the parking lot and the section of the yard where the sidewalks were laid out like a cross in the middle with a circle flower bed and in the middle a white cross. She stood there, the cross behind her.

"What do you know?" She asked.

"Not much," Ryder said reaching under his jacket and pulling out his notebook and pen he always had with him. A gust of wind whipped across the parking lot. "She wouldn't tell me." He looked up from his notebook, "Do you know anything about it?"

"No."

Ryder was looking down at his notebook and writing as he lifted one eye brow and gazed at her; that answer sounded very strange as if it were the truth but she was trying to hide something. So he asked, "Do you know anything about the club?"

"Is this for an investigation?"

"Not really," Ryder said. "Annie came to me last night upset. Said she was going to talk to me today about it, but she is not here. So what do you know about the club?"

Sierra set down on the edge around the circle and looked up at him. Ryder, wanting to make her feel comfortable sat down beside her. "I mean no harm; Annie is a dear friend if she is in trouble I want to help her."

"You know that the Crowder was once an army base?"

"Camp Crowder, during WWII. Yes, what does that have to do with it?"

"And it was much larger then, there were lots of buildings back then. Including one where the sergeants gathered with their wives, it was known as the sergeant's club."

"Annie wasn't even born then what does that have to do with her?"

"When it was turned into the campus the tales of the sergeant's club were told again, some students back then formed their own club, called the Sergeant's Club, had nothing to do with the Military anymore; it was more based on the Beatles album. The *Sergeants Pepper's* we would...they would all go to the dances and stuff together."

"You are part of this club?"

"Yes but I can't tell you anymore."

"But you and Annie are quite a few years apart in age." Ryder paused and then asked, "The club is still going?"

"Yes, it is one of the biggest secrets of Crowder College; you are not going to find out about it in the catalog or on line and most teachers will just dismiss it, that it is part of a legend. That it existed years ago, but no longer."

"But today?"

"It is still there, but you can't ask about it. You will get nowhere, you can't ask to be in it, if they want you they will ask you." Sierra stood up turned and faced out across the large field that was at the back of the church. She took a deep breath and continued, "But the Club you're looking into," she turned back to him and said, "it is not the same club as today. Today it is a group that goes to dances together, studies together. Back then it was something deeper." She paused for a short time and then said, "And darker."

"Darker?"

"It was more like a sorority or fraternity as it took both men and women, but it was told that they also mixed it with..." She lowered her voice and looked around to see if there was anyone close, there was not and she said softly. "I heard they did black rituals with candles, daggers, a golden goblet and something else"

"Like what?" Ryder asked once again writing in his notebook.

"This is just hearsay okay?" Sierra said nervously, her words quickened in speed. It is like the tales of when doors open or close by themselves, that it is the ghost of POW's. It is told by the members of the first Sergeant's Club, the one your mother and Annie were in, that they did a sacrifice. They...they ..." She struggled to get the words out, finally she pushed them out. "They killed someone. "

Chapter 11

Marissa wanted two parties for her birthday, one that was with the family and that was where Ryder gave her the gift of her day, what she wanted she got for the day. There would be no rules, yet Ryder knew giving a fifteen year old girl that kind of freedom, there had to be at least common sense still there. No booze, no drugs, no smoking. However there would be boys at the second party.

The theme of the party was Hawaii, complete with hula lessons, and of course a luau with roasted pig in a pit in the ground. It had to be one the biggest events in the area, as there were 21 teenagers roaming around the yard, including nine boys. There were shrill screams that only a teenage girl can produce, as they dashed about, most of them dressed in two piece bright colored bikini's the bottoms covered with straw colored grass skirts. Screaming even louder as they twisted to music or watched the boys dive into the swimming pool landing with a splash.

Ryder stood on the deck watching the party going on, his hands gripped on the wooden rail scanning the yard as if he it were a prison yard and he the warden. There was a mock-cocktail bar with fruit juice and water, and another bar for the food. Marissa stood near the drink bar wearing a purple with white polka-dot swim suit and a grass skirt and a lei around her neck with a flower in her hair. She turned and raised her glass that held a virgin banana daiquiri with coconut milk after the bartender he had hired served her drink. Another one of her classmates, Heather Bradley walked up to the bar and she turned and looked at Ryder. She was fifteen on her way to twenty-one in her mind. She wore a lime green and pink bikini that barely covered her teenage assets. She pushed her long wet hair back as she smiled at him.

"You have an admirer," he heard Alex say as she walked up behind him. She too was dressed for the party with a swim suit and her bottom covered with a grass skirt and a garland of flowers, around her neck. She took a sip of iced diet pop. "And from what I have heard around here, there is more than one." She took another sip and then with a smile she added, "Including a couple of their mothers." She gazed out across the yard as Heather approached the deck with two drinks in hand. "Hey Romeo your Juliet approaches."

"Where is Yakira?" Ryder asked

"Out there," Alex pointed to the group of women that were talking hula lesson, his wife shaking her grass skirt, Ceelia right next to her, trying to match the moves. "Guess I ought to be going to."

"Like hell!" Ryder snapped back. "You stay right here. You work for me. That is an order."

"So I am still on the clock?" Alex offered with a mocking grin.

"You don't get off the clock," Ryder said as Heather strolled up the steps that lead to the deck. Alex turned around, resting her seat against the deck railing.

"Hi Ricky," Heather said with a warm smile and tone that could charm a kitten away from its mother. "You want to 'Cuddle on the Beach?'"

"Say what?"

She held up a cocktail glass with a light orange colored drink in it. "A mock cocktail." She explained. She handed Ryder the glass, and noticed she had the same drink, "or you can put rum in them and we can have 'Sex on the Beach.'" At this point he heard a snuffle smirk from Alex.

"Heather—I think—I think you should go back to the party." Ryder muttered out. "Thank you for the drink." He lifted the glass and she lifted hers in a toast.

"Okay," she said turning and taking a couple steps away before she stopped and looked over her shoulder. "The dance is going to be after awhile, can you save me a couple Ricky?"

"I think my dance card is pretty well filled by my wife. And maybe it would be better to call me Mr. Ryder."

"Marissa said you didn't like that?"

"I—I—think it is just better if you do that."

"Okay, Mr. Ryder," she offered with a wiggle of her fingers. "Bye-bye." Then she walked back out into the yard.

"Oh young love," Alex said leaning up from the rail. "It is wonderful."

"Not when it looks like that," Ryder said as he watched the girl walked away, trying to wiggle every muscle she had. "You ever have a crush on an older guy?"

Alex lifted her eye brow as she said, "Mr. Roberts, he was a cool teacher, long hair, never wore a tie, drove a Corvette with side pipes and listened to Kansas and the Eagles. Every girl in school had a thing for him." Her tone change more seriously as she asked, "Did you get a hold of Annie yet?"

"Stopped after we got back, called a couple times but nothing." Ryder replied. Bubbie and Ceelia danced alongside Yakira. Ryder pointed at Ceelia as he said, "you know she is going into one of these in ten years and we will be having it for her. "

"She is starting to ask."

"About what?"

"Her daddy!" Alex said. "She wants to know who he is." Alex grabbed his arm and continued. "I think it is time we tell her. Or are you going to wait until she comes and tries to flirt with her own father?" Ryder didn't reply, he stood there looking at her, so Alex continued. "Come on Rick. Yakira knows, Bubbie knows, I am sure half the town of Cassville knows." Still he didn't reply. "She is our daughter. Sooner or later she is going to start her investigation or worse she is going to hear it from some kid at school. That little girl loves you. But if she finds out on her own…"

"I know!" Ryder snapped back. "She will end hating me."

"She will never hate you." Alex replied as she let go of him and Ryder finished his drink and set the glass down on the rail. "But she might question why was she robbed of the time that she could have had a daddy. And she will resent us both for that. Do you want that?"

"We will tell her when the time is right?"

"There is no right time!

"We will do it soon."

"When? Alex demanded.

"Sometime soon…" Ryder turned and faced the yard. Another teenage girl, Amanda, looked at Ryder, flipping her blonde hair behind her bare shoulder. The bartender poured crushed ice in the two hurricane glasses and then grapefruit and orange juice along V-8 Tropical blend with shot of simple syrup "A cat 1 Hurricane is heading your way," Alex said and he turned and looked at her to explain. "All the flavor but not the damage."

"And that is my cue to leave." He said as he took a step towards the steps.

"Rick, if Ceelia finds out on her own, you will have a true storm on your hands."

****

When Ryder moved here, he bought everything, the land, the buildings, the tractors, trucks, even the tools that were hung on the wall in the repair shed that was in an old building where an old Dodge farm truck usually sat. Now inside was a 1977 Impala 2-door coupe, it was covered in light gray primer, the middle of the top removed. Standing next to the car was a middle aged man with thinning red hair swept over in a desperate attempt to cover the ever creeping baldness, he was dressed in grease stained blue striped coveralls that pushed out a little due his protruding waist line. It was Gene Weston. He gazed across the open roof of the car inside was just a single bucket seat with brown cloth interior. He looked at Ryder and blinked eyes quickly.

"She's no beauty queen, but we can make her that way." Gene said as he rubbed his hand on the hood. "Engine no good; it is sucking up oil like a D-list star on the bench. You want old school, or new?"

What do you think?"

"I am thinking maybe LS7."

"But no outrageous horsepower," Ryder said. "Keep it under 400 she is only fifteen."

"Okay," Gene sounded disappointed. "Colors?"

"She likes purple."

******

It had only seemed like a few minutes, but the pool party had changed the other half of what Marissa wanted; a makeover party. Each teenage girl and their mother or lady of their choice, was given a chance to have a professional make over, with hair, makeup and a fancy party dress.

The D.J. had arrived and was setting up, Marissa walked up to Ryder. She was dressed in a light purple evening gown, with a glittery sleeveless top and a long flowing bottom that swirled around her feet barely revealing the purple high heels. Her face adorned with concealer, blush, lipstick, and her eyes beamed as bright as her smile that she flashed at him. He had never seen her in makeup, when she asked, he just couldn't bring himself to admit the fact that his little sister was quickly growing up. He just stood there gazing at her soaking in how she looked.

"Where have you been?" She asked, "the dance is about to begin." He didn't reply he just stood there, feeling a grin breaking across his face becoming a fully fledged smile. "What is it?" She asked confused by his glance.

"You are beautiful." He said. "I mean breath taking. You look all grown up."

"Really?" She replied slightly blushing. "But you have got to go get changed. Right NOW!"

"Yeah, okay." Ryder said, still standing there looking at her from head to toe.

"Will you go get changed!"

His eyes fell down onto the silver pendant that was draped around her neck with a large link silver chain. He lifted the pendant up; it was fairly heavy for a pendant of silver lace and in the center an oval shape dark red ruby. It was antique, and had to be expensive. "Where did you get this?" Ryder asked as he let the pendant fall back down on to her chest.

"Annie Harris."

"She is here?"

"No some guy with long hair and beard brought it and said it was from her." Marissa replied, picking up the pendant and looking at it. "Bubbie said that 'he brought it while we were at church.'" She dropped it back down and added, "It is beautiful!" She looked up at him and said forcefully. "Now go get changed. The dance is going to start in ten minutes."

Ryder walked into the house and up the stairs to the master bedroom and changed into a tuxedo. Having trouble with bow tie, he came back out into the bedroom. Yakira was there waiting for him, she was dressed in a pink evening own. "You are a great big brother." She said as she tied his bow tie for him. "You really went all out for her." She straightened the tie out and asked, "But what are you going to do for her sweet sixteen?"

"Don't know got a year to think about it." He replied then offered her his arm, "Mrs. Ryder would you care to join me?"

"I would love too." She took his arm and they made their way down stairs back outside.

A D.J. announced, "All right ladies. First dance. Ladies choice." The music began to play. Four teenage girls made a quick dash over to Ryder, asking him to dance, with Amanda and Heather pushing each other back, trying to be the one to dance with him.

"You have anything to say about this?" Ryder asked looking at his bride.

"No sweetie," Yakira grinned widely and then said as Marissa walked over to him holding her hand out to him. "It is my birthday," She said with a firm tone to the other girls, "I get the first choice." She took hold of her brother's hand and led him out onto the dance floor that had been put into place in the yard.

"Are you sure about this?" Ryder asked. "You can choose any guy you want here."

"And I am choosing the one I love." She said looking up at him. He put his arms around and they danced to the tune as others joined them; some fathers and daughters, others taking the chance to get the boy they liked on the dance floor. "Thank you for this day. You made all my dreams come true." She grinned mockingly as she tilted her head and looked up at him and laughed as she said, "How are you going to top it next year?"

"Maybe I will be broke by then; the best I can do is a cheeseburger at McDonalds."

"As long as you are there brother, then it will be okay."

Suddenly screams interrupted her and the dance quickly stopped, the dancers parting like the Great Red Sea, but it wasn't Moses, it was Annie parting it. She was staggering across the dance floor, covered in blood, her print blouse soaking, and blood dripping down her side flowing over her hand and a drop of blood dripping down on the bright colored dance floor. She looked at Ryder and Marissa and took and another couple of stumbling steps towards them. She was shaking, her legs trembling; finally, she took another step before collapsing face first into Marissa, knocking her down.

Ryder noticed there was a large dagger sticking out of Annie's back, the handle was gold, twisted with a leaf shape at the end. Marissa's gown was now soiled with Annie's blood. She looked at her and spoke forcing her words out, "Please!" She begged, holding her blood- soaked hand out to her, "Take the case!" She held a single dollar bill, the bill barely recognizable being soaked in Annie's blood. She placed the bill in Marissa's hand and just before collapsing said, "Before the others die!"

Chapter 12

The music played no more, the sound of cheers and laugher were now muted sobs of teen age girls, their faces buried in the father's shoulders or wrapped in their mother's arms. Grown men lost without words to comfort their families as they headed for their cars. Alex too comforted her daughter in her arms.

Ryder stood in the yard and held out his arms as he said, "No one can leave here!"

"That is bull!" Heather's mother said as she grabbed her daughter by the arm and started to push past him. "You do not have any authority to keep us here."

Ryder grabbed her arm and pulled her back, reaching for his wallet, he flipped it open revealing a brass five-point badge he said, "I still hold the position of reserved Deputy of Barry County. Now I want everyone to move over to the side of the yard. If you try to leave you will be arrested."

As the guests cleared the dance floor he looked down at his sister sitting on the bright dance floor, her dressed covered in Annie's blood. Annie face down as Marissa looked up at him. She didn't speak at first, instead she looked down at the dagger in Annie's back then she looked back up at Ryder as she said, "Just like mom."

"I know," Ryder said gently. "I want you to slide her out from under you and then stand up. Marissa did as she was told and carefully laid Annie's head down on the floor. Ryder removed his jacket and placed it over Annie. She was curled slightly and only her legs could be seen.

"Oy vey!" Yakira cried out feeling her heart racing and pounding at the veins in her neck. "What happened Ricky?"

"Where's Brian at?" Ryder asked as he hugged his sister.

"He and Thom went into town to get more ice." He heard Yakira say as she walked up next to them. "I gave him a call he is on the way back and was going to alert the department."

"She hired us to find her killer." Marissa said. And Yakira and Ryder turned to her.

"I think we should just leave this to Brian." Yakira said.

"No!" Marissa insisted. "This is my case she gave me the dollar." The blood soaked dollar was still in Marissa's hand. She gazed up at Ryder, "You said this is my day. That you will do anything I want."

"But..."

"But nothing! It is still my birthday. And I want to take the case." Marissa said. "Let's find out who murdered her." Sirens began to fill the air, many sirens and they were growing louder.

"Okay," Ryder said as Alex walked up to them also. "We have a new investigation."

Chapter 13

The red and blue flashes of emergency lights painted across the ranch like lightning bugs lowering towards the ground and flashed a return greeting of the brilliant flash of the camera as the investigating detective of Barry County would snap another photo.

Ryder sits on the steps of the deck. On the step between his feet was a small flashlight. On one side of him was Yakira on the other Marissa now dressed in a robe, her gown now bagged as evidence. He had his arms around both of them and they each had their head resting on his shoulders. He stared out across his ranch to the western sky and saw a flash of lightning creeping along the horizon. Followed by a low rumble of thunder he bet it was raining in Neosho, pouring down on Crowder College. His mother always told him that when someone dies if it rained, it was the town weeping. . Guess the college was weeping over the loss of Annie.

Brian Thompson was elected sheriff. Brian was the younger brother of Ryder's best friend in school, Thom Thompson; one of the greatest centers that the Wildcat Football team ever had. He was part of the championship team, which at one time was ranked the best high school team in the United States. Brian with round shaped face and hefty pouch in the middle looked a lot like his brother, just not quite as heavy. He was dressed in a tuxedo to dance with his daughter but had missed the dance. He walked up to Ryder on the steps; Ryder looked up at him as the man spoke.

"You have any idea who might have wanted to kill her?"

"Did you know anyone that hated Annie?", Ryder replied back with his own question that answered the question. Truth was Annie was one of the kindest, sweetest women you could meet. She was a college professor with the heart of a kindergarten teacher. She would sit down with students and go over the project step-by-step until suddenly it clicked in their mind. Ask Crowder students to name the one teacher they will never forget and the answer would be Annie Harris. If you met her pushing her cart out of Wal-Mart ® or coming out of Whitley Pharmacy on the square and you were to mention fishing, she would have a smile and story to tell. Fact was no one would want to kill Annie. But as Ryder looked down and saw Brian's big brother Thom the county Medical examiner zip close the body bag, there was one person that did.

"Ryder," Brian asked. "What did she say to you?"

"She said nothing to me."

"It was me," Marissa said lifting her head from her brother's shoulder. "She died in my arms. She hired us to find the killer."

"That is what she said?" Lightning flashed again in the sky and a small rumble of thunder was heard.

"No, she said, maybe we could save the others."

"What others."

"I don't know."

Brian looked at Ryder for more information, "I don't know who she meant, honestly, Brian." Ryder said.

"Did you see the dagger in her back?" Brian asked. "Did you ever see anything like that at Annie's?"

"No," Ryder answered simply before adding, "We have had supper at Annie's many times. She was a very simple person, simple flatware, plain white plates, and simple old hickory knife ware."

"Ryder, this is right up your alley" Brian paused and then added, "I want you as the chief investigator on this."

"I can't do that I am not..."

"You are a reserve deputy, you can be called in at any time," Brian paused and then said. "I am calling you in. What have you found?"

Ryder didn't reply he just stood up grabbing the flashlight and motioned for the sheriff to follow. Ryder walked back around the house and down the driveway, noticing the spots of blood on the stones that had been marked with numbers. The blood trail lead to Annie's car a light green Ford SUV, parked along the side of the road. The driver's door wide open. The gray interior stained with blood. The driver's seat back with two large spots, a bloody hand print on top of the door panel. Using the flashlight he shone the beam around the interior, noticing a set of keys lying on the floor and the position of the passenger seat.

The Sheriff put gloves on and Ryder asked "Got any more gloves?" And the sheriff handed him a pair of rubber gloves which Ryder snapped over his hands. He went around to the other side of the SUV and shone the light down on the road, seeing half of a shoe print. "Did you catch this shoe imprint?"

"Not much to go on?" Brian said as Ryder kneeled down beside the print. He spanned his hand next to it and noticed the shape of it. Sport shoe

Ryder said as he stood up. "I would say a size six or set or nine." He opened the door and then pressed the seat adjuster forward . "Someone was with her?"

"How do you know that?"

"Annie always kept the passenger seat all the way up, because…" Ryder opened the rear side door and shined the flashlight on the floor of the SUV. there three tackle boxes sat on the floor with four fishing poles in the back seat. One of the tackle boxes was lifted up slightly being pushed back against the seat back. "See the broken pole?" Ryder asked pointing to a broken red Zebco pole. "You know what that means? This was an unwelcome guest. No way would Annie allow a pole to get broken." Ryder squatted down and used the flashlight to look under the tackle boxes - there was something there. "Push the seat all the way up." The sheriff pushed the button and the seat moved forward.

"What…the…" Ryder question as he shined the light under the seat. He reached in and removed it, it was walnut stained wooden plaque, 8x10 with a playing card in the center 'the Queen of Spades' and below burned into the wood was a bible verse Deuteronomy 21:7 '*....Our hands did not shedd this blood, nor did our eyes see this done.'*

"What the hell is that?" Brain asked as Ryder turned it over, it was plain wood not stained and the small price sticker of $12.99 stuck to the back. "Surreal that would be here."

"You need to bag it and dust it for prints." Ryder said.

Brian stared at Ryder then out across the countryside again, watching the lightning flash again and a then single drop of rain fell and streaked down the windshield as if it were a teardrop. "I know that look Ryder, what are you thinking."

"Could be Cassville is about to get its first mad killer."

Chapter 14

The next morning Ryder found himself again in the kitchen making breakfast, simple scrambled eggs and toast with coffee. Yakira, who was again feeling ill, sat at the table in the kitchen, in her robe, one leg crossed over the other, a fuzzy pink slipper dangling from her foot. She held her head down in her hand, staring at the bowl of oatmeal in front of her. She let out a deep sigh and pushed it away from her.

"I think I will just have some tea and toast," she said. Ryder put some water in a pot on the stove to heat, and then walked back over to the table and sat down beside her. He reached over and patted her hand as she said, "I am sorry I can't go with you today. I am not feeling well anymore."

"Don't worry about it," he said tenderly. "Why don't you go see the doctor today? You have not been feeling good for the last three or four weeks."

"I am not bad enough to see a doctor." Yakira said. "I just got some kind of bug. Besides I don't know if I could get in."

"You are the wife of Richard Thomas Allen Ryder," he heard Alex say as she walked into the kitchen; she was dressed in gray sweats, and a t-shirt with the KC Chief's logo on the front. "One of the richest men in the State of Missouri, believe that when you call you will get in."

Alex walked over to the table. She went over poured herself a cup of coffee and walked back, pulled out a chair and sat down next to Ryder. "I take it you are not going either?" Ryder asked as the pot whistled on the stove indicating that the water was hot for the tea.

"I thought we were on vacation?" Alex said, as Ryder stood and then walked over to the stove. He poured some water into a cup and dipped a tea bag. Alex continued. "You know I was sick like this once."

Ryder put the cups on a saucer and picked it up and head for the table as he asked, "When was that?"

"Oh close to six-years ago." Alex grinned and looked back at her daughter playing in the floor of the next room. Ryder's fumble as he set the cup down spilt a little tea on the saucer. "I was like a little chipmunk looking in his hole." Ryder's eyebrows twisted down in puzzlement so she explained. "Toilet bowl, chipmunk hole."

"I can't be pregnant!" Yakira said. "You know what the doctor said after the accident. I couldn't get—I can't have a baby."

"He didn't say that," Ryder said as Yakira added some sugar to her tea and stirred it in. She raised the cup and took a sip as Ryder continued, "He said it be nearly impossible for you to have a child. He didn't say it was impossible."

Alex took a sip of her coffee and grinned mischievously setting the cup back down on the saucer and asked, "You too are having fun aren't you?" Neither Ryder nor Yakira answered but by the glow on Yakira's cheeks the question was answered, Alex added. "Then it is not impossible is it? Have you missed a certain monthly visitor?"

Again a warm glow flushed over Yakira's face as she said,"You know that explosion messed up my insides, the doctor said it was normal for me to miss some."

"But have you?"

Yakira picked up her cup holding it in both hands, "Maybe one or two or *four*" she muttered.

"Four!" Ryder exclaimed. "Four Months! You call the doctor right now!"

"They are not open yet.

"Don't worry," Alex said. "I will see she does. I will take her. I will see she gets in."

Ryder stood up from the table, he was dressed for work; slacks, matching dark navy jacket and white button down shirt, no tie and the top button open. "Well I guess I am on my own today."

"I am ready!" He heard his sister say and looked over as she walked down the back stairs. She stood there, looking as professional as she could. Dressed in smoke gray slacks, a half sleeve purple button silk blouse, with a smoke gray light weight jacket, on her feet black leather heels. She was wearing makeup, a couple of rings and the pendant that Annie had given her.

"For what?" Ryder asked

"To go on the investigation," she said walking over to him. "You said yesterday I could do anything I wanted.

"That was yesterday and…"

"I took the case. It is my case." Marissa said cutting him off. She reached into her jacket pocket and pulled out a small note book and pen. "I am ready."

Ryder knew his sister's hard will, it was the same as his, "Get in the car," Ryder said. And Marissa grinned, turned and quickly made her way to the garage. "See you in a little while." Ryder said as he leaned down and kissed Yakira on the cheek. He made his way back down the hall to the door that led to the garage and Alex quickly followed. Ryder had just grabbed the door knob when Alex approached.

"She asked again last night," Alex said. "Ceelia asked 'where is my daddy'?"

Ryder twisted the knob and opened the door before he said, "We will tell her tonight."

Chapter 15

Crowder College is a small community junior college, yet it is the one college everyone knows but knew nothing about. Its founding goes back to WWII where a large military base was placed, known as Camp Crowder, it was the base for the central signal corps training center, it was also a prisoner of war camp. It wasn't till after the war that it became a true star, mainly due to those that were trained here. It was where Rob and Laura Petrie met on the *Dick Van Dyke* show but if you ever picked up the Sunday morning comics the inspiration for the comic strip *Beatle Bailey,* was inspired by Camp Crowder.

Over 65,000 acres at its prime, the camp was a town inside of a town, with hundreds of buildings, everything from barracks and command headquarters to theaters, dance halls, churches, even its own hospital complete with named streets and its own railroad spur. As soon as the war ended most of the land was sold off or returned to the farmers it was taken from and the buildings torn down or moved. Yet a few still remain, many are part of the camp ground for the National Guard, and the rest is a charming little college in Neosho, Missouri.

Known as the "Flowerbox City" Neosho is the largest city in Newton County on the far western edge of the Ozarks and about 40 miles from where Ryder lived. There are many routes to Crowder College in Neosho, but driving a custom 1971 Dodge Charger, there was only one way to go, the back way. The roller coaster ride of Highway W to Wheaton, through Stella and then D highway, this was the way his mother would have gone back when she was young and attended Crowder.

Ryder guided the car off the highway and down a small street that lead to the college. A building filled his windshield; panes of glasses staring at him, watching as he twisted the steering wheel to the left, guiding the car to an empty parking spot.

Ryder got out and looked across the campus and over to the building strung right out across the street. The Arnold Faber building was the grand greeter to those coming to the campus; it stood there, the reflections in the window glass like a warm hello. He watched as a pair of students opened the front glass door. It was here that he was told he would be met by the president of the college.

He opened the car door for Marissa and they walked across the parking lot and into the first building on the left. Through a set of glass doors, and then another set into the large commons area. Ryder reached up and removed his sunglasses as a woman approached. She was attractive, well dressed with medium length dark hair.

"Mr. Ryder?" She asked walking up to them with her hand held out. "I am Judith Love, President of Crowder college. Welcome to the Neosho campus." He shook her hand and said.

"Just call me Ryder," He said as he turned to his sister and said, "This is my…" He paused for a moment not just wanting to say his sister and then continued, "Associate Marissa." Judith turned and shook Marissa's hand.

"We are all deeply saddened by the news of Annie's death." Judith said, "She was a great asset to this campus and she will be greatly missed. Everyone has heard of you mister…" She caught herself and said, "Uh Ryder, of the cases you have solved. And you are taking on this case now?"

"She hired us." Marissa spoke up. "Do you know anyone that would have wanted her dead?" There was a moment of pride there as he heard his sister ask that question, not who would want to murder but wanted her dead. It was the type of question he would ask, he couldn't help but puff his chest out a little and try to keep a smile from breaking across his face at her.

"No!" Judith said. "No one disliked her. The staff, the students, the students loved her!"

"No one?" Ryder asked. "She did say there was one student that gave her trouble. Something about a protest."

The president looked around the commons room and even though the spring semester had ended the summer one had begun and there were still a few students roaming around climbing the stairs up to the library. "Maybe I can show you around some," it was a kind way for her to say she couldn't talk here. Ryder agreed and she showed them out the back and to the yard. Ryder slipped on his sunglasses again as the sun was bright.

Perhaps this area was the jewel of the campus the sidewalks were laid out like a diamond and in the center of this jewel was the bell tower. Ryder followed the woman out to where she stood under the bell tower; at that point the bell rang out as students were dismissed from class.

"Yes, there was one student she did have trouble with. But so did all the professors." Judith said. Ryder reached into his pocket pulled out his note book and pen. "

"Do you remember his name?"

"Till after the day I die?" She replied her words firm. "Heinz Van Way. That is two words."

"You have thousands of students here every year, why would you remember him?" Ryder asked.

"Only student we have ever had removed from the campus by gun point."

"Why?"

"We are Rough Rider's we are proud of that. Van Way took black paint and painted the word 'Murderers' on the back wall of our baseball field. Just before we had a playoff game here. After that he chained himself to the cafeteria doors holding a knife to his throat. Demanding we transfer all the money from all sports to student aid. "

Ryder jotted this all down in his notebook. "Did he threaten Annie?" Ryder asked.

"He threatened everyone on this campus. Teachers, students alike, include me! And my family. While we were at St. Canera the word traitor was painted on the side of my car." Judith said. "But yes, Annie he really hated."

"Why?" Marissa asked as she too was writing in her notebook and she looked at President Love.

"Unlike the other teachers that grew tired of his protests and would just throw him out of class, Annie would try to challenge him. She would take whatever he said and confront him with facts. So he got the wise idea to turn it around from the way he thought she believed and she turned it around on him, he was pulled from her class screaming 'I will kill you! I will kill you.'"

"Where can we find this guy?" Marissa asked

"Internet," Judith said. "He has a show on there where he reads comments on line. You know the comments you can leave at the end of an article using a fake name. He responds and is very cruel about it. His show is called 'Van's Way'"

"Do you know anything about the Sergeants' Club here on campus?" Ryder asked.

"It is not an official recognized club of the college. It is just a group of kids that get together, they study together go to all the dances. Eat together ..."

Ryder interrupted her and asked, "I mean the early days when Annie was part of it?"

"I have heard that in the early days of the club it was much stranger, weird things would happen. It was reported that one of the professors complained the club had become very secret and that is the reason the club is no longer accepted here.

"Who would that have been?"

"Marion Morestein."

"Where is she?"

"Many years ago she just disappeared; her daughter is a nursing student here.

"Patrice, "Ryder said softy remembering the stripper he paid to attend here.

"But if you want to know more, you might want to ask Malcolm Davis, he was the president before me. He works part time at the newspaper here in town. He will know everything about the Sergeants Club."

A spring time breeze drifted across as the yard. "Ryder thanked her and turned to head back to this car. "Uh—Ryder..." Judith drew out, "...you did say something about a donation."

"Oh yes!" Ryder said as he reached into his inside jacket pocket and produced an envelope and handed it to her. She opened it and gasped as her eyes read the amount. "One million dollars!"

"For this amount we would be glad to honor you in a ..."

Ryder interrupted her. "I want nothing! That is to be in Annie's memory." Ryder turned and took a couple of steps before he turned back to her and asked. "You are already doing some improvements, where is that?"

"It is for the trucking school," she replied and pointing over her shoulder. "We are removing the maintenance building and going to put the education building there."

Back in the car Ryder drove past the baseball field, where workers were replacing the spoiled sign that Van Way had painted the word murders across. He turned to the right, following the cement roadway to the back side of the campus. Over to the left was a construction zone, sealed off with bright orange fencing. Ryder parked the car along the side of the road and stepped out, he watched as heavy equipment was being used to remove the trees and the grass alongside an older building that looked to be one of the survivors of the old Camp Crowder days. The diesel smoke bellowed up as the bulldozer ground its track ripping in the soft ground from the rain last night. The thick blade pushing into the flesh of a young tree, the roots snapping like bones, as its life ends, and its carcass is pushed over into a pile with its fallen brethren. Out of the corner of his eye Ryder caught movement; it was a construction worker walking down the street. He wore a workers uniform and a bright orange vest and hardhat. He told his sister to stay in the car.

"Excuse me!" Ryder said as the construction worker started to reenter the construction site.

"Could I ask you a few questions?"

Maybe it was the fact that Ryder looked like a cop, but the man said, "This about all the shooting going on around here?"

Ryder wanted to know if they had uncovered anything, but when the opportunity presented itself he knew to grab it with both hands. "Yes," Ryder replied "what can you tell me about it?"

"Well I don't like having my equipment messed with for one." The construction worker said. "Several times we had to hold up work because ignition wires were removed or hydraulic hoses cut. We spend the damn morning trying to get things back together, and then it is too late to get any work done. Now we are shot at."

"Shot at?"

"Yeah just yesterday. I sent some men up to start removing the roof of the old maintenance building. "Ryder looked at the old building and noticed a couple of sheets of the metal roof had been removed. "And they were shot at. This morning the same damn thing. I guess you are with the college security, any way you tell them we can't go on like this, we demand guards to be out here at night. And while we are working I am not going to have my men killed."

"Do you know where the shot came from?"

"Yesterday it seemed it came from the college, this morning down in that wooden area down there." He pointed down a crossroad. "Maybe near the lagoon."

"Thank you," Ryder said as he jotted what the man said down in his notebook.

"Hey do you want the bullets I found?"

"Slugs?"

The worker reached into his pocket and pulled a clear plastic sandwich bag. Inside of the bag were a few remains' of BQ potato chips and two heavily damaged light gray slugs. He handed them to Ryder who examined them as the man spoke. "I dug them out of the roof four inches away from one of my workers legs." Ryder slipped the bag into his jacket pocket and looked at the man who said angrily. "We have any more of this crap! And we are out of here!"

****

There was only one newspaper office in town and the red and white sign read 'Neosho Daily News.' It was an L-shaped building with the newspaper offices on one side and the printing press at the back. Published twice a week Tuesday and Friday, it was a busy time getting ready for the print run, the headline was one that the paper didn't want to run "Beloved Crowder College Professor Murdered", it was not the thing that a community like Neosho embraced. In St. Louis this would just be another murder, just another day. Here this was a face that they knew by name, and knowing that they would not see her again shook the town.

As he entered there was the reception area with a long counter to his left. There was an elderly man standing there, behind the counter, most of his hair gone, what was left was silver and pushed back. He was dressed in brown ribbed pants and camel sport coat with leather patches on the sleeves. He turned and looked at Ryder and he pushed the heavy black frame eye glasses up on his face. He was holding the uncut galley of tomorrow's special edition in his hands. "Rick Ryder, I presume." He said. "Judith told me you were coming." He laid the page down on the counter; there below the headline was a brightly colored photo of Annie behind her science desk in her room.

"And that would make you Malcolm Davis?" Ryder said as he reached up and removed his sunglasses. "You were once the president of the college?" Ryder asked as he let his eyes roam around the room. Inside the front door were also two chairs and a table between them for anyone who is waiting. There are two offices, one for the publisher, and the other for the bookkeepers on the right.

Straight ahead were two rows of four desks each with an aisle between them. In front of the desks is a conference room with a long table surrounded by chairs to the right. To the left, there are two unused offices now shut tightly. It became a hallway just where the old print crew office was, now it was being used as a break room. Beyond all that are the huge printing presses, sorting machine, machines that tie the paper so the paperboy could throw the paper. They sat there like ghosts from the past just shadows of when they would run at full speed, printing out the words that readers would be anxiously waiting to devour in a seven course meal of world news, local news, facts, comics, sports and gossip to be finished off with a crossword. Now it was instant news, everything jammed into 2 minute spots. Even though they made no sound Ryder could hear the machine humming and the smell of printer's ink that disappeared long ago with boys and girls on bicycles that tossed your paper on your front porch.

"And you are wondering why would I be here?" Malcolm asked as he stepped towards Ryder. "I am an old news man. I started out at the college teaching journalism. It was back in the days when these machines ran at full speed, not just our paper but all the local ones that now have become nothing but a foot note in history. Once you get this printer's ink in your blood you can't get it out." He walked back and sat down at one of the desks, on the desk was a coffee pot half full of hot water. He picked up the hot water and poured some into a cup that was printed with the words. 'My way is the way!" He then took an herb tea bag and dipped it in the water as he asked. "A cup of tea? Coffee?"

"No thanks." Ryder said following the man.

He dipped the bag a few more times then placed it to the side, on the tea bag wrapper, taking a sip he turned and faced Ryder and said, "Judith said you were investigating Annie's murder? And you had some questions." He paused and took the cup over to the desk and sat down before he said with a lift of his eyebrows, "About, the Sergeants' Club?"

"You were the president back then?"

"No," Malcolm replied. "I was the journalism teacher back then when your mother was there."

"You knew my mother?"

"She was in my class, one of the best students I had. She had the makings of a real reporter." He opened a desk drawer and laid out a photo on the desktop. The color had faded some over the years but it was of thirteen students. They were on a stage in the music room of the college. His mother was in the center of the photo sitting down, the stage on dark blue carpet, and the group forming a semi circle around her. She was sitting down, her arm across her chest, three fingers extended across her shoulder. Next to her was Annie, kneeling, her left hand held up, her fingers curled into the shape of the letter C. On the other side was another woman, holding her hand up her index and thumb extended like the letter L.

A man with long hair was kneeling on the other side of his mother, he held his hand up with the index and middle finger grouped together the others tucked down tightly under his thumb. Another man was kneeling behind Ryder's mother, he too had long hair that was held back with a colorful headband and long sideburns and dressed in blue and green tie-dyed t-shirt. He was holding his palm up the thumb tucked under his fingers. The others were standing in a group behind, one would have their fingers curled over their hearts the next one would have the same sign but it would be over the left side of their chest.

"That is your mother isn't it?" Malcolm asked as he pointed to her in the picture. "The main problem with your mother was she would forget that The Crowder Sentry was not the New York Times. Instead of covering the winners of the basketball game she wanted to dig up the possibility of poisonous gases that were left by the troops in WWII in underground tunnels under Crowder." Ryder picked up the photo and looked at how pretty his mother was.

"Where did you get this?" Ryder asked.

"Your mother Danielle developed it. But she left the negative. I made another copy."

"What are the signs they are doing, it looks like sign language."

"That is exactly what it is." Malcolm said as he took the photo back. "Sergeant," He pointed to Ryder's mother. "C, L,U B. " Then swiped his fingers across his chest. "Members. You should know others in there. There are some famous faces in here."

"Can you name them?"

"Some," Malcolm replied. "I will make a deal with you. I will tell you who these people are if you will sit down with our reporter and give us an interview about Annie."

"Deal."

"What you are looking at are some of the most famous and popular people to come out of Crowder college," Malcolm said again pointing at the photo. "Here we have Beulah Brawn, otherwise known as Cheri DeAmour the romance author that just released her last book that is about a group of kids at a Missouri College. And this beauty October Evans, the model and this guy you should know Paul Steel the lead singer for the rock band Steelace.

"You are kidding!" Marissa said excited. "Steelace. *Don't Need Love, When I'm Gone, In the Darkness* that band!"

Malcolm looked up from the photo at Marissa in disbelief as he asked, "Why would a young girl like you be interested in a band that hasn't had a hit in 30 years?"

"They have the number one album now. Rock Resurrection," Marissa explained, "all my friends listen to them."

Again Malcolm looked at the photo, "some of the faces I don't remember. Some I do just can't recall the names." Malcolm said as he started to hand the photo back to Ryder, "that is about all I remember, maybe if I heard the names I might remember. Now how about that interview?"

"Can I have this photo?" Ryder asked picking the photo up. He started to lead Ryder to the reporter that was sitting at the conference table when suddenly he whirled around and said:

"Where's that photo! I remember someone else." Ryder handed him the photo again. "Russell Edwards he was crazy! I mean brilliant crazy he never got anything below a 100%. But really crazy! It was like he still thought it was 1968, he was always dressing that way; listened to old 1960's bands. He really identified with Jim Morrison from the *Doors*. This is him!" He pointed to the man with the headband.

"Crazy can mean a lot of things," Ryder said as Malcolm handed the photo back to him. Ryder started to slip it back into his jacket. "Did he have anything against Annie?"

"He held a knife on her and threatened to kill her."

"When did this happen?"

"When they were students there," Malcolm explained. "For awhile he and Annie had a thing going. Then it blew up in this fight. And before you ask I don't know what the fight was about."

"You are talking R U Eddie aren't you?" Ryder heard a woman ask in soft voice. He turned, saw a middle-aged woman with round face and warm smile, it was the reporter that had gotten up from the table to meet them.

"R.U. Eddie?" Ryder asked.

"His middle name was Uptun the reporter said. "That is what we called him back then R.U Eddie."

"You went to school with them?"

"Oh Ryder, Malcolm said, "This is Millie Rollins. She is the lead reporter at the Daily News. She will be doing the interview. "

"Don't worry," Millie said. "I will be gentle."

"You knew my mother?"

"Yes we were in the same journalism classes." Millie said taking the pen she was holding and bit down on the tip of it. "Annie came in here a couple months ago wanting me to find out information about him." The reporter said. "I mean R.U. Eddie. She said he tried to contact her and wanted to talk to her ."

"About what?"

"She didn't say."

"How did she feel about that?" Ryder asked. "Happy? Sad?"

"She just said there was something that she had to talk to him about." Millie said

"She seemed scared," Millie said. "She said if he were to find out, she wouldn't be safe."

"Find out what?"

"I don't know."

After the interview Ryder reappeared and looked for Marissa, but she was not there. Thinking maybe she went back to the car he went outside and looked, but the car was empty. He went back inside, and there was another woman in the front office.

"Have you seen a pretty young girl..."

"Wow! My brother thinks I am pretty." Marissa said with a smile as she walked into the room holding the photo in one hand and a folded up newspaper in the other hand.

"Where have you been?"

"I got an idea," Marissa said as walked over to him. "I was thinking that a lot of news stories in the paper have to do with the college, and the students there. I thought you might find something in the back issues"

"Did you find anything?"

"They don't keep that many back issues," she replied. "But guess what? I found something else." She showed him the paper. "This is from last week. Is this woman here not the same woman that is here in the photograph making the letter L. Ryder looked at the photo, she was much younger and her hair was longer and darker, but it was the same woman. He read the article it was Charlotte Day- Leighton the owner of a dress shop on the square downtown. Marissa grinned broadly and continued. "Don't you think I need another dress?"

Chapter 16

The center of the 'Flowerbox City' is the square and in the center of the square where the courthouse is, the down town shops are circling around it with one way traffic. There, many different antique shops, insurance and lawyers' offices, surrounded the public square, in the center was the courthouse.

Ryder pulled the car into a parking spot in front of a quaint little shop with the sign that read "Day's-Leight Dress Boutique". It was a play on the owner's name, her Maiden name was Day, married name Leighton. Ryder rolled the power windows down, got out and held the passenger door for his sister, and they both headed for the storefront.

He pulled the front open and a bell hanging over the door rang. The first thing he noticed was the harsh aroma of starch in the new garments that were hung on the racks on both sides of the store. It was not a large store, and chrome racks were grouped together according to each garment, all the blouses, slacks, dresses, and jackets. Each one further divided by the sizes. On the wall to the left were racks holding shoes. To the other side were shelves that held all the under garments and nightgowns. At the back were the dressing rooms and the office; near this area were the evening gown, which was going to be Ryder's excuse for being in here, to buy his sister an expensive dress.

Ryder looked the shop over, there were no other customers. He reached up and removed his sunglasses and called out "Ms Day. Charlotte!" He called out her first name hoping to make it sound as if he knew her, so she would be more willing to come out. The only reply was that of a frazzled voice coming from the radio at the back of the store, it was tuned to the local Christian radio station KENO 91.7 FM, a woman was speaking. Again Ryder, called out, "Charlotte! Are you here?"

Not hearing her reply Ryder pushed further into the store towards the checkout counter. There was something strange going on. The radio lay on the floor, upside down, the speaker being muffled by discarded articles of clothing that had been removed from the racks. Tossed on the floor were empty boxes, which were used to wrap up the garments, plus the tape machine and a package of wrapping paper. It appeared the counter had been wiped clean. The drawer to the cash register was wide open, the money was still there. Leaning next to the cash register was a wood plaque 8x10 with the 'Queen of Diamonds', and burned into the wood a bible verse "Cursed is the one who accepts a bribe to kill an innocent person" *Deuteronomy 27: 25.* Ryder suddenly got this creepy feeling.

"Charlotte!" Ryder called out again this time with desperation. He looked down into the trash basket next to the counter, there were several items including a crushed Coke can on top and a couple of empty plastic cups.

"Ricky!" Marissa said in sudden outburst as she stood staring down at a dark colored spot on the floor. "Is that what I think it is?" Ryder walked over and bent down and touched the spot, and wiped it over his fingers, it was red when he lifted his finger up to his nose and sniffed, it was not chemical smelling. It was blood.

"Stay here!" He ordered as he stood up noticing another spot of blood a couple feet away.

"Shouldn't I..."

"Stay here!" He ordered again more firmly, he followed a trail of blood drops back towards the back of the store, each drop getting closer and bigger in diameter, splattering spread out. He walked past the bathroom and again he called out, "Charlotte!" No answer, his training as homicide officer was preparing him for he knew what he was about to see. Then he saw another splatter of blood on the office door, the door was closed and he pushed it open. Ryder stepped inside.

It was a small room, cramped with a couple of file cabinets and a large black metal desk the wooden top covered with papers. There were no windows, and it was dark, the only light showing was that of a goose neck desk lamp, that was lying on the floor behind the desk. Plus the warm glow of a black and white video monitor, below it an old style VCR tape machine, the tape missing, the video screen just a jumble of wavy lines.

He peered over the desk and saw the shape of a shadowy figure lying on the floor. Ryder was always a prepared cop, even though he no longer carried a badge. He reached into his jacket pocket and produced a white handkerchief he always had on him. Using the cloth he lifted up the lamp from the floor, letting the beam grow wider.

Charlotte lay on the floor, her body twisted in an odd angle. She was lying on her stomach; twisted at the waist, her legs bent, her bare foot bent down revealing her dark green toenails. Curled under her chest was one arm, the other curled up by her head which was twisted to the side and facing the right. Her cream colored dress soaked in blood, and sticking out of her back, looking as if it were growing out from the wound, was what looked at first like a Hawaiian Hibiscus, five large yellow pedals with a red center.

"Call 911 tell the dispatcher there 10-100 possible homicide. CSD is required." Ryder called out to his sister as he looked closer at the flower and noticed that it was in fact a steel pointed dagger with a handle that was shaped like the flower.

"What?" She asked walking back towards him. She stood in the door way of the office, her mouth dropped open as she stared down at the woman's body. Ryder stood up placing the lamp down on the desk. She turned to him and asked, "Is she…is she dead?"

"As much as a canned mackerel, call it in. All hell is about the break loose. Call it in."

Marissa called it in and then looked down at the woman again and said. "Ricky the flower. It is a Hibiscus."

"I know."

"But it is the same one that the Queen of Diamonds on the card in there is holding."

"What?" Ryder quickly dashed back to the counter and looked at the playing card that was mounted to the piece of wood. He looked closely at the Queen's hand, Marissa was right. "Do you know what the Queen of Spades holds?"

Marissa pulled out her cell phone and began searching the internet. "This," she said holding it over for her brother to see, "Doesn't that look like the dagger that was used to kill Annie?"

Ryder's ears were filled with the multitude of sirens that only the code 10-100 code brings. He looked down at the wooden plaque, he knew that his next step was going to be illegal, but he was the only one right now that saw the connection. It would just get overlooked, possibly even get lost in the overwhelming condition that was about to happen. It was nothing against the local police or Newton County, it was just the fact Ryder was the only one who saw it.

He took his handkerchief and carefully lifted the wooden plaque up and then picked up a white sack off the floor and dropped the plaque into the bag. He rolled the top down and turned to his sister who was standing there watching. "Not a word!" He said quickly making his way outside, the scream of sirens were bringing the town to a halt. The sirens just seemed to be echoing, coming from every direction because that was what was happening. Ryder tossed the sack with the wood plaque into his car, through the open window.

Customers and store owners alike were pushing the doors open and stepping out on the sidewalk to gaze at the police cars swarming on the square like bees to the only flower in the meadow, as Ryder's sister joined him outside. A black and white city cruiser slid to a stop in front of the store. The officer dashed inside.

As yet more screams of sirens made it hard to hear, another cruiser slid to stop next to the first city cruiser; this was a County Cruiser, dark in color with bright graphics on the doors, light flashing, catching in the reflections of the pane of window glass in the store. Each strobe from the light bar painted across the mannequin's face as it stood there staring, and the officer dashed towards the shop. He was dressed in uniform and Ryder recognized him as the Sheriff Ray Barker.

"Rick Ryder, what are you *doing here*?" Sheriff Barker shouted, having to shout his last words to be overheard by the scream of yet another siren that was arriving.

"I was going to buy my sister a new dress," Ryder replied. "Found the place empty, looked for the owner and found her murdered in her office. Since money is still here, nothing seems to be missing I would say robbery was not the motive."

"How do you know she was murdered?"

"Most people don't have a flower growing out of their back."

"A flower?" Sheriff Barker asked. "How do you murder someone with a flower?"

"Take a look, you will figure it out." Ryder replied as he slowly reached into his jacket and pulled out his sunglasses. He slipped them on and looked back at the sheriff and added, "I was here to buy a pretty dress."

"Yeah right!" The sheriff drew out in a disbelieving breath as another squad car slide to stop. And another siren could be heard in the distance approaching. "The money you have, you could buy an original in Paris so why would you buy something here in Neosho."

"I like shopping local." Ryder replied.

"Yeah right! And I guess cops don't eat doughnuts. Why don't you think it over and tell it to me later. And don't leave. " Sheriff Barker said.

Ryder pointed to his car and the squad cars parked behind it, "Where can I go you got me blocked in." He glanced over to a restaurant on the other side of the square. "We are going over there," Ryder said pointing to the shop "And get something to eat, because we haven't had anything since breakfast. That is where you can find us." Ryder reached down and took a hold of his sister's hand and added, "Come on sis."

They walked down the street, stopping as a city cruiser sped past in front of them, then continued across to *Cafe Angelica.* If one was to go by at normal speed around the square the cafe could have been easily missed. Sandwiched in between two other businesses, it was small but cozy. With lace curtains draped over the front window. The red and white checkered table cloths just seemed to be inviting them. They went up the three step and Ryder opened the door and they walked in. They were shown to a table right in front of the window and given a menu. The waitress introduced herself as Ada.

"What can I get you to drink?" Ada asked

"Sweet tea, a half twist of lemon." Ryder said

"Same for me." Marissa said.

Ryder grinned at the young woman, her raven hair tied back, held with dark blue ribbon. He handed her the menu. "I am new here pretty lady." She blushed as his hand touched hers. "What would you recommend?"

"Our specialty the Club Angelica. Ham, turkey, bacon, cheddar cheese with lettuce tomato with mayo on triple decker white and wheat toast very yummy, or our soups, they are homemade."

"Sounds good," Ryder said. "We will share the sandwich and bring us each a bowl of soup." Ryder glanced across the restaurant it was small with home style eclectic decor, the tables close together. They were the only customers in there. He turned and glanced out the front window and looked catty-cornered across the street watching as the County's command center drove up.

"What happened?"Ada asked as she brought the tea.

"A murder." Marissa said with glee as she took a sip of the ice tea.

"Charlotte!" Ada said as she pulled out a chair at the table and sat down with a thud. "That is what he wanted."

"Who?" Ryder asked leaning back in his chair and taking a sip of his tea.

"The guy that came in here. He wanted to know where he could find her." Ada said dropping her head down in her hands. "It is my fault. He said he was a friend that they knew each other in college. I didn't know."

"It is not your fault!" Ryder comforted her placing his hand on her arm. "It is the one who killed her. What did this man look like?"

"Scary!" Ada said lifting her head up. "That is why I should have not told him."

"It is okay!" Ryder said reaching for his note book in his inside jacket pocket. "But tell me more about him. How tall was he?"

"Tall but not that tall, say five nine five ten", she pointed to Marissa and said, very thin. Not attractive at all, long face, sharp nose, big round eyes. Brownish hair, long held back with a bright colored headband, it had big yellow flowers on it. He also had long side burns and a beard. "

"How old was he?"

"I don't know twenties maybe thirties."

Ryder was jotting this all down; he turned and asked her, "Anything else you remember?"

"Yes," Ada replied, "And it was strange. He went to shake my hand his hands were sticky like glue."

Chapter 17

Questions, and more questions that was what Newton county and the Neosho P.D. wanted from Ryder. But there were no answers, for Ryder had none to give. Finally coming to the conclusion that he had nothing to do with this murder he and his sister were allowed to go and they headed back home.

He drove into the driveway and parked behind Alex's sedan. As Ryder got out he looked at the dark blue Ford and wondered why it was parked here. Alex usually always parked down at her house down the hill.

"I am going to go take care of the horses," He heard Marissa say as she quickly opened the car door.

"Yeah, okay." Ryder said as he made his way towards the house. Opening the garage door and stepping inside, his mind suddenly flashed back to this morning and the fact that Yakira was going to see the doctor. He opened the door and stepped inside. Alex greeted him a she walked out from the kitchen into the foyer, an apron tied around her.

"How is Yakira? What did you find out?"

She didn't have time to reply before Ceelia came running to him with arms stretched out for him to lift her up in his arms. "Mommy is fixing supper tonight. Her BBQed chicken. He hugged the little girl and then set her down on the floor again.

"What is wrong with Yakira?"

"She has an ulcer," Alex said pointing up at the ceiling. "She is upstairs. Said she wanted to talk to you when you got in. She said 'there is something else that the doctor told her that she wants to tell you."

Ryder removed his sunglasses and took a couple steps up on the stairs when Alex asked, "Did you find out anything?" He stopped and turned to her.

"A couple of things," he said. "Marissa can tell you." His words were low and somber and as empty as a drunk's shot glass. He started up the stairs again.

"Rick," she called him by his first name tenderly. "Are you okay?"

"I am fine Belle," He said, calling her a shorten version of her first name, as he climbed the steps not even turning to her. He knew his words were a lie. Inside he was a child again just getting off the bus and walking through the front door. His mother had been to the doctor and those words were spoken to him, 'your mother wants to see you, there is something the doctor told her that she needs to tell you.' Eleven years old and have your mother tell you they found something wrong-she has cancer that she wouldn't live to see you turn 13 was hard.

As he stepped on to the second floor, fear had its hand around his throat and with each step he could feel the icy cold fingers of this beast squeeze a little tighter. He coughed, felt as if he couldn't take a deep breath. As he reached the bedroom door he reached up and unbuttoned the top button of his shirt.

He opened the door, '*God please don't let this be bad.*' He prayed in an unspoken voice and stepped inside. She was resting in bed, her eyes closed. His mind flashed back to his mother in a coffin lying in front of him and just before the lid was being closed down on her, he laid his most precious toy a stuffed cat next to her. Ryder stood there for just a moment looking at his wife. She always had such a connection to him, as if she knew what he was thinking. Yakira's eyes fluttered open.

"Don't worry I am not dying," she said with a grin, as he set down on the edge of the bed beside her and she continued, "I wanted you since I was eight-years-old. You think I am going to give up now?" She pushed herself up in the bed, brought her nose up to his and said, "You think I am going to die and let another girl have you? Ain't going to happen."

"I heard you had an ulcer are you okay?" With his question she leaned back on the headboard.

She took a deep breath and replied, "That is what I told Alex the doctor said. The test showed something else..." She paused for a brief moment before the large smile beamed across her faced as she leaned forward again and added, "He told me I am going to have to work on my guilt."

"Your what?"

She put her arms around his neck, kissed him gently on the lips. Her eyes gleamed like priceless gemstones under the bright light in a jewelry store and her smile revealed her slightly bucked grin. It was clear she wanted another kiss.

"Are you okay?" Ryder asked. "What do you mean you have to work on your guilt?"

Not getting the reaction she wanted she moved her face back from his. "It is what Jewish mothers excel at. I don't have a hole in my stomach I have a baby. I am four months pregnant!" He sat there, blinked his eyes a couple of times not knowing what to say. "Did you hear me?" He nodded but still didn't say anything. "He told me I have a 'high risk pregnancy'."

"What does that mean?" He finally managed to speak.

"She said 'we should treat our baby like a miracle from God. For that is what it is."

"What do you have to do?" Ryder asked, inside he could feel his heart pounding like a big bass drum as the parade was just about to begin, it was beating faster, so fast he knew all she had to do was look and see his shirt moving.

"I am to take it easy, no housework, no flying and no work." She said releasing him from her embrace.

"So you stay in bed?"

"No," she said that would be boring. "I just—I...I can't help you."

"Alright, I will stay here and…"

"*Sha!*" She said meaning hush as she gently brings her fingers up to his lips. "Don't speak my love!" She moved her fingers from his lips and cupped his hand in hers and continued. "You are an investigator. You are not my nurse maid."

"Then I will get you a nurse! I will hire the…"

Again she placed her fingers up on his lips and told him to hush, "I don't want anyone else to know this," she lifted her fingers from lips and continued, "I asked Bubbie to come over she will take care of me."

"Does she know?"

"You can't keep anything from her, as soon as I called she knew." Yakira said, "But she hasn't told mom and dad, and you can't tell anyone else either."

"Why?" Ryder asked. "I want to tell everyone I know."

"I just feel that if I brag about it I will jinx it." As she spoke Ryder took his fingers and brushed back his bride's hair out of her face, this child was going to be a mix of them, he loved everything about her, her face, her smile her…

"Eyes," he said as pushed her hair back over her shoulders. "She will have your eyes."

"No, he will have your eyes."

"He?"

"We are going to have son. A Jewish mother knows these things!"

He cupped his hands around her face letting his fingers trace around her lips, he always considered himself hardened, yes tears for sadness but happiness…he had never felt that before. But she was becoming blurry; he felt a tear roll down the side of his face. As he saw her eyes puddle she took her thumbs and carefully wiped away his tears, and put them up to her eyes as she said, "My tears are your tears. If I don't cry you don't cry but if I weep…"

"We weep together." They both said together.

"Now is it okay if I hugged you?" He said and he grabbed her in his arms and pulled her close. Soon there was a knock on the door.

"Ryder," he heard Alex say from behind the door. "Supper is ready. Yakira your grandmother's here. She brought you what you requested. "

"Cravings dear?" Ryder whispered.

"Just a chocolate doughnut with Jiff® Peanut butter and strawberry cream cheese," Yakira said.

"I will be there in a minute Alex," Ryder shouted back, then tuned to Yakira and softly added, "Going to be a few weird months isn't it?"

"Five fun filled months."

Chapter 18

Three more days had passed, it was the middle of June but the weather didn't seem that way. It was the day of Annie's funeral and it was raining, not a hard drenching rain, with lightning cracking and thunder rumbling over head. It was just a steady, rain, the type that would run down the rim of the umbrella, and gather in puddles, puddles that just could not be avoided, nor could the media that had encircled the Oak Hill Cemetery, at the top of the hill that looked down at the city.

Ryder could feel the squish of the soil under his shoes as he stepped off the pavement and into the graveyard. He could see the headstones dotting the lawn, and the white tent the funeral home set up, her family already gathering under it.   Ryder placed his arm around Yakira's waist and pulled her closer to him as with the other hand he held an umbrella over them as they made their way closer to the tent. Alex and Marissa following close beside them, each with their own umbrella, the pendant that Annie gave her hanging around Marissa's neck, shining on her dark colored dress.

There were several mourners as Annie was well loved, and that included many students, past, present and even those that were looking forward to having her. The small tent was jammed with them, and more were being stuffed in. Ryder guided Yakira over to the tent and she stood at the edge along with Marissa.

"Go on in there Rick," he heard a man say; Ryder turned and saw Thom Thompson, the funeral home director standing under a black umbrella behind him.

"Double T," Ryder said using his nickname. "You know me; I would rather just stay out here."

Thom was dressed in a suit and tie, as he always was on funeral days, he too held an umbrella. Pastor Woods brought the services to a start with the reading of Annie's obit. She had lived a grand life. Alex stood beside Ryder; she was in a dark colored dress with a lace inset. "Where is the little one?" Thom asked, meaning Ceelia.

"At home," Alex replied "with it raining and all, I thought it was best." She twirled the handle of the umbrella in her fingers. "What did you find out?" She asked, as the minster told more of Annie's life. Thom was also the county coroner, in fact he was a medical doctor and his specialty was pathology, but he preferred to be the small town funeral director, than the M.E. of a big city.

"Cause of death homicide." Thom replied. "Her left lung was punctured, sliced the pulmonary vein. How she made it to the back of the house I don't know. "I did find something strange in her blood."

"What?" Ryder asked as there was a rumble of thunder and the rain began to fall harder.

"Now don't get me wrong," Thom explained. "I don't mean to disrespect her. I test for chemical substances in all cases. But she tested positive for codeine. I had Brian check the trailer the only prescription was for Ziac® for high blood pressure."

"Drugs?" Ryder questioned as Pastor Woods paused the services for a hymn. "Annie? Annie Harris taking drugs? I can't believe it." As the crowd joined in on the hymn *In the Garden,* Ryder continued. "What was the amount in her blood?"

"Don't know yet that takes awhile. But she did have traces of codeine."

Students came forward to offer their memories of their favorite professor, as Ryder looked over the mourners, those sitting on the front row, her two sisters and brothers and in the middle her son Dr. Harrell Harris, general practice in the Physicians' Specialty Hospital in Fayetteville, Ark, as well as many cousins, but it was one person in particular that Ryder was looking for.

"The codeine, could someone have given it to her?"

"Also found traces of coke…I'm talking the pop here. It could have easily been mixed with that."

"What would have been the affects?

"Drowsy, slower breathing ...." It was then that Alex walked up, noticing Ryder looking the crowd over, she interrupted Thom.

"You really think he will show up here?" The rain was pouring down over the rim of the umbrella.

"There are two types that have to show up at a funeral," Ryder said. "Those that love that weep for the lost, and those that want to dance on the grave. He is definitely a dancer."

"So what does he look like?"

"Out of place," Ryder said. He saw him standing near the back of the tent, he was dressed in jeans and a t-shirt that had the word 'revolution' imprinted on the front. His hair unkempt and curly . Instead of being sad, he seemed agitated, ringing his fingers as the students spoke, his hair was a large afro styling with a droop down mustache. He looked around at the others under the tent, as yet another student came forward to express the fondness for Annie, the man seemed to become more agitated gritting his teeth as yet another student came forward. "Like that guy!"

Alex held up her cell phone and zoomed in and took a photo of the man. "I will see if I can get a match."

"Anyone else would like to say something?" Pastor Woods asked.

"Yes I would like to tell the truth about Annie Harris," the man said as he moved forward through the crowd.

"Well we may not have to," Ryder said as he watched the man reach the podium. It was Van Way, the person Ryder was looking for.

"So many kind things have been said about Professor Annie Harris," the man said calmly but the thing is…" He began to shout. "They are all lies! Professor Harris was a pig! She was part of the problem, she deserved to die!" Pastor Woods tried calming the man and moving him away from the podium but he pushed the minster down as he shouted,

"Whoever killed her should be given a medal. Ryder approached the tent, Van Way saw Ryder, he turned and ran across the graveyard. Ryder tossed his umbrella down and chased after him.

In football, Ryder was the player that the tacklers were always after, but that did not mean he was not taught to tackle. He leaped forward, extended his arms out, he wrapped them around Van Way's legs and they plowed down into mud. With Ryder twisting the man's legs, he forced him facedown and quickly moved up grabbing Van Way's arm and twisting it around behind the man's back.

"Let me go!" Van Way screamed, slamming his fist into ground. "I done nothing wrong."

Ryder pressed his throbbing knee down into the pit of the man's back as Sheriff Thompson walked up and said.

"Need these?" He handed Ryder a pair of handcuffs as a crowd began to gather. Ryder snapped the handcuffs around Van Way's wrist.

"What am I under arrest for?" Van Way asked as Ryder pulled him to his feet and Ryder said, "Disrupting a funeral for one and suspicion of murder."

Chapter 19

It was the funeral that was breaking headlines, images taken from cell phones, never knowing if they would reach   celebrity status in matter of minutes. Suddenly posted on Facebook and Instagram *Murderer Goes to Victim's Funeral* were circling the globe, as they were shared and comments posted over and over again. That the one who attacked those commenter's on line as being vile and stupid was now suddenly the fodder for all the other comments.

Once again the dollar a day billionaire was on the Yahoo news page and the media was descending like hungry scavengers on Cassville. Ryder handled it the way he had learned, a few questions answered, but no answers ever given.

"I am confident in the skill of the local authorities that they can wrap this up but this is an ongoing case and there are still many questions that need to be answered. We will keep you advised on further updates. But we are not taking any other questions Thank you." Ryder had learned that the press was like stray cats, you give them something to actually eat and stroke their ego they would stay around forever toss out a few table scraps, and they would eat and then leave.

Ryder was still in his muddy clothes as he entered the integration room at the Barry County Sheriff's Department. Van Way sat at the table clearly as fidgety as a tree frog on a hot plate. He swigs down the cup of water that had been offered to him. Ryder sat hunched down in the chair across the table from Van Way, next to Ryder was Brian the sheriff. Brian sat firmly with his back on the back rest of the chair, his elbows resting on the table top and his fingers stroking his chin.

"I did not murder her!" Van Way screamed out.

"We have your fingerprints, we found them." Brian said leaning forward and pointing his fingers at Van Way and continued with a forceful tone. "We found one of your prints in Annie's house and on her vehicle, we have you. You will head for death row."

"You are not going to find anything." Van Way said.

"Why, because you wore gloves," Brian asked as he stood.

"No because I wasn't there!"

"We found glove prints on the adjustment rail when you pushed the seat back. We also found them on the dash and the door panel. We can match them just as well as we can fingerprints." The sheriff tossed a clear bag down on the table, inside the bag was a pair of dark brown leather gloves size small. "We found those in your car. Hidden under the driver's seat."

"I—I— never seen those before." He stuttered out. "The locks don't work on my car, anyone could have put them in there. It wasn't me! I didn't kill her."

"You threatened to when you were removed from her class." Ryder said as he stared at the man. "We have fifteen witnesses in that class that have all said they heard you say 'you were going to kill her.'"

"Yes I said it. I hated her. But I didn't do it." Van Way said as he gripped his fingers with his other hand. "Haven't you ever been mad and said something dumb like that."

"But you have a habit of doing that, don't you?" Ryder said as he picked up a paper on the desk. "These are some of your comments to people online and read: 'To Darkline180, you have to be an inbred, your father and mother had to be related, otherwise no one could be that stupid.' 'To jkkiller, you have no reason to talk, you have no reason to live, and someone ought to shut you up.' 'To Simlpesimon101, without a doubt you are uneducated, uncivilized, fly over garbage, I am tracking you down, your real name is Trina Allaway 101 Golden....' Ryder stopped speaking in sentence and set the paper down on the table and stared at the man, watched him slowly push the head band off his head and clutch it in his hands. "And on show 107, you listed Annie's real name and her address. Stating..." Again Ryder read from the paper. "Annie Harris is criminal. A criminal to our goals. She is old school and needs to be eliminated..." Ryder set the paper down and then continued,

"Don't you get it, say that and if any of your listeners acted on that you are as guilty as they are."

"You have agreed to talk to us without a lawyer. Do you still feel that way?" Brian asked.

"I don't need no stinking lawyer! They are part of the problem. I didn't kill her," Van Way said. "I didn't know she was dead until I saw it on Facebook. It is like I told you I was online the night she was killed."

"Yes, spreading out this garbage!" Ryder said sitting up in the chair and leaning over the table. "Van's Way! We are going over all your shows if you have made a comment where you mention Charlotte Day by name or her online name and you are…"

"I don't know any Charlotte Day! And besides, they are haters I have a right to take them down anyway I can." Van Way said his lips curling into a snarl as he looked over at Ryder, as Ryder stood up placing his fist on the table.

"And nothing more that is full of hate than cold blooded murder RIGHT!"

"I was on line doing my show when she was killed." Van Way said. "If you look at it you can see that."

"And a show can be recorded and played back later."

"Not the way I do it! I pick an online article and I make comments while those on line are making comments at the same time."

The door to the room opened and in walked a Barry County Deputy, "Sheriff," the deputy said. "That witness is here."

"Some saw you go into the Day's store just before she was killed." Ryder said as he walked towards the door, then turned and faced the suspect. "If that witness identifies you, you are heading to death row, oh those guys there are going to love you, maybe you will have special affection from your cellmate. Confess to both murders we could see to it you get solitary lock up." Ryder's hand rested on the door knob as he looked at the man.

"Stuff it!"

Ryder knocked on the door and said, "All right we are ready." The door opened and out walked the sheriff and Ryder. There standing in the hallway was Ada from the diner in Neosho. "Okay Ada," Ryder said. "I want you to take a good look at him. Is that the man you saw asking you the questions. She stood gazing through the two way glass at him.

"No," she shook her head. "That is not him."

"Are you sure!"

"The nose isn't long enough and the face is wrong, and he is not skinny enough hair is all worng the guy I saw had long straight hair. Sorry but that is not the man I saw."

"We can still hold him for disrupting a funeral, "Sheriff Brian said. "And if someone was inspired to act on his words, he is still toast." Ryder stared at the man through the glass. "What is bugging you? " He asked.

"The plaques why leave them? What would they have to do with the murders?" He looked over at the sheriff and asked, "Did you get any prints on the plaque ?"

"It was wiped cleaned. And the bloody hand print was Annie's"

"That means it wasn't a gift, it was brought in by the killer."

Chapter 20

An eye witness can make or break a case and this one just shattered this one, but Van Way was off the air and was going to be cooling off for awhile thanks to Barry County. Like a child's game Ryder was sent spinning back to the start square, and the first space ahead was marked 'Sergeants Club'. This had to do with his mother, and the person that knew her the best was her brother, Father Anthony.

Ryder changed his clothes and headed to town to see his uncle. The rain had stopped and the sun was trying to break through the clouds. The area was left feeling like a steam bath as the mercury began to rise again. He pulled the Killer Bee into the driveway of his uncle's house.

His uncle was in the garage bent over the fender of his custom car, the fender protected by a cover. He was changing the spark plugs. He stood up; a ratchet wrench and deep well socket in his hand, a sparkplug in the socket.

"So you don't wear the collar to work on the car?" Ryder asked as he walked into the garage.

His uncle looked up at him and laughed, "I don't know, you think that might help?" He laid the wrench down on the fender cover, and added, "Rick you are on TV again."

"Did they get my good side," Ryder said as he reached up and removed his sunglass. "I need help Uncle Tony," the father put the socket down on the cover and Ryder continued. "How much do you about mom's time at Crowder?"

"Some," Father Anthony said as he turned and wiped his hands with a cloth. "She had a group of friends she hung out."

"Annie was one of them?"

"Yes, they were all in a club."

"I know the Sergeants' Club, but what was it?"

"She never told me, I was not part of it." Father Anthony paused as he looked up at the ceiling. "You know that before your mom and dad were married Danielle and I were close. Then when she got pregnant with you she had to drop out."

"She never got her degree?"

"No Ryan insisted she stay home with you," Father Anthony said. "While he went out and with every woman he could find." He dropped his head and used his fingers to cross his chest as he said, "I am sorry Heavenly Father, I have forgiven him. I have forgiven him. I have forgiven him. Please forgive me." He looked back up at Ryder and said, "She only had one credit to go, and he would not let her get it."

"What was her major?"

"English, your mother wanted to be a writer."

"She never told me," Ryder said with a grin. Father Tony continued, "I was the only person that she ever told. She said that no one else would have believed in her. She was involved in the *Crowder Sentry* and *the Quill* and she would have been a great reporter but that father of yours he never...again I forgave him."

"You also have a hard time forgiving him?" Ryder asked. "A priest?"

"I am also human just like you. And she was my sister. "

It is odd when you find out something about someone that you love and think you know everything about them, but you find out you don't even know about their deepest greatest dream. "Do you have anything that she wrote?"

Father Anthony looked up at the ceiling. "I think there is one of her boxes up there. He walked over to the far wall where a rope hung down from the ceiling. There was long bench pushed up against the wall of the garage. Father Anthony stepped up on the bench so he could reach the rope, he pulled on it and a ladder dropped down. Ryder watched as his uncle climbed up the ladder. He could hear boxes being moved around. Then Father Anthony descended the ladder.

"Here," He said as he handed the box to Ryder. The white box was covered with dust so much he couldn't even see the red and blue stripes and the words '*Three Musketeers*' printed on the top. Written on the sides were the words '*Crowder College years*'. The lid was tapped shut with masking tape that had dried out, yellow and so brittle that it broke when he applied a little pressure to it. He removed the lid and, there on top a white quill pen that she used to write with and under that was a piece of newspaper cut from the college newspaper.

Entitled 'When Barry Manilow meets Black Sabbath local band has a new sound.' It was all about Steelace and how Crowder Students Paul Steele and Stephanie Granger have formed a hard rock band that sings pop songs. It was written by Danielle Delany. Ryder sat down on the bench and picked up the folded up newspaper.

He unfolded it and there was the headline '*The Truth of Air Force Plant # 65*,' the featured article in the *Crowder Sentry,* again authored by his mother and Millard Snyder. He began to read the article. It was about the time when rocket engines were tested here, rocket engines that would send men to space and beyond. And the possibility that the government was storing dangerous chemicals in the underground bunkers that were the old blast pads and that these chemicals were leaking and contaminating the nearby towns including Neosho resulting in an increase in the risk of cancer for the residents. It took the whole front page and was continued on another page inside.

"Holly Hanna!" Ryder said as he looked up from the paper. "Uncle Tony this is the stuff she wrote? She was very good. Why didn't she…" She looked back down at the newspaper. "Is it because of me that she didn't reach for her dreams?"

"No kiddo," Father Anthony said as he walked over and sat down next to his nephew. "There was nothing more important in your mother's life than you were, she would have done anything to protect you, even giving up her life. She continued to write making up stories she would tell you and even had a column in the *Barry County Advertiser*. Father Anthony reached into the box and pulled out a folded clipping from the newspaper. It was titled *'Out and About' By Dannie Green.'* "She used her nickname at Crowder and our grandmother's maiden name." Father Anthony looked at the column and laughed as he handed it over to Ryder. It was light hearted piece about what the people in town were doing.

"It seems wild child of town Anthony Delany will be a father!" Ryder read. "No not the way you think. He has seen the light. Giving up his dreams he is heading to the seminary this fall." Ryder placed the article down on his lap and turned and looked at his uncle lifting an eye brow at him. "Uncle Tony what was your dream?"

"You will laugh at me."

"I would never do that?"

"Then you will think I am crazy."

"You are part of this family you have to be crazy." Ryder said.

"I wanted to be the lead singer of a rock band. Like Paul Steel" Father Anthony said. "I used to have this old broken handle of a badminton racket. I would go into my bedroom and use it as if it was microphone and sing along with all my records. Even tried to look like Ozzy Osborne."

Ryder tried not to laugh, to picture his uncle the priest singing heavy metal was hard to believe. "You are kidding right?"

Father Anthony stood up and walked over to the opened door and gazed out across the street and over to his church. He turned back to his nephew and began to sing the first two verses of Black Sabbath's 'Iron Man'.

Father Anthony walked back over to the bench and reached back into the box and pulled out a photo of himself and his sister, Ryder's mother and handed it to Ryder. They were standing in front of a

Cardinal Red 1972 with white interior and white vinyl top. Ryder's mother was in a two piece swim suit, Father Anthony was 15 years old and his hair long and straight parted in the middle, hanging on his bare shoulders, he was wearing swim trunks. Ryder looked closer at the photo; there were drawings on his arms and chest.

"Uncle Tony you don't have any tattoos." Ryder said.

"Daniele drew them on me." Father Anthony said as he reached over and took the photo from Ryder. He grinned looking at it and then said, "She was the greatest big sister there ever was." He laughed out loud. "The only thing is the ink washed away, and we got kicked out of the Cassville city pool." He laid the photo down in his lap. "The only one I told my dream to was her. You know she even wrote me song lyrics."

"Shut the front door!" Ryder said shocked. "My mother wrote rock and roll lyrics?"

Again Father Anthony reached into the candy box and at the very bottom was a small 5x7 spiral notebook with a faded red cover and her name written across the front. He flipped it open to what looked like poem.

The EYES OF DARKNESS

Now listen there is nothing to be heard-

Voices all around, but not one spoken word-

Silence comes but everyone has something to say-

I shout but nothing can be heard-

Death stumbles across the floor-

There is nothing left but loneliness-

I open the door-

And I see the eyes of darkness-

"I didn't know you had it in you, mom," Ryder said. As he looked into the box there was a clipping from a newspaper, this one was from the Neosho Daily News, and the page was yellowed, it was folded up. He carefully unfolded it and read it:

*A two month old infant was last seen at 11:30 p.m.
yesterday at Sales Memorial Hospital, in Neosho, MO.
Nurse Francine Hopper checked on the infant at that
time, ten minutes later the child was reported
missing. Neosho Police Chief Marvin Raystone
remarked there was a report of a group of young women
seen around the hospital at that time; however Newton
County Sheriff states they have no leads at this
time. Witnesses have reported occurrences of satanic
rituals being carried out on the grounds near Crowder
College, the remains of a young goat were found last
week near the old community swimming pool. Reports
are that the throat of the young goat was cut and it
was allowed to bleed to death. Anyone with any
information is requested to contact the Neosho police
department or Newton County sheriff's office.*

"You know anything about this?" Ryder asked as he handed the clipping to his uncle.

"There was talk and rumors at one time that there were devil worshippers there on the old Camp Crowder grounds, but the cops just figured it was just students playing a trick." He handed Ryder the photo back and then placed everything back into the box and handed it to Ryder. "Here, this is yours."

"Could this have been mom? " Ryder asked with a lifted eyebrow. "I am hearing tales that the club was into some weird like this."

"I don't know," Father Anthony replied. "You mother was a passionate woman back then she would have tried anything."

*****

Back at the house, he handed the box to Alex for her to look through as he went upstairs to check on Yakira, who had been told to stay in bed as much as possible, going to the funeral was all that she could do today. He opened the bedroom door. "How you doing mom?" He asked with a grin. Walking over to the bed where she was lying he sat down. "Can I get you anything?"

"No, Bubbie went to town to get me some tacos and those little Reese's Peanut Butter Cups." She explained just as the door opened and in walked Bubbie carrying a foam carton and a sack from Wal-Mart.

"You know what *Motek*," she said as she looked at Ryder. "Don't be surprised if three wise men show up in Cassville."

"Why do you say that Bubbie?"

"Because in the past two days I have bought strawberry ice cream and hot fries, and now tacos and peanut butter cups." Bubbie said as she handed the carton and the sack to her granddaughter. "One of them asked if I was expecting, if I am, then it is a blessed miracle."

Ryder laughed at her as he watched his wife open the carton where three tacos without cheese were, and then he watched her open the package of mini peanut butter cups and his mouth dropped open as he watched her take the mini candies break them in half and place them inside the taco. "I don't know about you *Motek*," Bubbie said quickly turning and heading for the door. "But I can't watch that."

"What?" Yakira questioned as she picked up the taco toward her mouth. "It is good." She offered it over to Ryder. "Want a bite?"

"No."

"If you love me you would."

Ryder stood up from the bed and said, "And if you loved me you wouldn't ask me that."

"Oh well more for me." With that she took a bite.

"Bubbie wait up and I will go with you." Ryder walked out of the room and closed the door behind them.

"I didn't want to let her know," Bubbie said as they stood in the hallway. "But it is getting around town. And it isn't me they are talking about. Pascal asked, I thought he needed to know he was going to have a grandchild. He is very happy man. Hope you don't mind?"

"I don't care," Ryder said. "I want to tell everyone, but that stupid superstition of hers." Ryder changed the subject. "Alex is making supper. You are welcome to join us."

"I can't Pascal is overjoyed by the news and Rebekah is madder than a wet hen that she has to find out this way. I am going to go over and try and smooth it out."

Ryder went down stairs, in the dining room Alex had the table set, Ryder was at the head of the table, his plate filled with a leg and thigh quarter roasted on the grille coated with a mild salsa sauce, a side salad, baked potato with butter and sour cream, corn on the cob and baked beans.

"I guess it is just you and me," Alex said. "Marissa said she was studying for her driver's test took her plate and went up to her room. How's is Yakira doing?

"Fine," Ryder. "Where is Ceelia?"

"My mom took her to Roaring River." Ryder pulled her chair out for her to the left of him as she seated herself she continued. "Remember you are coming over at nine tonight, we are going to tell Ceelia who you are?"Yeah, okay." Ryder said unsure.

"Come on you have been putting this off. Everyone that could be affected by this news knows already. Except the one that needs to know the most." She placed her hand on top of his and added, "Please, we tell her now". She lifted her hand and pointed to the notebook that was his mother's lying in front of Alex. Alex continued "I have been looking over this notebook." She said as she flipped the pages over. "Your mother was into some weird stuff. Something called the Sergeants' Club"

Alex flipped another page, "Such as the 'Night of Bones', this is how they picked their ranks. It happens in a dark room with all drapes closed. A round table is set up and black cloth spread over it. In the center a human skull is placed on a Lazy-Susan. A red light is placed inside the skull so that the light shone out through the eye sockets. A deck of cards is placed on the table with all cards removed but the face cards, and the 8 of spades. The members gather around the table and the Master of Death."

"The Master of Death?"

"That is the highest ranking member of the club, the one that holds the Ace of Spades, that one is not selected but chosen. Since it was your mother that created the club she was the first 'Master of Death'," She flipped over another page. "The Master of Death will be selected by the members, each one voting, but they cannot vote for themselves. However, if the offspring of the High Mistress of the Master of Death shall claim her inheritance, and the cards will it, then he/she shall be the Master."

Ryder was hungry but her words were more filling to him, than the chicken was. He sat hand tucked under chin, elbow on the table and his eyes glued to her as she explained another ritual.

"I told you there was some weird stuff." Alex said, "Like the Blood Covenant." Again she began to read out of the book. "Each member shall pierce their flesh and seven drops…"

"Wait a minute?" Ryder asked. "Annie was talking about a blood covenant, what is it used for?"

Alex looked through his mother's hand written notes in the notebook and she read, "When a sin is committed by one or more of the members, seven drops of blood shall be collected in the golden chalice, the giving of life shall be mixed with the witches brew, and then sacrificed to *Harpocrates*. While it is said, 'Life is given to trice. And all is given. The secret is right, but if told cannot be forgiven. And breaking the covenant, death must be the price." She looked up as Marissa walked into the room.

"*Harpocrates* is the Greek god of silence and secrets." Marissa said as she held the wooden plaque that they had taken in her hands.

"We were going to check that for prints." Ryder said.

"I did," Alex said. "There was one set on them and I have yet to have a hit on them."

"So what are you doing with it?" Ryder asked of his sister as she walked over to the table pulled out a chair and set down beside him.

"I got to thinking," she explained twisting the plaque around in her hands. "This is an odd thing to have. So I looked it up on line". She flipped it over and pointed out there were two small sideways marks on the lower right-hand corner. This is a design mark, it is done by an artist in Lamar, Colorado."

"We need to check with him." Ryder said.

"It is a she and I already have," she replied. "He said they were all sold to one place called Angel's Shop in Manitou Springs. So what do you think?"

"I think," Ryder said as he stood up. "You need to get to bed early. We are heading for Manitou Springs tomorrow."

Chapter 21

A new day rose over the Ozarks, the warm rays of the beginnings of summer gleaming over the fields, as the green stalks of fescue swayed in the gentle breeze. Ryder stood on the back deck of his house; sipping on a mug of coffee, made the way he always took it; cream and two sugars. Sunglasses covering his eyes, he gazed out across his massive ranch, listening to the heavenly song that was whistling through pine trees that were at the edge of the yard. He took another sip from the mug, lifting his head to the clear blue sky he watched a meadowlark, its wings fluttering as it lifted from the ground and took the air, his mind now going to the jet that was waiting for them at the Monett airport. He looked at the watch on his wrist, eight o'clock. They had to get going, they were to meet the plane in about 45 minutes, and Monett was a thirty minute drive to the north.

He turned around and standing there was Alex, the expression on her face soured. "Where were you?" She asked. Ryder didn't reply he just grabbed the sliding glass door and pulled it open and walked in the morning room. It was a small 10x10 feet room in the center of the room was a small table and four chairs and a wicker loveseat pushed up against the one wall that was not made of glass that could be opened and allow air to flow in. "I thought we were going to tell her." Alex said following Ryder into the room, and closing the sliding glass door behind her.

"I couldn't", Ryder said turning around and facing her again. "I just don't think she will understand."

"She has friends that have single mother's she can understand if her father…"

"Belle," Ryder said tenderly interrupting her, using a shorten version of her first name. "We are not exactly the same as those mothers. You work with me; you live just 200 yards away from me on my ranch. Your female best friend is my wife. This is not normal."

"Maybe Ceelia and I should move."

"No!" Ryder shouts back. "I don't want that. I love having her here. I couldn't imagine not seeing every day. "

"Every little girl needs a daddy." Alex said before she closed her eyes.

"That little girl will not need for anything," Ryder said as he placed the mug down on the table and his hands on Alex's shoulders he looked into her green eyes and continued, "she may not get everything she wants, she will get everything she needs."

"She needs her father."

Ryder started to pick up the mug of coffee, when the little girl dashed into the room. She tilted her head back to look up at him, her long dark wavy hair hanging loosely like sheer curtains over a picture window. She turned and faced her mother and asked, "Did you ask him?"

 Ryder turned to Alex, eyebrows knitted down, "Ask me what?"

"You ask him honey."

"Uncle Ricky," Ceelia said. "When you get back can we play fairy princess and have a tea party?"

"Sure darling! But it will probably be late, so maybe the next day." Ryder said, "We will have a grand party."

"Okay," she said, "I will go make the invitations." She dashed off again into the house.

"I love that little girl," Ryder said. "And I would even if she wasn't mine."

"I know." He picked up his mug and took a sip of the coffee and she added, "But she doesn't want a father she wants...

Suddenly Ceelia dashed back into the room. "Can I ask you something else?" She said with a serious tone. "It is really important."

Ryder kneeled down, and looked right in her face, she was so cute at being so serious he wanted to smile, even laugh but he didn't want to hurt her feeling. She was holding a folded up piece of paper and a pen in her hand. She took her hands and grabbed him by the side of the face. Her eyes were his eyes, gleaming brightly, she grinned flashing those dimples. He grinned, "How could I ever say no to this face."

With as much earnest that she could muster, she asked "Mr. Rick Ryder, when you want things to be legal you sign a contact right? When you *odobted* Marissa and became her gardener right?" Mispronouncing her words.

Again he wanted to laugh at the words she was having trouble with, but he kept a serious tone. "The word is contract, and I adopted her so I would legally be her guardian, but yes."

She took a deep gasp and unfolded the paper and hand it to him. "Then can't you do that to me? And I would become your kid? And I could call you daddy?"

Ceelia's words stuck Ryder as a speeding semi loaded with timber, he nearly fell over. She placed her hands on his shoulders and brought her face closer to his to where she was nose to nose with him and she said, "I need a daddy. And I think you can do the job." Ryder was not used to being stunned or at a loss for words. His lips opened but no words came out. He looked up at Alex, he wasn't sure if she was trying to hold back a laugh or tears. She let out a moan and then turned away, so no one could see her reaction

"You look over this *'contract'*," Ceelia said struggling to make sure to say the word correctly. Then she handed him the pen and said, "And if you agree we will sign it."

'This Contact is for Mr. Rick Ryder and Ceelia Alexander. You will be my daddy. This contact last forever.'

Ryder placed the paper on the table and used the pen to sign his name. And then handed the pen back to her and she printed her name. "Here mommy, you need to write your name on here too." Alex was wiping away tears from her eyes, took the pen and signed her name. "Now it is all legal." She stuck out her hand and he shook it, "Now you're my daddy we hug." Ceelia said wrapping her arms around his neck and asked again, "Can you bring me a surprise Daddy?"

"Yeah." He managed to mutter out as he watched the little girl dash into the dining room. He stood up and looked over at Alex and as asked, "Are you okay?"

"I am fine." Alex muttered out.

"Rick, are you okay?" She asked turning around wiping the tears from her eyes.

"I am fine." Ryder said trying to hold his emotions in check as he walked towards the doorway. He stopped in the doorway, taking a deep breath, trying to take control of his feelings. He turned back to her and said, "Since you are staying here, I want you to look into something for me. That article about the missing baby, can you check it out and see if you can find out anymore."

"Yeah sure thing daddy."

Chapter 22

Ryder had very little to say all the way to Monett and only what he had to say when he and his sister got aboard the private jet. He always rented the same jet from a company in Kansas City a white with dark blue stripes Embraer Phenom 100 and the same pilot Min Choe. Inside it was like being in a giant capsule with the white curved walls only broken up by the wooden trim. Four white seats, two facing forward and two-facing backward.

Marissa was sitting across from him; he was in the seat next to the window and gazed down upon the abstract artwork known as the state of Kansas. The criss-cross blocks divided by highways and country road, were patterned with the different shades of vegetation below. Fields of wheat and fresh plowed ground with circles made from the tractor appeared like the signature of the artist. Followed by the speckled dots of homes and business of a small town, sometimes grain elevators trying to reach up from them, but failing and disappearing underneath them, once again farm land, a splash of green that is lake, a wiggling line that is the river.

"Guess I am an Aunt huh?" Marissa said her words breaking his thought.

"What makes you think that?" Ryder said turning to her. His words being heard over the roar of the jet engines before he turned and looked out the window again at the fertile land below. "Did Yakira tell you? She said we were not to tell anyone."

"I heard Ceelia call you daddy" Marissa said. He turned and faced her, she was dressed again businesslike with slacks, and a light weight jacket. She had removed her shoes and had her legs curled up under her in the seat, a notebook in her lap. She gazed across at him then her mouth fell open. She uncrossed her legs and put the notebook in the seat next to her. She leaned forward towards him as she gasped "Yakira is pregnant!"

"You can't tell anyone," Ryder said. "Anyone! You hear me?"

"Why not?"

"Yakira got some idea that if she lets everyone know that something will happen to the baby."

"Is that something to do with Jewish culture?" Marissa asked.

"I don't know, you know how she is."

Marissa leaned back in the seat and rolled her eyes up to the rounded ceiling of the jets as she pondered and said, "Aunt Marissa!" She looked back at him and continued, "I like that." She tucked her bare feet back up under her legs. "But I am already Aunt Marissa ain't I? With Ceelia?"

"You know that too?"

"Alex told me about you and her when I moved in and what happened on that night with you and her."

"Are you sure this is something a brother and sister shouldn't talk about?"

"You said that when I moved in that there would never be anything that we couldn't talk about. Besides I know all sorts of things," Marissa said as she reached over into the empty seat and picked up the notebook, Ryder saw it was the notebook that was his mother's. "For example your mother was quite a poet. Did you know she could write poetry?"

"I didn't but I saw some of stuff ubthat notebook." Ryder said. "Where did you get that?"

"It was lying on the table in the dining room." Marissa said as she turned to a yellowed page with faded black ink handwriting, his mother's handwriting. "Strange thing about her poetry,"

"Believe it or not she was trying to write lyrics to a rock song." Marissa said as she looked down at the pages. She looked down at the page and read:

Who Needs Love?

"Who needs love when it's the demon that rob you of your control?

Who needs love when its knife cuts your flesh to the bone?

Love just makes you lose your soul.

Love just leaves you all alone.

Who needs love?

I don't need love.

"I have heard that somewhere!" Ryder said reaching over and taking the notebook from her. He looked down at the bottom of the page where there was some writing, this done in a different handwriting, it was Annie's.

Love is just a fine wine

It grows old with time

It reaches across time and space

Then slashes face

Who needs love?

I don't need love   A.H.

Then another verse this one by Charlotte Day

Love can stand the test of time

Or be wrapped up in a silly rhyme

It holds you tight-

Then it was his mother's hand writing again.

Then it leaves you in the middle night-

Cold broken and alone-

Right to the bone-

Who needs love?

I don't need love

I DON'T NEED LOVE

Marissa played the song by Steelace that was claimed to have been written by Paul Steele, it was the same exact lyrics. "This is the number one song on all the charts right now. Would you say that stealing lyrics could be motive for murder?" She grinned and guess where Steelace is playing tonight Colorado Springs.

Chapter 23

In Colorado the skies seemed just a little bit bluer, and the sun a little brighter the soil sandy, the grass not a rich carpet but sparse, mixed with a viper of a plant the world knows as 'sand burrs', ready to bite if one dared to go barefoot. Coming out of the airport in Colorado Springs the majesty of the mountains did not fit the windshield, and guided by the sign that reads 'Downtown 24', the on ramp twists around, as the mountains began their royal entrance, eyes quickly dart over to the large bison made of steel The artwork has rusted over the years and gives the appearance that it is truly the magnificent creature that raised his head from grazing to sniff the air and become aware of the American Indian on horseback behind him. Suddenly the Rocky Mountains fill the windshield, the mighty 'king of the mountains'-Pike's Peak appears standing out with its snow topped cap. Soon the rustle of traffic fills the ears under a bridge and the mountains drift over to the side, but before one can question 'is this Colorado?', the mountains welcome you again.

Manitou Springs and the mountains are just a little higher and little closer and the snow on Pike's Peak a little whiter. "So we are looking for 'The Angel's Shop'?" Ryder asked.

"No ," Marissa said. "There is no 'the'; it is just Angel's Shop."

Manitou Springs, also known as the "Saratoga of the West", was established as a resort community best known for its mineral springs and "wonderful setting" at the foot of the Rocky Mountains. The town is bordered by Mt. Manitou to the west, Red Mountain to the south, and rests at the base of Pikes Peak. Today still some come for the taste of 'heaven's journey' the mineral waters that all begin with a single raindrop, and end in anything from tangy to sweet, naturally carbonated water.

The houses grip as tight to the mountain slopes as a father hugging the prodigal son returning home. Gazing up at the homes they could look precarious and cramped as if they will tumble down a child's building block, but the picturesque" 19th century Victorian homes have stood the test of time, as they watched down from the decks and saw the town change from a resort area into a place where life and art mix together creating a unique masterpiece.

Downtown is a mix of new and used and the old - like gracious styling of the Baker's House - all meet, but further into the mouth of town the traffic thickens, and shops of all kinds appear, some made of brick, other with the adobe appearance, yet others are brightly colored.

"There it is!" Marissa said pointing to a nondescript red brick building. A semi circle sign with a winged angel and the word's 'Angel's Shop'. It was a small shop on the end of a much larger building. A large glass window was adorned with bright yellow signs pasted on it that read "70% off all items. Everything must go." But the neon sign that read open was dark.

There was only parking on one side of the street so, Ryder turned the car around and parked the car across from the store. Ryder opened the door for Marissa she glanced across the street. "I think it is closed," she said as Ryder shut the Mustang's door.

They crossed the street and stood in front of the store, the insides were dark and there was a sign that read 'closed' on the glass door. "That may be the problem," Ryder said as they crossed the street. He placed his cupped hands up on the window and looked into the store, it was dark but there was enough light showing through that he could see most of the shelves were bare, and what was left was odds and ends, porcelain figures and plaques.

He looked at the lock, it was a simple key lock, but it wasn't turned upside down, the tumblers were on the bottom, it would be easy to pick. As he twisted his head to the side he saw a white box on the wall, a red light blinking. It was an alarm. He had to find some other way to get information.

He heard a pair of women talking "Lets head for Seven Falls.", one said. He turned as he saw them come out of the shop across the street; they were carrying a shopping bag.

"No I want to go there at night." The other woman said, "Besides we may not get back to the cog railway. Let's just have some lunch." He watched as they got into a dark gray sedan with Kentucky license plates on it."

"Tourists!" Ryder said out loud. He reached for his wallet, and pulled out two hundred dollar bills. He handed them to Marissa. "Time for you to go shopping," he added nodding towards the store across the street. "Who knows more about what is going on than your neighbors?"

Inside the store was a mismatch of odds and ends, cups with pictures of Pikes Peak, and 'Garden of the Gods' and Seven Falls, t-shirts with the same photos, calendars and dishes, pens, note pads, toys of all kinds and all ages. While Marissa shopped Ryder talked with the gentleman who owned the store.

"Visitors to our area?"
"Yeah, from Missouri," Ryder said.

"Just you and you're a daughter?" With the differences in age he got this a lot.

"She is my sister, "Ryder said. "Love the mountains. Where would you recommend we go?"

"With that Mustang out there try Gold Camp Road it is a nice drive, and Helen Hunt falls," the owner said as Marissa placed several items up on the counter.

"Guess business is doing good?" Ryder asked as Marissa handed him the two bills. "Benjamin's huh and in cash." He took a pen and said, "No offence but we have had some fake bills going around town. He checked the bills with the testing pen and they passed.

"Is that what happened to the store across the street?" Ryder asked as the owner placed the bills in the register and gives Marissa back the change of seventeen dollars. "She took in too many fakes?"

"No she fell on some hard times, "The shop owner said. "Her daughter Angel who the store is named after got cancer, the town pulled behind her, but the little girl died two months ago. Then Trina, that is the owner Trina Allaway, she spent so much time away from the shop she went bankrupt."

Trina Allaway, that name swirled around in his mind but he couldn't place it right then and there. The owner continued, explaining as he placed the items in the bags and handed the sacks to Ryder. "They found her dead at the Garden of the Gods." They say it was suicide but..."

"But what?"

"Well," the store owner said. "I am not one of those guys that watch across the street all the time but the day before they found her there was this man she had to throw out of the store. And he was screaming about how he was going to kill her."

"Who was it?"

"I don't know but Rita might know."

"Rita?"

"Rita Williams," the store owner explained. "She used to work for Trina. She now works up at the pancake place, Uncle Sam's, it's right on the main drag, you can't miss it. "

Chapter 24

There are many signs that indicate that a restaurant serves good food; one could be the aroma that drifts out, or word of mouth or the fact the parking lot is jammed packed with cars. Uncle Sam's Pancake House fit all the above, luckily there was one spot left and Ryder guided the car into the spot. It was all American, red, white and blue stripes around the back wall of the parking lot; the main building an A-frame with a red metal roof.

After locking the shopping bags in the trunk they made their way to the front door passing by the black bear statues wearing a red, white and blue top hat. He opened the glass door, as they stepped inside Ryder removed his sunglasses. The hostess showed them to their seats. The insides of the restaurant continued the patriotic theme with a red and white checkout counter, with the American flag on the wall. Wide blue stripes, bright white paneled walls. There were several customers seated and the young hostess led them to the back of the restaurant and seated them at a booth with red tucked vinyl bench seats.

"Karen will be your server." The hostess said

"Is Rita here?" Ryder asked as he looked up at the young lady and grinned.

"Yes, do you know Rita?"

"We had friends that stopped here and they told us how wonderful she was." Ryder said as he picked up the menu.

"I will send her over."

"That name Trina Allaway !" Ryder exclaimed as he lay the menu down and reached for his notebook in his inside jacket pocket. "I know I heard that name before he said it." He began flipping through the pages, going back. "Here it is! " he said looking up. Van Way got into an argument with her online, he give out her name and an address. If someone …"

In a short time a young woman with long platinum hair, straight as the interstate across the dessert, stood beside the table. She placed two glasses of water on the table and asked, interrupting him, "I am Rita, what would you like to order?"

Ryder looked up and quickly closed his notebook and said, "What would you recommend?"

"It is all good, I really like the Eggs Benedict, I'd kill for that Hollandaise Sauce."

"Sounds good," Ryder said placing his hand down on his notebook "Bring us two of those and two coffees."

"So you had friends that stopped here, who were they?" Rita asked.

"Trina Allaway." Ryder said. "You worked for her right?"

"You were friends of Trina's." Rita said. "May I?" She asked pointing to the bench seat and Marissa slid over and she sat down. "It was so heart breaking how she died."

"Do you believe she was murdered?" Ryder asked.

"You mean that screwball that was screaming at her for using the money the town collected. No Trina was well armed and well trained, if they got near her she would have blown him away."

"You were working at the store the day she was killed?" Ryder asked. "And there was a customer she was trying throw out of the store. Do you know who he was?"

"Are you kidding?" She smirked. "Everyone knows him. It was Paul Steele lead singer of Steelace."

"What did he want?" His question seemed to make her face grow pale. Ryder scooted his glass of water over to her.

"He was upset about something that was sent to him." Rita took a sip of the water and continued. "It was a plaque with a playing card and a bible verse on it. Trina had a special deal with the artist that made them, that she was the only one that sold them"

"Them?" Ryder asked, opening up the notebook and jotting everything down in his notebook.

"Yes, there was a bunch of them, a lady came in bought all of them,"

"Who was she? Ryder asked. "Did you get a name? Can you describe her?"

"She was pretty with long dark hair." Rita said. "I said she took all of them I was wrong. She left one. It was when Steele saw what was left he went crazy."

"Why?

"I don't know?" Rita said, "I really don't. He just started screaming, when Trina showed him the notebook."

"What notebook?"

"Trina liked to get the names and addresses of her customers, so she could send out emails she even would send them e-cards for their birthday. 'Customers were family', she would say." Rita took a few more sips of water.

"Can I see that notebook?"

"Yes, but I can't go there now." Rita said. Ryder reached for his wallet and took a hundred dollar bill, tore it in half and wrapped it around one of his business card and handed it to her.

"When you get time give me a call, and you can get the other half."

*****

Ryder drove back into Colorado Springs and turned right from Colorado Avenue onto Cascade Avenue, it was late afternoon, clouds and a haze were filling the sky, the mountains were now bluish gray, and appeared like storm on the horizon. He parked in front of the Pikes Peak Center for Performing Arts. He noticed the parking meter and checked his pockets; he never kept anything like coins.

"Got any change?" He asked as he got out and walked around the car to open the passenger door for his sister.

"I got seventeen bucks" Marissa said as she checked her pockets.

At this moment a young man walked by. "Excuse me!" Ryder said. "Got any change? Need it for the parking meter."

"I don't know?" The young man said.

"Give me four quarters I will give you a five dollars."

The young man quickly produced four quarters and Ryder handed him the bill that Marissa was holding. Put them in the meter and then they headed for the front door, walking by a large sign flashing with red letters 'Tonight Steelace'.

There were three sets of glass doors, Ryder grabbed one and pulled it open, and then they went through another set of glass doors into the lobby. It was longer than it was wider curving around the front portion, with large windows that look out across the lawn and the street. Over to the right was a set of steps that led to the entrance to the auditorium. Ryder could hear the sounds of hard rock music being played; the band was doing a sound check for the concert tonight.

A set of double doors flew open as a stagehand exited, Ryder grabbed the door and held it for Marissa and followed her in to the auditorium. It was large and grand, with 1,171 seats on the main floor, 290 seats on the mezzanine level, and 528 seats on the balcony level.

The proscenium was open and revealed the 116 foot wide stage made of plywood and covered with maple. It was complete with a bright red grand piano, a drum set and behind that a wall of speakers. There were six members on stage, lead guitarist Stevie Lace jamming on her Gibson Flying V, the rhythm guitarist David Simmons on a Les Paul, on key boards Sara Conway and the lead singer Paul Steele was singing.

> *"Now listen there is nothing to be heard-*
> *Voices all around, but not one spoken word-*
> *Silence comes but everyone has something to say-*
> *Everyone just trembles in fear-*
> *Everyone shouts but nothing can be heard-*
> *I stumble across the floor-*
> *There is nothing left but loneliness-*
> *I open the door-*
> *To see the eyes of darkness-*
> *OH Darkness—"Oh the darkness comes to me!"*

Just at that moment the head of the roadies walked up to them. He was older, heavy with dyed long hair, but his beard was heavily seasoned with a salt and pepper look, it appeared he had seen many years of this work with many different bands. He was wearing a black T-shirt with the Steelace logo on the front but the back and his arms were covered with a long sleeve shirt.

"You can't be in here!" The roadie shouted to be hard over the deafening music. "You have to leave!" He put his hand on Marissa and tried to force them to the door.

Ryder pushed back, he wasn't going anywhere. "I need to talk to Paul Steele now."

"I will get an autograph for you if you just leave now!" The roadie insisted grabbing Marissa by the arm.

"This isn't about a damn autograph," Ryder said. "It is about murder!"

"M—m—murder?" the roadie questioned letting go of her arm. "Are you a cop?"

"Private," Ryder replied. "You tell Steele Rick Ryder wants to see him. It is about the Sergeants' Club."

Steele stopped singing and as the female lead guitarist began a solo, Steele was dancing around the stage as the guard climbed the steps and spoke. Steel became motionless as the guard pointed at Ryder.

"Stop!" Steele screamed out. "Let's take a break!" He put the microphone back on the stand and walked backstage. Stevie stood the guitar in her hands, clearly confused as to what happened, as there was more rehearsing to do. Ryder watched as the roadie went up and whispered in her ear and pointed at Ryder. She set her guitar down and then disappeared back stage as the main sage green curtains drew closed.

The roadie returned and led them onto the stage behind the main curtains and the black velour legs, the curtains that hid the back stage. He opened a door that lead further into the guts of the center, into a maze of long hallways and doors that led to the greenroom and dressing rooms. The door to the greenroom was opened and Ryder turned and saw the female guitarist standing in the doorway, she stared at him and then closed the door. The roadie led them down to hall to the second door on the right. He knocked on the door and said, "Mr. Steele your guests are here."

"Let them in", the muttered reply came from behind the door. The Roadie opened the door and they stepped into the private dressing room. Steele was sitting in a swivel chair at a sink in front of the mirror. He looked at Ryder's reflection in the mirror not turning around. "You are Danni's kid! I see her in you." His age was showing, lines in his face his skin drooping, his eyes tired from the 70 day 65 city tours, his hair as long as it was in the photo that was taken decades ago , and still just as black. Dressed in a t-shirt and jeans, he slowly turned around in the chair and faced them.

"Mind if I smoke?" Steele said as he stood up and walked over to a love seat that was flanked by an end table that was on the other side of the room where a brown leather jacket laid. He picked it up and pulled a pack of cigarettes out of the pocket, took one and lit it up using a lighter that was in the same pocket of the jacket. He took a big drag off the cigarette and blew the smoke towards them.

"Yes I do!" Ryder said, he took the cigarette away from him and crushed it out in the ashtray on the end table.

"All right how much do you want? To keep quiet?" Steele said as he flopped down on loveseat. "That is what you are here for to blackmail me?" Steele stood and marched over to the sink, ran some water in the sink. "I will give you the same I gave Charlotte, a hundred thousand. After all I guess I owe it to you since you are Dannie's kid." Steele scooped up some of the cool water and splashed it on his face.

"Is that why you murdered Charlotte?" Ryder asked.

Steele quick turned around, "Murdered! " He shot back with shock glaring at Ryder. "Charlotte is dead?" He stumbled over to the loveseat and sat down again. "Oh my Dear God!" He said dazed as he lowered his head and rubbed the back of his neck with his hand. He looked up at Ryder and asked, "When?"

"The day after Annie was murdered," Ryder said. "You did know about Annie?"

"Yes," Steele said. He placed his finger on his temples and stared down at the floor as he moaned, "Oh dear God what did I do?" He looked back up at Ryder who was standing in front of him. "I knew it was wrong. Taking the lyrics, if I would have just given them the credit." Again he held his head and stared at the floor and continued.

"My mother's lyrics? For Darkness also" Ryder asked.

"Of course! I figured that it was so long ago no one would remember. Your mother always gave me a copy to see what I thought!" He said looking up at Ryder. "The last time I seen you, you were a baby!" He looked over at Marissa, "Is this your daughter?"

"My sister."

"You know what it is like to be on stage and look out and see that most of your audience can join AARP and collect their Social Security?" He pointed at Marissa. "I just wanted you to like me." He turned back to Ryder, "Now they are singing our songs. I tried to write new material, but it was crap! I remembered the copies that Dannie gave me, Stevie was able to put the music to them, and she didn't remember them so I thought I was safe. I faced every kind of demon there is, alcohol, drugs, women. You know what the most addictive drug is? It isn't cocaine or heroin. It is the roar of that crowd. It is seeing your picture on magazines. It is fame...once you have it, you do anything to keep it."

"Including murder?" Marissa asked.

"Yeah," He replied with a somber tone. "But I didn't! I didn't kill Charlotte I just paid her off."

"And Annie?" Ryder said.

"I would never do anything to hurt Annie! I would do everything to protect her. I did everything to protect her."

"What does that mean?" Ryder asked.

"Nothing!" Steele said as he stood up and walked over to a bar and picked up a low-ball glass, dropped a few ice cubes into it and then mixed together gin and diet coke and poured it into the glass. "Want a drink?" He asked Ryder. Ryder shook his head. He walked over to the loveseat and sat back down. "What we did we did for all."

"The Blood Covenant of the Sergeants Club?" Ryder asked.

"Then you know it cannot be broken, I pledged all my earthly goods, my life to it. "What was the Sergeants Club?"

"Most clubs on any campus, including Crowder are for the popular, the smart ones, and the elite. Your mother wanted a club for the down trodden, the crud under the shoes of the elite. We started just having a table near the jukebox and drinking Dr. Pepper while we played spades. But we started meeting in the old building and weird things began happening."

"What old building?"

"The Maintenance building." Steele explained took another sip of the bitter sweet liquid and grinned mockingly as he said, "that is when we started getting the rank in the cards, we became like a secret society, even having a secret greeting." He stood up holding his hand out but before Ryder shook it he drew it back placing it flat over his heart then curling his little finger and thumb down he drew them across from his shoulder to the other side of his chest.

"What about Angel's Shop in Manitou Springs," Marissa asked. "Were you there?"

He took two more quick swigs of the drink and downed it. "You wouldn't ask that unless you know I was. Yes, I was there." He stood up and walked over to where a suitcase laid open on the cart, he dug through his clothes and at the bottom pulled out a 8x10 inch wood plaque. "I wanted to know where this came from." He handed it Ryder.

Decoupage to the wood was the King of Clubs and burned into the wood was the bible verse. Deuteronomy 27:17 *'Cursed is the man who moves his neighbor's boundary stone.'*

Ryder handed it back to the singer. "What does this mean?"

"I haven't the slightest idea."

"What about the card?"

"I guess," he explained as he filed his glass again with diet coke and gin. He took a sip and walked back to the loveseat and reseated himself. "In the club we each had a rank according the cards. "I was King Caesar."

"Caesar?" Ryder asked.

"The playing cards are based on real people; the King of Clubs was Caesar."

"And Annie?"

"She was Athena the Queen of Spades."

"And Charlotte? The Queen of Diamonds?"

"Yes, Rachel you know from the bible," Steele said then took a drink before asking, "How did you know that?"

"Annie and Charlotte both got things similar to that right before they were found murdered." Ryder said. "Someone is murdering those in the Sergeants' Club, you could be next."

"I got protection!" he lifted his shirt up and revealed a Smith and Wesson Body Guard 380 tucked into the waist band of his pants. He pulled his shirt back down. "Nobody is getting to me!"

"Did you murder someone back then?"

"What!" Steele snapped back, "How dare you ask me that. I have had enough!" Steele said grabbing them both by the arms and pushing them towards the door. "I have to get back to sound check we have a big show tonight and then we are heading to Seattle."

Is that what happened?" Ryder asked. "You killed somebody! Is that what it is about you killed someone in a ritual and you buried them on the campus right where they are digging right now. They are going to tear down the old maintenance building."

"What! They can't do that!" With that Steele pushed them out in the hall and slammed the door.

Chapter 25

The winning championship and having the Cassville Wildcats ranked as the best team in America when Ryder was in school allowed many on that team to be offered scholarships all over the nation. One who was offered a scholarship was Timothy 'Wildman' Knight, the crazy cowboy who went on to become the Medical examiner now working in Colorado Springs, but his heart belonged to his ranch a few miles outside of the city limits, where the plains rolled out under a clear blue sky, the red colored pavement stretched out between green fields, the mountains just being a distant shape on the far horizon. Hair flows in the breeze that circles around the seats in the convertible with the top down, eyes must be shielded from the sun that was beginning its final performance for the day.

Ryder saw the sign warning of a sharp curve to the right that was his clue to turn off the road. He pressed down on the brake pedal and guided the car off on to a small single lane dirt road. The light red chat crunched under the Mustang's tires as the dirt road became nothing more than couple of well-worn paths, a driveway created by tires, coming and going. He passed under the shade of a couple of trees that stood at the edges of the driveway welcoming visitors. Ryder pulled the Mustang up behind a dark green three year old Ford pickup truck. Ryder stepped out of the car and let his eyes scan over the ranch.

There were 120 acres that was home to a heard of bison that was in the far field, in the yard was a log house and a few feet away the essential red barn, complete with rooster wind vane on the top, which squeaked as the wind caught it making a change in directions. The wind was making the tail of Ryder's jacket flap as he searched for a sign of his friend. Suddenly he heard the sound of a high whining VW engine. He caught the site of a bright red sand rail dune buggy speeding past the barn, leaving a dust trail behind it. It was heading straight for them, then suddenly veered off to the right around the back of the Mustang and over into the yard where the buggy did doughnuts going one way and then the other, throwing grass, and dirt high into the air, creating a dust cloud so thick it nearly hid the dune buggy. The driver straightened the steering wheel and raced right at them. Turning the wheel hard to the right and slamming on the brakes, the buggy slid to a stop a couple of feet away from the side of the Mustang. The driver who was wearing jeans, Lynyrd Skynyrd t-shirt, cowboy boots and topping his head with a Stetson, looked up at Ryder and as the dust settled said, "How you doing Pale Ryder?"

"Nobody has killed me yet Wildman." Ryder said as the man stepped out over the rail. He was the same age as Ryder, shorter but stoutly built, his once golden hair had darkened, his face was triangular shaped and covered with a weekend growth of whiskers, after all he was on vacation, why shave? Ryder drew his hand up like a paw and said, "Once a Wildcat..."

"Always a Wildcat!" The man replied drawing his hand also.

"Long time, no see, Wildman" Ryder said holding out his hand.

"Ah heck! Is that the way you greet someone who protected your butt from the big bad Bears?" Tony said referring to the fact that Tony was an offensive lineman when they were in high school and protected Ryder the quarterback against the rivals, the Monett Cubs. He grabbed Ryder and gave him a manly hug with a pat on the back.

"I want to introduce you to my sister Marissa."

"Have you heard the tales of how this guy was in high school?" Wildman asked Marissa. "Like when he rode on the roof of the car naked."

"Really?" Marissa laughed.

"Wildman that was you, I just drove the car."

Wildman laughed, "Backwards around the square."

"I was going around it the right way," Ryder said.

"But in reverse," Wildman laughed out loud. "Let's head on up to the house, I got the grill going, and some of the best steaks you will ever eat."

The beautiful log home was picturesque of the mountain life as if it had been taken out of a magazine and pasted there, with its bright blue metal roof and cedar steps that lead up to the covered deck, and looked out to an oversized two car garage. There was a long rectangular glass top patio table with seating for six. As Ryder stepped up on the deck he was greeted with the sweet aroma of the grill, hickory. Wildman wasn't using store bought charcoal he was using hickory wood, in the large grill that was in the back yard. His wife Kristi pushed the glass doors open and stepped out onto the deck. She was pretty, a few years younger than her husband, her hair medium length and the color of Kansas wheat at harvest time. She looked at Ryder, her brown eyes twinkling as she handed the tray of t-bone steaks she was carrying to her husband, and he went down the back steps to the grill.

"Double T tells us you got married"? She said, "And we were not invited."

"It was sort of a quick thing."

"And you're the sister?" Kristi asked. "How old are you?"

"I am fifteen."

"Know your way around the kitchen?"

"Some," Marissa responded.

"Good you can help me."

As the women went back into the kitchen, Ryder walked down the step and over the grill where four large 2 inch thick steaks were sizzling on the grill. Tony looked at him, "You are chasing a wild goose buddy!"

"Why do you say that?"

"Allaway's death wasn't murder." Wildman said as he turned the steaks 90 degrees to get that perfect cross hatch pattern on them. He invited Ryder over to one of the two steel chairs that were resting up next to the house; in between them was a small table with a file folder lying on it. Ryder sat down in one of the chairs and Wildman the other and he opened the file folder. "It was suicide."

"You positive?"   '

"One hundred percent!" he explained. "Of course you know about the little girl and her business going under. Her husband left for a younger woman, nineteen years old and built like you know what and now he gets everything. And if that isn't enough evidence for you buddy." He handed Ryder a photograph. Ryder stared at it, it was of Trina Allaway, a blue rope around her neck. He handed Ryder another photo a close up of the dead woman's neck. It showed a deep groove cut into her flesh, high upon the neck just under the jawbone, and crossing over the front of the neck in a diagonal direction, a larger marking on the neck for the knot on the rope on the left side. "Notice the small black and blue marks along the edges where the rope was, meaning…"

"Meaning she was alive when she was hung." Ryder said.

"Her neck was not broken nor was the hyoid bone." He handed Ryder the report. "As you can see I listed cause of death, as Asphyxia due to hanging. Also her prints were the only ones found on the rope, and the anchor in the rock. The detectives found receipts where she bought the rope just two day before. And lastly there was a note left. Typical goodbye can't live with 'my Angel', Good bye cruel world. Hope everyone can forgive me." Wildman stood up and walked over to the grill and flipped the steaks over. "Sorry if that puts a damper on your investigation. Or you can continue."

"Have no reason to doubt your word." Ryder said as he handed the report back to him. "But it still doesn't erase the fact that two people were murdered back home."

"Been seeing you in all the newspapers and magazines, 'the billionaire that solves murders for a dollar a day', what is it the New York Times is calling you? Oh yes the Budget Detective! What are you working on now?"

"You remember my mother?" Ryder asked.

"Yes, every boy in school remembers your mother, she was hot." He said as flipped the steaks over.

"Never thought of my mother as hot," Ryder said. "You think she could be capable of killing someone?"

"Murder?" Wildman questioned. "No not her." Ryder's cell phone rang, he saw it was Alex calling so he walked a few feet away and answered it.

"Ryder," he heard her say. "Got the results back on the tox-report for Annie and Charlotte, both have traces of codeine in their blood. Annie barely had enough to affect her, but Charlotte had twice as much in her system. Thom said that with that much she would have been so drugged she could have barely walked. She would have been bumping into things and knocking things off if she tried to walk."

"That makes sense of what I saw," Ryder said. "we have one other thing to check out and then we will be heading back."

Chapter 26

After supper, Ryder, and Marissa returned to Manitou Springs, Rita Williams had called them and asked them to meet her at Trina's store, she still had keys to the store and had it opened and the lights on when Ryder arrived. The other stores were closed, and the street was nearly deserted, the only thing on the pavement now was the warm glow of the street lights.

Ryder pulled the Mustang convertible over to the side of the street and parked right under the street light, the golden radiance filling the convertible's interior. They got out and walked across the street. He pulled the door open and held it open for Marissa.

Trina's plan was not an original one, it was just another shop where tourist could buy a porcelain figurine, collector thimbles, plaques and other collectables, that they could gaze at and remind them of their trip to 'serenity town' of the mountains. Now it was mostly empty shelves, racks with hangers hanging naked, longing for the cover of another gimmicky t-shirt with Pike's Peak or Garden of the God's photo, knives, swords and other medieval objects.

Rita stood behind the sales counter over to the side near the front of the store. She was turning a wire rack that was half full of colorful postcards, the rack letting out a moan as she twisted it around. She turned the rack and looked at Ryder.

"You said 'you wanted more information about the plaques?' "She asked stepping out from behind the counter.

As she did, Ryder walked around the store looking at the items that were still for sale. He picked up a glass vase and looked at the price on the bottom, $17.99 marked down to $5.40, the price sticker included a small drawing of angel. He set the vase back down and then picked up a wood plaque. It was the only one of its kind left. A wood plaque with a portion of a bible verse 'The fruit of your womb will be blessed…" Deuteronomy 28:4 above it a playing card the Ace of Spade, Ryder held it up.

At first he found it very odd that this plaque was the only one left, as it was mother's rank in the Sergeants' Club, but she was   the only one that was dead. If someone was killing members of the club and sending them the plaques they wouldn't need to send her one.

Ryder set the plaque down, and then he picked it back up again and walked to the counter.

"I will take this," he said as placed the plaque on the counter and reached for his wallet.

"Forget it!" She said with wave of her hand now that Trina is dead it will be her husband getting any money we make here. She looked over at Marissa and said, "If you find anything you like you can take it too. He doesn't deserve anything." As Marissa looked around the shop, Rita bent over reaching under the counter and placed a records book on the counter and then held up the half of the torn bill he gave. "You said I could get the other half of this if I showed you this." He handed the other half of the bill in his pocket and handed it to her. As she taped the bill back together, he looked down at the names that were recorded in it, there several listings for religious figurines but for the card plaques there was only one name listed. As he read the name his face turned red with anger and he looked up at her and growled out "That is not possible!"

"That is the name we got." Rita said looking down at entry.

"And I am telling you that is freakin' ass impossible." He slammed his finger down on the name on the paper and shouted even louder. "I am telling there is no damn way that woman could have walked into this store." Ryder grabbed the sack that Rita had placed the plaque in and headed for the door. He had just pushed it open when Rita again looked down at the entry and spoke.

"I don't get it. Who is Danielle Delany?"

Chapter 27

Ryder stormed out of the store and across the street, got into the driver's seat and slammed the door. Marissa followed shouting, "Ricky, Ricky!" She walked up to the car. "Are you okay?"

He turned to her and bellowed, "Get in the damn car!"

"That is your mother right?" She asked and he didn't reply to her. "It is just someone trying to play a bad joke. You know it could be one of the people from the Sergeants' Club. Maybe it is one of them trying to get rid of the others." She opened the door and sat down in the seat. "I was thinking maybe if one person did the murder and the others were covering up for them and they are afraid they talked they would..." She stopped speaking as she pulled her seat belt, out of the corner of his eye he caught her looking over at him, and she timidly asked, "Want to go somewhere and have a milk shake and talk it over?"

"HOME!" Ryder shouted back. "I just want to get the hell out of here!"

"I just wish we could do something else. I am having fun being with you..."

"How dense do you have to be?" He glared over at her; "We are investigating a murder not having fun." Dejected Marissa leaned back in the seat and snapped the belt around her. She didn't say anything else, just rolled her eyes over to him, her lower lip in a pout.

Ryder fired the car up and sped away, leaving a smoky trail of rubber behind them, all the way well over the speed limit. Maybe it was lucky, maybe the sign that God was still with him as the first time he saw a cop car was when he had turned off the freeway under the sign at the airport that read 'Rental Cars.' It was then that he spoke. "Dead women don't buy things."

He pulled the Mustang into the large parking lot that was used for rental cars. "You know you could be right! It could be one of them is the murderer and they are trying to silence the others. But I don't get the plaques what do they mean? " He looked over at his sister; tears were rolling down her cheeks. He sat there staring at her watching as she used her hands to wipe away the tears. She sniffed and unbuckled the seat belt and grabbed for the door handle.

"Let me out of here!" She said opening the door. "You don't want to be with me. I don't want to be with you!" He reached over and grabbed her arm and gently pulled her back into the seat. She turned her head and looked at him but didn't respond, she just looked more hurt, eyes red, lips still pouting. He carefully took his thumb and wiped away her tears.

"Your tears are my tears..."

"But I am the only one crying," Marissa said interrupting him, her next words like a dagger through his heart. "You are just like dad was." Ryder's father was hardly ever around always finding a new woman starting a new family. That was how Ryder and Marissa found each other. He dropped his head down ashamed that the one person he never wanted to be like, he had become.

He lifted his head and grabbed her in embrace, but she didn't return it. "Marissa, I never wanted to hurt you. You mean everything to me. I have to say I was having fun with you too." She slowly placed her arms around him and returned his embrace. The embrace ended, and he continued. "When I saw her name it all came back to me that last night in the hospital, watching my mother die, and all my life I have been afraid."

"Of what," Marissa asked.

"Death, he said with a serious tone.

"You are scared of death?"

"Not my own, but someone I love," he explained. "I'm afraid of feeling pain that if I love someone, they go away." Ryder shook his head and glared out through the windshield his hand resting on the steering wheel. "What am I doing telling this to a 15 year old kid for?"

"I am not a kid I am your sister," she said. "And I know what you mean. You are scared that one day that you will wake up and find out you are alone in this world." He turned to her and she continued. "That there is no one there for you. For Christmas it is nothing more than just a TV dinner warmed in the microwave. Or when you want to cry there is no shoulder to lean on. That you just don't want to wake up and find out this was all just dream."

"You are pretty deep for a fifteen year-old." Ryder said, he leaned over and gave her a kiss on the cheek. "I am sorry Marissa. Don't know how good of a dad I am going to make."

"When the baby's born you are going to be one great daddy and Ceelia…"

"Oh shoot!" Ryder said. "Ceelia! I forgot to get her something."

"Well good thing you have Auntie Marissa," Marissa said stepping out of the car. "Pop the trunk!" He pushed the button and the lid popped up and he got out. Marissa reached down in the trunk, pulled out one of the shopping bags. She reached into the back and produced a small purse, made of leather, dyed purple with bright red flowers on the front and shoulder strap covered with sequins.

"Now I really feel bad."

"Good," Marissa said with a mocking smile, "that makes it all worth it." She leaned over on him and grinned as she handed him the purse. She reached back into the bag, and pulled out another item. As she held it up, Ryder couldn't help but laugh. It was an outfit for a new born. Black with red lettering on the front, that Ryder's read out loud.

"Daddy's Little Detective."

"Got you something too," Marissa said as she reached into a different sack and pulled out an extra large bright red t-shirt, with white lettering, that read. 'World's greatest big brother because…' 'And got myself something', she again went to the second bag, and pulled out another t-shirt, that was just her size and she held it up in front of her. It read '… I am his little sister.' "Fitting, don't you think?" She asked with a smile. He reached in to the trunk and grabbed the shopping bags, places his arm around her shoulder.

"Perfect." He said, and led her away from the car.

After checking the rental car in, they had to wait for the jet to return as the jet that had been waiting for them was commandeered for a quick escape by Paul Steele; it seemed that fame screamed louder than money in this case.

As they boarded, he was met at the doorway of the jet by a Korean woman in her early thirties. She was attractive with long dark hair that was tied loosely behind her back and flowed down from the captain's hat she was wearing that was part of her uniform, the dark blue jacket with white stripes on the sleeves. She greeted him with a warm smile as she spoke, as Marissa pushed past her and seated herself. "Sweet tea right? I just made some fresh. I hope you will forgive me for taking another flight."

"It is okay Min." Ryder said sat down in the seat across from his sister. And Min closed the door and headed for the cockpit.

Flying at night is a different feeling, over the farm land one is encased in darkness, just like when eyes are closed and sleep is trying to enter. The lights on a train trailing like a glowworm below, moving too slow and is left behind becoming a dim glow that can no longer be seen.. Towns with lights twinkling like a swarm of lightning bugs, others so small they are but just one flash of light.

Ryder leaned back in the seat, and relaxed with a glass of ice tea, sweet but not sickly sweet, but also not where it wanted to make him gag from the bitterness, it was just perfect. He took a sip and as he held the glass in his hand, he closed his eyes.

"Oh gosh! I can't believe it," Ryder heard Marissa say. He opened his eyes. Her body hidden in the darkness of the interior of the jet her face illuminated by the bluish glow of her cell phone. 'Look!" She held the phone up for him to see. "This happened tonight."

It was Paul Steele on stage at the Pikes Peak Center, telling the world:

"Steelace has other shows planned, but I am going to have to take a short vacation due to unseen events." It was the reaction of the other members of the band that made Ryder wonder what was going on, they were shocked. The lead guitarist Stevie Lace slammed her Gibson to the floor and stormed off stage.

Marissa turned the video off on her phone and asked, "What could have made him do that. Steelace has the number one album and number one song right now. They are the hottest band out there."

Ryder placed his glass down in the holder beside him and stood up and walked up to the cockpit. He pulled the curtain back. He could hear the roar of the jet engines, and the warm multiple colored glow of the high tech instrument panel. The computer like monitors showing their location over eastern Kansas, while through the windows was complete darkness. Min was over to the left at the controls.

There was a set of headphones draped across the co-pilot, just like the ones that Min was wearing. Ryder slipped them on and sat down in the seat beside. "Min you want to make this up to me?"

"You want to fly again? Take the controls." She said as she turned to him.

"No," Ryder replied. "I will leave that to you." Ryder looked out into distance and below them miles away he could see a light flashing atop a TV broadcast tower. She and turned her attention back to the flight path ahead. "Tell me, where did you take Steele?"

"I shouldn't tell you that but..." She paused and turned to him again. "I owe it to you. I took him to the Joplin Airport."

"Joplin?"

"Why Joplin?"

"That was the closest I could get to the airport he really wanted."

"Which was?"

"Neosho."

"Thanks Min." Ryder said standing up. He removed the headphones and went back to his seat. His sister was busy searching the internet again.

"I have been thinking you are putting too much into this." Ryder said as he sat down.

"It is my case!"

"Marissa you are fifteen years old, you are not a detective." Ryder shifted himself in the airplane seat and leaned over towards her and continued, "We are not talking the case of a missing grandfather's clock here. We are talking about cold blooded murder. This isn't what a teenage girl should be doing; you should be doing normal things."

"Like what?" Marissa said, "Hanging down at the lake in my swimsuit, acting like an air head when a boy comes by?"

"I am Rick Ryder's little sister!" Marissa said, "There is nothing normal about that. My brother is nearly 30 years older than I am. We didn't even know each other existed until my mother was murdered. Now I live in his house with his wife, who has had a crush on him since she was eight years when he dated her older sister. Also on the same ranch is my brother's partner who is his former girlfriend, and who had a child together. And there is a woman that we all call grandma who is only blood kin to my sister-in-law. But she takes care of me and Ceelia when my brother, Sister-in-law and partner go out to investigate murder cases for a dollar a day because he is the biggest Powerball jackpot winner of all time. And to top it all off, the girls at school want to be my friend so they can come over and pant like a dog looking at my brother. Ricky we are not the Nelsons, the Cleavers, or the Bradies, heck you need a score card to figure us out. And if you are talking about boys, my brother is also a former NFL QB and my sister-in-law owns the gun shop in town, so all but one of the boys is scared to death to talk to me. I have had teachers that wanted to know if I could get a photo of you in the buff and she would give me an A. I have a coach that thinks because my last name is Ryder I should be able to throw a ball without breaking windows. Then there is Mr. Davis, the biology teacher that instead of having me dissect the frog to find out how the frog died, I am the only teenager that ever had to fill out a police report on her biology project. And you want me to be a normal teenager?"

"Are you done?" Ryder asked calmly as he leaned back in the seat.

"Yeah."

"I was talking about getting your driver's permit?"

"Oh that," Marissa said. "I guess I could get that. I have been studying."

"They are in Cassville on Thursdays, can you pass the test?"

"I know how to drive." Marissa said.

"Do you have the driver's guide downloaded?"

"Yes but—."

"Is that what you are doing now?"

"Yes, I am studying right now."

He held his hand out for her phone. And she handed it to him. One the screen was police records. 'Newton county years ago, about missing persons.'

"Missing persons?"

"If someone was murdered," Marissa explained, "they would likely have been reported missing, right?"

"Yes." Ryder said as he handed the phone back to her.

"I looked at police records for the two years your mother attended Crowder, I checked Newton, McDonald and Jasper counties." She looked down at her phone and brought up the note section, "During that span there were three missing person reports. One was an elderly man who walked away from a nursing home in Anderson." Ryder shook his head it just didn't sound right, and Marissa next words confirmed that "He was found a day later near Indian Creek, trying catching minnows; he was going to go fishing; another was a missing teenager from Joplin." *Now that had promise* Ryder thought.

"Male or female?"

"Female."

"Found?" Ryder asked

"No," Marissa replied. "She was last seen hitch hiking on highway 71 trying to get to Kansas City. But it is the next one I really found interesting, as it happened in Neosho," again Ryder's interests was peaked, he drew his finger across his chin as he listened to her explain further. Jordan Hansson 24 years old, a carnival worker from Sedona, Arizona last seen at the Newton County Fair, reported missing from the Roy Jean Carter Memorial Fairgrounds in Neosho, Mo and was last seen in the company of three other individuals who got into a red 1972 Pontiac GTO. He is described as around five foot eight, stocky built, 190 pounds, dark hair and full beard, had tattoos, one in particular was a spider web with spider with the face of a woman that has no eyes."

"A spider web interesting." Ryder said.

"Does that mean something?

"It can mean he was in prison."

She looked up from her phone and added. "Didn't you tell me that your mother had a 1972 red GTO?"

Chapter 28

Back home and in bed Ryder awoke to the song of sparrows greeting the new day, he rolled over to embrace Yakira, but instead found her side of the bed empty. He stood grabbing a light weight red robe with black stripes on the sleeves, slipping it on as he walked over to the French doors that led out on the balcony and opened them and stepped out. From across the road in the field he could hear the whistle of red-tailed hawk and his eyes drifted up to the clear blue sky. There was not a cloud to be seen, the thermometer that was mounted to the side of the house pointed to 80 degrees, and by the clock on the nightstand by the bed it was 7:00 a.m., it was going to be a hot day. He stepped back inside and closed the doors and made his way down the back stairs into the kitchen. As he got halfway down, he caught the sweet aroma of fresh baked bread.

As he descended into the kitchen the aroma grew stronger, he realized it wasn't bread it was bagels, not store bought but freshly made. Without even seeing who was in the kitchen he knew. "Bubbie," He said gently before taking the last step to the bottom of the stairs.

"Right here *Motek*," she said with a term of affection. As he looked across the kitchen and saw her standing at the island in the middle of the kitchen, at that moment, she looked the essence of what a grandmother should be. As if she was a living breathing version of a Norman Rockwell painting. An apron, all the furls tied around her and a smudge of flour on her forehead. Behind her was a large pot of boiling water, the steam rising up like a cloud making her take a cloth that was in the pocket of her apron and dab away from her brow. She turned to her helper beside her, the five year old Ceelia who was standing on a box so she could reach the counter, "Got to get the *shmutz* off."

In front of her on the counter was a cookie sheet sprinkled with corn meal, and fresh dough, on one side were those that were all ready formed into circles. On the other was the dough that was rolled out into a log, speckled with dried cranberries, which Ceelia was picking off and eating. He moved closer to the island and Ceelia who taken another sweet berry and put it in her mouth.

"I am helping, daddy!" Ceelia said.

"I see you are," Ryder said looking at Bubbie. "And a big help you are. Guess you know?"

"Know what?" Ceelia asked with the innocents that only a child could know.

Bubbie smiled as she pinched off a bit of the dough and said, "That you call Ricky daddy now. You couldn't have picked a better one." She rolled the dough out and placed it in front of Ceelia, "Now make it into a circle." The little girl grabbed an end a twisted the dough around and Bubbie sealed it together.

"I am the circle maker." Ceelia said as Bubbie carefully placed the formed dough on the other side of the counter.

"And a good one you are." Ryder said as he watched as Bubbie carefully placed the raw bagels into the boiling water, then flipping them over then she scooped them out of the water, and placed them on a drying rack. At that moment the timer went off on the oven, Bubbie turned and using a pot holder removed a corn dusted cookie sheet with fresh warm bagels on it. Ryder inhaled, that was the aroma he had been smelling, "Is that..."

"Peanut butter," Bubbie said placing the tray down on the counter. And using tongs quickly placed the bagels on a plate. She covered them with a cloth. "Guess who wanted them? With lox." She handed them to Ryder.

"I'll see she gets them." Ryder said took the plate, and leaned over and kissed Bubbie on the cheek and said, "You know if you came with a price tag I couldn't even afford the down payment." She grinned.

Bubbie helped Ceelia down from the wooden box she was standing on.

"Come on daddy!" Ceelia said, taking hold of his hand, she led him out through the dining room and the morning room, and outside on to the deck. Breakfast was being served *al fresco*, under the shade of a dark green umbrella over a glass topped patio table with room for six, along which were Yakira, Marissa, Alex, each with a plate and mug of coffee. In the center of the table was a serving tray with a small tub of strawberry cream cheese, plain cream cheese and packed on ice, a container of smoked salmon, next to it another tray with a pot of coffee and a small pitcher of cream and a bowl of sugar. The little girl pulled out a chair for him and Ryder placed the plate of bagels on the table and seated himself.

Alex started to reach over and started to grab one.

"Peanut butter."

"Yuck!" Alex said drawling her hand back. Yakira quickly reached over and took one and using a knife that was lying beside the plate sliced it , then spread some strawberry cream cheese and topped it off with some of the salmon. Yakira took a bite and moaned with delight. Alex looked at her and then back to Ryder. "It is chilidog!"

A chilidog?" Ryder asked confused

"When I was expecting, all I wanted was chilidogs," she turned back to Yakira and said. "You're pregnant!"

"Oh my gosh, really Yakira. I am going to be an aunt?" Marissa asked looking up from her cell phone, her tone unconvincing that she was just now finding out.

"You told them!" Yakira said looking at Ryder who was pouring himself a cup of coffee into the mug in from of him. He replaced the pot on the tray and scooped two spoonfuls of sugar and a splash of cream from the smaller decanter of cream. Using a spoon beside him she stirred the mixture.

"You can't keep a secret around here," Ryder said as he took a sip of the sweet coffee. "The whole house is filled with detectives." You are eating peanut butter and fish, a blind man could figure it out."

"If she has a baby what is it to me?" He heard Ceelia ask and turned to the little girl standing next to him.

Ryder looked over at Alex who had taken a plain bagel and placed cream cheese and lox on it and had just taken a bite. "If you can explain this I will give you a hundred bucks." Ryder said.

She swallowed wiped her mouth with a napkin and turned to her daughter and said, "Since Rick is your daddy but Yakira is not your mother it will be your half brother or sister, but in this family we don't do things half way. So he or she will be your brother or sister."

"Okay," Ceelia said.

"So where is my money?" Alex holding her hand out.

"I don't have it with me. I will get it to you later." Ryder said, then turned to her daughter and asked. "What do you want a brother or a sister?"

"I hope it is a boy. We have too many girls around here."

"That is my girl," Ryder said as he reached down, picked her up and placed her on his lap. He hugged her and made her giggle. Remembering the gift he had for her, "Marissa," he asked and Marissa was staring at her phone and didn't hear him. "Marissa!" He said a little louder. She looked up at him, "Did you wrap up the package?"

Marissa reached down and handed him a package, which she had wrapped up in bright purple paper and a pink bow. She handed the package across the table to him, and then went back to her phone.

"Is that for me?" Ceelia asked crawling down from his lap

"Yes."

She stood at the side of the table ripping into the paper and opening the box and looking inside. "Wow!" she said with excitement, her blue eyes as wide as the skies above her. She lifted the purse out and said, "Look mommy! I am a woman now." She draped the strap of the purse over her shoulder as she stood up, she pushed her long dark locks back over her shoulder and looked up at him as she added in the most serious tone she could manage, "Doesn't it make my eyes sparkle."

With a small laugh he said, "Yes darling it does."

"Ceelia what do you say?" Alex said.

"Thank you, Daddy," The little girl said stretching her neck to look up at him. He kneeled down in front of her. And she wrapped her little arms around his neck and hugged him tightly. He looked at Marissa who was head down engrossed in what was on her cell phone.

"You are welcome," he said as she released him. "Marissa picked that out for you. Go give her a hug."

The little girl dashed over to Marissa, who was face down in the cell phone. "Thank you Aunt Marissa." Marissa didn't notice the little girl; instead she was scanning through news on the internet. Ceelia stood her arms out waiting for a hug.

"Marissa!" Ryder said firmly as he stood and Marissa looked at him as he pointed to Ceelia.

"Oh," Marissa said hugging the little girl with one arm. "No problem kiddo."

Ryder reseated himself at the table, when Ceelia walked up beside him again and said, "I can take this to our tea party."

"Sure," Ryder said as he lifted the coffee back up to his lips.

"It is going to be fancy," Ceelia explained. "So you have to get all dressed up."

"Okay," Ryder said taking a bite of the chewy bread, tasting the sweetness of the cream cheese. "Why don't you pick me something out?"

"Okay!" She said with delight. "I will fix my room up." Ceelia and her mother lived in the foreman's house at the bottom of the hill but many times due to investigations that would lead her away, Ceelia would stay at the main house, and Ryder just gave her one of the rooms for her very own. She turned and ran into the house. As he looked across the table at his sister who was still immersed in what was on her phone. Ryder lifted his mug and took a sip and gazed out across the freshly cut green lawn and clear blue skies. He looked over at Alex as she was about to lift a bagel up to her mouth and he asked.

"Did you mow the yard?"

"This yard!" She said with amazement because of the sheer size of the lot. It was nearly an acre. "I was too busy getting the information you wanted."

Ryder placed his elbows on the table and cupped his fingers around each other and brought them up to his chin as he eagerly asked, "And what did you find out?" Before she could reply, he once again gazed across the table to his sister. He eyes still fixed on the screen of her cell phone, a bagel with cream cheese on it, only one bite taken out of it. "Just a minute, Ryder said to Alex. "Marissa," He said, not getting to answer he shouted, "Marissa!"

"Huh?" She asked looking up.

"Turn your phone around where I can see it."

"Why?"

"Just do it." He said.

"I was just texting some friends," She said nervously. "To ask questions about the driver's test."

"Turn it around."

"Okay I was texting a boy it is kind of personal."

"Turn it around!"

She reluctantly turned her phone around and he saw what she had been doing. Ryder put his hand out for the phone and she handed it to him. He looked down at the screen and the name of the receiver and said, "Odd I didn't know that you were friends with the Sedona Red Rock News." He handed her the phone back and added, "So what do you talk about with the cute boys in class?"

"I did some more research." Marissa said as she took her phone and laid it down beside her on the table. "I found out the carnival worker that was missing was from Sedona, AZ, I asked to see if he had any arrest records."

"I told you no more investigating. You have to study for the driver's test."

"I know how to drive!" She snapped back. "I drove to Kansas City by myself."

"Yeah, and we will not discuss that one." Ryder said. "This isn't about how to drive, it is about the rules. You don't pass the written test you can't get the permit."

"I know all about that."

"Okay," Ryder said leaning back in his chair. "You answer three questions with get two right and you don't have to study anymore."

"I am ready!"

"First question 'the minimum age that a person must be in order to obtain an

Instruction Permit is…"

Before he could finish she replied, "Fifteen!"

"Good, now you got to get one more right. Second question what does SATOP stand for?" A blank expression ran over her face. "Don't know?" She shook her head.

"Substance Abuse Traffic Offenders Program"

"That is not going to be on there. Give me a driving question and I will show you."

"Okay, now you get this wrong and it is hit the book 'when may you pass another vehicle by using the shoulder of the road?'" He waited watching eye brows knit down in frustration.

"I have seen it a lot, and have seen you do it." She said with reassurance, "When the car is turning left." Ryder slowly shook his head. "But— I have seen cops do it."

"It is never legal to pass on the shoulder," Ryder said pointing to the inside of the house. "Hit the books."

"It isn't fair!" Marissa complained, "This is my case!"

"Make a deal with you. You pass the test; I will let you back on the case." She took her cell phone and went inside. Ryder turned to Alex. "So what did you find out?"

Alex stood up and walked back into the house and was holding a yellow legal pad in her hands. She sat back down and flipped a page over and began to read from the notes she had made. The child, a boy, was born Caley Kalhoun, but the reports in the paper were wrong, he was not born there, but was a patient there. His mother Brenda Kalhoun, a mother of three was well known for her drug habit, the state had to remove the kids from her custody, including newborn Caley, who was in need of medical care. Caley was to go into foster care the next day, but…"

"A description that matches my mother was seen walking away with the child."

"No that was wrong too," Alex said flipping over a page in the legal pad again she read from her note, "According to the records the father James Kalhoun signed the child out. However, at that same time

James Kalhoun was being arrested for DUI by the Missouri Highway Patrol, in Dade County." Alex said.

"Are you sure?" Ryder asked

"Positive!" Alex said. "The parents had seen jail before. For him two arrests for drunk and disorderly, another for theft. For her prostitution and procession of illegal substance. He was a booze hound, she was a snort queen."

Ryder had finished his bagel, and was getting another one, when he asked, "You know where Kalhouns are today?"

"901 East South St, Neosho, MO."

"That is where they live?"

"It is where they lay. The both died." Alex said, looking at her notes, "Brenda thirty years ago from a drug over dose, James last year, cirrhosis of liver. The nurse on duty back then gave me a description of the man who took the kid. Around five foot eight, stocky built, 190 pounds, dark hair and full beard, had tattoos, one in particular was a Spider web with a spider with the face of a woman that has no eyes."

"The missing carnival worker. That is why he disappeared, kidnapping is life stretch."

"Jordan Handson was never seen again, However ten years ago a Jordan Henry was struck and killed in an accident in New Orleans he had tattoo a spider web with a spider with the face of a woman that has no eyes. That is a rare tattoo Rick."

"So our missing carnival worker is dead, and the only missing person left is the baby."

"You said there were rituals in that club," Alex paused before saying, "You think they killed a baby?"

"I don't know, " Ryder took another sip of coffee. "Did you dust the plaque?"

"Yes, there were many sets on there, too many to identify." She paused, and said, "Rick there was one other thing," She paused again flipping the pages back into place on the legal pad and holding it close to her chest as if it was something that she didn't need to read to remember, as she continued. "Don't know if I should tell you this or not. There is no hard proof that was—but it was a—I don't want to upset you."

"For gosh shakes Alex what is it."

"She said the man that took the baby." She took a deep breath before she spoke. "That he got into a red car with a young dark haired woman, the car had hood scoops. Like a GTO."

"Danielle had a red GTO," he heard Bubbie say as she walked out the door holding another plate of bagels. Ryder turned and looked at her over his shoulder. "I helped her buy it." She set the plate of food down on the table and continued. "Ricky you really don't think your mother was involved in this do you? The stealing or killing of a child!"

"I don't know what to think Bubbie." Ryder said as Bubbie set down at the empty place where Marissa had been sitting. "Every time I turn around her name pops up. And nobody wants to talk about this club that she created." Ryder reached across and grabbed one of the fresh bagels she had just brought out, they were plain and still warm and she had already sliced them open.

"The Sergeants' Club?" Bubbie said, "The brothers and sisters of the covenant."

"What do you know about it?" Ryder asked and he smeared plain cream cheese and put a slice of salmon on it.

"It is a Blood Covenant *Motek*," Bubbie said as she grabbed one of the bagels and cut it open. "You remember doing that with Annalisa when you were kids?"

"No."

"You remember, you would have secrets and you would take each other's blood and mix it together."

"Like blood brothers?" Alex said.

"Yes, but you sanctified it to God." Bubbie said. "It cannot be broken."

"Is that what they did?" Ryder asked, "Sanctified it to God, that is why they won't tell?"

She took a bite of the bagel and quickly changed the subject as she looked out over the lawn. "I think he did a good job."

"Who?" Ryder asked, inside he heard the land line phone ring.

"The young man I hire to mow the lawns, fifty bucks! Special price. He is using your lawn mower and gas." Inside the phone rang again.

"Bubbie back to the covenant!" Ryder said, "what do you know about it? "

"Nothing I am not one of them. Only if you are one of them can you know.

"Marissa get that please!" Ryder shouted. "Bubbie there is a missing child, and Annie was afraid that was going to be uncovered at Crowder. They sacrificed a child. Didn't THEY!"

Ryder was interrupted as Marissa stormed out the door; her voice was trembling as she spoke. "Ricky—the sheriff of Newton County is on the phone, he wants you to help him. There has been another murder." She handed him the phone. "It is Paul Steele; he was found murdered at Crowder College."

Chapter 29

Ryder quickly dressed and since it was to be in the 90's, he chose light gray colored slacks and a short sleeve white shirt and light weight gray jacket. Busily stuffing all the things he normally carried with him, notebook and pen, small clear plastic bags and a white handkerchief. He stood in the kitchen, where Bubbie was busy cleaning up.

"You don't mind staying here?" He asked as he slipped his sunglasses over his eyes.

"You have to do what you have to do *Motek*," She said as she wiped down the island. "Marissa is studying and Ceelia is in her room. I will make them a nice lunch. I will also watch after Yakira. It is kind of nice to be needed again. Since you two got married, I feel sort of *on a nutsn*"

Bubbie you are far from useless, "Ryder said. "We couldn't make it without you."

Ryder pulled his sunglasses down on his nose and watched as Yakira entered. She turned to her grandmother and asked, "Bubbie could you fix me a bowl of love?" Meaning Matzo Ball soup.

"Of course *nekhdah*." Bubbie said, which meant granddaughter. "You just go and get back in bed and I will take care of you. Yakira smiled, gave her grandmother a hug and Ryder a kiss and went back up the stairs.

"You know," Ryder said removing his sunglasses. "When the baby gets here things are really going be hectic around here. How would you like to move in?"

"Oh Ricky I don't know," Bubbie said. "I would just be in the way here."

"Nonsense!" Ryder shot back. "I have the room, the maid quarters are right off to the side of the kitchen. There is a separate living area and bathroom, you are cleaning up and cooking you might as well be..."

"Motek," she replied. "If you say get paid for it I will knock you out."

"Ceelia would love having you, Yakira would," Ryder grinned. "And I would too." Ryder put his sunglasses back on his face. "And there is going to be a new baby to spoil. Don't want that to be a part time thing, do you?"

Alex descended the stairs into the kitchen. Alex was dressed professionally, light blue skirt, and matching jacket over a white silk blouse.

"You ready?" She asked putting on her sunglasses.

"I will think it over!," Bubbie said

******

Ryder again found himself at Crowder, according to the report he heard the body was found behind the main portion of the campus on Laclede Avenue. He slowly guided the red Dodge across the bridge and saw a couple of students sitting in the grass under the shade of one of the trees that line the street. They were dressed for summer in shorts and t-shirts. They gave him a glance as they passed by the brand new sign that read *"Home of the Lady Rough Riders."* He twisted the wheel over to the right and guided the car down the street, the tires clicking under the slabs of dividing strips of cement slabs. Two teen girls were jogging along the side of the road and they turned and glanced smiling at him as he drove by.

"Cool car!" One of the teens yelled as they passed by the soccer fields. He came to a point where the cement strip was to go four ways; it was the hopes and dreams of a college reaching for an ever expanding campus, but the dreams had not been realized yet, as the street made a hard turn to the right, and in front of him the base of a road that was nothing more than just a scar torn into the ground, a makeshift road for heavy equipment that was to add the next step to the campus, a new home for the trucking school.

Ryder twisted the wheel to the right, over to the left was the remains of the maintenance building. Its secrets could only be told if one was looking at an old Camp Crowder map. In the 1940's it was bustling with thousands of soldiers. Long trains pulled black locomotives vomiting smoke in the skies, as another group of young brave lads stepped off from the cars. They were from all over the nation willing to give all for freedom, as another group boarded wondering if they would give all.

There were hundreds of buildings dotting the swampy grounds that would be forever burned into the memories of those that entered. If you stood still, even today, and listened carefully one could swear that you heard the sounds of Guy Lombardo and His Royal Canadians or the Andrews Sister singing "Shoo-Shoo Baby" or the swing of G.I. Jive bellowing out from the dancehalls. As Doll dizzy soldiers danced with Ducky Shincrackers USO girls.

Ryder parked the car, and tried to listen but the ghosts didn't have anything to say, all he could hear was the squawk and buzz of the police radio of the squad car he parked behind. He walked over and opened the door for Alex, as she stepped out he noticed her gazing across the street at the building behind the chain linked fence and behind that student housing, even though it was the summer months and the housing was not being used, a group had gathered in the yard and was watching all events that were unfolding. Ryder approached the restricted area that had a yellow piece of tape across the street.

"This is a restricted area!" The young deputy said as he held his hand up.

"Ryder!" Newton County Sheriff Roy Barker shouted out as he saw Ryder, he walked over to the young deputy and continued, "Son don't you have an inkling of who you have here? They are the ones that tracked down the Kansas City Butcher; this is Rick Ryder and Isabelle Alexander. One of the most vicious bloody serial killer of all time and they caught her." He held the tape up for them to the bend down and walked under it.

"What do you have Barker," Ryder asked as they walked down the street past the construction site. The bulldozer was perched and ready to go, a dump truck sitting next to a backhoe, it's bed only half filled. The last remaining structure, its white stone frontage stripped back down to its beginning, showing the 1940's styling. The metal roof was removed its insides exposed to the heavens.

"Biggest frigging case I ever had in my life," Sheriff Barker said as he led them down through a maze of emergency vehicles, their lights flashing, spanning over them. "We have had some big cases here, like the shooting at the church but this is a frigging world class rock star." He stopped walking and turned to Ryder and added, "Just got word that the media is on their way here. Fox News, MSNBC, CNN, ABC, CBS, if it has gosh blasted letters they are on their way here. That is why I called you in. How do you handle this stuff? I mean I have done KODE KSN but this is the big shots from New York."

Ryder placed his hand on the man's shoulder. "Ray," he said calmly using the sheriff's first name. "You have to stand firm in your core beliefs. These people are different than your local anchors or the reporters for the Daily News. They don't care about truth or facts; all they want is everyone tuning in. They are going to make you think you are the grandest star of all time. They are going to act like they are hanging on your every word. But if they can throw you to the wolves to make people tune in to their report instead of someone else's, they will. They will want you to do all kinds of interviews, and when you don't, they will claim you are hiding something." Ryder placed his other hand on the other shoulder and continued, "but you stick to your guns. You give them only what you need to, you leave them hungry and wanting more. You fill them up and like feeding a wild animal, they become dangerous." Ryder lifted his hands from the man's shoulders and asked "Where did you find the body?"

Sheriff Barker turned back and continued walking down the narrow strip of pavement. "That is sort of the odd thing," the Sheriff said as the passed by the parking lot where several semi's parked, each cab lurking steel gray, the box trailers adorned on the sides with the Crowder College logo. Parked in front of one was a brand new Nissan sedan. Tennessee plate. "We found him face down, down here in a ditch."

They turned left and walked down another street, it too lined on both sides with squad cars. "You know my grandfather was stationed here. He was a sergeant," The sheriff continued. He again stopped and turned back to Ryder and Alex who were following him and explained more, "Back during WWII, when it was Camp Crowder." He turned and began to walk again, still explaining, "When I was a kid we would drive through here and he would tell me about all the building that used to be here. You know it was a big camp. Went clear down to the interstate, there was a prisoner of war camp, a hospital." the sheriff pointed over to the right at the lagoon, "that was where a PX was and there the swimming pool, it was even the city pool for a while."

As Sheriff Barker continued to speak Ryder leaned over and whispered to Alex, "Run the plate of the Nissan. "

"You have reason?" Alex asked whispering back.

"Yeah it doesn't look right?" Ryder said softly back and then Alex stepped away from them.

"There were six theaters, fourteen chapels. But his favorite place was right here," he said as he pointed to the other side of the road, "the Sergeants' Club."

Ryder quickly stopped in his tracks and grabbed the sheriff by the arm as he asked, "The what?"

"You know the Sergeants' Club," Sheriff Barker said. "Where the sergeants would gather, you know, like the officer's club, it was the backbone of the army the Sergeants of the army."

"That is it," Ryder said softly.

"What is?"

"Never mind," Ryder said looking back at the construction site. "Where exactly was it?"

"The one they are tearing down," Sheriff Barker said. "But that doesn't have anything to do with this case. The sheriff followed Ryder's gaze to where he was staring at the old remains of the building. And then he added, "Does it?"

"I don't know," Ryder said as they passed by the main command center unit. Over to the left was a field, according to the sheriff, during its military days it was the parade group and during rainy days, like it had been, this area would be muddy and thus Mort Walker called it Campy Swampy. Just behind the fence along the side of the road was a ditch that was full of muddy water. There was a metal bar gate and it had been pushed open. In front of the gate was a white ambulance with blue stripes, with "Newton County" painted on the sides of it, the strobe of red and blue light on the front flashing back and forth. On the ground in front of the ditch of water laid a body covered with a white sheet. Ryder kneeled down beside the body and grabbed the coroner of the sheet.

"Son, you better have a strong stomach," He heard a man say as he glance up at him. He was standing there next to the body dressed in kaki slack and a three button red short sleeved polo shirt, with the words Newton County Coroner Jackson Patterson stitched over the breast. "Already been a couple of officers who heaved it up."

"Jackson," Sheriff Barker said. "This is Rick Ryder."

"The billionaire that goes around solving murder cases," Jackson asked, "That Rick Ryder?"

Ryder lifted the sheet, the body was still face down, and there was a gash two inches wide on the side of the head just above his right ear, blood had dripped down on the side of his face and gray brain matter was trying to ooze from the wound. The hair was plastered with blood, and he reeked of the muddy stagnant water.

"Got any gloves?" Ryder asked

"Here, Jackson said as he handed Ryder a pair of blue latex gloves. Ryder put the gloves on and then carefully grabbed the man's shoulder; he was stiff and cold, his face frozen in death, the skin waxy and purplish eyes sunken back. Ryder laid the body back down and lifted the dead man's arm up, the top of the arm was white in color, his finger tips blue.

"How long do you think he has been dead?" Ryder asked as he looked at the dead man's other hand.

"By the rigor mortis at least four hours," Jackson replied. "But the water he was in was cold, it could have affected the timing."

Ryder looked closer at the man's left hand; he noticed there a gash in his palm and under his nail a large splinter in the end of his pinkie. "Did you notice these splinters?" Ryder asked holding the dead man's hand up.

"I figure it is defense wounds."

"But this one in the finger looks old, and it has finish on it. It looks like as if he was trying to pry a wood floor." Ryder dropped the hand down and stood up allowing the sheet to cover the body again. His gaze fell on the remains of the old building.

"Trying to pry up what?" The sheriff asked.

"Never mind," Ryder said as he turned to the sheriff and asked, "What was the murder weapon?"

"A double edge sword." Sheriff Barker said. We found it stuck clear through his head. He was pinned to the ground. You need to take a look at this." The sheriff walked over to the command center and picked up a large paper bag and handed it to Ryder. Ryder opened and reached inside and produced a golden colored cutlass. A board blade two edge bladed sword), the handle was gold plated and adorned with colored stones.

"Rubies and sapphires," Sheriff Barker said.

178

Ryder held the sword up and the bright sunlight caught the stones which gleamed like glass, as that was what they were. Ryder said, "Fake." As he held it up he saw the price sticker on the handle with a small little angel on it. It was bought at the Angel Shop in Manitou Springs. "The suicide king." Ryder added.

"The what?"

"He was the suicide king, the King of Hearts," Ryder said. "His killer is the same one that killed Annie and Charlotte."

"What?" Jackson asked.

Ryder noticed the stale water and there was something wrong, the color. Blood is thicker than water was not just a saying, it was fact and the amount of blood that sunk into the water here just wasn't enough, not for a head wound like this one. He went back to the body and again lifted the sheet. Just above the dead man's ear was gash just as wide as the blade of the sword, his skull was caved in, the other side was untouched the sword hadn't gone all the way through. There was just not enough blood.

He dropped the sheet down again. "Any sign that the body could have been drug here?"

"None," Sheriff Barker replied. "What are you thinking he could have been murdered somewhere else?"

"There is just not enough blood."

"I would have to agree with that," Jackson said. "There should be a lot more blood."

"Ryder," he heard Alex say as she walked up behind. "We got a hit! It is a rental from the Springfield airport. Guess who rented it?"

"Sheriff," Ryder said as he turned back around. "Do you have his personal effects? Can I see them?"

The Sheriff orders one of his deputies to get the personal effects, and he returned shortly with a clear plastic bag. He opens the bag and pours the contents of the bag out on to the hood of a squad car as Ryder looks over the items, "What are you looking for?" The sheriff asks.

Ryder looked the items, over; rings, gold watch, billfold…"Car fob!" Ryder said as he picked them up. He pressed down on the alarm button and the horn on the Nissan sounded. He turned it off and they walked back to the parking lot. Ryder pushed the lock button and the horn on the Nissan sound.

After walking back to the car, Ryder pushed the button on the key fob and unlocked the door. He sat down in the driver's seat and began to search the interior. And Alex asked if she could borrow his car, there was something that she wanted to check out.

"Again what are looking for?" Sheriff Barker asked.

"The reason," Ryder said as he pulled the glove box open, and then the ashtray. "The band was going to do more shows, suddenly he quits. Not one of the band members knew he was going do that." Ryder looked at the sheriff standing next to the car and added, "Why come to Crowder College in the dead of the night?" He looked down at the floor mats on the passenger's side and there was a wet stain four inches in diameter, it was clear and odorless and at the edge of that stain was a sales slip from Wal-mart® . It showed that Steele had bought two items, a pry bar and a shovel. Ryder pushed the trunk release and the lid popped open. He got out of the car and looked down into that trunk; it was clean except for one thing. The discarded plastic wrap that was around the head of a new shovel, "No dirt," Ryder said standing up and looking across the street at the remains of the old maintenance building and muttered, "The Sergeants' Club that is it!" as he walked across the street the sheriff followed. "He bought a shovel and a pry bar. Yet they are not in the trunk, there is no dirt so he didn't return them.

The construction area was surrounded by a bright orange webbing fence, but there was a gate and he opened and stepped inside, again the sheriff following him. He carefully stepped along the clawed up ground past the backhoe and over to the remains of the old building. The windows had been removed as had the door and the metal roof, the bare skeleton of the roof joints stared down on the antique wood plank floor.

Ryder stepped inside, the wood planks moaning under his weight, He could see the shadows of where heavy shelves once rested, protecting the floor from the sun fading them, leaving their outline behind. A few feet away he saw something lying on the floor. It was a shovel. He kneeled down beside it. The handle was bright and shiny, at the end of the blade were sharp notches, in between the notches was dirt. Ryder picked up a chunk of the dirt. It was dry and light brown on the outside. He squeezed it between his fingers and it easily clumped together. This dirt had not been here this long. Yet as he looked around the floor, there was no sign where anyone could have been digging. The soil did not match the clay that was being exposed in the yard.

His gaze fell down upon the planks in front of him. Something struck him oddly about the pieces of wood. There were signs that they had been recently pried up. Chunks of wood were missing, exposing the raw wood and a large gap between the planks. As he looked closer it was something bright and shiny that really caught his attention. It was nails. Some had recently nailed this plank back down.

As he scanned the floor once again he saw it, thrown over to the far wall-the pry bar. He stood up and walked over and picked up the bar and returned. "What are you doing?" Sheriff Barker asked grabbing Ryder's arm as he prepared to pry the boards up. "That is evidence."

"Is this the murder weapon?" Ryder asked clearly annoyed. "You got the proof he bought them. I guarantee the motive behind these murders is under the planks." The sheriff lifted his hand from Ryder's arm and he pried up one of the boards. "There are legends in this county of buried confederate gold; it would be worth millions today. That would be a reason to kill someone."

Sheriff Barker knelt down beside Ryder and together they lifted the board out, the bright nails moaning as they ripped from their new home. "Tales are that it is in a small wooden box." The sheriff said as they pulled up the last board.

Ryder leaned down on his hand, looking down into the hole; there was a fresh pile of dirt, the same dark dirt that was on the shovel. Taking the shovel Ryder pulled the fresh dirt away, he was down about a foot and a half when he came across harder dirt and the same type that was being exposed in the construction. It was hard and compact; using his foot he applied pressure to the back of the shovel and scooped out another shovelful. The dirt was mixed with the top soil. He knew that the soil had been disturbed before. He had dug another two feet when-THUD!

The tip of the shovel hit something. Sheriff Barker jumped down in the hole and using his hands he began to uncover the object. It was a wooden box; two foot long and 18 inches wide. Ryder dug around the box; it was about a foot deep. On one side were rusted hinges and the other side had a rusted latch, it was nailed shut, with no new nails, but nails that were modern and forged. On the ends of the box were rope handles. Ryder grabbed one rope and the sheriff the other. Ryder prepared himself for a heavy weight; if this was the gold it was going to be very heavy. He was shocked by how little it weighs, it was barely the weight of the box itself. They placed it on the floor and Sheriff Barker quickly climbed out of the hole.

"It is the gold!" The sheriff cried out. "We found it!" He grabbed the pry bar and began to pry the lid open. "I am going to be so famous!"

"Sheriff," Ryder said calmly as he pushed himself up out of the hole.

"Okay, Okay! We will be famous."

"Sheriff it is not the gold," Ryder said walking over to him. "It is not heavy enough. Plus…" Ryder used his hand to wipe the dirt from the lid revealing the letter 'Camp Crowder 1944.'

"But they buried it here. Has to be valuable!" Sheriff Barker said as he pried the last nail free and the lid popped open. It reeked and the first thing that he saw was the remains of an old jersey, with the name Crowder across the front, it was the number 15. "I don't get it!"

"I do," Ryder said as he carefully lifted the jersey he realized there was something wrapped in it. He lifted it up, revealing dark colored bones. Rib bones, pieces of a skull, tiny leg bones, and arm bones the size of chicken leg and a pelvis, Ryder looked up at the sheriff and said. "Congratulations Sheriff, it is a boy."

Chapter 30

Summer is a shapely beauty who indecently flirts. She dresses in sky blue but barely wears anything at all, her eyes the bright sun. She demands that you show skin, then covers you in warm dry kisses as beads of sweat drips down from your face, she leaves a sting kiss on one's eyes. And you slip from her fingertips going inside giving over to her nemesis-air conditioning, she waits for you outside the door, like a gun mall as the iron door of prison slams behind you, she says "*I will wait for you.*"

According to the clock on the bell tower the hands pointed to 1:00 in the afternoon; according to the thermometer it was 96 degrees. Ryder was glad that the college had allowed the sheriff to set up a command post inside the Arnold Farber Building on Campus in the Bob and Mary Wright Conference Center. It was upstairs, and just to the left, further down the hall was the grand Bill and Margot Lee Library.

The Conference Center was one large room that used folding divider walls that could separate it into three smaller rooms. It was currently divided a larger room and a smaller room to the right, of the door way. As Ryder entered, the first thing he noticed was the large arch shaped window that looked out onto the Bell Tower. In front of the window was a line of white fold up tables. Between the tables and the window stood Sheriff Barker gazing out across the campus, his hand folded behind his back. Outside the bell was ringing, but it couldn't be heard inside. Without turning around he spoke, "At the academy they teach us how to look at bodies, all sorts they put before us, man, woman, decayed, floaters," he paused and then said, "Except for one."

"A child." Ryder said solemnly as he walked over to the window and he too gazed out the window and down at the green lawn below them. "Except for one officer," he paused then said, "me. They showed me a kid."

"Have any kids Ryder?"

"A little girl." Ryder replied. "And another one on the way."

"Me too," Sheriff Barker said as he turned and faced Ryder. "Not that I have two. I have six."

"Six!" Ryder exclaimed as he also turned and faced the man.

"All girls! My youngest will be starting kindergarten my oldest starts here at Crowder next fall." Sheriff Barker walked around the table and continued. "Let me buy you a cup of coffee?" He headed across the room and past the dividing wall where a table was set up with a couple of large coffee dispenser. The sheriff picked up a white foam cup and asked, "Regular or unleaded?"

"Doesn't matter." Ryder said as the sheriff placed the cup under the dispenser marked Decaf, he pressed down on the lever a couple of times and filled the cup with rich dark brown liquid. He handed it to Ryder and Ryder mixed in sugar and cream as the sheriff fixed himself a cup. "I better make mine unleaded. It is a damn thing getting old."

Ryder took a sip tasting the rich warm sweetness of the coffee then he asked, "Sheriff are you trying to make small talk, or do you want to know something?"

"I need help!" Sheriff Barker said as he too took a sip of his coffee. "I don't know what the hell is going on here. But you seem to know everything about this." Ryder took another sip and turned and walked back into the larger room and the sheriff followed. "What does this have to do with Annie and Charlotte?"

"Nothing," Ryder said. "Maybe everything. "

"What does that mean?" Sheriff asked as he sat down at the table, positioning himself so he could see out the window.

"You know that Annie started her college education here?" Ryder asked and he turned and saw the sheriff nodding his head and he continued. "She was here at the same time Charlotte Day and Paul Steele were here along with my mother. They started this group called the Sergeants' Club. Not one of them will tell me what happened in this club. There was a missing baby about that same time."

"Caley Kalhoun, son of James and Brenda. It is still one of the unsolved cases in Newton County.

"There were reported sacrifices back then." Ryder said as he took a sip of coffee

Sheriff Barker asked thunderstruck. "You think they murdered this child?"

"I don't know," Ryder said "there is still part of this puzzle that is missing.

Chapter 31

The late afternoon shadows were beginning their daily exercise stretching across the sidewalk reaching for Davidson Hall on the Crowder campus. As Ryder pushed the front glass door open he felt summer's jealous rage against him for cheating on her with air conditioning, feeling the slap of heat across his face. According to his phone the temperature was now 99 degrees but in the Ozarks it isn't the temperature that rings sweat out of you like a maid's fingers around a dishrag, it is the humidity. With the humidity it felt like 117 degrees. However, he quickly found some solace in the shade, where a little comfort could be had.

He leaned back on the bricks of the building and closed his eyes listening to the silence. It seemed that it had been awhile since he had heard nothing, but it had only been this morning. Maybe life could escape reality for just brief moments; the sounds of a siren broke the tranquility. He opened his eyes and turned his head and watched the ambulance zoom by on the highway in front of the college. He reached into his jacket pocket and pulled out his sunglasses and as he slipped them on, he looked up at the sky and wondered if even in paradise he will hear the sirens?

"Ryder," He heard his name spoken and he opened his eyes seeing a friendly face looking up him. At first he didn't recognize her. She grinned again and then added, "It is me, Patrice." He remembered she was the former stripper from Kansas City that he had given the money to go to school here.

"How things going?" He asked.

"Great, but I'm so sorry to hear about Professor Annie. She was my favorite teacher here. We got to be friends. She even invited me to her granddaughter's wedding. That is when something really strange happened, " She leaned in closer to him and said, "I heard Annie tell this guy that was his son."

"He told her that that he knew about she and the pthers did."

"How did Annie react to that?"

"Thanks Patrice," Ryder said. "You have been a big help."

As the siren faded he heard the rumble of dual exhaust and saw the shark like nose of the Killer Bee coming down Brown Street. He walked to the edge of the street and mockingly put his thumb out as if he was hitchhiking and lifted his pant leg to reveal his leg. The Killer Bee pulled up next to him and Alex rolled the window down.

"Going my way?" He asked looking in at her behind the steering wheel.

"Heading home," She replied.

"That is my way."

"Want to drive?"

"It's all set up for you," Ryder said shaking his head and grabbing the door handle. He opened the door and sat down in the gray and black striped leather passenger seat. He had to admit it was strange being on this side of his car. Staring down at the red and yellow nameplate 'Killer Bee' and the angry Bumble Bee on the dash, feeling the shoulder strap go over his right shoulder instead of the left it almost made him want to change his mind and drive. But Alex was all ready heading back to the highway. But she turned right instead of left.

"I thought we would grab a burger at Sonic®" I haven't had anything to eat since breakfast. I am hungry." She said as she rolled up to the stop sign to wait her turn to make the hard left bend onto D-highway. A gray Nissan drove past the driver, his head turning to gaze at the high winged Charger. Alex twisted the steering wheel and made the turn and then gunned the engine, suddenly over 800 horses came alive, and he had never noticed how hard the car shifted through the automatic gears. The road came to a point where the road split to the left for Interstate 49, to the right, it was the aorta that lead to the beating heart of the town- Neosho Boulevard.

She pulled the Charger up into the Sonic® drive in and parked away from other cars. She pushed the button and ordered, "Two double quarter cheese burgers with everything except ketchup, two Cokes one diet and a large order of fries."

"Because fries are meant to be shared," Ryder said.

"You haven't asked." She said as her fingers wrapped round the leather rimmed steering wheel.

"Do I need to?" Ryder asked. "All right what did you find out?"

She let go of the steering wheel and turned to him and spoke, "Each victim has something in common."

"I know," Ryder replied. "The Sergeants' Club."

"I mean how they died."

"Of course it is like the cards; Annie the scepter, Charlotte the flower, Steel with the sword."

"No I mean…" She stopped speaking as a young teenage girl approached the car with their order. Ryder started to reach for his wallet. She grabbed his arm. "No I got this! I need some tax deductions too." She grinned and reached for her wallet that was in her jacket she was wearing and handed the girl a fifty. "Just keep it."

"Thank you so much ma'am!" the teen beamed with glee as she folded up the fifty. "This is a cool looking car. But what is it?" She asked as she handed them their drinks, two large Route 44 cokes. Diet for her and regular for him, he needed something cold and wet to drink, he had just taken a long sip of the sweet cold liquid when Alex said, "It is his."

"It is a 1971 Dodge Charger Killer Bee." He explained.

"I have never seen anything like this." The teen said as she leaned down on the window and looked across to Ryder.

"And you won't," Ryder said. "It is a custom one of a kind."

"My dad would go ape crap over this. What kind of engine?"

"Hellcat hemi! Underneath is all modern suspension four-point suspension, it will handle like a Ferrari and go like a rocket." Ryder explained.

"Can I get picture of it for my dad?"

"Sure," Ryder said as he opened the sack of burgers and handed Alex hers.

"I don't get it, men and cars." Alex said as she took her burger.

"That is just like my mom," the teen said. "You remind me of my mother. Same hairstyle, the same style of clothes and she just turned fifty this year." The teen took the photos of the car and then helped up the fifty and said, "Thanks again for the tip!" Then she left.

"I lost my appetite," Alex said looking down at the burger.

"What is the matter?" Ryder asked.

"Fifty?" She turned to him. "Do I look fifty years old?"

"No you look maybe 30," Ryder said as he unwrapped the paper from his burger.

"Anybody ever tell you you lie a lot." She said turning back and staring out the window, noticing the cars that were there. "You are the guy with the cool car, I am just..." She sighed and looked over at him again. "I could be her mother. I am just a typical mom! Like all the others here."

"So, how many mothers like hers have had shoot outs with international terrorist? Spend the day hanging out in the morgue." He reached over and took a hold of her arm as he added, "How many mothers parked here have to wonder when they say goodbye to their little girl that they may not be coming back?" He said grace and took a bite of his burger and enjoyed the warm salty taste. "So what was it you were trying to tell me?"

190

"They were all drugged!"

"Drugged?", he asked confused. "Are you telling me they died from drug overdose?"

"No, their methods of death were what they were but Charlotte, Annie each had traces of Codeine in their system." Alex said as she took a bite of her burger.

"Codeine?"

"In the blood but not in their stomachs."

"No injection?"

"No injection marks."

"Steel also tested positive for codeine in his blood, but also found traces in his stomach," Alex said as she took a sip from her drink.

"He was a known drug addict…"

"Save you sometime," Alex replied. "There were no traces of filler material in his stomach. I searched the car and his belongings; I found a prescription for lisinopril it is used to control blood pressure and a bottle of OTC acetaminophen but no sign of codeine anywhere on his person. I talked to Double T, he said, it sounds like it was in liquid form, if small amounts were given it would be absorbed into the blood, but if large amounts were given, it could still remain in the stomach after death occurs. They have to wait until the tox-report but…" She paused and then said, "But Jackson is stating that Steel was dead before he was stabbed in the head. He said the amount of codeine he found in his stomach was enough to kill him."

"He find anything else in Steel's stomach?"

"Oddly enough he found the same in Charlotte and Double T found it in Annie," Alex said reaching into her jacket pocket and pulling out a notebook. She flipped through the pages and then read out loud,

"Acetaminophen also phosphoric acid, sucrose, vanilla extract, Critic acid , caramel coloring, nutmeg, orange oil, coriander…"

"What is that?" Ryder interrupted her.

She looked up from her notebook and reached over and picked up his drink and said. "You are drinking it, Coke." She closed the notebook and put it back into her jacket pocket. "I was thinking that if we could find that bottle of codeine…."

"We need to get back out to Crowder."

****

The sun set like a song bird on the top branches of the trees of the far horizon when they got back to Crowder. It seemed like it would be a simple thing to look for an empty prescription bottle for liquid codeine, tossed in an outside trash can. However, that raised the next question. 'How many blue barrels are there on this campus….answer including the five that were near the construction site-well after the tenth one Ryder quit counting.

In the middle of a heat wave, digging through trash cans is not the ideal thing to do, and the things people throw away, half eaten sandwiches, crumpled papers, test scores that were not what was expected, empty water bottles, soda cans of all kinds, Dr. Pepper, Pepsi, Sprite, Wal-mart brand, beer cans, even empty amber prescription bottles, antibiotics, empty birth control packets, female products, even empty opioid analgesics- just not the one they were looking for.

Ryder was hot and tired, he and Alex had gone through all five cans around the construction site and nothing was found. His hands stunk, his clothes stained with sweat and dirt. He sat down on one of the bleachers just outside of the baseball field. Sipping the rest of his pop he looked over at Alex who was going through another trash can. The sun was just beginning to drop down behind the line of trees, creating a brilliant masterpiece of reds, yellow, deep orange and brilliant blues that filled the spattering line of clouds. The shadows were as long as the day itself. The fence around the ball field created a game of tic-tac-toe, but the sun did not want to play and dropped down past the horizon and the shadows began to fade away. He too looked through another trashcan. With the sun gone it was a little a cooler, the heat index was no longer three digits.

His jacket hung draped across the side rail of the bleacher, his shirt stuck to him as if it was a second skin. He unbuttoned his shirt; the hair on his shirt was stuck down. His hair plastered to his scalp. What he needed now was cool shower, but there was none around, none that he could use…well wanted to use. Instead he went to the bathroom and ran some cold water and splashed it on his face and on the back of his neck. He came out of the bathroom he saw Alex standing there a wide grin painted across her face. She held up a clear plastic bag, inside of it was an empty brown 16 oz bottle with the words Codeine and Acetaminophen printed on the label.

"Found it!" She said. Her face beet red, what makeup she had been wearing was gone, streaked down her cheeks with the sweat, her hair losing all of its body and plastered to her as was her blouse. The top two buttons were open revealing the top of the black bra. "This bottle is empty. It has a code number on it, we can trace where it came from."

At that moment the sheriff drove up. "Hide it!" Ryder said. Alex turned around and placed the plastic bag in her blouse and buttoned up her blouse and pulled her jacket up around her just as the sheriff walked up, he was carrying something in his hand.

"What in the world is going on here?" He asked looking at them at how dirty they were. "I got a report that a homeless couple was going through the trash cans looking for pop cans.

"We were looking for a pop can crush a certain way," Ryder said, "Where one end is pushed over one way and the other end the other way. The sheriff looked at him confused. Ryder added to his lie. "We saw a bent can like that at Annie's house. Thought it could be left by the murderer. If we could get some prints."

"Did you find anything?"

"No, nothing," Ryder said. "Think we will head home and get cleaned up."

"Well I got something." Sheriff Barker said, as he handed Ryder the newspaper in his hand. "That is tomorrow's edition of the Daily News."

He unfolded it, printed across was the headline 'Former Crowder Student found murdered in her Apartment.'

Cynthia Hayes of Burke, Va was found dead in her apartment this morning. Authorities believe foul play is involved as she was found face down in her kitchen with a spear like object sticking out of her back. Ms. Hayes received a degree in Business Administration at Crowder College here in Neosho. At the time she was enrolled at Crowder she was part of an underground club of students known as the Sergeants Club.

This club according to a source that will only be known as Monica practiced strange rituals that boardered on witchcraft. According to our source in this club, each member is given a rank according to the face card in a deck of playing cards. Ms. Hayes was the Jack of Diamonds-Hector. In Greek mythology and Roman mythology, Hector was a Trojan prince and the greatest fighter for Troy in the Trojan War and the greatest warrior of all, it is reported that the spear used in the slaying is similar in design to that the mythological Hector used.

Ryder looked at the byline it was Millie Rollins. "How would she know all this?" Ryder asked looking up from the newspaper.

"Oh one other thing," Sheriff Barker said as he reached into his pocket and pulled out a folded up piece of yellow paper. "I ran into Malcolm. "he said to give this to you, it was the names you wanted".

Ryder unfolded it and read through the names, right at the top was his mother's name, below that Annie, Charlotte's, Paul Steele, Cynthia Hayes, he kept reading through the list, but there was no Monica, at the bottom was Millard Snyder. "As in Millie Rollins?" Ryder asked as he held the newspaper up, and added, "as in the same person that wrote this article?"

Chapter 32

Alex convinced Ryder that it would be best if he went to see Millie tomorrow as the way they looked, and smelled, it would be better if they just waited. It was already dark when Alex drove the Charger into the driveway at the ranch. She stopped in front of the garage door and Ryder stepped out, it was a little cooler here maybe it was because it was night, maybe because it was in the country and it wasn't surrounded by pavement, maybe because it was home. He rubbed his hand over his day old growth of whiskers and stared out across the yard and watched as lightning bugs dipped down, flashed their greeting and then disappeared on to see another big flash and another greeting. He looked at his phone; it was down to only 10% power.

"You might as well just stay here tonight," Ryder said as she stepped out. "I have a big guest room. Has its own bath nice big tub. You could just soak this day away."

"Sounds inviting," she replied as they headed for the garage. Ryder pressed an amp on his phone and the garage door rose up and light filled the garage. "I think I will just grab Ceelia and go home."

"It is ten o'clock," Ryder said as they entered and pressed a button on the wall and the garage door closed. "She is probably fast asleep." They walked towards the door that leads into the house and he opened it for her. She stopped and turned to him.

"The guest room it has that big tub doesn't it?" Alex asked. "I think I will take you up on that offer. Thank you."

"Belle," He said tenderly using a shorter version of her first name. "You know you are always welcome here." She grinned; he could see her face smudged with grime; her clothes stained with sweat and dirt. The light in the garage went off and only the light from the hallway spilled over her. Her hair was stuck to the side of her face and he pushed it to the side. "You are the mother of my child, my friend. I know if I get in trouble you are going to be there to back me up. Even if you get married, you are all welcome here." He took his finger and rubbed the dirt from a spot on her face and then leaned down and gave her a kiss on the cheek.

She handed him his keys back and they stepped inside the hall. "Of course I must approve of him first," he joked as they walked down the hall.

"Really?"

"Didn't you have to approve of Yakira?" He asked as they laughed as they turned and walked into the kitchen, it was fully lit and Bubbie was sitting at the table, reading a magazine sipping on a cup of tea and eating a cookie that she took from the plate that was on the table in front of her. She looked up at them.

"Shalom," Bubbie said. "You two must be *raav*." Meaning they were starving. "Can I fix you something to eat?"

"Too tired Bubbie," Ryder said. "Just want to get cleaned up and head for bed."

"You at least got to have a cookie," she said as she stood with the plate and offered them one. Ryder had learned when a Jewish grandmother offers you a cookie, you take one no matter how full or tired you are. He took a cookie and it was rich but so good, cream cheese sugar cookies.

"Thank you Ms Rosen," Alex said reaching for a cookie on the plate.

"What have I told you about that?" Bubbie said pulling the plate back from her "I am just Bubbie to everyone."

"Thank you Bubbie," Alex said and Bubbie handed the plate back to her and she took a cookie. She took a bite as Bubbie added, "The secret my dear is the cream cheese, it has to be the perfect temperature."

Ryder took another bite of the cookie as, he asked, "So how is our patient?"

"Which one?" Bubbie asked. "The one that put cheese dip in her soup or the one that is suffering from heartbreak because of being stood up for her date?" *Marissa* he thought. "Again huh? Some boy let her down huh? Some jerk."

"I wouldn't call him a jerk," Bubbie said. "He is pretty good most of the time. He just got side tracked on this one."

"We will have a big brother to sister talk in the morning," Ryder said as he headed towards the back staircase.

"Wrong heart," Bubbie said as Ryder stopped and turned back to her.

"Ceelia?" Alex questioned. "My little girl? Who broke her heart?"

"The one that she loves the most," Bubbie said.

Ryder still didn't understand. "Take a look in the trash." Ryder turned and looked down into the trashcan that was near the stair, lying on top was her purse, two tiaras each glistening with bright simulated stones, a tea play set, and two sheer like scarf's one red and one purple. Ryder picked the can up and carefully laid each item out on the counter.

"Oh damn," Ryder said with remorse. "The tea party. I promised her. I feel like the slime under a slugs butt."

"Motek," Bubbie said. "You got a very sad and mad little girl upstairs." She walked over to him and explained. "She stood right there on the bottom step, where you are and said. '"A daddy never breaks his promise." Ryder let out a deep sigh as he dropped his head down and rubbed his fingers over his eyes. He felt almost like crying and felt a sharp pain in his chest.

"It is all right Rick," Alex said. "I will explain to her that work came up and there is going to times when..."

"No," Ryder said. Cutting her off and lifting his head. "I am the one who let her down and now I have to pick her back up." He looked down at items in the trash and then at Bubbie. He bent down and picked the items out of the trash. "Bubbie while I get cleaned up can you lay out my tuxedo and uh…" he grinned as he added. "Make me and my date some tea?"

Ryder went upstairs took a shower, shaved, brushed his teeth, styled his hair and dressed in his tux that Bubbie had laid complete with cufflinks as he was finishing up the bow tie. Yakira who had been asleep in the bed woke up and saw him.

"Where are you going dressed like that?" She asked pushing herself up out of bed.

"I have a date with a beautiful girl," he said as he checked his cufflinks one more time.

"What?" Yakira said as she stood up and he walked towards the door. "What girl?"

"The one down the hall," he said as he opened the door and stepped out into the hall and Yakira followed after him. With tone as serious as he could be he added, "We have a date for tea."

He walked down the hall two doors down and opened the door; it was Ceelia's room when she stayed here. The walls were painted light purple with murals of unicorns. He turned on the light; he felt that tug in his chest again as he looked at the room.

Ceelia had decorated the room all by herself. Using red streamers taped to the walls, stretching them across the room, through the headboard of her bed and over to the wall on the far side, the streamers were not that far off the floor, only as high up on the wall as a five year old could reach. The louvered closet doors were pulled back. Tossed on the floor was a princess dress. And in front of the closet was a small white metal table with four small chairs placed around. In two chairs were stuffed animals, *Mafoo*, a dark blue elephant and Cotton, a dingy pink dog. On the table spread out as a table cloth was a bath towel and in the middle a stick that was stuffed into a pot of molding clay. But there was one thing missing Ceelia.

"She is in my room," he heard Bubbie say. He turned and saw her standing in the door way, she was holding the items on a tray. "She said that Mr. Ryder could take all this stuff down and that this was not her room anymore."

He picked up the princess dress and walked out of the room; he grabbed the crowns on the tray, and turned to Bubbie. "Bubbie can you set the table?" The room that Bubbie used was the maid's room down stairs. That was at the back of the kitchen behind the stairs.

Ryder opened the door and walked in. There were two rooms to the maid's quarters, the main bedroom, which was at the back and a living area that was decorated with a couple of chairs and a sofa. There was an end table with a lamp on it at the head of the sofa.

Through the moonlight that was shining through the window he could see the little girl asleep on the sofa, covered with a blanket and her head on a pillow. She was curled like baby, her hands tucked under her head.

He sat down on the sofa bedside her and turned on the lamp. He took hold of her arm and gently said, "Hey beautiful princess wake up. Wake up beautiful." He said a little louder and shaking her again.

Her bright eyes beamed opened and she looked up at him, at first she smiled then she remembered how mad she was. "Mr. Ryder so you are back now?"

"I am here for our date."

"That was hours ago Mr. Ryder." Ceelia said crossing her arms in front of her as she sat up, her lip stuck out in a pout as she added, "And you were not there Mister Ryder."

"I thought you called me daddy?" Ryder asked. "Please honey! Don't call me that."

"Daddy's don't break promises Misters do."

"Now young lady I didn't break my promise to you," Ryder leaning his face closer to hers. "I said our date was for today." He looked over at the clock on the nightstand. "Well Cinderella it is 11 o'clock there is still an hour to go in the day." He laid the dress down beside her and said, "Now you get dressed and I will meet you outside." He stood and as he walked towards the opened door, he a heard a scuffle of feet moving away. He turned to her and said. "Daughters have to keep promises too."

As he stepped outside he knew he was being watched, "All right!" he said. "You don't have to hide." Peering around the corner of the stairs was Alex, Marissa and Bubbie who held in her hand the two scarves, she handed them to Ryder. The door opened and out stepped the little girl now wearing her princess dress with its purple skirt and sequined top. Ryder kneeled down in front of her, placed the jeweled tiara on her head as he said, "Your crown my princess." Then he took the purple scarf and placed it around behind her and it flowed out like a cape. "Your wrap your highness."

"Oh darling!" Ceelia said with mocking upper crest tone. "This simply will not do. We must fix you up." She laced the other crown on his head and stuffed the other scarf around his collar as she said, "And yours too, daddy."

He stood and held his arm to her and with his lips perched, "May I escort you to the tea party?"

"Yes you may." She said taking his arm. They walked past the others and up the stairs to Ceelia's room. She went to the closet and pulled out two pairs of high heels, which she had retrieved from her mother's closet. She handed him a pair of the stilettos and said, "We have to wear heels, this is a very fancy party." Alex wore a size seven shoe and there was no way they were going to fit his feet. But he removed his shoes and stuffed at least his toes into the bright red shoes.

"Have a seat *deary*," Ceelia said as she pulled out a chair for him. "And I will pour the tea." Ryder took a couple of steps, the shoes twisting under his feet nearly falling he caught himself.

"Oh my poor shoes," He heard Alex say and turned and saw them standing giggling in the hallway.

"I will buy you another pair," Ryder said as he saw her lift her camera up to take a photo. "I will get you designer shoes, made just for you if you don't take that photo."

"I don't care if you give a million dollars, this is a keeper!" Alex said with grin and a laugh as she took the photo. Bubbie and Marissa also raising their phones to take a photo. Ceelia marched over to the door, the shoe flopping on her tiny feet. She grabbed the door and said forcefully, "This is a private party. And you are not invited!" She slammed the door.

The little girl walked back to the table and picked up a domino and acted as if it were a lighter using the stick as the candle. "Imagine them trying to crash our party." She poured tea, which was water into the cup and handed Ryder a cookie. She poured herself a cup and a cookie. She took a small bite of the cookie and took a drink of the pretend tea, making sure her pinkie was sticking out. Ryder did the same.

"Tell me about your day *deary*." Ceelia said with a flip of her hand and batting her eyelashes.

"Oh it was nothing *deary*," Ryder said mocking the same movements she had done as he took a sip from the tiny cup that nearly disappeared in fingers. "You are the princess you surely had a more exciting day. Do tell me all about it."

"It was just dreadful. Just had to do so many princess things everybody wanted something. Oh and help is just so hard to find." She took a sip of the pretend tea, then a small nibble of the cookie dabbing her lips with a napkin. "*Mafoo* told me that Cotton was missing and she hired me to find him. I told her it was a dollar a day." Ceelia again took a sip of the pretend tea, dabbed her lips again with the napkin then continued," "Could you not believe it *Mafoo* could not even come up with a single dollar."

"Did you help anyway?" Ryder asked as he crossed is legs, the napkin spread across his lap. Hands that were made to toss a football down field or hold a Glock were now gripping a tiny tea cup. He brought the cup up to his lips and took a sip and dabbed his lips.

"Yes I did," Ceelia said. "I found him hiding in the closet down stairs." She shook her head as she said, "Cotton can be so weird." She took the napkin from her lap and placed it on the table as she said. "But, enough about me. Let me do something for you." She reached over and grabbed his hand pulled it over closer to her and said, "Those nails are awful let me fix them for you."

"Oh could you *deary*?"

Ceelia carefully painted Ryder's nails bright blue, and then her own nails in the matching shade. Nearly an hour had passed and Ryder reached up and removed the crown and placed it on the table. He kicked off his shoes as he looked at the clock on the night stand. The hands of the clock were almost standing straight up.

Downstairs he could hear the grandfather clock start to chime, "It is midnight Cinderella," he said using his regular voice, "Time to turn back into my little girl. Go get ready for bed and I will tuck you in." She stood and slipped out of the shoes she was wearing. He reached down and picked up one shoe. "I will keep one shoe so I can find my princess again." She disappeared into her bathroom. As she brushed her teeth and dressed into pajamas he removed the streamers and pushed the table back into the closet. When she emerged she was still wearing her tiara.

He lifted her up and put her in her bed pulling the covers up around her. He took the crown from her head and placed it on the nightstand beside the bed. "Good night darling." He said giving her a kiss. He headed for the door and turned off the light and just opened it a crack when he heard her say, "You are not a mister, and you are a daddy."

"See you in the morning."   He closed the door behind.

He made his way down the hall and opened the door to his bedroom and was quickly met by Yakira who planted a hard kiss on him, "What was that for?" He asked, as her eyes sparkled like a mountain stream in the sunlight.

"You are a good dad!" She said. She placed her hand on her tummy and added, "And this little one is going to love you so much."

Ryder walked over to the bed, removing his jacket and bow tie he sat down on the bed, and looked at his fingers and said, "I have a question for you. How do you get finger nail polish off?" Yakira smiled even wider and sat down beside him as she said.

"Correction the greatest dad!"

Chapter 33

Next morning Ryder awoke. He was lying on his back. Yakira cuddled up next to him on her side, her arm draped across his bare chest. Her other hand was down to the side and she held on to his hand. Her head tucked up next to his. With each breath he could take in the sweet aroma of honeysuckle perfume. He heard her exhale as her hair dropped down over her face. Using his free hand he carefully pushed her hair back exposing her ears.

"Why did you do that?" She asked as she woke up. "Don't look at my ears." She pushed her hair back down covering her ears. "My ears are ugly."

"They are not." Ryder again uncovered her ear and kissed it. "Everything about you is beautiful. From your ears," he tossed the covers back exposing her bare legs and feet and he crawled down to the foot of the bed and picked up one of her size five feet and stubby toes, and continued, "down to the cute little toes…" He kissed the top of her foot. With her underneath him, he crawled on his hands and knees back up to her and looked down into her eyes. "And back up to this gorgeous face." He kissed the end of her nose and then his lips savoring for a moment the taste of her, he said " How you doing mommy?" He smiled and then he moved down to her stomach. She was wearing panties and one of his old KC football jerseys to sleep in. He lifted the jersey up and revealed her bare tummy and the bump that was their child. He used his finger to lightly trace around her tummy.

"Hey little one," he whispered into her belly. "I am your daddy. I can't wait to see you. I am going to tell you it is one messed up world out here. And when you go to school and start telling about your family the teacher is going to be left with a dumb look on her face. So let me see if I can explain this. I am a believer in Jesus but your mother is Jewish so being born to a Jewish mother, you will be born Jewish. Your grandparents are also Jewish, as is your great grandmother, oh but she is a delight. But your great uncle is a Catholic priest, now my little sister is going to be your Aunt Marissa, when we are out most people will think she is your sister because she is young enough to be that. In reality she is your half aunt because we had the same father but different mothers. You will also have a big sister, Ceelia, whose mother you will call Aunt Alex, but her real name is Isabelle, but everyone calls her Alex. In reality she is not your aunt, but Ceelia is your sister, because I am yours and her father. Then there is the thing about your aunt Annalisa…" Ryder could feel Yakira's tummy shaking and he looked up at her.

"How are you going to explain that one?" She asked laughing, holding hand over her mouth. Her tummy jiggling with each giggle.

"We will wait until you are little older," Ryder said again looking down at her tummy. "Say—about when you are thirty. But anyway growing up you are going to have a Christmas tree but at the same time you will celebrate Hanukkah. You will celebrate Passover but you will also have an Easter basket and hunt for Easter eggs. I know—I know. You are freaking now and saying I am just going to stay in there. But you don't want to do that, you see all these people I told you about, you don't have to worry about who they are to you, but only what they are to you- family. Kid when you get here we will love you more than you could ever possibly imagine."

Yakira lowered her hand from her mouth and placed it on her stomach. "He is right, there are a lot of people that will love you, but not as much as me."

"Daddy," he heard a small voice say from behind the door. He pulled Yakira's jersey down, rolled back onto the bed and said.

"Yeah Darling come on in."

The door knob twisted and the door pushed open and Ceelia trotted in. Her head was down staring at the floor; in her hands was the purse that Ryder had given her, she lifted her head there were tears in her eyes. "It is broken!" She whimpered as she held the purse up. She crawled up on the bed next to him and said, "Make it better. Fix it please."

He took the purse and examined it. The strap that was attached with a rivet had broken. "We can glue this back together." He said has he placed his hand behind her head rustled her hair.

"Ricky!" He heard Marissa say, Ceelia had left the door open. She was dressed standing in the hallway and looking in. "Why aren't you ready? We need to get to town!"

"What for?"

"It is Thursday! My driver's test!" She said with force stepping into the bedroom. "I have been studying. Now I am ready! I want to get my permit."

"First I have to fix this for Ceelia and get some breakfast made..."

"NO!" Marissa bemoaned. "You told me if I pass this I can be back on the investigation. And I want to get started."

"Here," Yakira said reaching over taking the purse. "I will fix this you go with her." Yakira stood and held her hand out for Ceelia to take, which she did. Hanging onto Yakira's hand Ceelia leaped off the bed. Yakira cried out in pain grabbing her back.

"Are you okay?" Ryder asked quickly standing and running over to her.

"I'm fine," she said. "I just probably didn't drink enough yesterday it was so hot." She continued to lead Ceelia out of the room.

Ryder got dressed and headed downstairs where he was met by Marissa waiting with a cup of coffee and a doughnut for him for breakfast. Alex was wrapped in a light colored robe, which was part of the guest room. She sat at the table reading the Barry County Advertiser sipping on a cup of coffee and snacking on a doughnut, her legs crossed and her bare foot swinging back and forth. She looked up from the paper as Marissa grabbed him by the arm and was pulling him through the kitchen not even giving him time to eat or drink the coffee.

"Can you print that bottle?" He asked.

"Got it in the fish tank as we speak," Alex explained referring to the fact she was using the vapors of Super Glue ® to get the fingerprints off the bottle. "Also running the control number, should hear back in an hour or two."

"Let me…" Ryder tried to say, Marissa still pulling at him and leading him towards the garage.

"Come on!" Marissa demanded. Alex stood and walked over to the hall.

"When we get done there I am heading over to Neosho!" Ryder said as Marissa pulled him out into the garage.

He drove her into town and as he made the turn onto highway 248 and crossed the bridge, he looked down at Flat Creek. How many times he had seen the water rolling along and pushing up out of its banks, but today it was just a gentle stream. However, it wasn't a gentle stream flowing through his little sister. He heard her take a deep quick breath as he turned the car into the spot where the testing area was. Two more quick breaths as he stopped. He looked over at her and her face was pale as she sat holding on to the door handle. He stepped outside, it was only ten minutes after ten in the morning but already he could feel the summer heat baking down on the valley. He walked over and opened the passenger's door. She let her hand fall from the handle of the door as she sat staring out the windshield at the building that she was to go into.

"You are not telling me you are nervous about this are you?" He asked as she didn't reply and just looked up at him. He took her by the hand and pulled her up and out. "You got this! She looked at him forcing a small grin to her face. He let go of her hand. "You got your birth certificate?" She nodded her head and walked towards the door of the office; she took a hold of it and raised his voice so she could hear. "Marissa! You got this!"

She was in there for a little over an hour, it was just enough time, for Ryder to do what he wanted to, make calls. He felt a little proud himself as she bound out of the building. "I passed!" She said with glee holding up the test. "Only missed one." A trip back up town to the DMV to get the permit and as soon as she exited she said what any teen would, "Can I drive?"

"No not right now," Ryder said as he led her back to the car. "This car has got way too much horsepower for you.

"Can we get a breakfast burrito?" She asked. "I was so nervous I couldn't eat this morning."

"I was just thinking the same thing," Ryder said. "We will go to the Sonic."

Ryder pulled into the drive-up at the Sonic and passed by several empty parking spots, instead he chose to drive around and park up next to another car. He ordered drinks and breakfast burritos.

The car that he parked next to was a custom one of a kind; a 1977 Impala coupe; painted purple metallic with broad white twin stripes with ghost flames that ran down the center of the hood and the trunk. The center portion of the roof was removed and opened to the sky. Behind the opening in the roof was a spotless white vinyl roof and the rear quarter windows were covered with slotted louvers. He looked at the Chevy and said, "Isn't that a good looking car."

"Love the purple." She said bending forward so she could see it.

"I have got to take a closer look at that!" Ryder opened the door and got and walked over to the car. He went around gazing at it. He looked at the front end, at the sloped down nose and blacked out grille with the SS logo in the center. It was a modified 1992 Monte Carlo SS front end. Molded into the hood were twin hoods Mach I style hood scoops, he used his fingers to push the flaps in as he said. "These things are functional."

At this point Marissa quickly got out of the car, "Ricky!" She warned. "What are you doing?"

"Just checking out a cool car," he said walking around the car and Marissa followed him. He continued to walk around the car, at the back the taillights were three custom round inset old Impala taillights. And a lip like rear spoiler with the SS logo painted in between the white stripe. Ryder walked around the car to the driver's side. He placed his hands on the Targa roof and looked down at the white bucket seat interior. The back seat was custom, to make room for a padded roll bar.

"Ricky!" Marissa said grabbing his arm trying to pull him back. "This is somebody's car! They are going to freak out."

"Look at this!" Ryder said sitting down in the seat.

"What the hell are doing?" Marissa said. "You can't get in somebody's car!" as he sat down in the driver's seat and looked down at the custom dash, the round speedometer and tachometer, the other gauges, the console that housed a custom shifter that controlled the automatic transmission.

"The instruments are laid out like a 1968 Corvette." Ryder said, "And what a stereo system." He ran his hands over the SS logo that was embroidered into the head rest. "I wonder what this thing has under the hood. He looked around and reached down and popped the hood latch and the hood popped up. he got out and lifted the hood and there perched under the hood was a custom small block fuel injected 350 Chevrolet powerplant with chrome valve covers, but the fuel injection was hidden under what looked like an air clearer from a 1969 Camaro.

"Ricky!" Marissa pleaded with him. "You are going to get arrested."   About that time a county cruiser turned into the Sonic driveway and turned on emergency light as it pulled in behind the custom car.

"I am glad you are here sheriff!" A woman said as she pushed the door open and stepped out from the Sonic. She seemed irate as she stormed up to the car and Brian stepped out of the cruiser. "This guy has been all over this car. And it is not his! You know how hard my dad and I worked to get this car looking this way?"

"Oh chill out!" Ryder said shutting the hood and turning to the woman.

"I want him arrested!" The woman said to Brian.

"You do know who this is?" Brian asked.

"Yes Rick Ryder, but I don't care how much money he has. He just can't touch someone else's car."

"Please!" Marissa begged of the woman. "Can't we just forget about this? There was no harm done. Please don't arrest my brother!" She turned and begged of Brian.

"I will tell you what, I will buy the car," Ryder said. "Name the price!"

"Some things are not for sale!" The woman shot back "This was a gift!"

"Everything has a price!" Ryder said. "Name it 50 thousand, hundred thousand..."

"It was a gift! Given by a brother to his sister," the woman turned to Marissa and asked. "But if you want to sell it what is your price."

"Well I would..." The woman held the keys up to a dumbfounded Marissa. She was still not understanding what was happening, even when the staff of Sonic came out cheering and clapping along with a middle aged man with thinning red hair swept over in a desperate attempt to cover the ever creeping baldness. It was Gene Weston the man who built the car and the Killer Bee.

It didn't make sense to her until Ryder took the keys from Mrs. Weston and dropped them into her hand and said, "Happy Birthday darling."

"This is my car?"

"I thought about waiting until next year but you need to get used to it. Gene didn't have it done on your birthday." Ryder said.

"This is my car!" She asked still confused.

"Her name is Karla," Gene said as he walked up to Marissa. "Say hello to her." To Gene each car he made was a work of art that had soul and life, and needed a name.

"Hello Karla," Marissa said as he placed her hand on the side on the hood.

Gene walked over to the Killer Be and whispered to the car, "Lisa this is Karla, she is going to come and live with you. But don't worry you are still my great beauty." He put his hand on the purple car and added. "Karla this is Lisa."

"Gene," Ryder said. "Can you take Lisa back to my house for me? Keys are in her. We will take this one."

After eating, at Marissa's insistent they ate at the tables outside of the drive in, then with her driving headed for Neosho. Riding in a car with an open targa top is much like being in car with a t-top, you just don't have that center bar, the wind swirls around in the interior messing up hair, but it is worth it. Gene had made two different tops, one a canvas that could be snapped into place if you got caught in a rain storm, and back home in the garage was the hardtop, that was made of smoked glass. Marissa pulled into the parking lot of the Neosho Daily News.

Before he could open the door, Marissa had walked around and opened it for him. "My car!" She said as she opened the door. "I open the door for you." Ryder turned and grabbed the roll bar that was right behind the front seats and stepped out and she closed the door behind him. "So what are we here for?" Marissa asked pushing her hair back out of her face.

"To see a reporter," Ryder said. "Ask a few questions of our own." He grabbed the front door of the newspaper offices, opened it and continued inside. "We are here to see Millie Rollins." Ryder said as he removed his sunglasses. They were shown back into the guts of the news room, to a small office where he was placed in a chair in front of a small desk that was piled with papers around a computer terminal; Marissa was seated next to him.

Mille entered and Ryder stood greeting her and she returned the greeting "Mr. Ryder—uh Rick—I mean Detective Ryder." She remembered he did not like being called mister and she quickly corrected herself. She sat down and he did too and she continued. "You said this was about the Sergeants' Club at Crowder? I would be very interested in what you know about it. With my other source…"

"You mean yourself."

She took a deep breath and leaned back in chair, and it let out a squeak followed by a moan, "I was never part of the Sergeants Club!"

"Don't lie to me."

"I am not!"

"Again," Ryder said. "That is you. You are your source. I checked you out. Journalism was your major at both Crowder and University of Kansas, you excelled at it. There are only two ways your source could be used, either it's you or you made it up. You are too good to lie. So…" Ryder reached into his pocket and pulled out the list of names that Malcolm had given him. "This is a list of the names that were part of the club." He handed her the list and she looked at it. "I checked the records at Crowder, there was only one Millie Snyder registered at the school during that time. That is you." He reached into his pocket again and produced the photo of the group in the music room. "However, when I look at the photo I don't see you in it."

"Because I wasn't part of it."

"How many positions are available in the club?"

"Fourteen."

He slid the photo across the desk to her, "Count how many are in the photo." She did as she was told and then said.

"Thirteen." She replied handing the photo back to him.

Ryder slid the photo over again to her and said, "Count them again, there are fourteen in this photo the thirteen in front of the camera and the one behind it. You are the one behind it."

"You are wrong," Millie said. "That is not me. She turned and lifted up a pile of paper and produced a playing card, it was turned face down. She slid the card out and as she spoke she turned the card over. "That is my rank." Ryder looked down at the card it was an 8 of clubs.

"I don't understand," Ryder said picking up the card. "The way I understand this club, there were kings, queens, jacks, jokers and..."

"The ace of spades," Mille replied. "Your mother, I knew her." Millie leaned back in her chair. "Unlike any other club, the members didn't choose if you got in or not, or your rank, it was left to the fates, the fates of the card. Fifteen people were selected I chose the wrong card I was black balled and had to leave. For a while everything was the same, I was even invited to Annie's baby shower, but after her son was born. Then no one in the club would even say hi to me in the halls. It was like I died and didn't matter anymore."

"How did you hear about the thing they did?"

"I spied on them." Millie said. "There are many structures, including tunnels on the old Camp Crowder grounds. They used one of those tunnels for a meeting place. I saw your mother cut each of their palms collect the blood in silver cup and each of them drank from it. Swearing their allegiance to each other, and the secret that they buried."

"All of them?"

"No," Millie said with a shake of her head and said, "Only seven of them. Your mother, Annie, Paul, Charlotte, Beulah, Monica and…" Millie picked up the photo and pointed to it and the one that is behind the camera, Stephanie Granger better known by her stage name Stevie Lace."

Chapter 34

"Stevie Lace cannot be found!" The Fox News reporter said. *"The lead guitarist for the rock band Steelace has not been seen since her band mate, and front man of the group Paul Steele was found murdered at Crowder College in Neosho, MO two weeks ago. Police are not considering her a suspect in Steele's slaying, however friends and family members are concerned about her well being. Steele and Lace were a credited song writing team that were responsible for such hits as "Give Me Your Love, Gone, Gone, A Little Good News and just recently, Don't Need Love. Lace is to sing the National Anthem at the St. Louis Cardinal's home game tonight for the fourth of July, but no confirmation has been heard that she will show. I asked her management group, do they fear she could be suicidal, but they refused to answer."*

Some time had passed and clues were becoming nonexistent. The Super Glue test revealed no prints on the bottle at all it had been wiped clean, and the control number checked back to being delivered in April of this year to the University of Arkansas for Medical Sciences in Little Rock.

The next few weeks were easy going, just trying to wrap his mind around the fact that new life would soon be in his crowded house. As he sat there leaning back in the soft comfortable recliner in the living room; he thought about it. Yakira said it was going to be a boy. A son would be nice he thought, "My boy!" He said softly to himself.

"Reece," he heard Yakira say as she walked into the room. He picked up the remote and turned off the TV, he laid the remote back down on the end table that was between two easy chairs. He watched as she walked into the room, clearly showing now. She stood in front of him and continued, "That was what you were thinking names for our baby? I like Reece. It fits you know. Reece Ryder, and if it is a girl it would also work."

"I like it," Ryder said as he reached up and took a hold of both of her hands. "So how is he doing?"

"Sleeping I guess," she said. "The past few days he hasn't moved much." She looked back over her shoulder at the blank TV screen and asked "You think she is dead?"

"Who?" Ryder asked as she carefully seated herself in the other recliner.

"Stevie," Yakira said as she pushed out the footrest of the chair and leaned back. "You told me you think someone is murdering the members of the Sergeants' Club and she was a member."

"I don't know," Ryder said as he stood up and walked over to the window and gazed out across the front lawn. "This killer is unusual. It all seems tied together. Yet each one is different. Annie murdered in her car, another in their home their homes, Charlotte in her business, and Steele was left so public." Ryder turned back to Yakira and added, "I have to think there was some reason for that."

"Maybe because he is the bigger name," Yakira said. "Everyone knows who he is?"

"Why is it every one of the victims have codeine in their system? The tox-report shows more than 3000 mg in his system."

"Isn't that a lot?"

"Enough to kill," he heard Alex say as she walked into the room in her hand was a written report. "And if it was mixed with something bitter say gin you would not even know it. A quick check of Rolling Stone magazine shows Paul Steele's favorite drink was gin and coke. Ryder, I checked the toxicology reports again, for something they all had in common and each and every one tested positive for a trace of alcohol."

"But Annie didn't drink," Yakira said pushing herself up from the chair. "We had her down for the Passover meal, she wouldn't even drink wine."

"But was she always that way?" Alex asked. "An alcoholic can't even get near the stuff. What if the reason that Annie barely had any codeine in her system is because she recognized the taste of the booze and wouldn't drink anymore. And you know that stain we found in Steele's rental car? It was codeine. Someone spilled it."

Out of the corner of his eye he caught movement, someone else was walking into the living room, it was his sister Marissa. She too was holding a printed out page. "Alex," She said as she entered. "I got that information you wanted me to look up."

"Steelace was playing the Merriweather which is just outside of Baltimore at the same time *Cynthia Hayes* was killed." Marissa said. "And when Annie and Charlotte were killed Stevie was being placed in the special section of the Hard Rock Hotel as part of Oklahoma's Hall of Fame just a few minutes away in Tulsa. She was born and raised in Oklahoma."

"And what about Steele? " Ryder asked.

"I asked Min a question that you didn't?" Marissa said. "It seems he was not alone. Stevie was with him. Min told me that Stevie said she was going back home to Lenapah, Oklahoma. Yet no one has seen her there, it is small town."

"That gives her no alibi," Alex said.

"You think she is the killer?" Ryder questioned. "What is the motive?"

"I don't know." Alex said. "But I think we need to visit Lenapah, OK."

"What about the professor at the University of Arkansas, did you check him out?"

"Not today!" He heard Bubbie say as she walked into the living room, dressed in her apron. "It is our country's birthday. *Take the day off!* Her last words more of a warning than a suggestion. Bubbie was right, it was Independence Day, the Fourth of July, the day that America grew a year older, it wasn't a time of murder and mayhem, but a time to reflect what, as a nation, America stood for, the true bright shining star on the hill. To fire up the grill and cook hamburgers and kosher hotdogs, serve it up with potato salad, baked beans, and potato chips that end up in the hands of three five year old girls that scream to the heavens as they dash at full speed through the sprinkler that has been set up in the yard, and screams even louder as the cold water hits them. And even louder screams from teenage girls lounging in swim suits by the pool as they are hit by the stream of a water gun wailed by the said five year old girl who screams as her fifteen year old sister was after her with another water gun.

As adults sat under the shade of the large oak tree, legs stretched out from lawn chairs that circle the sacrifice of every Fourth of July; a large striped rattlesnake watermelon in a galvanized tub of ice water, waiting until dark, when it will be sacrificed under the blade, its sectioned corpse craved into wedges and passed out to every hand there. The only question left was whether to use salt or not.

And it seems then that the celebration slows as all wait for darkness, here it is summer nights that just tick by. "Is it dark enough for the fireworks?" Ceelia asks

"No not yet!"

"How about now Daddy?" a struggle faced face asks desperate to see the show in the sky. And a smile can only be generated again by lighting a bamboo sparkler and allowing the child to paint the night air. "How about now?"

Nine thirty five p.m. "It is time!" Ryder said which brought cheers from the guests. There was Brian Thompson and his wife Lee Ann, and their daughter. Brian's brother Thom and his son Zack who had brought Marissa a soda, and even opened it for her; she invited him to sit on the blanket on the ground beside her, bringing giggles from her three girl friends. Also there, seated in the lawn chairs was Yakira's mom and dad Pascal and Rebekah and of course Bubbie. Also there were a couple more friends that were on the Wildcat football team that live in Barry County and from Kansas City during his days of being a homicide cop, his friend Captain Ben Malloy, now the head of the K.C. homicide and his wife Jeannine.

"Need help?" Malloy asked sitting in a lawn chair, his arm draped around his wife.

"Malloy," Ryder joked. "I need someone who can run. You try and I would end up having to air-a-vac you out of here." Ryder looked over at his other guest, who was just standing there sipping on a can of soda; it was his uncle, Father Anthony. "You are elected!" He and his uncle went down the hill to a spot where he had cleared off and made a pad so that the fireworks could be shot off.

Roman candles zoomed into the air creating a dazzling sparkle of color, rocket shot into the air exploded into streams of red, green, yellows, and oranges and a haze of smoke drifted across the fields, it smelled like a battlefield and another rattling crack of pops and bangs, that come in between cheers from the crowd.

Ryder could see his uncle's face in the glow of the punk lighter that he was using. He picked up a large rocket, "I can take care of this," he said and I will wire a few of these things up together along with some whistler, you go be with your lady." He grinned. "We are Irish son, we believe in the luck and kissing your true love under fireworks will bring you double good luck." As Ryder walked back up the hill, behind him was an array of fireworks that was to be the grand finale. He walked over to where his bride sat in a chair.

The air grew still like after a major storm and she asked, "Is it over?"

"No," He said, then raising his voice so the crowd could hear. "Everyone stay put! This grand finale is going to take a little while to get it ready. It will be worth it." He lowered his voice and held his hands out and Yakira took them and he helped her to her feet. "Uncle Tony told me that kissing your true love under fireworks would bring good luck. Not sure if it is a Jewish thing or not, but you want to try?"

She grinned broadly and said, "I don't need fireworks, we always made them." With that he lowered his mouth to hers and enveloped her in a kiss. Rocking gigantic bursts of fireworks slammed into the sky and he could feel each burst in his chest. But again he was not sure if it was the fireworks or what he felt for her. That was how she made him feel. He finished his kiss and held her close, cheek to cheek they gazed up at the sky glowing in red glitter, gold white glitter, with a sea of blue filling the sky as more and more and more shot into the air, followed by whistles and scream with bangs and booms that seem to shake the very ground under their feet.

Suddenly Yakira grabbed her stomach and let out a moan. "Are you all right baby?" Ryder asked.

"I just shouldn't have had that extra piece of watermelon." She replied as he helped lower her back in her seat, behind them the fireworks shot up again, mortars speeding into the air and exploding with fury over their heads, as sparkling low red, white and blue shined close to the ground. He could see her face wrinkling in pain. As she cried out louder bending over holding her stomach, it also caught the attention of her mother and father who stood up.

"Yakira are you okay?" her mother asked.

"I—think—I—I over did it." She held her hand up for her husband to take it. He helped her to her feet as again." I think I will just go lay down." Ryder was helping her to the house, as crackling tails sparks shouting out their screams as they soared into the air exploding into stars and green and blue bouquets and ending with a gigantic white spiral of flowers. As it was filling the air Yakira cried out, her scream drowning out the pops and bangs as she grabbed her tummy. She was wearing shorts; something was running down her leg. He put his hand down on her leg and raised it up to his eyes

"Blood!" he cried out the fireworks lighting up the entire area. Thom rushed over, he looked at her as she cried out in pain and she held her arms. "Someone call an ambulance!" He shouted as held he held her tightly. Marissa stood up and got on her phone and in tears she was trying to tell the 911 operator what she needed.

Thom dashed over to her; he saw the blood running down her legs. "Ricky," his tone was so somber and serious. Thom was always joking even during an autopsy and his calling him that name made it even more serious. Yakira's whines were coming in short burst in between her shallow breaths. The fireworks were over yet no one saw them, the crowd had gathered around Yakira.

"She is having a miscarriage!" Thom said his voice cracking as he grabbed her wrist to take her pulse. It was a warm summer night, yet as Ryder felt the side of her face she felt cool. "Damn it!" Thom said letting go of her wrist and placed his fingers on her neck.

"Ambulance is on the way." Marissa said her voice cracking as tears ran down her face.

"Ricky," Thom said. "She is going into shock." He rose up and shouted. "Somebody get a blanket! And some pillows." Bubbie dashed into the house as Thom took hold of Ryder's arm. "You got to let go of her. We have to lay her down." Ryder felt heaviness in his chest as he laid her down and let go of her. Bubbie returned with the blanket and Thom spread it over her. He placed the pillows under her feet.

"Where is that damn ambulance?" He heard his sister curse. He stood up and felt her arms grip around him squeezing tighter and tighter and tighter as she began to cry. He grabbed her too, trying to hold it together but he couldn't, he felt tears run down his cheek as he lowered his face to the top of his sister's head.

Thom lifted Yakira's hands and checked her fingers and lips. "Rick she isn't going to Cassville. She's got to go to Springfield. She has to go by chopper. Now!"

"Brian call it in!" Ryder said turning to him.

"I don't know if they will come here."

"Call it in Sheriff!" Ryder shouted back. "You tell them if they want their damn money. They better get their gosh dang asses here! They can use the field across the road it is flat and open. We can use the emergency flashers on the car. Tell them to get here!"

Brian started to dash off to his car to radio the call in, when Thom stopped him by saying. "Sheriff if you have a portable oxygen tank I could use it here."   He looked up at Ryder still holding on to his sister. "I will do my best."

Chapter 35

Standing in front of the window on one of the upper floors in the South Cox Hospital in Springfield, he gazed out over the Queen city and placed his forehead on the cool glass. He closed his eyes and he could see visions of the chopper landing in the fielding in between an area marked off with the cars and the ambulance, Yakira being loaded aboard, and feeling the blast of the rotors as it took off.

"I am so sorry son," He heard a fatherly voice say, he turned around and saw Pascal, a stocky set man with graying hair along the sides of his head, the bald spot covered with a dark colored kipah-skullcap, he usually wore one of the suits that Pascal would make himself by hand, there wasn't a man in Barry county that didn't have one of Pascal's suit. And you can assure yourself that in court, the judge, the D.A. and attorney were all wearing one of his suits. "They did all they could but…they lost him."

Today was different he was in light blue shorts and matching t-shirt. Ryder felt the man's hand rest on his shoulder. That is all he could say, there was no magical words he could say, that would just wipe the pain away, like an eraser over a chalkboard. The pain would remain etched into his heart as if it were a tattoo. "Are you okay? " Pascal asked.

He had asked that question himself, *what a stupid question. How can anyone be okay?* To hold what was once a living breathing part of you and a part of the one you love the most. This was not some glob or mass of cells, there was a face, and fingers and toes, a heart beating that beats no more. He looked down at his hands where he had held him.

"How is Yakira, Ryder?" He lifted his head to the sky and could see the fireworks rising up on the horizon making no sound, but displaying their great beauty in the sky.

"They are still working with her; they can't get the bleeding to stop."

"I can't lose her," Ryder said calmly watching as another stream of glittering lights shot up into the air.

"Have you said a prayer? Pascal asked.

"I don't know if I can..." Ryder slowly turned a back to his father-in-law and added, "I still don't feel that God and I am able to do that. That he wants to hear from me."

"He always wants to hear from us."

"Do you pray for her?" Ryder asked

"I started the day she was born, and haven't stopped since." Pascal said as Ryder could feel the man's hand tighten on his shoulder muscle. "She is my child. And as much as you love her, I loved her first. But the prayers she needs the most now are yours."

"How can you have that much faith?" Ryder asked. Pascal lifted his hand from Ryder's shoulder; he placed his hand on Ryder's palm and then pushed Ryder's fingers close. Ryder could feel something in his hand.

"Reality is a fist," Pascal said "Knowing we must fight our way through the life. Open your hand." Ryder opened his hand and looked down to see it was Yakira's wedding ring; the ER staff had removed it and gave it to him. "Faith is believing that there is something worth fighting for."

Ryder lowered his head and said a soft prayer. "Heal Yakira; don't take her away from me."

"Come on," Pascal said. As he placed his arm around his son-in-law's back. "Come and be with the family." He led him back down the hallway and into the waiting room.

Another damn waiting room! Ryder thought as he entered. *Why is it that I spend so much time here?* Everything was going through his mind, but nothing was leaving his lips. As Pascal went over and sat next to his wife Rebekah, she too was dressed for the fourth of July in blue culottes and print sleeveless blouse. Ryder continued to walk over to the other side of the room. It was a great room which divided his family and friends on one side, and the Rosen's on the other. Thom sat leaning back in a chair, his legs pushed out in front of him, his hands crossed on his lap over a clipboard; sitting next to him was his son Zack. Two chairs over was his uncle Father Anthony and next to him his sister, she was still wearing her swim suit but covered with a long sleeve shirt. Her bare legs showing, she rested her head in hands, her hair falling down to the sides. And standing there in the middle was Bubbie. She saw him and walked over to him.

"*Motek*," She said softly as she wrapped her arms around him. She released him and looked up at him, tears in her eyes as she added. "My heart is broken for you." She lowered her voice and continued, "I saw how you talked to him."

He heard Thom clear his throat as he stood up. Out of the corner of his eye he could see him walking up to him. "Ryder," He said. "I am talking to you as the county coroner of Barry County now. Cause of death will be considered accidental due to miscarriage." Ryder swallowed hard, as he turned to him. "The hospital wants to know what you want to do with it, the fetus."

"Thom," Ryder said softly fighting his emotions. "I…"

 "You want me to take care of things for you, the funeral and burial or cremation." Thom said.

"No cremation!" Pascal said upset as he stood up quickly, walked over to where Ryder stood. "Please Rick, no matter how you would have raised him. He was born to a Jewish mother, he was a Jew. It was his heritage."

Burial, right next to his grandmother," Ryder said as he swallowed again, trying to not show any tears.

"She would have loved him," Bubbie said.

"Do you want a name or just Baby Ryder?"

"Reese," Ryder said his voice just at the point at cracking. "His name is..." His voice cracked even more as he fought back tears and corrected himself, "His was Reese Pascal Anthony Ryder." He took a deep breath and then said, "And you list all his relatives every aunt uncle, friends that were family and make sure you list his sister Ceelia." Ryder quickly signed the papers and then walked over to Marissa. She looked up at him as he held out a hand and said, "Come on sis let's get out of here, and get you something to wear. Something has to be open in this damn town." He pulled her to her feet and they headed for the door, just as Alex walked in. He looked at her. Ryder and Marissa had ridden up with Father Anthony. "I have got to get the hell out of here Alex!" She reached in her pocket and pulled out a set of keys, the hex head Chrysler key hanging from a fob in her hand that went to the Killer Bee.

"It is down in the parking lot across from the main entrance." Alex said. "He had just taken a hold of the keys when the nurse appeared and said.

"She is awake if you want to see her."

Ryder turned back to Alex, she took the keys back, "Go on," She said with a nod of head. "I will take her and find her something to wear."

As he walked into her room she was sitting up in bed, her hair a mess as she held her head down. She must have heard him or maybe it was that she just felt he was there, as she turned her head and looked at him "My baby is gone." She said in solemn tone. "I never got to hold him." Tears were running down her eyes as she asked, "Did you see him?"

"Yeah," Ryder managed to get out as he moved closer to the bed she was in.

"Was he beautiful?"

"Just like his mother," he said as she stood next to her.

"Oh Ricky!" She moaned "I lost him," Suddenly her tone changed to anger. "It was because I was going to be a lousy mother a horrible wicked bitch that doesn't deserve to..."

He sat down on the edge of the bed as he grabbed her face in his hands and looked down at her, saying sternly, "NO! We are not going to do that! I am not going to have you thinking this is your fault. We are not going to blame each other. You hear me!" He removed his hands from her face and grabbed her hands. "We get through this together!"

"How?"

"By holding onto each other even tighter than we have before," He let go of her hands and took the ring that Pascal had given him and slipped it on to her finger. "Forever and ever." She quickly grabbed him around the neck and embraced him tightly.

Together they cried over the loss of their child. That dam of tears that had been held in were released and flowed like a flood. She released him from her embrace and he reached over, pulled out a few tissues from the box on the nightstand, and taking some he dabbed her eyes, then using the same tissue he placed them up to his eyes as he said. "My tears are your tears."

She grinned as he took a tissue from his hand and dabbed his eyes as she said, "If I don't cry, I don't cry." Then they both said together, "But if we weep. We weep together." Then she kissed him. "Still doesn't explain why this happened?"

"It was His will." Ryder heard Rebekah say, as he turned and saw her and Pascal entered the room. The room was mainly dark only the light from the hallway shone over them as she moved closer to the bed and she continued, "whatever the Merciful One does, He does for the best.' This is so, even when those we love die."

Yakira pushed back from her husband and stared at her mother narrowing her eyes as she did, "Do you mean to tell me that it was God's will that my baby should die?" She laughed but it wasn't one of humor it was one of disbelief. "Dear mother," she said. "You are telling me that God wanted me to feel the most pain I have ever felt in my life?" Yakira's voice was rising louder. "That is God's plan for me! I should be grateful? You have been telling me that all my life." She pushed Ryder away and swung her legs around; she was dressed in a hospital gown. She placed her bare feet of the floor and stood on shaky legs as she confronted her mother. "When grandpa died, it was God's will. When Annalisa was murdered, it was God's will. When I broke up with Ricky it was God's will. Now my child dies and it is *God's will*?" She shouted those words. "If this is your God I don't know if I want Him!"

"He is your God, our Lord."

"*No! Mother*," She shouted even louder. "I want a God I can feel. He is not here."

"He loves you child!"

"No, a God that loves me wouldn't do this to me! To make me hurt this much." She screamed out, bringing in a pair of nurses. "If that is God's love I don't want it." She took a step towards her mother and her legs buckled. Ryder grabbed her scooping her up in his arms. He spun her around as one of the nurses tried to escort her mom and dad to the door.

"You will have to leave please you are upsetting the patient." One of the nurses said.

"But she wants her mom and dad." Rebekah said, as they were forced to the door.

Bubbie stuck her head in the door, and said "What about me?"

"I want everyone out of here!" Yakira screamed again as Ryder laid her down on the bed. The other nurse started to escort him away, but she quickly reached and grabbed him by the arm. "Not you! You are all I have." He could feel her fingers tighten around his arm and pull him closer. "Don't leave me." As the nurse pushed her parents out,

Ryder sat down on the edge of the bed again and then she said, "I have never felt so alone in my life Ricky. I feel empty inside. Hold me!" He wrapped his arms around her, he kicked his shoes off, put his feet up on the bed and laid back with her still in his arms. "Tighter," she said. "I still feel alone."

Chapter 36

It was a long night of tears and a never ending embrace of a father holding mother. Ryder awoke with Yakira still in his arms, a blanket draped over them, one of the nurses must have spread it over them, he reasoned. Yakira's head was resting on his shoulder, his other arm draped across her. He needed to get up, so he slowly slid his arm out from under her. Not wanting to wake her up, he crept out of the room and went down the hall to a public restroom, where he went to the bathroom and washed his face and hands.

He just stepped out of the bathroom when he met Father Anthony who asked, "How is she doing?"

"She keeps asking questions," Ryder said walking back down the hall, his uncle by his side, his hands folded behind his back. "Well one question."

"Why?" Father Anthony asked rolling his gaze over to his nephew. "Why would God allow this to happen?" Ryder stopped and turned to him. "And before you ask, I don't know either. Why it is that a hundred year old man that has lived a good life gets to walk out of these doors, but a child that has yet to live is carried out not in the arms of his mother but a box. I can't answer that."

"But you are…"

"A priest?" He replied with almost a laugh. "The one that is supposed to know everything about God? I know no more about Him than you do." Father Anthony said as he placed his hand on Ryder's arm. "I know the words He spoke, how He came here, why He came here, but I kneel before Him just like you do."

"That is not very comforting Uncle Tony."

"You want me to give you whole ten yards about how you will see your son again and he is being held in the arms of the Father. You know there are no magical words to take away the pain. I am not here as a man of the cloth. I am here as part of this family. So how is she doing?"

"She is giving up," Ryder said.

"What?"

"She has lost her faith."

"You mean in God?"

"In all things, you know what she ordered for breakfast? Bacon and sausage. When they told her she couldn't have that, she wanted oatmeal and a piece of toast soaked in bacon grease. She said if I really loved her I would go get her Spare ribs in Kansas City. Her mother came in and saw her again last night and she threw the water picture at her."

"Ricky?" He heard Yakira scream. Ryder dashed into the room, Father Anthony right behind him. "Where were you?" She asked breathless her arms open wide as she grabbed him in an embrace and drew close to him, so close he could feel her heart beating next to his. "I woke up and you were not there! Why weren't you there?" Her hand moved up to the back of his head and her fingers wrapped around his hair. "Don't leave me!"

"I am here," he said softly holding her as he looked over his shoulder at his uncle, confusion sweeping over his face. "I can't take it if you leave me." She released him from the embrace only to grab his face and add in desperate tone, "If you do I will die!"

"I am here!"

Suddenly like the switching of a channel on a TV her emotion changed, she grinned as she released her grip on his face. She leaned back on her pillows and said in pleasant tone, "I am hungry. When is breakfast going to get here? I can just taste that bacon now."

Father Anthony stood there for a moment staring at her then he moved closer before asking, "Have you given up your Jewish faith?"

If she had been taken over by a demon she couldn't have flashed a smile that was more wicked, as she said, "You mean be the good little Jew, and follow all the rules that Moses gave us. Well screw him! Besides…" She laughed in the same manner as her smile, and added, "Did Jesus make everything clean?"

"So you believe in Jesus now?'

"Can't," She said. "For Jesus to be real He has to be the Son of God. There is no God."

"Why do you say that?"

"Because all my life I have heard God loves me," Yakira said her lips turning down into a frown as she added. "No God that loves me would have let this happen." She shook her head and offered that same creepy grin, as she said, "So there is no God!"

Chapter 37

The Dog Days of Summer was a time when Greeks and Romans connected with heat, drought, sudden thunderstorms, lethargy, fever, mad dogs, and of course bad luck. It was the heliacal rising of the star Sirius. When it would become the brightest star in the dark liquid that was the night sky, it was time when the day didn't want to end and night just refused to come. Fans buzzed, and compressors heaved from the work load. Ice cubes in glass were only a small sliver of relief. The moon seemed so close that you could reach out and touch it, but before the face of God could be stroked, the moon would bow its head and sink below the horizon, yet the sky was an inky dark. It was at this point there was just a hint of liberation from the heat, the blast from a fan could find a person sleeping, deep rattling snores emitting from an open window falling on the deaf ears of a city, that has only the glow of the lights that remained, as signs that a red 'closed' beamed their message, throughout the town. The town was Cassville and the town was asleep, except for one light that shone from the back of the Thompson Funeral Home.

There was stillness in the town, it was broken only by the rumble of dual exhaust as the headlights from a 1971 Dodge swept across the back of the funeral home, In an instant the tranquility and darkness returned as Ryder shut the car off and stepped out, the light of the interior of the car spilling out on to the parking lot. He shut the door and headed for the back of the funeral home, the door was unlocked so he opened it and walked inside.

Besides the one single light in the hallway, the funeral home was dark. He swore if he just stopped and listened he could hear the voices of those that never left here. However, that was not the reason he was here. Over to this side of wall were the doors to an elevator. He pushed the button and heard the rattle of the cables as it pulled the car up from the basement. The doors opened and he stepped inside the car. He pressed the button marked 'down'; the doors closed and down the car went. The doors opened and he is in the basement, the coroner's lab. With that blast of cold air that always seemed to blow down the back of his collar and the white walls, it was like feeling he was cold cuts in a refrigerator.

Thom was standing next to the metal table that was in the middle of the room a sheet covering the item that was lying on the table. Thom was dressed in a white lab coat. Coffee bubbling in a beaker over a Brunson burner, Thom put on a heavy glove and carefully poured it into two smaller beakers. He put some sugar and cream in one and handed it to Ryder. "Just the way you like it." He said as Ryder took a sip. "Don't spill any, it might show up on that suit." Ryder was dressed in cream colored slacks and jacket with a bright blue shirt. Thom continued, "I have to ask why you want to do this in the middle of the night?"

"I didn't think Yakira could take it yet, it has only been three weeks since…we lost him." Ryder took a sip and set the beaker of coffee down on a file cabinet on the other side of the room. "Can we get this over with?"

"Welcome to the Valley of the Dead." Thom joked as he lifted the sheet. "Ezekiel is going to connect those dry bones." As he lifted the sheet it revealed the bones of the child's body that was found buried at Crowder. Thom continued, "You mind if I don't play this game?" Ryder looked down at the tiny skeleton; it felt as if someone slugged him right in the chest making his heart stop for a moment. Thom looked over the table at him, and asked, "Are you okay? Sure you can do this?"

"Let's get on with it," Ryder said. "How was he murdered?"

"He wasn't," Thom's blunt and brief answer made Ryder's eye brows twist down in puzzlement. "As far as I can tell, the child suffered no blunt trauma, there was still marrow left in the bones, what little hair I could find showed no signs of long term poison."

"What about the skull?" Ryder asked, "It had come apart wasn't it crushed?"

"A question I missed on my test in medical school. It was tricky question 'How many bones does a human have at the most in their lifetime?"

"That is easy 206."

"No, not when we are born, we have 270 or more, they fuse together shortly after birth." Thom explained, "Some of the bones are not even solid they are cartilage and it turns to bone." He turned and picked up a beaker of coffee he poured for himself and took a sip and then asked, "How old did you say that missing child was?"

"Eight weeks."

"Something is wrong here," Thom says. "Ossification starts right after birth. This is not the skeleton of a two month old infant. It is that of new born. I would say two weeks at the most." Thom walked to the back of the room where a desk was. He sorted through a stack of files and then returned. "There is another question, I used the bone marrow to do blood typing, the child here is AB Negative but according to death records the parents of the missing child were both O Negative."

"AB negative is a rare type," Ryder said. "Double T, we have had this conversation before when Annalisa was murdered. That same type is also mine."

"You know Newton County sent everything over in the box ," Thom said as he picked up a bottle up of his desk, "I found this in the box under the child's body."

"A baby bottle?" Ryder asked seeing the rubber nipple was still intact and there was a dried up dark colored liquid inside the bottle.

"What is interesting is what is in the bottle," Thom explained. "Coke mixed with codeine."

Chapter 38

When Ryder got back to the house, he was met by Yakira who was dressed and wanted to go the cemetery. It was where hers and Ryder's family were all buried. Right across from a small country church, it had no denomination, everyone was welcome through red painted doors, the symbol of the ultimate sacrifice, the symbol was blood. He opened the car door for Yakira and helped her out. In her hands was a single red rose wrapped in baby's breath.

As Yakira continued across the graveyard, Ryder stopped and looked back at the small white country church. Excessive heat warnings were already being issued by NWS out of Springfield, actual temp to be 108 and heat index in the 120's and daybreak was only beginning as the sun broke across the horizon and the rays backlit the church peering through the steeple. It almost gave Ryder a bit of comfort, that maybe; just maybe God hadn't forsaken him.

As the sun rose just a little higher the warm rays caught the stained glass, and it almost seemed to glow, brilliant red, and blues. He turned and watched as his wife kneeled down in front of the small grave, the grass disturbed and a mound of red clay and flint rocks still showed. There was no headstone yet, just a simple metal marker with the name Ryder, Reese with the year of birth and death the same.

There was not a breath of air that could be felt, and already he could feel droplets of sweat forming on his forehead as he stood and watched Yakira drop to her knees in front of the fresh grave. She laid the flowers down on the red rocky soil, next to several other dried decay stems that were once flowers that she brought each day.. Then she dropped her head down and sobbed. "I never got to hold you! But there will never be a day I don't love you." He felt so helpless there was nothing he could say or do for her to ease her pain. He felt the loss of his child, but never what she could be feeling. He placed his hand down on her back. She looked over her shoulder at him, her eyes swollen with tears.

"Are you going to tell me that life goes on?"

"Never," He replied as he helped her to her feet.

"But it does, doesn't it?" She asked looking up at him. "I mean my world comes crashing down but the damn world it keeps on spinning." She looked down at the grave marker. "Those that didn't know him are just going to walk past him and never think of the pain it caused. All that will be said is 'look he died on the same day he was born.' They will never know how much he is missed." She lowered her head on to his chest, and he held her close. "Why did God allow this to happen? She looked up at him and continued, "… all the bad people out there that kill and rob they get to live and he doesn't? "

"I don't know."

"But you are the guy that is supposed to have the answers." She wrapped her arms around his chest tighter, and then said, "But life goes on, including ours. I want you to get back to the investigation and find out who killed Annie."

****

It was going to be a long day and Ryder had hoped for an early start, on the road before 8 a.m. but as the only saying goes 'good plans get changed'. It seemed every time he was ready something came up to change that. First was Ceelia who decided her art works might look better as make up and that she wanted a red dress not a yellow one, which involved a bath and a dress soaking in the sink and after the bath she decided that a hair cut was needed, hers. Four inches falling to the floor, followed by the scream of "Ceelia what the hell did you do!" from a frantic mother.

Yakira agreed to take her to see her hair dresser at Cut-A-Above in town hoping that her hair dresser Andrea could work her magic out of this disaster. After Ceelia's bath and cleaning up the painted mess Alex now needed to change clothes again, Ryder was walking the floor like a convict waiting for his release as he waited for Alex to change.

"I am ready," he heard Marissa say as she walked down the back stairs into the kitchen. Ryder turned to her, it must have been the expression on his face that told her, "I am not going am I?" she sounded disappointed. She walked towards him, dressed in her business style with slacks and a light weight jacket.

"You are fifteen years old Marissa you should be having fun."

"I told you I wanted a job this summer, and you gave this to me." She twisted her head slightly to the side and continued. "If I was working at the Sonic would you be telling me to have fun or go to work. What if you owned a business down town, wouldn't you allow me to work there? Isn't this our family business? Murder?"

"Okay," Ryder said. "But I need you to do something for me to here."

"What is that?"

He walked across the kitchen and over to the refrigerator, opened the door to pull out a pitcher of ice tea. "I want you to go down the list of those in the Sergeants' Club and find out what their blood type is."

"How do I do that?" She asked as he poured the ice tea into a thermos.

"I am not sure," he replied as he screwed the red cap back onto the thermos. And then opened the cabinet door and grabbed a pair of plastic glasses. "First start checking with public records then if you can't find anything, I left the name of a friend of mine in the State Health Department over there on the table. He might be able to help you."

"Why do you need to know this?" She asked as he took the thermos and headed for the hallway that leads to the garage. And she followed him.

"If the baby that was buried wasn't the one taken," Ryder said. "Then who was the child and more importantly whose child was it?" He paused as grabbed the door knob of the door that lead into the garage then said, "Tell Alex I will meet her in the car."

Chapter 39

There is something about a summer day when the thermometer clicks on that 100 degree mark yet the atmosphere is so thick it feels that you could reach up, grab it and ring it out like a wet dish rag. It is then that the air conditioning is nearly running constant and the button pushed to maximum on the dash just to stay cool. The pavement blistering up like a second degree, the flesh being ripped by the tires leaving their prints behind as Ryder parked the car in the lot.

Overhead were clear blue skies, except for a couple of fluffy clouds on the distant horizon that look as if they were rejects tossed from a bottle of aspirin. Something that Ryder needed desperately from the relief of this headache that the heat and this case were giving him.

The University of Arkansas was a large campus, a city of over 30,000 in itself surrounded by the city. It was the home of the Razorbacks. There were many lions, tigers and bears but there was only one named the Razorbacks they are the pride of an entire state. Generations of students, alumni, fans, and entire families would always hold their allegiance till the day they died to the Razorbacks.

It wasn't Ryder's first visit here, in fact when he graduated from Cassville this was one of the many universities that tried to recruit him. At first it seemed odd that when he called the university the president Timothy J. Hacker requested to meet him here. However, standing there on the fifty yard line of the Donald W. Reynolds Razorback Stadium with the large red logo of the razorback under his feet it started to make sense. The razorbacks need a quarterback to cement their trip to the National Championship, but Ryder decided to go to the University of Missouri and that hope didn't come that year.

Ryder stood there with Alex next to him. His eyes shielded by his sunglasses gazing up into the empty red seats, and the bright red lettering under the booth 'The Home of the Razorbacks'. Suddenly there was a flood of lights as the field lights came on and at the end of the field the giant "*PigScreen*", a 30 by 107 foot LED display came to life. With Ryder and Alex larger than life on the screen, Ryder looked around trying to find the camera, but his eyes drew back down to the field as a tall man wearing a light beige suit approached them from the end zone right down the middle of the grid iron. He was tossing a football in his hands, looking at Ryder and getting closer. In a flash the stillness was shattered as a voice boomed over the loudspeakers on the field.

"Now playing quarterback for the Arkansas Razorbacks Number 7, Rick Ryder." With that the tall man threw the football at Ryder. Ryder caught it, his fingers gripping around the laces. The man stopped a few feet away from them and   Ryder noticed he was an older man in his early eighties, his hair Spartan and gray, a large bald spot on top of his head. He had lost a lot of weight since the last time Ryder had seen him,

"Coach Heningway?" Ryder asked.

"Do me one thing." The coach said. "Throw that ball as far as you can."

Ryder stepped back a couple of steps, drew his arm back and using the power of his whole body flung the ball in tight spiral, the ball zoomed down the field and landed in the end zone, right in the second 'R' in the end zone.

"Damn," the coach said. "I could have slept like a baby tonight if you still couldn't have done that. You know how bad I wanted to hear that being said here. Instead you became a Tiger. I could have taken the championship that year, but you see…"

"I was supposed to meet President Hacker here," Ryder said.

"Sorry Rick," He heard a voice say from behind him, as a heavy set man approached from the other end of the field, his hair slightly gray and neatly cut, dressed in a light gray suit with a bright red tie that hung down to his waist. The fragrance of his aftershave arrived first. "He just insisted that he meet you first."

"Coach it was nothing personal," Ryder said turning and facing the man. "I just didn't want to be a Razorback."

"What degree did you get?" The coach asked. "They don't offer criminal justice."

"Art History," Ryder said and Alex looked at him strangely twisting her head around and drawing her mouth up in a half twisted smile. He turned to her and continued, "That's right. I know all about the old masters the Gothic/Proto-Renaissance, Neoclassicism, Romanticism. Giorgione's *Sleeping Venus* and of course Francisco Goya's *Yard with Lunatics.* Guess that painting was the setting for life, as I have been chasing the lunatics ever since." Ryder turned the coach, "I wasn't sent there to get an education, I was there to hold up that crystal football," Ryder said referring to the old national championship award. He turned and looked at President Hacker, "It wouldn't have mattered if I was a Tiger, Razorback or a Hurricane, you didn't care what went into my brain, only what I could hold in my hands." He turned back to the coach and said, "Coach you were no different. Not once when you were trying to get me to come here did you ask me 'what do you want to do with your life?' No, it was all about the how all those in the stands would be cheering for me, all the equipment you had, all the girls you had on campus. I started out a business major, started failing and the school made me change my major, so I could pass with flying colors. All they cared about was I could throw a football 78 yards, with the gentle drop right into a receivers hands. If I failed another class they would move me to an easier class. You know why I chose law enforcement as a career because here I can't fail, if do some will die." Ryder shook his head. And his tone changed. "But that is enough about me. I came here to find answers. I want to see Professor Russell Edwards."

"I couldn't tell you this on the phone." President Hacker said. "He is not here."

"When will he be back?"

"Never," President Hacker replied causing Ryder to twist his eye brows down in puzzlement, so Hacker explained further. "He is dead!"

"Dead!" Alex spoke up. "When did this happen?"

"A few months ago."

"When exactly?" Ryder asked as he reached for the notebook he always carried with him.

"May the 14th," President Hacker explained further. "His daughter found him in his office."

"Murdered?" Ryder asked looking from his notebook as he jotted down the information that Hacker was telling him.

"No! Oh heavens no! His daughter found him. He was just slumped over at his desk. He was going over his plans for the summer classes."

"Was an autopsy done?" Alex asked and Hacker turned and looked at her.

"I don't know, Campus police looked into the matter as did Fayetteville P.D. they found nothing that would indicate murder. He had heart trouble. A couple of years ago he had a heart attack."

"His office, was it given to someone else?"

"No. It was just like he left it."

"Can we see it?"

The Bell Engineering Center was one of many buildings and schools that were on the complex. From the front it favored Mercury's helmet, the sides reaching up like the wings, the windows the empty expression of a face, the structures of the building stood out like the feathers of Mercury's wings, four stories tall.

Standing on the door steps was a man, African-American, the same age as Ryder, stocky built, but about four inches shorter than Ryder. He was dressed in a dark blue suit with a dark red tie done in a Windsor knot and a light blue button down shirt; it was not exactly a uniform but might as well screamed like a madman with a bull horn - law enforcement. As Ryder approached, he saw a small grin break across the man's face, the thin mustache on his upper lip twist upward. As President Hacker introduced him, "This is the head of Campus Police Lyle Canon, Lyle this is…"

"Rick Ryder also known as the 'Pale Rider' for when he comes to town he brings death to the other team."

Ryder was curious of this man's tone, it sounded sarcastic at the least and reprisal at the most, he reached up and pulled down his sunglasses on his nose and stared at the man and asked, "Have me meet before?"

"Once," Lyle drawled out. "On the gridiron." He pulled his jacket and continued, "I was wearing blue then too...Kansas Blue. I was a defender. I read your eyes right down field. I knew right who you were going for, then without looking you sent a bullet downfield the other way to seal the game. So the last time you came to my home you brought heartbreak, what brings you to my town now?

"Murder," Ryder said in a firm tone as he pushed his sunglasses up on his face.

"Murder?" Lyle questioned as he opened the glass door and turned to face him, there was a look of shock on his face. "Professor Edwards? There was no sign this man was murdered." He led them inside and into the elevator, the doors closed and he continued, "What makes you think he could have been murdered?"

"Four others have been, including Paul Steele." Ryder explained as the doors opened and they stepped out.

"The rock star!" Lyle stopped walking down the hall and turned to Ryder. "I heard about him on TV but what does he have to do with the professor?"

"They were all in the same club at Crowder College," Ryder explained. "Now they are being murdered and I have a reason to believe that it all has something to do with the Sergeants' Club."

"He never mentioned anything like that," Lyle said as he returned to walking down the hall. They came to a door that was locked and he unlocked the door and turned on the light. It was a small office, with a desk dominating the room, in the middle it was covered with papers. Two blue added arm chairs were in front of the desk. Behind the desk was a large dark brown high back, tucked button leather judges' chair with a sport coat draped across the back. Behind that a bookcase full of books.

Ryder reached up and removed his sunglasses and slipped them into his jacket pocket as he looked around the room. "Has anything been touched in there?" Ryder asked as he walked around behind the desk. Lying on the desk was a desk pad calendar; he was differently old style, with grade books and with notes written on a sheet that read May, a corner of the page was torn off.

"Nothing has been moved," Lyle said as Ryder searched through the papers. "What exactly are you looking for?"

Ryder continued to search as Alex asked, "Was a tox-report run?"

"Yes."

"Did it show any drugs in his system?"

"*Rosuvastatin, Benazepril* and *Hydro-chlorothiazide*" All drugs used to treat heart trouble.

Ryder checked the pockets of the jacket and there was nothing, he turned to look at Lyle and asked, "Cause of death?"

"Cardiac arrest, so if you are looking for murder here, there is nothing here." Lyle explained as Ryder looked at the bookcase.

It was full of books, mostly about Electrical Engineering and scientific research. Including a couple that Professor Edwards authored himself. Each book neatly placed in its position arranged alphabetically according to author and the title and subject as there was a shelf full of romance books all by the same author Cheri DeAmour, his former Crowder classmate.

"I know it looks odd!" President Hacker said as he moved closer to the bookcase, "Romance novels, but they were all written by a friend of his from Crowder college. The books were pushed up between a pair of lions head book ends. At the end there were two books leaning together *Zula's Time* and *Simona's Rose*. "Hey there is one missing *Wildflower's Passion*"

"How do you know that?" Ryder asked.

"It was the last one, he had just got it." President Hacker said, "There was something odd about that book after reading it he got very upset."

"Why?"

"He said that he couldn't believe that she would write about this."

"What?"

"I don't know," President Hacker said. "He just said 'that she didn't have any right to tell this secret."

Ryder pulled out his notebook and jotted the title of the book down and replaced the notebook in the pocket of his jacket. He looked down at the torn page on the desk pad calendar the quarter portion of it was gone. He looked into the trash can next to the desk, there were a few pieces of wadded up paper, he bent over and looked through them smoothing the wadded up papers out, they were notes of his coming classes in the summer, no corner page of the calendar.

Ryder turned his attention to the phone on his desk. He lifted the receiver and pushed the button marked redial, on the other end it rang.

"Hello." He heard a man's voice say on the other end.

"Who is this?" Ryder asked.

"Dr. Harrell Harris who may I ask is calling?"

"Harrell this is Ryder, are you at your mother's house?"

"Yes, I am getting it cleaned up. Packing her things up." He heard Harris say.

"Sorry I still have your mother's number in my contacts, I must have hit it by accident. Talk to you later." Ryder hung up the phone and looked at Alex. "Odd thing huh? The last person he called before he died was Annie

"President Hacker," Ryder asked. "This is going to be an odd thing to ask. But it is vital I know this." Ryder reached for his wallet and pulled out a business card. He handed it to the man and continued, "I need to know what his blood type was, nothing else about his medical history just the blood type." President Hacker took the card and had just slipped it into his pocket.

"What the hell is going on in here?" Ryder heard a woman's voice say. He saw a young woman in her late twenties, her legs just seemed to start at her neck and moved down like a long stretch of a dessert highway, there was not a curve to be found. Her face, soft and lean long with pouty lips, hook nose and doe like eyes. Her hair was like a Milky Way ® bar, chocolate brown with hints of caramel on the inside. She appeared annoyed as her lips parted showing the slight overbite. "I am asking again! What are doing looking through my father's desk?"

"Flora," President Hacker said trying to calm the situation. "This is Rick Ryder. The billionaire investigator you hear about in the news. He is investigating a murder."

"What murder! My father wasn't murdered. He died of a heart attack." She said as she stepped into the office, "Because of what that woman did to him and our family."

"What woman?"

"The author! That nasty romance author DeAmor. She wasn't satisfied just making things up she had to spill all the secrets."

"About what?"

"Why don't you read the book yourself Mr. Ryder?" Flora shot back. "Names were changed but it's all in there. Including about your mother!"

"Did you take anything out of this room?" Ryder asked as he shut the desk drawer and took a step closer to the woman. She didn't answer so he asked again. "Did you remove anything from here?"

"What difference does it make? He was my father.

"Like it or not Mrs....?"

"Ms. I am single mother. You can just call me Flora."

"Flora, four of your father's friends have been murdered. And they were all members of a group that your father was part of." Ryder said.

"The Sergeants Club, right?"

"Your father told you about it?" Ryder asked as he pulled out one of the padded chairs in front of the desk and offered it to her.

"Right before he died," She said as she seated herself. She was dressed in denim shorts and she crossed her long skinny legs, letting a flip-flop dangle as she let her foot rock back and forth, she continued, "he told me they were the best friends he ever had." Her foot stopped rocking as her tone changed harsher, "Some good friends." She said her gaze dropping from his face onto the speckled title floor. "When he died not one of them showed up, not one of them sent flowers or even a damn card. She looked back up at Ryder and said, "Yeah I took something from this room. A photo of my father and mother that always sat on his desk, she stood up stuffing her foot back down into her shoe. "What blood type are you?"

"Why should you ask that?"

"Nothing personal," Ryder said. "Just wondering since you are your father's child."

"I am not going to tell you anything! How dare you ask me that! Her face twisted up as she asked, "You didn't even see me there did you? At Annie's funeral, I was there." Flora paused gazed across the room for a minute and then back to Ryder. "Want to know why?" She paused, Ryder wondered, did she really want you to ask, but she continued. "She was the love of his life, not my mother. That was just someone he settled for. Annie was the one he dreamt about at night. He told me about my brother, my brother I never got to know.

"Harrell right?"

"Huh? " She looked at him confused for just a moment then replied. "Right, see I don't even know him enough to remember his name. Now if you are done with your questions may I leave." Ryder nodded and she stood up and walked to the door before turning around and adding, "Detective Ryder if you really want to know the secrets of the Sergeants Club I suggest Cheri's latest book they are all in there."

Chapter 40

Ever want to see a strange look on a woman's face behind the counter of a bookstore, when a man lays down a romance novel on the counter, that has a review from the New York times that reads 'like summer heat wave it will take your breath away'. Then she asks 'For your wife?" And you reply "No just a little homework." The eye brows lift even higher. Ryder exited the store and got back in the car as Alex was pouring some ice tea from the thermos into one of the plastic glasses and she handed it to him.

As she poured herself a glass of ice tea, and twisted the lid back on the thermos, he handed her the book and said, "I need you to read this and report back to me." She placed the glass on the seat in between her legs. She flipped it open and read a passage, "His manhood engorged and he…" She shut the book and looked over at him. "Are you kidding me? This stuff could have saved the Titanic. It would have melted the iceberg." She handed it back to him. "I am a good girl I am not going to read that stuff. Get Yakira or Marissa to read it."

Ryder took a sip of the ice tea and then said, "I am not going to let a fifteen year old read that."

"My dear friend," Alex replied as she lifted the glass up to her lips. "She is probably already reading these things and her and her little friends are getting turned on."

"I don't need to know that!" Ryder snapped back. 'You read this that is an order!"

"No way," Alex said, "there is nothing in my job description that says I have to read steamy books and then go jump in creek to cool off." You read it!"

"Gun, knife, bomb?" Ryder asked, it was their version of rock, scissors paper. Gun kills knife, knife cuts fuse on bomb, and bomb blows up gun. They shook their fists out towards each other each pointing out their index fingers, knives they had to do it again. Ryder held out his index finger and thumb straight up and Alex her fist.

"Boom!" She said quickly opening her fingers. "Bomb blows up gun. Happy reading. Now can we get moving it has to be 120 in this car?"

U.S. Highway 412 heading west through Tonitown, Robinson, Pedro, there were always signs that you were still in Arkansas forests, farms and just off the main road, a used car lot. The four lanes come together, it was the sign of something ahead, the town of Siloam Springs Arkansas. Past the town and in the blink of an eye 412 says goodbye and a new number rises US Highway 59, it is in Oklahoma. Turn north at Kansas, not the state but the town, Welcome to Cherokee Nation, where green fields abide and trees stand at the edge of the road, and towns are nothing more than a convenience store. It was almost a treat to actually see a town appear in the windshield.

The town in Oklahoma that claimed to be the hometown of the top ten world's greatest guitarists and ranked best female guitarist of all time, was Lenapah, Oklahoma. A town of nearly 300 souls located in north central Nowata County, it was where, if one was to stand on their roof on a clear night one could peer into Kansas. Its name is an adaptation of *Lenape*, the name of a Delaware Tribe of Native Americans. It was mostly made up of the working class, where workers returned, tired from a day's work, wanting supper and just a chance to relax before the next day began. However, most were never too tired to tell their story of their favorite famous resident Stevie Lace, or as the older ones remember her, Stephanie Granger .

Just like the graves of Elvis or Jim Morrison, it had become a tourist attraction, people that would have no other reason to come to this small town were showing up, turning on highway 10 also known as 4th street and traveling the road that she traveled growing up here. Signs in front of houses, claiming like the father of the nation, that she slept here, she partied here, she played here.

Including that little church where she first drew down power chords to '*I'll Fly Away*' and created a hard rock version, that she still plays in concert today. Back then the elders came up out of the graves and declared it blasphemous, but today they will tell you how they got up and danced to her music. Many of the streets are narrow strips of pavement, some were even gravel covered, including the one where Stevie grew up, the town had turned the house into a museum honoring her. They debated over paving the road, but it was decided that they would keep it just like when she lived there, so that others just like her, could strap a guitar to their back and walk down the street barefooted. A girl that could outplay any man she was the thing of legends.

The house from the outside was unexceptional, wood frame, and siding painted mint green, it was faded and peeling, a clear coat was applied to keep it looking like the house that she grew up in. It was small and faced the railroad tracks. Across from the tracks, it just all seemed a perfect reminder of the little girl that grew up poor and became a star.

Ryder pulled the Killer Bee into the parking lot that was once the yard, but was now pavement; maybe they did change some things. Built on to the back of the house was a new addition that served as the entrance.

It was late afternoon, and well over 105 degrees. As he stepped out, he heard the horn of the train blast through and looked across the road and the field and saw a faded orange Union Pacific locomotive chug by, pulling behind it black tanker cars and grain bins. In the road was a teen age girl, about the same age as Marissa, dressed in jeans and a tie-dye t-shirt, a head band holding her hair back, a guitar strapped to her back, she was beginning the walk down the road and into town.

He held the car door open for Alex as he watched the teen trying to step quickly, the hot rocks cutting into her tender bare feet. Alex stepped out turned and looked at the teen girl and then at the puzzled look on his face and asked, "What is the matter?"

"I don't know," Ryder said as she shut the door.

They walked to the entrance and Ryder pushed the glass door open. Inside it was cool, air conditioned, illuminated by fluorescent lights. It was a large gift shop, with the glass shelves filled with all sorts of collectables that included everything from Steelace and Stevie Lace albums to dolls that look like her. At the front, just when he came in, was a counter where a ticket could be purchased.

"Welcome," The lady behind the counter said as they entered. Ryder reached up and removed his sunglasses and looked at her. She was in her late fifties, salt and pepper hair, pushed back with slight curls on the side. She was Native American, and was shorter than either Ryder or Alex. The name tag on her dark green vest read "Salali".

"A beautiful name," Ryder said offering a smile.

"It means squirrel," She said, "my parents said they named me that because I was always a little nut. Do you wish to purchase tickets to see the museum?"

"Sure," Ryder replied as he pushed his folded up glasses into his jacket pocket.

"Will it be a general pass or the guided pass?"

"What is the difference?"

"With the general you just go through yourself, guided we lead you thorough and explain all the things and answer your questions."

Ryder had learned when things like this happened you didn't over look them, as his uncle would say, it was gift from God. "We will take the guided tour."

"That will be fifty for two." She said and Ryder handed her a fifty. She walked out from behind the counter over to the other side of the room, where a green wooden screen door was and she pulled it open and then stepped into what was a small back porch. It was eight feet long and six feet wide, in the middle of the room was a vintage Kenmore wringer washer, it was white, round with a stainless steel tub, a pair of jeans was run half way through the wringer. A line was strung across the room and the various articles of clothes were hung up with wooden pins.

"Stevie grew up as Stephanie Granger," Salali explained. "Her mother was a full bloodied Cherokee and her father left them when she was five years old. Stevie grew up pretty much on her own, her mother worked as a cocktail waitress in a bar in Coffeyville Kansas. When she was 12 years old she made a deal with the owner of a pawn shop, doing his laundry in exchange for her first electric guitar and amplifier. She kept that up for two years, every week paying for her strings and better amplifier at fourteen. She would hop the train, head for Coffeyville and played for tips in the same bar where her mother worked. Now we will head on into the kitchen."

Salali pushed open a white wooden four panel door, the room was bigger than the porch, 12 feet by 12 feet. On the wall next to the porch was a line of white wooden cabinets with glass doors. Inside were various products, canned goods, and spices that all dated back to when Stevie was a young girl. Below the cabinetry were matching counters with metal tops. In between them was the propane stove, on the stove were two cast iron frying pans with plastic food in them. Over on the other side of the room, looking out over a single pane window was a Beauty Queen sink painted white, steel cabinet 5' by 24" with a 60" Cast Iron double bowl sink and double drain boards. There were several photos of Stevie when she was young, she was thin and pretty with long dark raven hair that hung down her back and highlighted with a colorful headband adorned with Cherokee symbols for life and peace.

"While you will see a bathroom in the master bedroom, it was only a toilet. Stevie had to bathe here using a wash cloth." Next to the sink was a stand holding posters with several photos, of Stevie washing dishing, eating at the green Formica and chrome table and chairs that were pushed over into a corner of the room. And standing on a chair an apron tied around her, she couldn't have been more than eight, a cast iron frying pan in her hands. "And you sir might enjoy this," Salali continued as she pointed to the enlarged photo on the poster. "We have pictures of Stevie taking a bath." The photo she pointed to was of a 12 year old Stevie trying to hide behind a towel her long hair hiding her where the towel could not, the headband still adorning her like a crown.

She moved over to the Antique China cabinet, painted white, with stoneware dishes that could be seen through the glass doors. Leaning up against the cabinet in between the wall, was a three-point fishing gig. Ryder walked over and picked up the gig. "This was how Stevie fed herself." She walked over to the stove and pointed to the frying pan, where simulated frog legs were in the pan. "You will notice there is a large pond down the road, she would go down there and gig frogs, and fish."

So she is good with a spear?" Ryder asked as he set the gig back down.

"Oh yes very good!" Salali said as she held the door open for another doorway. "That and liverwurst and cheese sandwiches is what she survived on growing up." She walked through the doorway into what was the living room. It was moderately furnished, with a sectional sofa covered in a Harvest gold fabric. Pushed up against the wall across the room was a pair of matching swivel rockers. A simulated walnut coffee table in front of them and over to the side of the room was a pot belly stove. There were many photos of Stevie with an older woman standing in front of this house, Stevie a teen at Christmas getting a new Gibson guitar, packing up and heading for Crowder. She was now a full grown woman, a Cherokee princess of the world. Her raven hair now to the middle of her back divided in the middle and held back with a headband that had bright colors and symbols.

"Did Stevie every have a boyfriend?"

"Several," the woman replied. "But she would use them up like candy. She wouldn't ever let things get serious. Once the L word was used, love, she would dump them."

The tour continued through the master bedroom, which was now a room that was dedicated to everything Stevie Lace and Steelace with copies of her gold and platinum records on the wall, photos from concerts, appearances on TV shows. Ryder noticed in every photo she was wearing the headband.

The tour ends with Stevie's bedroom which was just big enough for a bunk bed. She could turn around across the room and dress on the other side. Covered on the wall were posters and magazine pull outs of Eric Clapton, Jimmy Hendrix, Brian May, the entire greatest guitarist. On the wall were pictures of Stevie various ages, from eight to eighteen. Ryder gazed at the photos. There was one of Stevie when she was only a little girl, eight at the most, she was standing on the porch with a Native American woman. In the middle of the eve of the porch was a carving of a large owl.

"This is a different house," Ryder asked. "Where is it?"

"That would be the old Granger farm in Elliot."

"Where is Elliot?"

"It is a place that is not anymore."

"No offense but that sounds stupid. Is that Cherokee babble?"

"No," She replied. "It means years ago it was a town a stage coach stop, today just a couple of houses."

"This one," Ryder said pointing to the photo. "Is it still there?"

"Yes."

Alex looking over at him then back to the woman and asked. "How do we get there?"

"Head back up 169 till you come to EW05, turn left, follow the road till it makes a sharp bend, the old farm house is off to the side."

"Ryder that is where she is staying at."

"You are Rick Ryder," Salali said shocked. "The guy that investigates all those murders. What are you trying to do?"

"Stop a murder!" Ryder said.

"Whose?"

"Stevie Lace's"

Chapter 41

Unlike in town where there is a sign marking every little aspect of her life, there is no sign that marks Elliot, Oklahoma or that this was her real hometown, a town that long disappeared, no such street, no such number no such code, when traveling by horse and carriage there was a hitching post, today only an unmarked intersection. Ryder saw the small green sign that read "EW05", he slammed his foot down on the brake pedal. There was a scream of tires and smoke billowing up into the air as the custom four wheel disc brakes slid the car to a stop.

Over the railroad tracks they left a trail of dust behind them. There was a 90 degree turn in the road to the left, and there just on the right was a long driveway that was only wide enough for one car. Ryder grabbed the shift lever and pulled it down into the lowest gear and began the trek up the drive following a single track that had been mashed down in the center of the drive.

The driveway was over grown with Indian rice grass, the tiny yellow and green blossoms swatting the sides of the car, the Pink to purple blossoms and long, delicate seed heads of the Plains Lovegrass tickling the belly of the Killer Bee Bumblebee logo on the quarters of the car and the Burrograss wrapping around the driveshaft. Ryder could smell the smoke as it melted against the hot mufflers when they pulled up into the parking area that was surrounded by buffalo grass. As Ryder got out, the smell grew stronger; he crawled under the car and pulled the grass clear of the driveshaft and muffler, so that it would not catch fire. As he stood, he brushed the grass and dirt from his jacket and stared over at the house.

It was the same silence that could only be found in a graveyard, the only thing that could be heard was a gust of wind as it swept across the plains, swirling into a dust devil in the road, sucking up the dust and working its way across into a field.

"Do you think she is still here?" Alex asked breaking the stillness.

"That track in the grass was made by a motorcycle coming in, it never went out." Ryder said, his eyes covered by sunglasses looking over the area. There were two buildings on the property, the house and an old barn. Both were large two-story structures, the wood panels on the barn and the siding on the old house were both gray in color.

"How do you know that?"

"The grass it is only bent over once, showing her driving in but not driving out."

A gust of wind whipped across the yard and he heard a moan of a weather screen swinging open in the wind and then slamming shut. He stared up at the house, there were two windows just under the gable, they were wide open and curtains flew in the wind. He just couldn't help the fact that these windows looked like soulless eyes staring down at him wondering why he came here.

They moved closer to the house and he placed a foot on the step and the wood let out a groan, again he heard the back screen door slam shut. He gazed up at the eve and there in the center was a large wood carving of a great horned owl. The front porch was as long as the width of the front of the house and supported by six large round pillars. The wind howled as it swirled around the front porch, just as they stepped up on the wooden floor of the porch. It caught the shutter hanging like injured bird's with broken wing. It slammed in the wind and Alex drew closer to Ryder.

"This is a scary place." She said grabbing his arm as they stepped up to the front screen door.

"It is not a five-star hotel that is for sure," he said as he peeked through the screen of the door looking into the front room. He could hear the buzz of a fan, the blade turning at high speed, as he spotted a white box fan set in the floor near the window. Ryder banged on the door and said, "Stevie we would like to ask you a few questions." There was no reply, Ryder turned to Alex and then back and opened the door and they stepped inside.

The front room span ran the entire width of the house, and it was twice as wide as it was deep. The walls were covered with paisley print wallpaper, the ceiling was eleven feet high, and the floors a dark green linoleum, which was beginning to curl up at the edge. It was sparsely decorated with a loveseat, sofa, and a couple of high back wing chairs, and over in the corner of the room was a 19 inch Black and white Philco ® TV, placed on a stand, The simulated wood grain cabinet, showing no dust, the yellow close pin connector still attached to a flat cable that ran out the window and up to a TV antenna.

In the center of the room was a large oval woven rug that was different shades pinks, blues and greens, and in the center of the rug right in front of the fan was a plastic divider plate. On the plate were a half eaten pork chop and a scoopful of Kraft ® macaroni and cheese. Also on the plate was a fork and knife. He knelt down and picked the plate up and sniffed, it didn't smell rancid.   He set it back down and used the fork and knife to cut off a small piece of the fat of the edge of the chop. He tasted it.

"Shake and Bake ®" Ryder said.

"What?"

"This is still warm and fresh."

"So," Alex drawled out. "She is around here somewhere."

"Someone is," Ryder said as he stood up. He walked through an arch passage that led into the dining room which had smoky gray painted walls and a wooden table with four ladder back chairs positioned around it. There were sheets of hand written music on the table. At the back of the dining room were the kitchen and a back porch. On the other side of the dining room was an open door that lead up to a staircase, it was steep and went nearly straight up.

At the top of the staircase were two rooms, one that opened up into the stairway and the other to a room on the right that was accessed by an open door way. On the right was a twin size bed, covered with light green woven blanket. Ryder moved over to the bed and picked up the pillow and sniffed, it smell of perfume.

"Well it is a woman staying here." He said as Alex pulled the closet door open.

"Ryder!" She said as she reached inside and lifted up a Henry rifle Big Boy 357 with a scope mounted to it. She replaced the rifle and picked up an empty holster. "She is armed." Ryder walked over to the window, pulled the curtain back and looked out the open window. He watched as he saw a dark haired woman pull the barn door open and disappear inside. He turned back to Alex and said, "You stay here I am going out to the barn."

"Remember she is armed!"

He went back down stairs and through the kitchen and mudroom and out the back screen door where a path went around the house and lead to the barn. He pulled the door open and stepped inside. It was hotter than ever, no wind could make it inside and it was only illuminated by the sun that was peering through an opening at the side of the barn. He could see that pictures from magazines had been removed where they were attached to the wall, so that it could appear like an audience with hundreds of different faces staring at him. By the looks of the discoloration of the paper it was done a long time ago, back when she was a kid. Sitting in the middle of the barn was a brand new Harley Davison motorcycle, next to the bike was an old fender Stratocaster and Marshall Amplifier. He placed his hand down on the unit, it was still warm.

He felt straw fall down up on him from the loft above and looked up and could see gaps in the boards over head from where the straw was raining down. It wasn't that he could see anyone, but he could feel her. He could feel her stretched out on the floor above gazing through the crack at him. Her weapon clutched in her hand, sweat running down her brow, trying to hold her breath, so that he could not hear her breath.

"I mean you know harm Stevie," Ryder said as he slowly reached for his wallet. "I am not a cop." Ryder opened his wallet and pulled out a business card. "I am Danielle Delany's son. You might have called her Danni. I have reason to believe you could be in danger." He bent down and placed his card on top of the amplifier. "I am leaving you my card." He closed his wallet and replaced it in his pocket. He headed for the door and pushed it open. He looked back in the barn and added as he looked up at the loft. "Stevie, my home, my cell, email it is all on that card. Please get hold of me. Someone is murdering the members of the Sergeants' Club and you could be next."

Chapter 42

Heading back east the sun was dropping in the sky, the day was slipping away and hunger was calling, screaming both their names, but small towns did not offer much in the way of restaurants just long stretches of pavement and convenience stores where the tank can be topped off and a couple of soft drinks and a bag Green Onion potato chips, was all that was offered. The other side of Welch, Oklahoma the clouds began gathering and the heat began to drop a few degrees, at least it was now under three digits. The further they traveled down the road the more clouds began to cover the sky, to the point where the sun no longer shone; it was hidden behind a dark veil of clouds.

Ryder reached up and pulled his sunglasses off and laid them down on the console between the seats. It was at the point where US 59 crossed over Cow Creek that Ryder said, "Looks like it is going to rain." He hadn't more than just said that, that droplets of rain began to hit the windshield and spread up over the glass, then another drop and another drop, the drops were becoming bigger and faster and soon Ryder flipped on the wipers and the headlights just as they hit a down pour. He flipped on the lights and he could hear the rush of water pouring down and see a streak of lightning bolt followed by a loud rumble of thunder. He twisted the switch on the dash and the wipers were now working at full speed swatting at the glass like it was giving the storm a standing ovation.

"You think she will call?" Alex asked her question, followed by another rumble of thunder, it was early evening but it was so dark that her face was hidden in shadows. However, he dared not take his eyes off the road as the water was beginning to run off and roar in the ditches.

"She might, if she trusts us and doesn't want to be killed." Ryder said, having to let up on the gas and slow the car so he could see where he was going. The rain was being pushed across the highway in sheets, and small hail began to bounce off the hood and the windshield and he could hear the ting, ting of the ice bouncing off the roof. It was raining so hard he could barely see a hundred feet in front of him and the hail was getting bigger. They needed to pull off the road, it was then he saw a distinct outline of an awning off to the side of highway.

It was an old convenience store, now abandoned, but the awning did offer protection. He drove under it and put the car in park and turned the wiper off. Alex took a sip of her soda and then said, "There is another possibility…." Alex paused and then said "she could be the killer". A streak of lightning ripped down from the sky striking a tree a few hundred feet away, the flash was nearly blinding and the crack afterward rang in his ears.

Ryder looked at his cell phone. The time read 5:59 p.m. but it also showed no service. They were in a dead spot. The hail was getting bigger, now the sizes of marbles, they were bouncing like ping-pong balls collecting in pools on the ground and rolling off the top of the awning. "Think about it Ryder?" Alex asked, "It is possible that she could be the killer. He had to admit she could be right, as quick as the rain began it stopped and they continued on.

Entering Miami from the west you are greeted by what looks like the largest white foam cups in the world, grain bins that reach high into the sky. Once again the skies were darkening to the point that the street lights just came on and the rain droplets were falling onto the windshield, when Ryder saw a sports and grille bar just off the side of the street. He pulled in and quickly got out, opened the door for Alex and they dashed to the front door. They had just entered the front door of the grille when the heavens unleashed into a down pour. He heard the rush of the water on the roof as he took a seat in the back.

There was a string of large screen TV's behind the bar. The waitress wanted to know if he wanted anything, a beer or cocktail, but Ryder waved it off, just asking that she bring them ice tea, sweet with a half twist of lemon, and a larger order of Nachos topped with chicken that they could share, they just needed a little something because Bubbie would have supper waiting for them.

The Nachos were fresh tortillas topped with tomatoes, olives, green onions and a melted blend of Monterey jack and Cheddar cheeses, and chicken and sour cream. As Ryder took a bite of the savory mixture it hit the spot, and the perfect wait to ride the storm out. The street became like a river, the water rolling down the pavement with traffic creeping though and lightning streaking across the sky followed by a rumble of thunder. Alex had laid her phone to the side of her plate and suddenly it caught a signal and it began to ping and ping over again. She picked up a tortilla chip and put it into her mouth as she picked up the phone and checked her messages. Ryder pulled out his phone and checked it, there was no messages from Stevie; he began to wonder, was it all a waste hunting her down?

Alex looked up from her phone at him with a smirk on her face, "Your wife!" She said firmly picking up another chip. "I blame you for this!" Ryder was confused until she turned the phone around and she added, "It seems that I have a new addition to my house." He saw a picture of a small black and white kitten, her blue eyes shining right into him, small pink nose and grin on her face, sitting on a red blanket in a basket on the seat of Yakira's truck. "It seems that Ceelia was upset because she had to get her hair cut. And Yakira stopped and got her a kitten." She turned the phone around and continued, "And now you know who is going to be cleaning up." Alex pointed to her chest.

Ryder laughed, "Every little girl needs a cat to love. So what did she name it?"

"Pistol," Alex said. "Because her mom and daddy carry pistols, so she wants to carry one." Ryder laughed out loud so much he got choked and had to take a drink.

"That is precious!" He said starting to reach for another tortilla chip as Alex checked her other messages. "You are going to have a great time with Pistol."

"Yeah," Alex drawled out, rolling her gaze up from her phone over the table to him. A small grin broke out across her face and was washed away by even a larger one as she said, "Well you are going to have an even better time. Meet Rifle!" She turned the phone around again and showed him a video of a border collie puppy, fluffy black and white, with a black beauty mark on his snout just under his right eye. He was inside the house running down the hall, tail wagging so hard that it nearly knocked him over as the puppy runs to Bubbie, and got so excited he peed on the floor.

Alex turned the phone back to her and continued. She laid the phone back down on the table then asked him, "Rick are you happy?"

"That is sort of an odd question to ask," he said as there was a rumble of thunder outside. "Why do you ask that?" He took a sip of the tea and said, "Because I have more money than I can ever spend?"

"No, are you happy?"

"Well I am married to the woman I love..."

"No," She said interrupting him. "I mean are you happy?"

"I don't know." Ryder said leaning back, with the glass of tea in his hand and said, "I don't know." He repeated. "It is crazy I have more money than I would ever need, because of investments I have more money now than I started with. "There are times that I seemed the most blessed person in the world, but there are other times when I just want to close my eyes and leave this place. So I can't really answer your question. What about you, are you happy?"

"When I look into my child's eyes yes. But others times...she turned and looked out the window, it was slacking. "Well the rain has stopped what you say we go home?"

Chapter 43

Back home Ryder had guessed right, Bubbie had made supper, a chuck roast with carrots, onions and mushrooms covered in a rich beef broth and diced tomatoes with her mashed potatoes cooked in chicken stock with fresh chopped chives and for dessert apple and golden raisin turnovers. Ryder was right it was worth not eating to come home to fill up on the wonderful meal. However, there was one thing that disturbed Ryder about the meal, it was nothing that Bubbie made, but the fact that Yakira would not seat herself at the table until after thanks was given, and she didn't give thanks afterwards as her heritage told her to, instead she took Ceelia by the hand and they disappeared heading to play with the kitten and have a tea party.

After supper Ryder dismissed himself to the living room, where he stretched out in one of the recliners and began to read the book he had bought. It was set at a fictional university, Midwest Missouri Central University or MMCU, but the fact that the university was once an air force base left no doubt that it was in fact Crowder College.

The names had been changed and it was set in the 1970's but the heroin of the book Sunflower, the flower child, was Annie. She was the care free spirit, into the music of the Beatles and the Doors, just looking for love. Johan was Paul the dreamer who wanted to be a singer, his pal Vonnie the musician, trying to break into a business that was dominated by men, was Stevie. And then there was Tammy the head of the 54 Diamonds, she was strong willed and inquisitive but she whimpered down when it came to her boyfriend Luke. As much as she tried, Tammy couldn't stop Luke's wandering eye, he was making moves on the Indian Maiden - Vonnie.

"Ricky?" He heard Marissa ask, shattering the make believe world. He set the book down and looked up at her, darkness was just beginning, she stood there in the living in front of him, and in her hands was a yellow legal pad. "I got as much information about blood types as I could. You want to hear it?" He marked the page in the book and placed it on the end table next to the recliner, pushed the footrest down and stood up.

"Let's go to the office," he said walking out of the living room and she followed. They went back through the kitchen, where Yakira and Ceelia sat on the floor playing with Barbie dolls and the Dream camper and a similar sized metal vehicle that had been Ryder's when he was kid; he had retrieved them from storage and had given them to her. One doll sitting in a pool, Yakira looked up at him and smiled. It was comforting to see her smile again. Ryder went around the corner and down the hallway towards the garage, instead of going out into the garage he turned left and opened a door, he flipped on a light. It was his office, it was comfortably styled room with a desk, a leather sofa and a large TV mounted on the wall. There was also a large blackboard on a stand and a cork bulletin board mounted to another wall. Thumb-tacked to the bulletin board were photos of those that had been murdered, and taped to the other blackboard, beside their names, written in chalk were photos of those still alive that were part of the Sergeants' Club. "So what did you find out?" Ryder asked as she stepped inside and shut the door behind her. "Was any of them AB negative?"

"It is very rare to get AB negative blood," Marissa sat down on the sofa and began looking at her yellow legal and the notes she had made. "For example you have AB- negative blood. But I have AB positive. Alex is A positive, Ceelia got your blood type she too is AB negative. My mom was B negative and had to take some drug so her blood wouldn't kill me. Even though our dad was AB negative, our grandpa was B positive so that is where I got that…"

"I know all of that," Ryder interrupted her. "I am remembering it from biology class in high school. Was there anyone who had AB negative blood?"

"No one in the Sergeants Club has AB negative blood."

"So the child didn't belong to anyone in the club?"

"You don't have to have AB negative blood to get AB negative blood. If your blood is positive you can be carrying both a positive and a negative gene, to be negative you can only carry both negative genes. So to produce an AB negative child, both parents would have to be carrying a negative gene. That is way too much I can't get into if someone's grandparent was negative. However I can narrow this down, to have an AB child both parents would either have to be A, B or AB, types. If the parents are O positive or O negative they couldn't have a child that was AB negative. Many of these members have type O either positive or negative. But it did narrow the field to four women. It was women that you asked me to check out."

Marissa got up and walked over to the chalk board and beside Stevie's photo she wrote down AB positive, then she laid the chalk down and walked over to the bulletin board three of them are right there. Annie had type B negative blood, Charlotte type A positive blood, your mother type A negative," she walked over to the chalkboard picked up the piece of chalk again and drew a circle around Stevie's photo as she said, "Only one of these women is still alive."

Ryder stood staring at the blackboard and then over at the bulletin board, then back again at the blackboard. He remembered the book and the tale that was going on with Luke, that he felt was based on his father. "If the mother is AB positive and the father AB negative what are the chances they would have a child that was AB negative?"

"Still rare, it would depend on things such as if she was carrying a recessive negative gene."

"Is it possible?"

"Yes."

Suddenly there was screaming from the kitchen, "I don't want to go!" It was Ceelia, she was in tears. "I don't want to go home mommy! I want to stay here and play with Yakira!"

"Ceelia pickup your toys and let's go!" He heard Alex say firmly.

"No! I stay here and play!"

"Ceelia, you are going to get into trouble!" Ryder and Marissa had just made it to the door when he heard a loud crash of the sound of glass breaking. He dashed to the kitchen; there stood a five year old girl in front of a broken window. She had picked up the metal camper and slung it through the kitchen window. A kitten running as fast as its little legs could take it into another room, the puppy crawling in behind Bubbie's legs.

Ryder stood there watching his daughter; the teeth firmly clinched together, her sapphire blue eyes trying to rip into her mother's heart. "I don't need you mommy; she looked up at Yakira and said, "You can be my mommy right?" She looked back at her mother and added. "She is nicer than you are! She lets me eat what I want and buys me things!"

Alex looked over at Yakira and said, "We have a problem here! You are ruining my kid!"

"I didn't mean anything by it…" Yakira looked over at Ryder and then said. "I was trying to be nice to her. I…" She turned and looked at Ryder and stumbled over her words. "I—"was –just…" She turned and looked back at Alex and then Ryder again, before breaking into tears and running up the stairs.

"Can't I stay here daddy," Ceelia said as she looked up at Ryder, her hair now cut to where it ended just below her chin.

"You broke that window," Ryder said pointing to the broken glass. "Do you know what that will cost?"

"You are rich, that is what all the kids at school say. You can afford it!"

"Ceelia, you go over to your mother and you get out."

"You don't like me now that I have short hair?" The girl said.

"No," Ryder as he kneeled down in front of her. "Ceelia I still love you but I don't like you right now because you are a spoiled rotten little brat. And whatever punishment your mother deals out to you I am all for, you understand. And until you do understand you are not allowed back in this house."

"But I want to…"

"Ceelia!" Her mother snapped cutting the little girl off. "Let's go now!" She walked and Alex grabbed her daughter's hand. With that Alex scooped her child up in her arms, and they headed for the door, Alex turned back to Ryder and said.

"Rick I will…"

"I'll take care of the window and put piece of plywood over it."

She turned back to her daughter and warned, "You and I are going to have an old fashioned mother and daughter talk."

****

Things quieted back down, the broken glass was swept up, the toy confiscated and the window covered with a sheet of plywood which left the kitchen dark when the light was turned off. Ryder took the book he had been reading and found his way upstairs to the bedroom. Yakira had changed into her nightgown and was in bed, she was not asleep but sitting up, a pillow behind her back, watching TV. He got undressed and then into his sleep-pants. He crawled into the bed next to her.

"I didn't mean any harm," she said almost like a child. "I was just—I just…" she dropped her head down not wanting to look at him. "I miss him so much. And I will never get to play with him like that!" She spoke of her lost child. Her words again turned to sudden anger as she looked up at Ryder. "How could God do that?"

Ryder had just opened the book; he placed it faced down on his lap so as to not lose his place. "You have got to get over that."

His words seemed to anger her even more as she snapped back at him, "You want to get over being upset because I lost my child? My baby! Possibly my one and only chance to have a baby! You want me to get over that? Get over him!" She again turned away from him dropping her head down, letting her hair fall down to the sides of her face.

He reached down and with care he stroked her hair back out of her face. "No baby," he said in a soft tender tone. "We will never be over it. We will always remember Reese." He placed his arm around her and she laid her head down on his shoulder. "You need to get over being mad at God. Things happen, God didn't do this."

"So you want me to ask for forgiveness? "

"No I want you to give forgiveness."

She turned and looked at him, her hand in her laps as she asked, "How can I?"

"Did you ever forgive your dad for the things he did? " He asked, her lips parted as she was going to speak but she didn't, so he continued. "Then why couldn't you forgive your Heavenly Father?" The tears began to flow even more and she turned her head and looked across the room, he saw her reach over and grabbed another tissue and wiped her eyes. "Then you forgive yourself because that is who you are really blaming isn't it, yourself?"

"It was my fault! If I would have just stayed in bed, and not went out to see the fireworks. I should have never moved. The doctor told me I had to take it easy." She turned back to him and sobbed. "I am sorry Ricky! I am sorry! It was me I am the reason we lost him."

"No baby!' He said taking her face in his hands. "This was not your fault; it wasn't because you got up. It is because…" He lifted his hands from her face and placed them on her shoulders. "I wasn't going to tell you this but I had Thom do a autopsy, his heart was malformed it stopped beating, he wouldn't have live no matter what."

"Oh god, my baby," she said somberly letting her hands slide up the sides of his face, she took her thumbs and wiped across his eyes as she said, "Your tears are my tears…" She placed thumbs up to her eyes. "If I don't cry you don't cry." She placed her hand on his check as she said, "But if we weep…"

"We weep together." They said together and then she fell down into his arms sobbing. He just held her, letting her cry nearly non-stop for the next fifteen minutes. She became quiet, sniffed and then lifted her head up.

"I am going to go wash my face," She said swinging her legs out from under the cover and standing up. Ryder went back to reading his book, after washing her face she came back, she was dressed. He put his book down on his lap as he looked at her; she was dressed in jeans and a blouse. She sat down on the edge of the bed and slipped on a pair of tennis shoes.

"Where are you going?"

"I am going to see Uncle Tony." She said as she tied her shoes.

"You want me to go with you?"

"No I have to do this myself." She stood and left the room.

Ryder continued reading the book of how the rituals were performed near a cemetery, blood being dripped into a golden cup and each member would drink from it. He wondered, was this what the Sergeants' Club did or was it creative license, but it was the sub plot of the individuals that really caught his interest and the affair that was taking place between Vonnie and Luke all the while Tammy found herself expecting, Vonnie was also expecting. Johnny would not have this ruining his life with Tammy, and forced Vonnie to abort the child. They then buried the child on the campus of MMCU under the floor of the old care takers house.

272

He was starting to get sleepy when he looked over at the clock; it was 1 a.m. when the bedroom door opened. It was Yakira and she seemed to be happy. "Guess what, I found something."

"I found something too." Ryder said.

"What did you find?" Yakira asked.

"That the baby we found at Crowder could be Stevie's and my father's," as he explained she didn't seemed pleased so he asked. "What did you find?"

"A way that I can forgive God."

Chapter 44

The next morning Ryder awoke to find the kitten curled on the pillow next to his head and the puppy lying on the bed in between him and Yakira, his head resting on Ryder's leg. As Ryder awoke Rifle raised his head and looked at his master followed by the wag of a tail as he crawled up to him and wanted to be petted. Ryder gave the puppy a good scratch then got up. He showered, shaved and dressed. As he exited the bathroom; he was dressed in light gray slacks and a jacket that was slung over his shoulder. He headed down stairs, Rifle shooting off the bed and following him down the steps. He opened the front door and let the puppy out, he ran around for a while, while Ryder slipped on the shoulder holster making sure the Glock was in good operation, stuffed into the holster and then slipped on the jacket. He opened the door and yelled for Rifle who had gone to the bathroom and ran back inside.

It was so still, he could hear the clangs of pot and pans in the kitchen. Bubbie was beginning to cook breakfast. As he entered she was mixing sugar, eggs, milk and water together in a stainless steel bowl, she then gradually added flour and salt to the egg mixture and whipped it till it was smooth, then added a little vanilla. She was wrapped in a fuzzy pink robe.

"Good morning *Motek*," she said looking up from her work as he entered the kitchen. "Thought I would make some Cheese Blintzes," She said and then pointed at the coffee pot on the counter and said, "Coffee is made if you would like some." Ryder got a mug out of the cabinet and poured coffee into it and stirred in milk and sugar. Then over to the table and sat down, Rifle following right behind him. He took a sip of the coffee and looked at the plywood that was still covering the window. "I got some small curd cottage cheese, been letting it drain overnight."

"Ceelia loves your Blintzes," Ryder said noticing how he could hear every little sound in the house. Bubbie opening and closing the refrigerator door, Rifle chewing on a rawhide bone under the table, even the air conditioner kicking off. He took another sip of coffee and said. "Why is it I hear everything today?"

"Because there is not a five-year-old screaming her head off," Bubbie said.

Ryder set the mug down on the table and looked back over at the plywood and how dark it was in the kitchen before he said, "Maybe I was too hard on her."

"No," Bubbie said walking over to stand beside him.

"I guess it is called tough love huh?"

"It is called raising a child." He felt her place her hand on his shoulder and continued, "You are not to be their best friend. You are to praise them when they do good, punish them when they do bad, pick them up when they fall, and love them know matter what." He turned and looked at her and watched as she turned and went back to the counter to mix together another large bowl, mix the small curds of cream cheese together, then add the egg yolk, lemon juice, honey, vanilla extract and sugar.

"Why don't you take your coffee out on the deck, I will bring these out when they are ready." Bubbie said as she began to cook the crepes in a small non-stick skillet.

Ryder headed for the deck at the back of the house, when he heard the door bell for the front door. Ryder had made arrangements to get the window replaced and thinking it was the repairman, Ryder walked into the entry hall and opened the door. He expected a middle aged man with a beard, what he saw was a five-year-old girl. He wanted to scoop her up and hug her, but he remained strong. "Ceelia," he said without a hint of emotion.

"I am sorry daddy," she said, she was dressed in old jeans and a light green t-shirt. She dropped her head down. "I am here to work and pay for the window," Ryder watched as her mother who had been standing off to the side walked up behind her.

"What else Ceelia?" Alex said as she placed her hand down on her daughter's shoulder.

"I also want to say I am sorry for back talking you and mommy. I was a bad girl." Ceelia looked up at him tears in her eyes.

"Since she messed the house up," Alex said looking at Ryder. "She is going to clean it. You said you would go along with whatever punishment I decided. Do you?"

"Yeah," Ryder drawled out." He placed his hand down on the back of his daughter's head and said, "But young lady, I don't want no more of that from you. You understand? "She nodded her head. "Have you had breakfast?" She shook her head. "Then go have some."

"Can I mommy," she said looking up at Alex.

"Yes."

Ceelia raced into the kitchen. Alex walked into the house and he shut the door after her. "Did you spank her?" Ryder asked.

"I thought about it," Alex said. "But, no I didn't.

He led her outside on to the deck and seated her at the table. Bubbie had already placed the pot of coffee on a tray, on the glass top table along with the rolled blintzes. Alex poured herself a cup of coffee and put a blintz on a plate. Ryder also placed a couple of blintzes on his plate, topped them with blueberry compote and a dab of whipped cream, said grace and then he took a bite of one, savoring the sweetness.

"I thought about selling her toys, but Bubbie suggested letting her help clean the house. Have you heard anything from Stevie?" Alex asked scooping up a bite of the blintz.

"Nothing yet," Ryder replied as he lifted his cup of coffee up to his lips. "How about the author, did you find her yet?"

"No," Alex said taking another bite of the blintz. "Her agent says she is somewhere working on the final rewrite of her next book." She looked around and then asked, "Where is everybody?"

"Bubbie is in the kitchen. Yakira and Marissa went shopping, back to school you know."

"Already!"

"I am not ready! It starts so quick anymore," Ryder started to lift the fork to his mouth but stopped, laid the fork back down on the plate.

According to the book three students in the club were pregnant, my mother, Annie and Stevie who had an affair with my father."

"No that can't be." Alex said. Thom said the bones show that there was no Native American parent both parents were Caucasian, that child can't be Stevie's child. In fact I have done some more research into Stevie's life. The tale is she was repeatedly molested when she was 12 years old, which drastically affected her mentally and physically, she can't have kids.

I only see two that were pregnant in that club, your mother and Annie. You are here, Annie's son is here. So who is the baby?"

"I don't know."

Ryder heard the front door slam. "Ricky?" He heard Yakira shout out.

"On the deck!" He shouted.

"What if the book is true, but she didn't just change the names she changed the facts and it is another woman that had an affair with your father?"

"Then who? Charlotte? Monica?"

"How about Millie?"

"The reporter?"

"What if the reason she got that card was because your mother made it that way."

"Then we need to find Cheri De Amor."

"Ricky!" Yakira said with exasperation. "I found her!"

"Who?"

"Cheri De Amor! She is at a cabin in Parkcliff just outside of Roaring River."

Chapter 45

It was a good test for the Killer Bee's new 4-link suspension, hanging tight to the twists and turns of Highway 112 and then down the hill into the park as soon as he crossed over the bridge of Dry Hallow and then back on to Highway 112 that went through the park, up the hill past the hotel.

It was a simple street that turned off the highway and led into Mark Twain Forest; the cabins were well secluded and safely guarded by the trees. If you didn't know they were there you wouldn't have found them. There was peacefulness where he could hear the songs of Eastern whippoorwills; it was odd to hear those three notes over and over again and it was a sound that could quickly become as unnerving as a siren wailing in the distance. As Ryder stepped out of the car he heard the wailing three notes *'whip poor will'*. What made it truly odd was usually the song was only heard at night. However, there was a legend that if you heard the song in the day the bird was looking for a soul to take and when it took flight it took it up to heaven. As Ryder shut the door, a small dark colored bird took to flight, it circled around almost to the point he could reach up and grab it, circled twice more than sailed up into the sky and disappeared into the forest.

"It is the one over there," Yakira, said pointing to a cabin as she stepped out of the car followed by Alex from the back seat of the Charger.

"How did you find this out?" Ryder asked staring at the cabin. It was a simple construction of cedar logs, but it seemed to fit the area, it looked as if it belonged here. If it hadn't been for the power lines and modern roof it would have appeared as if they were back in the 1800's.

"She likes to have Mexican food when she writes," Yakira explained. "The restaurant in town made a delivery here. We saw them at Wal-mart this morning. It was the same person that would deliver to me."

There was a front porch with a rail, Ryder stepped up, knocked on the door and said. "Ms. De Armor." He knocked again. "Beulah," he said calling her real name. "I am Rick Ryder, Dannie Delany's son, can we talk to you?" He looked back at the parking lot and saw a Mercedes parked there. He reached down and twisted the door knob and the door opened.

Inside it was fully furnished, two bedrooms, a private bedroom on the main level and a semi private bedroom in the loft. Both rooms had a queen size bed and there is a wooden beam sleeper sofa and a matching chair in the living room. All were done in the wood motif with deer or mountain prints.

Windows were all around the living room, allowing the sunlight to peer in yet all the lights were still on, including the deer antler chandelier over the rectangular dining table with six high back chairs. One chair over to the side next to the window was pulled out and the chair on the other side was turned over. Sitting on the table was her laptop, the screen was up but the computer had gone to sleep. Ryder took his pen from his pocket and tapped the enter key and the laptop came back to life.

"Want me to look around? Alex asked.

"Yeah."

Ryder looked down at the screen, it was a work in progress, a tale of a woman falling in love but this draft was being edited and there was a large blank space between the paragraphs "According to acknowledgements in her last book she always comes here for the final rewrite of her books, thanking a person named Dallas for her help while she was here. Go see if you can find her and ask her a few questions." Alex turned and walked out. Ryder took his handkerchief and pushed the keys Control and Z to paste and up popped the line.

'We buried him'.

"Ricky!" He heard Yakira say as she looked into the sink in the kitchen. "There are two clean glasses in here. Using a paper towel she opened the dish washer there were a few plates and glasses in the washer but certainly room for two more glasses. She looked down into the trash can that was under the sink. "And an empty Coke can and a small bottle of gin." Yakira walked out of the kitchen and back into the bedroom.

"Ricky!" He heard Yakira shout from the bedroom. He raced to the bedroom.

The deer motif was carried over into the bedroom. With exposed wooden logs, the bed frame, the end tables and the dresser were all made of wood. The room was only lit by a single lamp on one of the end tables next to the bed, the other lamp laid broken on the wooden plank floor. The bedspread was pulled off the queen sized bed, crumpled in a heap at the foot of the bed and tangled in with the top sheet that was half off the bed. Yakira was kneeling and holding up a corner of the sheet. Ryder could see a woman's leg sticking out from the cover.

It was Cheri De Amour, dead. Face down her arms stretched out over her head. The sheet was soaked with blood and there was a dagger with a flower like handle sticking out of her back. Ryder, using his handkerchief, turned on the overhead light and got a better look at the body. Her legs were bluish, almost a purplish cast. She was dressed in night clothes, a light weight pink top and matching shorts. Her nails were pale. He touched her arm and it blanched out, the skin was still warm and she was not stiff. She had been dead about a couple hours at the most.

"You better alert Brian and Double T." Ryder said as he stood. "Tell them there is another murder."

"Ricky!" He heard Yakira. "Look!" She said pointing to a plaque that was laying on the floor, attached to the plaque was a playing card, the Jack of Diamonds. Burned into the wood were the words "But the perverted tongue will be cut out."

"That is from Proverbs 10:31." Yakira said, as she laid the plaque back down on the floor.

"We need to get out of here," Ryder said and they headed back into the living area. Ryder walked over to the computer and looked down at the screen. The line that was written just seemed out of place. Using the handkerchief again he tapped the keys and another line appeared.

'How can it be? This child could be still alive.'

Chapter 46

Soon the wail of sirens shattered whatever peace there was. County cruisers swarmed like angry bees. Ryder sat on the hood of his car, Yakira next to him. He looked across the yard as the Barry County deputy's investigated the murder, Alex stood across the parking lot talking to one on the maids that work there.

"Ricky with her murder, this only leaves Stevie, is she next to die or is she the killer?"

"I don't know." Ryder said.

Alex walked up to the Charger. "I found out something very interesting." She said standing in front of them. "I found Dallas."

"Who?"

"The person that acknowledged that she helped, she is a maid here. She said the last person to visit here was a man, thin with long hair and long side burns and a colorful bandana headband."

"Why did she notice all that?"

"One main reason, the gloves he was wearing. It has been over 100 degrees and he was wearing ski gloves."

"Ski gloves?" Ryder questioned. "Anything else?"

"She asked who he was? He said he was Annie's son."

"Really?"

"That is strange," Yakira said. "About a couple days ago the good Doctor Harris asked me where a good Mexican place was. I told him about *El Mariachi* where Cheri ordered from."

"I say we go talk to the good Doctor." Alex said just as Thom walked up.

"Ryder," Thom asked. "Did you notice anything odd about the body?"

"Besides the dagger sticking out of her back?"

"The fact that her tongue had been cut out," Thom said. Ryder slid off the hood and stood up; the forward inch and a half of her tongue was surgically removed."

"Why do you say surgically?"

"Because it was done with a very sharp instrument like a scalpel," Thom said.

"You mean like a doctor?"

Chapter 47

A trip back to town revealed they had just missed Dr. Harris; he had been packing up his mother's stuff at her trailer, but had taken a lunch break. Dr Harris' favorite food was Mexican and his favorite place was *El Mariachi* in Cassville and he agreed to meet Ryder and the others there. Since it was right on the way back into town Ryder pulled the car into the parking lot and headed for the building.

In a time when Ryder's mother was a little girl it was the Piggly Wiggly grocery store, and then it went through changes and many names. Now it was painted half red, and the other half bright green. The bright green half was the restaurant, the red a flea market. Ryder held the door open and let the women walk in first. As he stepped inside he removed his sunglasses. It was bright and clean with an arch shaped opening with painted red bricks. The hostess met them and asked, "Three of you?"

"We are meeting someone here." Ryder said scanning over the restaurant for the doctor. He saw him sitting at a booth near the back. "Him," he said pointing to the doctor.

The young woman guided them back to the booth. "Rick Ryder, " Dr. Harris said looking up at him. He was fairly tall a little over six foot and stocky built with short curly brown hair. "Please join me! "Regular or mild salsa?"

"I don't do hot." Ryder said as he took a quick look at his menu and ordered "an ice tea, sweet with a half twist of lemon." The others also ordered their drinks and chips and salsa were brought, the salsa in small little bowls one for each, except for Dr. Harris who ordered the regular salsa which came in a bigger black bowl. Alex ordered a taco salad with chicken; Yakira tacos without cheese, Ryder ordered the combination steak and chicken fajitas. "Order what you like, doctor, it is on me." Ryder said and with that the doctor ordered the cheese enchilada dinner.

"I have been meaning to get hold of you Rick," Dr. Harris said as he took a chip and scooped up some salsa and took a bite. "I have been cleaning out mother's trailer. Since her place is next to you. "I thought you might like to buy the land and trailer?"

"Maybe," Ryder said as he picked up a chip and took a bite of his salsa, he paused before taking a sip of tea then asked, "What are you asking for it?"

"Two and half. That is the trailer and 30 acres."

"Two hundred and fifty thousand," Ryder said. "Sounds fair. Ryder lifted his glass of tea and added, "I guess we have a deal." They clinked glasses. Ryder took a sip of tea and set the glass down and then asked, "Your mother ever tell you about her days at Crowder with my mother?"

"Yes," Dr. Harris said wolfing down more chips and salsa. "She told me your mother was her best friend back then, and they hung out together."

"She ever tell you who your dad was?"

Dr. Harris hushed as the waitress brought the taco salad, Enchilada dinner and Yakira's tacos. Dr. Harris had just cut off a bite of his enchilada and was raising it to his mouth when he stopped and replied, "Once when I was eleven years old I asked where he was. She told me he was a man that didn't love us and we were better off without him. I joked with her, what if I had a rare blood type and needed a transfusion."

Ryder could hear the unmistakable sizzle of his lunch arriving on a very hot skillet, after the waitress left and Ryder scooped up some of the steak, chicken and veggies to put on a corn tortilla, Ryder asked, "What blood type do you have?"

Dr. Harris had just taken a bite and had to wait to swallow, before he replied, "Type O positive the most common there is. So there went the big thrill having that happen."

Ryder took a bite of the fajita and then asked, "Did she tell you much about the others that were in the Sergeants' Club?" He waited for the reaction of the man to see if he had heard of this group.

"Some," He said. "But not until just recently. I was here for Christmas last year. She said there was someone, a woman that was going to be writing a book that could be about the days at Crowder College. That I shouldn't believe anything in it; it was just a bunch of lies."

"Cheri DeAmour?"

"Yes, that is the person."

"Did you read the book?" Ryder asked.

"No, I didn't want any part of it."

"Did you meet her?"

"Who?" Dr. Harris asked.

"Cheri DeAmour, at her cabin at Roaring River?" Ryder asked again watching the man's reaction, it was one of surprise.

"She is here!" He said dropping his fork to the plate.

"You are sure you didn't visit her early this morning?"

"No," Dr. Harris replied. "Why are you asking me this?"

"Cheri DeAmour was found murdered at Roaring River this morning."

What!" He shouted out. "Murdered!" His shout caused the others in the restaurant to look at him. "You think I killed her?" His questions made a couple that were seated only two booths away suddenly get up and leave leaving half the lunch uneaten. He lowered his voice and said, "I didn't have anything to do with it. This is the first I have heard about."

"Cheri's book was supposed to be based on true events that happened at Crowder College and your mother was the lead character in the book. You are telling me you didn't have any interest in it?"

"Rick," Dr Harris said. "I know all about it, my mother told me. She said she fell in love with the wrong man. She said he was the most handsome man she had ever seen, the kind of guy that would never pay attention to her. When he did, she gave herself to him. Then he could care less about her. When she told him about me, he wanted her to get an abortion, she couldn't do that." Rick my mother did it all on her own, I didn't need a father then and I don't need one now. I had the greatest mother."

Ryder's cell phone dinged. He reached into his pocket and looked at the incoming message:

Need help.   Scared I am next.

Meet me at the Hard Rock in Tulsa 9:45 p.m. tonight.

come ALONE- Stevie.

Chapter 48

Back at the house Ryder is getting ready for his trip standing in front of the mirror on the dresser in his bedroom. As he smoothed the collar of his purple button-down shirt he could see Alex sitting on the edge of the bed in the mirror, he could see the worried look on her face as she looked at him petting Rifle who sat on the bed next to her.

"I don't like it Ryder," she said as she stopped petting the black and white puppy. "There is no way you should go in there alone."

"She said come alone." Ryder said as Yakira came into the room. She was holding a weapon in her hands. A semi-automatic pistol in a belt mounted holster. A Glock G43 9 mm she got from her store in town. "But that doesn't mean you don't go unarmed."

Alex looked over at Yakira and asked, "You going to let him do this?"

"When have I ever been able to stop him?" She asked handing him the weapon. "Here take this."

"It is a gun free zone. I don't want to draw any attention to myself, it could scare her off." He replied handing her the gun back.

"When have we ever allowed suspects to deem what we do?" Alex said as she stood up from the bed. "You said it yourself you could be walking into a trap."

"It is the only way we are going to find the truth." Ryder said as he walked across the room and picked up a white jacket that was lying on the bed. He picked it up and slipped it on. "She knows the truth of the secret of the Sergeants' Club."

"What makes you think she is going to tell you?" Alex asked

"She is ready I know it," Ryder said heading for the door. He stopped and brushed some lint from the leg of his white slacks.

"What if she is reeling you in for a kill?" Yakira said grabbing his sleeve. "Where does that leave me? I have lost my child and I might lose you too?"

"She is not going to kill me," Ryder said walking out the door and towards the stairs, Yakira and Alex following him.

"What if you are the real intended victim?" Alex asked. He stopped and turned to her. "What if the real secret is that Stevie was abused again and the club kept quiet."

"What would that have to do with me?"

"You are the son of the woman that is responsible for the Sergeants' Club." Yakira said. "Would that be enough?"

"Not buying it!" Ryder said firmly as he walked down the stairs.

"Ricky," Yakira begged hurrying her steps down the stairs to catch up with him. Again she grabbed his arm as she said. "Let me go with you."

"No!" He said. "She will be watching. "I don't want you two going with me." He leaned down and placed his hands on the side of his wife's face. "Understand? " Then he grinned. "Don't go with me." He looked over at Alex and added, "Understand?"

Chapter 49

Undercover surveillance requires a way of fitting in with the area that one is watching. If in a poor part of town you don't want to be in a high dollar car, likewise if driving into a casino you don't want a junker yet you also don't want a high dollar car looking like a high roller. Yes you would get the tip-top attention from the casino but that is not what you want. This was what Ryder got when he drove up in the Killer Bee with the Valet parking.

For those reasons Alex and Yakira wanted to fit in just like another visitor. Alex chose the light gray sedan, a 2013 Chevrolet Impala LTZ that was a perfect way to blend in. Alex pulled the car into the parking lot, Yakira stretched her neck staring up at the tower through the windshield at the bright glowing sign '*HARD ROCK'*®. At the top of the tower, circled in red, the red dash of light on the side of the casino, they made her think of the flashing lights on the slot machines that beamed out winner. As Alex twisted the car into the parking spot, Yakira could see the bright lights of the sign that alerted all those on Interstate 44 who was here, the bright blue glow of the screen reflecting in the lake, the fountain spraying up into the air.

"Remember," she heard Alex say as the interior light filled the compartment when she opened the door, "we are just a pair of friends here to have some fun for the night." Yakira followed Alex and they walked into the casino, they purchased some coins, each taking a hundred dollars worth. With Ryder dressed in white it was easy to spot him in the crowded casino, Yakira watched as he moved in between the brightly lit slots and poker machine, and the screens were a buzz of activity, as sounds of bells, buzzer and excitement of winning filled Yakira's ears. They put on cards that could be used in the casino and followed Ryder back into the casino near a line of slot machines.

"You still hooked to his phone? "Alex asked.

"She texted for him to go to the *Mr. Big Money Bags*® and take three turns."

Yakira positioned herself on another machine where she was hidden but could see Ryder at the machine. He won $25.00.

Ding another text came in.

'Go to Queen's Knight slots play till I contact you again.. '

As Ryder moved Yakira and Alex did also and went to another machine to watch. She could hear the bangs, bells and roll of the machine she watched as he looked at his phone. He had won $378.00 when another text message came through.

'Leave!'

Yakira and Alex stayed back not wanting to alert Stevie that they were following. Yakira watched as he disappeared into another room. *Ding,* another message.

'Go to a table'

Ryder went to an empty spot at a Blackjack table, he sat down and began to play. Yakira and Alex watched as he played several rounds. When a woman walked up to him carrying a drink on a tray, she handed him the drink and a folded up piece of paper. She watched as Ryder looked at the paper then cashed out and stood up and walked back towards the front of lobby where the memorabilia was located. He went to the place marked the 'Oklahoma Wall of Fame' where a large poster of Stevie Lace and one of an autographed Gibson guitar hung on the wall.

There he stood starting at the poster. As others would pass by he still stood there staring at the guitar and at the poster of her in her black leather skin thin cat suit encrusted with red rhinestones playing a riff on stage. Others would look and moved on. Yakira moved onto another display where she could occasionally let her gaze drift over and see Ryder.

He was standing alone in front of the wall, when she saw a woman approach; her face was nearly covered with dark sunglasses that were two times too big for her face, on her head was a panama hat the brim pulled down low. Her dark hair pushed up under the hat, but there were a couple of strands falling down showing the blonde tints at the end. In her left hand was a drink. It was Stevie Lace.

Yakira moved a little closer, to where she could hear her speak, making sure she kept her face turned to where Stevie could not see her. "Could I buy you a drink?" Stevie asked. "Maybe we could go up to my room?" Stevie said as she took a sip of the drink. "Maybe you would like to go there? She trailed off and then added, "Right now!" She wrapped her arm around Ryder's and led him away from the wall. Yakira knew she couldn't just follow behind them, so she counted to ten slowly; it was the longest ten seconds of her life she thought, but she turned and followed them deeper into the lobby. The crowd of visitors was like a wave coming in on the beach and it swallowed them up. Yakira's head twisted around trying to spot Ryder all dressed in white.

"Where is he?" She heard Alex ask as she walked up next to her.

"I don't know," Yakira replied, worried as she pushed through the people trying to push a tall man to one side. She had never regretted being 'height challenged' but right now she wished she was six feet tall. "Pardon me!" Yakira said as she pushed another person to side. "There Alex! There he is." Yakira said pointing to man dressed in white, he was heading back into casino and she and Alex followed. The man was alone.

"Where did Lace go?" Alex asked as they followed the man back into the table room. The man sat down at the table with his back to them. Yakira walked up to him and placed her hand on his shoulder. He turned and faced her, it wasn't Ryder.

"I am sorry," Yakira said. "I thought you were someone else." They quickly back tracked to the hotel. They couldn't find him. She looked at Alex. "She said she was taking him up to her room."

"Yakira there are over 400 rooms in this hotel," Alex said looking over the crowd. "We lost him!"

Chapter 50

On the shiny steel doors of the elevators were the words *"Love in an elevator"* *Aerosmith.* As soon as the elevator doors opened on the upper floor of the hotel, Ryder knew that he was on his own, that because of Stevie's quick steps he had lost his tail. He had to use his own wits. Stevie led him down a long hallway with bright lights mounted on the side highlighting the carpet that looked like it belonged on the walls of modern art instead of a floor, with intersecting circles of red, green and tan. She led him to her room and opened the door.

It was dark and cozy when she turned on the cylinder shape lights that were on each side of the king-sized bed. The light spilled down onto the bed revealing the black, white and silver theme of the room that was carried on the bedspread, pillows including those on a smoke gray sofa pushed up next to the wall next to red drapes. The drapes beamed against the dark blue wallpaper.

She released her grip on him and shut the door behind them. She moved deeper into the room removing her sunglasses dropping them down on the pine coffee table that was in front of the sofa. She removed her hat, and her hair fell down on to her shoulders, she dropped the hat down on the red leather settee that was at the foot of the bed. She was dressed in her style of fashion, that from the early sixties, a fuzzy avocado green turtleneck sweater and green paisley crop pants that zipped up in the back, on her feet black short ankle boots. She finished her drink with two large gulps, and then went over the phone and picked up the receiver and ordered.

"This is Stevie Lace, can you send up a large Bloody Mary and…" She turned to Ryder and asked, "And bottle of gin and a can of diet coke."

Stevie's bright smile gleamed across her Cherokee skin, the light from above the bed making her dark course hair seem to glow, and the blonde ends that started at her shoulder and ended just above her breasts, were gleaming like strobe lights. Across her forehead was a headband that was made of a strand of pearls with red rubies that looked the pedals of a flower with a larger pearl in the center. She was old enough to be his mother, but in the light of this room she looked thirty years younger. "And a glass of sweet ice tea with half twist of lemon." Her smile dropped down into a pout as she looked at him and hung up the phone.

"So it was you?" Ryder asked as he walked over and set down on the sofa. "You are the one that killed them?"

"I didn't kill anyone," She said as she removed her boots and then stretched out on the bed using the black and gray pillows to rest her head. "They are after me." She grinned at him again and added, "Want to know how I knew that you like sweet ice tea? . Because you don't drink alcohol because according to *Sports Illustrated* you tried it once when you were in high school and didn't like the bitter taste and you also don't like spicy food."

"So you read my interview?"

"I know many things about you," Stevie said. "Of how people follow me and buy every magazine I am on, I have done the same with you. You can say I am your number one fan."

"Really?"

"Yes, like when you were listed as American All Star, interviewed by ESPN after winning the national championship, I was watching the night you went down at Arrowhead. When they interviewed you on FOX NEWS when you caught the Kansas City Butcher, won the big bucks, stopped terrorists with your little team, of Isabelle Alexander and your wife Yakira. The ones that were following you around the casino, they were so careful to not let me see them they are very good, but they were so busy looking forward they didn't know I was following them. The same ones that are trying to find you but never will because I checked in using my real name."

"Stephanie Grainger?"

"Grainger was my grandmother's name My Cherokee name is Adsila Redfox, yes that same Redfox he is my cousin."

There was a knock at the door and she got up and went to the door and opened it, there was a woman standing there carrying tray with the drinks on it. "Just like you requested and the sweet ice tea." The woman said.

Stevie took the drink including the bottle of rum and coke, closed the door and handed Ryder the ice tea and said, "Should be the way you like it." She set the bottle of rum down on the coffee table in front of Ryder, and the can of diet coke next to it. Then took her Bloody Mary and returned to the bed. She pulled her feet up on the bed and rested her arms on her legs as she took a sip of her drink.

"Have you ever been so damn tired you just don't want to go on?" She asked him looking over at him. Ryder had questions to ask her, but this was not the time it was best to just let her go on, maybe she might just give the answers on her own. "There are times that I wake up and I want to curse God for letting me live another day." She took a sip of the tomato juice based drink and continued. "What I hoped for was one of those typical rock and roll lives. You know 'Rock legend Stevie Lace found dead in her hotel room.' Record sales would have soared, and I would have become a legend, with fans laying flowers outside of my home. They would cry for Stevie Lace. All my life I have been someone else. I have never been myself."

"Stephanie?"

"Stephanie, Stevie, the pride of my heritage," she took another sip of her drink placed the glass on the nightstand and continued, "You know what the first thing I turned to play on the guitar?" She twisted her lips into a partial smile. "The opening chords to *Smoke on the Water* "Da-da-da, Da-da-da, Da-da-da-DA" She sung out the tune as she acted out the movements with the hands. "I was so proud of myself; I played it over and over again till I made people's ears bleed till they screamed 'GET OUT'. Then I started doing scales slow at first then I got faster, and faster, I could even do it faster than the guy on the record, and I learned if I switch chords around and use two hands to do those scales, and then hit a power chord I create my own sound. Suddenly I was somebody people would give money to hear me play. I was not some Indian girl.

Steelace' first performance was part of a class assignment, when we started playing, every classroom came out, we emptied the place, kids were standing in the street in the parking lot and after that a teacher came up to me and said, ' you are a great guitarist…and then it came 'for a girl.' I have had to live with that all my life-'For a girl.' And if I die that is what it will be she was great female guitarist. Maybe if I would have been part of the 27 club instead of the Sergeants' Club. Dead at 27 but God don't listen to fools prayer or those of a little girl that begs him to let her die."

"How long have you wanted to die?"

"Ever since it started." She said, then she reached over and picked up the glass and looked down at it in her hands, "He sold me the guitar and I showed him what I learned and he took me into the backroom and…" She trailed off and then said, "I wasn't even a woman yet, I still slept with a light on. "I told my grandmother and she said "I was just an Indian girl what I said happened would not matter. Then he let his friends touch me." She lifted her glass up as a toast and said with grimace, "Here is to all the bastards."

Ryder lifted his glass and took a sip of the iced tea; it was not as sweet as he would have liked it to be. "So were any of them in the Sergeants' Club?" Ryder took another drink of the tea.

"Only one guy there tried. I put him down on the ground and threatened to kill him, if he ever touched me again. "Stevie said as she took swig of her drink.

"My father?"

"He never understood that some women didn't want him."

"In Cheri's book you knew him well."

"Oh that damn book! She has ruined my life with that thing. I could have killed her for it."

"Did you?"

"I didn't kill anybody!" Stevie said as she slid off the bed and set her drink down again on the end table. "And I didn't have your father's child. But I know who did."

"Who did?" Ryder asked feeling light head.

"I can tell you that right now?" As she spoke he looked up at her, it felt so dizzy it seemed that she was moving yet she was standing in front of him. "You are not one of us yet."

"How—do—I become one of you?" Ryder held his head as he tried to push himself up off the sofa.

"In time."

"Who is the baby that was buried?" Ryder asked as he took a couple of steps stumbling over the coffee table.

"Are you okay?" He heard Stevie ask her words seeming to echo in his heads. "Maybe you need to lie down." She helped him over to the bed, he placed his head down on the bed trying to support his weight, his head was swimming, his legs could support him no more everything went black.

Chapter 51

Ryder wasn't sure how long he had been out, had it been minutes or hours. As his eyes opened he could tell he was still in the hotel, but wasn't sure it was the same room, it was dark and the glow of candles could be seen. The candles seemed to be floating in around him in mid air, positioning around the perimeter of the bed. "Did you get all the stuff out of my car?" He heard Stevie say.

"Yes," he heard another voice say it was Flora.

"He is awake," he heard a man's voice say from out of the darkness. Ryder realized the candles were not floating, the candles were being held by a group standing around him.

"We are ready King Charlemagne? Known as Charles the Great" Ryder heard a female voice say from the darkness on the other side of the bed.

"Yes, Queen Pallas, known as Athena, Goddess of Wisdom. Do you wish to present the cards of fate?"

"I do!" Ryder could hear the woman's voice say and saw her hands. In one was a candle the other held seven playing cards all face down the dark red back ground showing. "These cards shall deal your fate. Only death shall erase that, which the blood of the cup has sealed. Pick your fate." She held the cards out in front of him

"What the hell is going on here?" Ryder asked as he pushed himself up in the bed. As he looked out past the glow of the candles he could see the dark blue wall covering and knew he was in the same room. There were eight spots of light around him three on each side and two at the foot.

"Do you wish to allow a question, joker of the night?" He heard the man say.

"It shall be allowed," he heard Stevie say from the foot of the bed. "The one called Ryder you wish to know the secrets of the Sergeants' Club, and then you must become one of us. The cards before you hold but one rank, that of the one whose blood you carry in your veins-the Master of Death. Pick any other card before you must leave. Become the master and all questions will be answered. Now pick three cards."

"Pick your fate." He heard the one called Queen Pallas say again. He picked three cards and laid them face down on the bed in front of him. "Now the fates shall be picked. Pick one card." Ryder reached down and flipped the middle card over it was of the Ace of Spades. "The fates have chosen Richard Thomas Allan Ryder as the Great Master of Death, King Charlemagne." The woman said as she picked the card up and handed it the man on the other side of the bed.

"The fates have chosen you as the Great Master of Death, our leader. Do you accept this that the fates have selected for you? If so say 'I do.'"

"I do," Ryder said.

"King Caesar bring forth the Dagger of Commitment," The one known as King Charlemagne said, a man that was standing next to him turned and then returned with a silver colored tray, lying on the tray was a jewel handled dagger and an unlit candle to the man who set the tray down on the bed along with his candle.

"King Alexander please bring forward the Chalice of Life."

Ryder could see another person at the foot of the bed holding a candle turn and walk back a few feet and then return holding a small silver colored cup. He walked up to the one known as King Charlemagne kneeled before him and handed him the cup. The king took the cup and placed it down on tray. "Great Master of Death you shall now be sealed in the 'Blood Covenant'" Give me your right hand." Ryder held his hand over to the man as he picked up the dagger. The shiny blade gleamed in the candle light. "Do you accept that your blood shall be bounded in this covenant and the secrets that shall be here shall be carried with you to the grave? If so say' I Shall'."

"I shall," Ryder said and with that Ryder could feel the razor sharp blade slice through the flesh of his index finger. He moved Ryder's finger over the silver chalice and let seven drops of his blood drop into the cup. He slit his own finger of the hand that held the candle. After seven droplets of his blood drop into the cup on top of Ryder, he blew the candle out.

"Queen Pallas Come forward." King Charlemagne said as she walked around the bed and up to him. "Do you accept that your blood shall be bounded in this covenant and the secrets that shall be here shall be carried with you to the grave? If so say' I Shall'."

"I shall!" With her words he sliced her finger and let seven drops of blood fall into the cup. Then she blew her candle out.

"Queen Judith Come forward," Ryder heard as he watched another woman walk around the bed. "Do you accept that your blood shall be bounded in this covenant and the secrets that shall be here shall be carried with you to the grave? If so say' I Shall'."

"I shall." Again he sliced her finger and let seven drops of blood fall into the cup and she too blew her candle out

"King Caeser, come forward. Do you accept that your blood shall be bounded in this covenant and the secrets that shall be here shall be carried with you to the grave? If so say' I Shall'."

"I shall, "Ryder heard a deep voice man say after his blood was placed in the cup he blew his candle out.

"King Alexander come forward. Do you accept that your blood shall be bounded in this covenant and the secrets that shall be here shall be carried with you to the grave? If so say' I Shall'."

"I shall," Ryder heard a female voice say he had heard this voice before but was not sure where. Again blood was drawn and seven drops placed into the cup, after that he blew his candle out.

The process continued through the remaining jacks and the joker of the night-Stevie being the final one, but instead of blowing her candle out she kept it lit. The blood was about an inch deep in the cup, when King Charlemagne took the card that Ryder had selected, folded it twice and placed it in the cup on top of the blood, the card quickly soaking up the precious life fluid. Stevie lowered her candle to the unlit candle and said, "I use my light to give you light Master of Death." The other candle lit, she brought her candle up to her lips and blew the flame out.

In the darkness Ryder could hear the sound of the rum bottle being opened along with the can of diet coke and it being poured. "Now that only one light shines, bring the brew of bitterness." Charlemagne said. Out of the darkness someone came into the light of the flame. Ryder could tell it was the hands of a woman the golden ring with the topaz setting, he realized who the woman was, it was Edwards's daughter. She was carrying the chalice that had blood in it. She raised it to her lips and took a sip and then handed it to another who took a sip, going around the group till it came to Stevie who handed it to Ryder. Ryder took a sip, it was awful, bitter at first then sweet, it was certainly strong in alcoholic content and the saltiness of the blood.

He handed it back to Stevie who handed it to Charlemagne, who took the Ace of Spades card and held it over the last lit candle lighting it on fire, he dropped the card down into the alcohol mixture as he said "Let the flame of the Great master of death consume it all." The drink arose into a blue flame, as it burnt the card and the blood. The blue flame died down and was gone. Charlemagne lifted the candle and held it in front of Ryder. "Now let it be sealed forever, "Charlemagne added and Ryder blew the flame out.

He was surrounded in darkness. Only to be broken by the light of the hallway as the door opened and several people left. The door shut again but darkness was short lived. As Stevie turned on the lights Ryder looked around the room, there were four others in the room including Stevie who sat on the bed next to him. Across the room on the steel gray sofa was a still beautiful woman, October Evans the model, she had appeared on many magazines and was the face of many products that ranged from lipstick to readymade stuffing, but that was in her heyday, now she was just remembered as the crush of many boys that grew up and now their heart's desire was their grandchildren. Her hair like dark chocolate, her eyes like gleaming violet jewels.

Next to her was a man dressed in National Guard military uniform silver eagles upon his shoulders, and over in the corner another woman, she was plain looking with gray hair that was tied back behind her back.

"We are the ones you are looking for," the man spoke and Ryder recognized his voice, "I am King Charlemagne also known as Colonel Leroy Sims, this is October Evans, and Sherrilyn Keystone, of course Stevie you know along with Annie, Charlotte, Paul and the others that were murdered and your mother we were the ones that buried the baby."

"Whose baby was it?" Ryder asked as he stood up.

"Annie's." Colonel Sims said.

"But Annie's son is still alive."

"No that is a different child."

"Maybe we need to get back to start." Ryder said walking in front of them. "Was the child murdered?"

"It was an accident," October said. "You have to believe that! No one wanted that child to die. Every time I look at my daughter it brings it back. It was my fault."

"It was all of us," Sherrilyn said placing her hand on October as she leaned down and placed her face in her hands. "We all did. We all hid it. We all take the blame for it Mr. Ryder." She continued to comfort October as she continued. Back then your father was the best looking man that ever walked the face of the earth. But he was also a jerk. He flirted with Annie and used her and when she got pregnant he told her tell Russell that it was his."

"Russell was starting out his career he had just got a scholarship to Rolla, he wasn't going to be tied down to a wife and kid." Colonel Sims explained. "He told her to have an abortion. When she refused he threatened to kill her. He even held a knife on her."

Sherrilyn said. "So we all decided to take care of Annie. After the baby was born we even took turns taking care of him."

"That is when I had a bad toothache." October said looking up at him. "I had pain and an infection, I never could, still can't swallow pills. The doctor gave me a liquid form of codeine. It was so awful he told me to mix it with coke. But drinking it cold and out of a glass made my teeth hurt. I know it sounds dumb but I found if I put it in a baby bottle and warmed it I could suck on it and get it down. It was my turn to take care of him. It was late at night; my tooth was hurting so bad. The baby cried and I fixed a bottle, but I also fixed a bottle for my tooth. I took them both in there. I…" October gasped and placed her hands over her mouth as she continued, her voice muffled some by her hands." It was dark—I picked up the wrong bottle." His next feeding Annie came in and he didn't move… October wiped the tears away from her eyes . She lowered her hands and then said under her breath. "He went to sleep and never woke up."

"We got scared!" Sherrilyn said "They would have busted us all. We were just kids!

"We were afraid we were going to go to jail." October said. "

"It was then that Edward wanted to see his son," Colonel Sims said. "We tried to put him off but he said that if we didn't do it he was going to call the police. It was then that your mother got the idea. She had heard about this couple that was abusive to their kids and they had just had a baby. We all put our money in together to pay this guy at the fair to go and pretend to be the father and sign the child out. That became Annie's kid."

And the child that died?" Ryder asked.

"We wrapped the child in Annie's basketball top and waited until the dead of the morning," Sherrilyn said. "We picked the lock on the door pried up the floor panels and we found a box there." She looked at Ryder and in a begging tone said, "We had a funeral. Your mother read something out of the bible and we all cried."

"We just did what we thought was best," Sherrilyn said. "We saved the kid from the life he would have had, they were going to put him an orphanage. Annie loved that kid like he was her own flesh and blood."

"A brother," Ryder paused for a moment and then replied pacing the room. "I know who the killer is."

Chapter 52

Ryder wrote down everything he was told and then stepped out of the room and shut the door behind him. Immediately the whole case was running through his mind like water through a sieve, and nothing was sticking. He knew who the killer was but only one thing made sense.

"Deep in thought?" He heard Flora say. She was standing in the hall leaning up against the wall. Her hair was pulled back, held in place behind her back with a larger red rubber band. Dressed in jeans with flared legs and white and green print blouse there was a gauze pad taped to the side of her face, just to her ear on the right side of her face. A large handbag draped across her shoulder.

"Mr. Ryder, "she said with a somber tone and offered her hand out to him "I must apologize to you. I know you are just trying to find the truth in all this." He shook her hand and noticed it was sticky. "I am sorry I spilled a drink on my hand."

"That is all I ever want Flora, the truth." Ryder said wiping his hand "I don't mean any harm to you or your father's memory. I just have to know what happened."

"My father did say something," Flora looked down the hall. "Buy me a drink I will tell you."

He led her to the elevator and into the car and pushed the button for the casino. "How did you hurt your face?"

"Cooking," She said with a grin as he placed her hand on the bandage. "I love to deep fry. It popped up and got me."

The elevator doors opened and the action in the casino was still going on, he could hear the bells and whistles, but not as loud as it was before. The crowds were beginning to thin, it was late, after 1 a.m. The sports bar was not the place to talk and at this time there was only one place open the Center bar.

Center Bar was right in the middle, it was the place to see and be seen. Stylishly designed bottles of fine premium liquor were suspended in unique ice collars. But it was the curved 80-foot bar, that was the show point. It was the midst of summer, but here it was winter the year around, as there is a thin layer of ice always on the bar, looking like fresh fallen snow on a country road, "See you come back Flora," the bartender said with a smile. "She has been my customer all night."

"Bring her whatever she has been having and bring me a sweet iced tea with a half twist of lemon." Ryder said. The bartender pushed the glasses like snowplow over to them; vodka on the rocks for her and sweet ice tea for Ryder.

"We will tell you when we need another drink," Ryder said as he held up a hundred dollar bill. Ryder raised his glass to the woman, "To your father."

"He was a really good man, Rick," Flora said taking a sip of his drink. "I can call you Rick can't I?"

"It is my name," Ryder said as he took a drink noting how cold it was, the glass was almost too cold to hold.

"I mean he really helped students learn if they were having trouble, he would stay until 9 or 10 o'clock at night. He was a great father," She set the glass back down in the ice on the bar. "He always had time for me. I remember one time I was in a play at school. I usually did the makeup , but I got this one part, I was a troll in a wooden box and all I did was raise the lid up a couple of inches and speak. I had one line. 'You can't come this way!' She ran her hand over her face as she added, "I glued fur to my face everywhere, you could barely see me, but when I lifted up the lid I could see him watching and after the show he brought me roses. He was also a wonderful grandfather. It was when Tucker died that he had his first heart attack it was just too much for his heart to take."

"Tucker was your child?" Ryder asked taking a sip of his tea.

"Yes, he was three years old when he drowned." She stared down at the glass on the ice covered bar in front of her. "Losing a child is the hardest thing in the world. It is just something that you just can't get over."

"I know," Ryder said. "My wife and I recently lost our son."

"How old was he?"

"It was a miscarriage she was a little over five months."

"It doesn't matter what age," she said lifting her head and looking up at the TV above the bar. "Three years old not yet born or just three weeks old, a parent cannot ever forget." She lifted the glass up to her lips and stopped before taking a drink and then said, "I know about him and Annie."

"What do you know?"

"That dad got Annie pregnant in college, and he left her." She took another drink and set the glass down. "He reasoned it would have ruined his life to have a wife and kid, he was heading for great things. When that child died that was his first heart break. He told me he blamed himself for it. There were times I would catch him out on the deck looking out across the yard just wondering what it would have been like if he had a son and I had brother."

"But Annie's son is still alive."

"I mean the baby the one they buried as if he were a pet. In the middle of the night."

"So you know about that?" Ryder took a sip of his drink and looked over at her. "How did you find out?"

"The book. I questioned Cherri, she told me the truth."

She picked up the glass and took a big drink and it spilled out on to her hand. The bartender quickly came over and handed her a napkin. She wiped up the mess and the bartender returned with a new drink.

"I am such klutz," Flora said. "Surprise that I am a nurse."

"Really where at?"

"Same as dad was, University of Arkansas, like dad I became a teacher." She brought the glass up to her lips and stopped staring straight ahead.

"Your father committed suicide didn't he?"

She took a sip of the drink and said with little emotion, "How do you know that? I took the note on the calendar and the empty pill bottles."

"Because that was your mistake you took the bottles. He was a heart patient, was on Digoxin, yet I found no bottle in his desk. No emergency drugs that you are required to have with you at all times. The tox report shows it in his system but it also showed it in his stomach. It was because of the child right?"

"Ricky!" He heard Yakira scream and stood and saw her dashing towards him, she grabbed him in an embrace and planted a kiss on his lips. "I thought she got you?" She released him just as Alex strolled up.

"We lost you in the crowd," Alex said as she walked up. "Who would have thought there would be two dressed the same way. Next go for neon orange. By the way we found what we were looking for; right where you thought it would be." Alex laid down a wig and make up box on the bar. Along with a pair of black ski gloves.

"Stevie?" Flora asked. "Stevie Lace is the murderer? Did she kill those people?"

"No you did." Ryder said

"What! Are you crazy?" She slammed her glass down on the bar.

"What proof do you have?"

"Sticky hands."

"I told you I spilled a drink on my hands."

"You have been drinking nothing but Vodka on the rocks." Ryder said as he lifted up her glass. "There is nothing sticky about this."

"But you found them in Stevie Lace's car"

"How would you know that?"

"She just said she found them there?" Flora said. "You are trying to pin this on me because you and Stevie have something going. What motive would I have?

"For what you think they did to your father." Ryder explained. "It was you that was trying to shut down the building site, it was you that signed as my mother and it was you that used the makeup kit to transform yourself into Annie's child."

"You can't prove any of that?"

"Stevie doesn't have a car; it was a car I arranged for her to have. Right next to a camera that caught the whole thing of you putting this case in that car, " Ryder said. As he saw a Tulsa police officer heading this way he said, "You killed them and you drugged them with codeine because the child was drugged that way. Flora I place you under arrest for murder."

Chapter 53

It was the next day almost 1:30 in the afternoon; the sun was again breaking out in clear blue skies over the plains of Oklahoma. The soft rising trill of an Upland Sandpiper could be heard as it landed in the fresh cut driveway of the old homestead property. The bird took a few steps twisting its head to the side looking for grasshoppers. Grabbing one in its beak it stood on one leg and watched the flickering of a sparrow in the sagebrush. The small bird took flight circled the barn once before it flew off into the meadow as heavy sounds of an electric guitar rumbled out of the lower loft of the barn, sounds that could only come from one guitarist- Stevie Lace.

Ryder opened the barn door, she had her back to him and she finished up and he applauded. She turned back to him and smiled. "I wanted to thank you for helping catch the killer. Now I was hoping you would help me with catching another one."

"Really who?"

"You?"

"ME! Who did I kill?"

"Muller at the Ghost light." Ryder explained. That wasn't a car with one headlight it was your motorcycle. You fired at the same time that Yakira did."

"Why would I kill him?"

"He's the one. The one that touched you when you were a kid."

"He was a bastard!" Stevie broke down. "How he was always making me do things reach down into his pants or take mine off! I thought when I was grown and a rock star he would leave me alone, but he came back stage paying people off and he grabbed me... I wasn't going to have him touch me anymore. He told me that if I didn't do what he wanted he would bury me at the Ghost Light and I would become part of the legend. Paul came in and ran him out. But I wasn't going to have it anymore. I was so hoping you would kill him, when he tried to run. I knew I had to do it. Yes I killed him, but you don't know what I went through, how he let his pals do the same to me. He was nothing more than a rabid dog. He deserve to die."

"You are going to take her in Ryder?" Deputy Redfox said. Ryder stood there for moment starring at each one of them and then out the barn door watching the tall grass sway in the breeze.

"You have dollar on you?" Ryder asked turning back to her.

"Yes," Stevie said as she reached into her pocket and handed it to him. "What is this for?"

"You hired me as a Private Detective." Ryder said putting the dollar in his pocket. What is said between a detective and his client is confidential." Ryder grinned and then said. "Have a good life Adsila Redfox."

Epilog

Spring time is the time of birth when new life begins to emerge from its safe cocoon and for the Ryder ranch it was also true. New foals were pushing up on unsteady feet, new calves being fed on bottles. And in the house after a long winter, each month being a new adventure of late night runs into Cassville for cheeseburgers, or how a couple of Ben Franklins got a Mexican restaurant to open again, Tonight Yakira cried out in pain. Ryder rose up like a green-horn private meeting his first general.

"I think it is time Ricky!" He heard Yakira moan. He leaped out of bed dressed in only sleep pants.

"Are you sure this time?" He asked as he pulled the blankets back to reveal a very pregnant wife.

"Positive!" She said "I have been having pains all night. I had another just a few minutes ago."

He dashed to the bedroom door yelled as loud as he could. "RED ALERT! RED ALERT!" he then dashed back to his wife helping her up out of bed. He went over to the side of the dresser and grabbed a black bag that had been prepared just for this occasion. Just at that time Marissa who heard the call burst into the room.

She dashed into bathroom and swung open the closet door and took a coat, she quickly returned and held the coat out for Yakira. It was April but it was still cool out at night. "Ricky you need to get dressed." Yakira said as she slipped into the coat.

"Marissa, get me something to wear." Ryder said. Again she dashed into the bathroom to the closet, just as Bubbie raced up the stairs and into the room. "And call Alex."

"I called the ambulance they are on the way. " Bubbie said. "Also called your mom and dad they are on their way over." Yakira's pregnancy was considered high risk and she was to go by ambulance when it was time.

"Here!" Marissa said as she tossed her brother a t-shirt and a sport coat. He slipped the t-shirt on and he could hear the approach of sirens. "Did you forget something," He said referring to his pants. "Never mind! "He said dashing into the bathroom and slipping into underwear and pants. He slipped on his coat and Marissa helped Yakira take each of the steps down the stairs to the entry way.

Boom! The front door opened. It was Alex. "I brought my car up; Ceelia is in her booster seat". Outside the scream of the siren was deafening as the ambulance pulled into the driveway, the red and blue lights spanning across the house and Alex's car as they helped Yakira out the door. The white lights flashing brilliantly as Rifle, the now full grown Border Collie was barking and running all over the yard, unnerved by all this going on.

"Rifle at ease!" Ryder shouted at the dog and he came up to Ryder's side walking with them as they led Yakira to the ambulance. The door now wide open and the cot pulled out they sat her down on the cot as yet more sirens could be heard. It was two patrol cars that stopped along the side of the road.

"Cox in Springfield right?" The EMT asked.

"Affirmative!," Ryder said as they placed her in the ambulance. "Run her up hot!"

"You got it!"

The sheriff of Barry County Brian Thompson came running up. "You ready to run hot?" He asked Ryder as the ambulance took off lights and sirens going.

"You can't run out of Barry County that way."

"I got a state car over here waiting." Brian said.

"How are you going to get away with that?"

"Rare blood types aren't you?" Brian grinned. "We will make an old fashioned blood run." He led Ryder to a waiting Missouri Highway Patrol vehicle. Brian placed his hand on Ryder's shoulder and added, "Take care of him Rusty!"

It didn't take long for the cruiser to catch up with the ambulance. The sirens wound down as they drove off National down under the bridge, the door to the emergency room quickly rolled up and both the ambulance cruiser drove inside, the door rolled back down as they wheeled Yakira through the doors of the hospital and a doctor was waiting there. "We have surgery room one waiting for her." The doctor said.

"What is going on here?" Ryder demanded to know as he grabbed the doctor by the arm. "Surgery? She is going to have a baby."

"Are you the father?"

"Yes what the hell is going on?"

"She is having trouble! She can't have them naturally. We have to rush her to emergency surgery."

"Doctor is the baby going to be all right?"

"We don't know yet."

There is nothing more intimidating or stressful than a waiting room at a hospital all by yourself, it is like being adrift on a raft on a still ocean. You can hear every sound made, every squeal of a wheel on a cart, every moan of a door being opened. You wait wondering when the others will be there. Then you hear familiar voices a little of the feeling leave.

"What is going on Motek," Bubbie asked as she entered the room followed by Marissa, and Alex and Ceelia. "Why aren't you in there with her?"

316

"They took her to surgery." Ryder said.

"The baby?" Marissa asked.

"They don't know yet." Ryder said as his sister wrapped her arms around him.

"She is going to be all right," Marissa said, I have been saying prayers all the way up here.

At the nurse's desk someone else asked about Yakira, it was Father Anthony who had stopped by to pick up Rebekah and Pascal, he offered prayer in both English and Hebrew. He had been in surgery for over an hour and during that time more and more of Cassville was showing up. Including Brian and his brother Thom. It got to the point that the nurse was asking "Ryder baby" even before someone asked.

"So what are you having a boy or girl?" Thom asked who was sitting next to him and Ceelia. "Another girl that is what you need around your house."

"I don't know Double T." Ryder said. "We didn't want to know anything about it. We wanted to be surprised. But a son would be nice."

Thom leaned over to Ceelia and asked, "You are going to be a big sister. What do you want to have?"

"A girl!" Ceelia said firmly. "You can play with girls. You can't play with boys."

"But your daddy is a boy, and you play with him."

"But he is a daddy," Ceelia said. "He has to!"

Ryder stood and walked around the room and looked up at the clock. "What is going on? Why haven't we heard anything?"

"You want me to try?" Thom said. "Sometimes in these places it is how you ask the question. I might be able to find out something."

Thom left and walked down the hall figuring him also being a doctor he could say the right things.

Ryder stood up and walked down out of the room, then down a hall. Once again he found himself staring out a window looking out watching the end of the night fading as the new dawn of a day broke across the 'Queen City'. He leaned his head on the glass, prayed softly that everything would be okay. Of how bad he needed an angel right now.

He heard the sound of footsteps behind him but he didn't turn, he just stood watching the light of the day grow bright with each tick of the clocks hand. It was then he felt a hand on his shoulder, a touch that was so tender and loving as was the female voice that said,

"Don't worry God has heard your prayer." He turned back and saw a woman standing there; she was in a black dress with a lace inset at the front. A large bag hung over her shoulder. Most of her face was covered with a large black lace hat and dark sunglasses. He could see her smile and he felt so at ease as she continued. "He knows you have had a hard life but Yakira is going to be okay."

"You know me?"

"Everyone knows Rick Ryder," she said staring out the window instead of looking at him as she continued, "The billionaire that solves mysteries for a dollar a day." She reached into the bag and pulled out a package and handed it to him as she said, "This is for the both of you." He took the pink and blue package with its white curled ribbon.

"Why give me this?"

"I am a great fan, I have followed you for a long time, from your time in high school to the university, to the Chiefs, to being a cop, I have been proud of you all this time. But it is the family that you have I am most proud of." She placed her hand on the side of his cheek. "If your mother was here she would be so proud of you too" he placed his hand on hers, and looked at the woman smile as he heard Thom yell.

"Rick!" Thom stood there in the doorway to the waiting room his face as pale as the wall of the hospital, his expression brought silence to the visiting crew that was gathering behind him. The woman removed her hand from his face and walked a few feet away leaning back against the wall keeping her head down. Thom grinned. "You are a father old man! Congratulations." Thom held out his hand to Ryder walking down the hall, with the crowd following him.

"And Yakira, how is she doing?"

"Great she is in recovery and doing fine."

"And the baby?" Ryder asked beaming.

"Which one? "

"Tw-two—twi-twi—" Ryder tried to say as his knees shook and he fell down onto the floor, Marissa and Alex rushed over to help him up.

"Twins!" Marissa gushed.

"A handsome boy with dark hair and brown eyes and a beautiful blonde haired blue eyed girl."

"Have you picked out names yet?" The woman asked.

"Danielle Rose Isabelle for the girl Anthony Thomas Pascal for the boy."

"Danielle Rose?" the woman gasped placing her hand on her chest. "After your mother. She would be so happy." She walked up to him and embraced him, giving him a kiss on the cheek. Then she turned and walked down the hall towards the stairs.

"Who was that?" Thom asked.

"I don't know," Ryder said a fan. "She gave me this." Ryder held the package up.

Ryder pulled the ribbon from the package and ripped the paper and opened the box and reached inside and pulled a small yellow and black stuffed tiger. It was dirty and tail twisted around, it fit in Ryder's hand.

"It is Stripy!" Bubbie cried out as Ryder slid down the wall and sat down on the floor. "How?"

"I don't understand?" Marissa said squatting down and taking the stuffed critter from her brother's hand.

"It was my favorite toy when I was a kid," Ryder said he looked up at her and said, "I gave this to my mother, I placed it in her coffin. He looked down the hall seeing the door to the stairs closing. He stood up and dashed down the hall grabbed the door. He raced down the stairs catching up with the woman he grabbed her arm and swung her around he grabbed her hat and removed her sunglasses, then breathless, "Mom!'

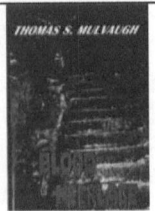	Rick Ryder has just won the biggest Powerball jackpot of all time One billion in cash. His high school sweetheart comes to Kansas City ofr help, but not getting what she wants she steals his sports car and ends up murder in the car at Roaring River State Park. Ryder returns to his hometown to find the murderer. What he finds is policatal coruption and secerts that are best left burried.
	A serial killer is loose in Eukera Springs, Ark. Thing is notes are being left just like burtal serial killer known as the Kansas City Butcher. But Ryder put away this killer years ago, is it a copy cat killer or is the butcher back.
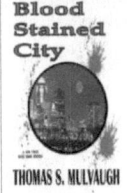	A sniper is loose in Kansas City Mo. And the city is held in terror. Can Ryder find the sniper before they kill again, or is this just a cover up for something even bigger?